DATE DUE

NOV 2 9 2002	OCT 1 4 2003
DEC 1 4 2002	
JAN 1 7 2003	
FEB 0 6 2003	
MAR 7 2003	
APR 0 1 2003	
MAY 2 2003	
JUN 1 3 2003	
JUN 2 0 2003	
JUL 2 9 2003	

Carnegie Public Library
Big Timber, Montana

RULES

1 Books may be kept two weeks and may be renewed once for the same period, except 7-day books and magazines.

2. A fine of two cents a day will be charged on each book which is not returned according to the above rule. No book will be issued to any person incurring such a fine until it has been paid.

3. All injuries to books, beyond reasonable wear, and all losses shall be made good to the satisfaction of the Librarian.

4. Each borrower is held responsible for all books drawn on his card and for all fines accruing on the same.

X

"A chilling murder mystery." —*Romantic Times*

"A spine-tingling novel that will grip readers and hold them captivated . . . Jones yet again proves herself a force to be reckoned with . . . amazing." —*New-Age Bookshelf*

"Chilling . . . a wonderful thriller . . . a truly fascinating book—don't miss it!" —Heather Graham,
New York Times best-selling author of *Long, Lean, and Lethal*

"A fascinating blend of historic murders and contemporary intrigue. You won't want to put it down!" —Lisa Gardner,
New York Times best-selling author of *The Other Daughter*

THE ISLAND

"[A] fast-paced story . . . [with] well-drawn characters and a few unexpected plot twists." —*Library Journal*

"A magical escape into a realm steeped with legend." —*Bookpage*

"Top-notch entertainment to die for!"
—*The Belles and Beaux of Romance*

"Mesmerizing . . . a page-turner from start to finish."
—*Old Book Barn Gazette*

CIRCLE OF THE LILY

"Her clever and compelling plot twists will keep . . . readers riveted." —amazon.com

"Dramatically enthralling . . . another notch to Jill Jones's growing list of surefire hits." —*Romantic Times*

"Impossible to put down." —*Rendezvous*

ESSENCE OF MY DESIRE

"A unique and utterly spellbinding story to savor . . . a true original."
— *Romantic Times* (4½ stars)

"An alluring tale of suspense and erotic enchantment."
— *Publishers Weekly*

THE SCOTTISH ROSE

"Seamlessly blends the elements of romance, time travel, adventure, and danger with truly spectacular results." — *Romantic Times*

"Exciting, absorbing, one of the top books of the year."
— *Affaire de Coeur*

"A unique page-turner, sure to win a favored place on bookshelves." — *The Belles and Beaux of Romance*

MY LADY CAROLINE

"A truly remarkable story." — *Publishers Weekly*

"A bewitching ghost story . . . This is an author to watch!"
— *Romantic Times*

EMILY'S SECRET

Winner of the prestigious "Maggie" Award from
Georgia Romance Writers

"A magnificent novel!" — *Affaire de Coeur*

"Beautifully written and compelling . . . I loved it . . . A must-read!"
— Heather Graham

"Lovely! It's the book I've always wanted to write."
— Marion Zimmer Bradley

St. Martin's Press Titles
by Jill Jones

Remember Your Lies

Bloodline

The Island

Circle of the Lily

Essence of My Desire

The Scottish Rose

My Lady Caroline

Emily's Secret

EVERY MOVE YOU MAKE

Jill Jones

St. Martin's Press

This is a work of fiction. Any resemblance of the characters to persons living or dead is coincidental.

To Eve, Sybil, Truddi, et. al.

ACKNOWLEDGMENTS

Many thanks to Marsha Briscoe, a long-time supporter of my work, and to Judy Lipp, LCSW, for sharing her experience as a mental health professional working with patients who suffer from more than mental illness.

My great appreciation goes to Stanley Hilton, native San Franciscan and author, who provided much of the "flavor" of the City by the bay for this book.

As always, I thank my husband, Jerry, for being there for me, and for the wonderful meals he prepares. I thank my family, especially my daughter, Brooke Cundiff, for their support and ideas.

And finally, I thank two people whose continual support and talent allowed me to write this book — my editor, Jennifer Enderlin, and my agent, Mel Berger.

I may write the words, but it takes many others to create a book.

EVERY MOVE YOU MAKE

I

The beat of the music, hard, hot, and heavy, struck a chord in the heart of the murderer. His pulse quickened, his heartbeat shifted to match the rhythm. A sense of righteous vengeance surged through him, and he trembled. The bitch would never hurt him again.

His gaze penetrated the smoky atmosphere of La Habanera, one of San Francisco's hottest dance clubs. He was repulsed by these clubs, but he chose to come because he always found her in places like this. He looked around and spotted her instantly, the woman with red hair and long red nails who danced with abandon beneath the flashing disco lights. Hatred seeped from his pores, bringing with it a sheen of cold perspiration, and the scent of death.

He approached her and began to dance beside her, not knowing or caring if she was with someone. She would leave with him. She always did.

The tempo of the music hit a frenzied pitch, and the woman, now fully aware of the man's attentions, moved her lush body in sizzling, seductive motions designed to hypnotize and beguile. He'd seen her dance like that before, and he knew what obscenities followed.

The rhythm reverberated in his head, hammering at him with such violence that he thought his brain would split with the pain.

Ka-thud.
Ka-thud.
Ka-thud.

He fought back the pain, knowing it would end soon. Thankfully, the torrid dance number ended, as well. When the music rolled into something more sedate, he took the woman by both shoulders and drew her to him. "Let's blow this place and go somewhere we can talk."

She raised her eyelids slowly and smiled knowingly up at him. "Talk?"

He didn't answer but returned her sultry smile.

They left the crowded dance club by a side door that opened into an alley. The woman was a little unsteady on her feet, so he took her firmly by one elbow and steered her through the dark passageway.

"Hey, where you takin' me?" The woman's voice sounded shrill in the relative quiet outside the club. All that penetrated beyond the walls was the pulse of the bass.

Ka-thud.
Ka-thud.
Ka-thud.

"How about a moonlight walk by the bay? Someplace we can be alone, just you and me."

They made their way down the alley to another dark street, and then another. This part of the city, which had experienced something of a renaissance during the dot-com boom, still retained its dark side. That's why the man liked it here.

They reached his preplanned destination, a small, secluded park, a copse sheltered by shrubs and bushes. "Come here," he said, taking the woman in his arms.

"You want to do it here? Sorry, but I'm rather partial to using a bed."

Her petulant attitude turned up the volume in his head and heated the rage that had been building inside since he'd seen her on the dance floor.

Ka-thud.
Ka-thud.
Ka-thud.

The rhythm consumed him, filling his body, absorbing his

brain, drowning all other thought or sensation. He began to dance to the beat only he could hear, and he forced the woman to dance with him. She tried to pull away.

"You crazy or something? What're you doing?"

The man's hands moved from her shoulders to her throat and tightened around her fair skin. "Dance," he ordered, still moving to the rhythm. Holding her by the neck, he made her sway with him, as if she were a puppet or a rag doll.

Her eyes bulged, and she struggled to get away, but he was far too strong for her. They danced as he strangled the life from her, and when she was dead, he let her fall to the ground. His cock was hard, not for her, but rather for the final step of the dance.

Reaching into one of the bushes, he drew out a baseball bat he'd placed there earlier. He turned the woman's body over so that her face was up, and she was staring at him with sightless eyes. He raised the bat and brought it down across her face with as much force as he could muster.

Ka-thud.

He heard the crack of wood splintering bone, saw blood spurt through the night air. The music in his head played louder.

Ka-thud. Ka-thud.

He beat the woman's body in time to the music, and with each blow, his desire built until it was at a fever pitch.

Ka-thud. Ka-thud. Ka-thud.

At last, he reached a climax, and as his body shot a stream of warm, wet semen into his Jockey shorts, he shivered and sank to his knees. He stared at the woman and felt no remorse. If anything, he felt elation at the sweet release of the rage. The pain in his head was gone now, too.

But, he knew, they both would be back.

2

The earth from twenty thousand feet above the Nevada desert was brown, scarred, and appeared as parched as the face of Mars. Regan McKinney leaned closer to the window of the 747, seeking a better view through the milky-hued glass. The captain's voice had awakened her from an uncomfortable, neck-straining sleep in her cross-country flight, announcing that they were approaching Reno. They would arrive in San Francisco a few minutes behind schedule, he apologized, due to unexpected headwinds.

Regan tapped her fingers impatiently on the armrest. It had been a long flight, and she was tired. Tired, and ready to get on with her life.

The acid of resentment rose in her throat as she thought about what she was leaving behind, and she swallowed hard. She hated the anger, but it was the anger that had gotten her through the nightmare of her divorce. She wasn't about to let go of it now, when she had little else to sustain her as she, at age thirty-four, pushing middle age in her own mind, was starting over.

I want a divorce.

The words echoed in Regan's ears as clearly as they had when her husband had uttered them six months ago. They'd been in their bedroom, having just returned from a formal party, a fund-raiser for their favorite charity. Theirs hadn't been the most loving of marriages for some time, but she was totally unprepared for his little bomb.

What'd you expect me to do? Keep waiting for what's obviously not going to happen? I want a kid, and I'm not getting any younger.

Regan still felt the shock and disbelief that had rocked her when he'd said those cruel words. Adam had sounded as if he were unaware of all that she'd done to get pregnant. He'd acted as if his infidelity were her fault. As if it were his right to deliberately get another woman pregnant and walk out on their fourteen-year marriage. The fact that the "woman" was little more than a girl didn't help matters, either.

The anger reared its ugly head again and roared. Regan caught herself grinding her teeth and consciously relaxed her facial muscles. Her dentist had warned her if she didn't stop that, she'd end up with jaw problems. She knew why she'd developed the bad habit—the injustices and humiliation she'd endured over the past six months made her want to go out and bite somebody.

Reno crept beneath the wings of the plane, its buildings looking like so many squarish cookies roasting on the huge brown ʼcookie sheet of the desert below. But only a few minutes later, the landscape changed, became greener, more hopeful, and the plane began its descent into San Francisco.

San Francisco. A city a continent away, a place she'd never been, where she knew no one except her sister, Kat. Regan hadn't seen Kat since their father's funeral more than ten years ago, and the sisters were as different as night and day. She might be making a colossal mistake in coming here, but Kat was the only family she had. And Kat had made it easy for her.

"Get your butt out here," her sister had insisted in her typically blunt manner. "You can stay with Blair and me until you figure out what you want to do next. We've got plenty of room in this big old monstrosity we call home." Then she'd added the zinger that punched a button somewhere deep inside of Regan. "It's high time you got a life."

Regan had always thought she had a life, but she'd been wrong. She'd had Adam's life, not her own. And Adam had shattered that life, ending not only their marriage but also destroying the only other thing she'd really cared about, her small antiques business, which she was forced to close as a result of the divorce.

Kat was right. It was time for her to get a life all her very own. But anxiety rippled through her. What if she hated San Francisco? What if she and Kat didn't get along? What if she couldn't find a job? After losing her shop, she had no desire to go back into the antiques business, but she had no idea what she wanted to do.

Regan took a deep breath, calming herself, not giving in to the fear she knew lurked deep inside. She couldn't allow that fear to surface. Not now. She'd cling to the anger instead. It was far more empowering.

Regan felt the thud and heard the screech of the huge wheels as they engaged the tarmac, and she was thrown forward slightly as the giant aircraft slowed. When at last the silver beast seemed to be tamed and began to roll complacently toward the terminal, Regan felt a bubble of excitement replace both her snarling anger and the menacing, quiescent fear.

Kat and her daughter, Blair, Regan's niece, had promised to meet her plane. She hadn't seen them in so long. Would she recognize them? Suddenly hopeful for the first time in months, Regan retrieved her small carry-on bag from the overhead compartment, bumped her way down the aisle and into the jetway, and hurried eagerly toward the terminal, heart pounding.

Kat was indeed there, and Regan had no trouble recognizing her. She was the tall, leggy one with spiky, short, really-red hair and spiky, high, really-red heels. In between head and heels, she wore a trendy black sweater dress that made Regan feel downright frumpy in her baggy denim jumper, even if it did carry a designer label.

Regan wasn't surprised at Kat's flamboyant appearance. Kat had always been the "wild child" of their family, two years younger than Regan but always the stronger and more daring of the two sisters. When they were children, Regan had often found herself following Kat's lead instead of the other way around.

Kat's ultra-red lips broke into a wide smile when she saw Regan, and she ran to her sister as fast as she could in those ridiculous shoes.

"Oh, my God, it's you! You're here! You actually came!" Kat hugged Regan so hard it nearly took her breath away.

"Of course I came," Regan whispered, struggling to control her emotions. She'd missed her sister, but she hadn't known how much. "I always did what you told me." The day grew a little brighter.

It became brighter still when Regan spotted a pretty, shy-faced girl watching them with a grin that revealed a mouthful of braces. A girl with long, strawberry-blond hair instead of her mother's short, fiery crown, but whose face Regan recognized in an instant. Except for her hair, she looked exactly like Kat had as a teenager.

"Blair." Regan murmured the child's name and turned to the girl, still clinging to Kat with one arm. She was stunned. This was Blair, the love child, the reason Kat had bolted from their zealously religious and judgmental parents when she'd been little more than a child herself. The reason their father had disowned his youngest daughter.

Regan had seen Blair only once before, at her father's funeral. Blair had been a small child then and had remained so in Regan's mind all these years. Now, she was startled to see her niece was a beautiful adolescent, a budding young woman. How old was she? Regan did the math. Fourteen? She couldn't be. But then, neither could Regan be thirty-four.

Regan drew Blair into her free arm and crushed both the child and the mother against her. And then, the tears she'd repressed beneath her anger refused to stay dammed inside any longer. She was with family, real family, people who loved her and whom she could trust. It was the oddest sensation, like she was coming home, even though she'd never been here before. For the first time since that awful night when Adam had pronounced her fate, Regan McKinney felt alive once again. And for the first time, she cried.

3

FBI Special Agent Sam Sloan stared down at the battered corpse of a killer's latest victim and felt the unwanted but familiar twist of grief in his gut. He had no right to feel grief or anything else for this woman. She was a stranger, as were all the victims of the brutal crimes it was his job to investigate. He should have managed to harden himself against such feelings by now, but with each case, it seemed to get worse.

He shouldn't have taken this assignment. He should, in fact, resign from the agency. What good was an FBI profiler who'd lost the ability to detach from the horror, who grieved for the victims and their families as if they were his own kin? Who suffered nightmares, and who, until recently, too often found solace in a bottle?

Sloan clenched his jaw and stuffed his hands into his pockets. He didn't want anyone to see that they trembled.

His last case. This would be his last case, he promised himself.

But then, he'd promised that before.

With enormous effort, Sloan shuttered his emotions and spoke to the medical examiner in a cold, professional manner.

"I see there's bruising around the neck. Was she strangled before the beating?"

"Looks that way. Just like the other two."

Sloan had been called to San Francisco when this, the third murder victim in as many weeks, had been discovered beneath a pier in a seedy part of town. The SFPD suspected the women had been kidnapped, taken somewhere no one would see what was happening, then strangled and bludgeoned with some kind of blunt instrument until their bodies were almost unrecognizable as human beings.

"There's no question in my mind the deaths are related," the ME went on. "I'm pretty sure we've got a serial killer on our hands."

Sloan thought so, too. That's why the SFPD had called the FBI in on the case, why he, in particular, had been assigned to it. Serial killers were his specialty, and these three murders were too much alike for it to be coincidence. The women were all in their early thirties, all had red hair, and all had been beaten savagely after being strangled. None had been raped, however, which Sloan found interesting. Sociopaths with this much anger often started with rape as the initial degradation of their victims, then took it from there.

He turned to the young officer, Inspector Brad Kelly of the San Francisco PD's Night Investigations bureau, who had accompanied him to the ME's office and who at the moment looked a little green around the gills.

"Where were the other bodies found? Anyplace near where this one turned up?"

Kelly shook his head. "They were all found in the Bay Area, but not near one another. I'll show you on a map when we get back to my office."

Sloan scribbled some notes. "Were the victims killed on site, or had their bodies been moved?" Sloan purposely referred to the dead as "bodies" rather than by the victims' names or even personal pronouns. It was one way to keep a distance, to keep from caring too much about those who had died. Sometimes it worked. Most of the time, it didn't.

"We believe the killer must have lured the victims into his trust, kidnapped them and taken them to wherever he committed the murder. Then he moved them again, probably in a vehicle, and dumped them. They were all found at various places in the bay, but at the water's edge, not out in the bay itself. So we don't think a boat is involved."

Sloan noted that the killer had gone to a lot of trouble, moving the victims twice. Why not just leave them where he'd killed them? Did he have a headquarters where he took them? Sort of a "murder central"? If he did, he was a pretty organized kind of guy, and would be harder to catch.

"What else do the murders have in common? Were the victims nude when you found them?"

"Nope. All were fully clothed."

"What were they wearing?"

"Good clothes. Fancy, sexy dresses. We've got the clothes, or what's left of them after the beatings, in the evidence room."

Interesting.

Had the women gone out dressed up in good clothes, or had the killer made them don the attire before he murdered them? He underlined the word "organized" on his notepad.

Sloan gazed down at the dead woman. She knew what had happened, but she could never tell. Her eyes were sealed forever with bloody bruises. Her mouth no longer existed. "Where were you going," he asked her softly, "all dressed up like that?"

"I bet it wasn't to church," the ME remarked dryly. "You finished here?"

Sloan nodded, and the man covered the remains of the dead woman. "Let's go," Sloan said to Kelly and held the door open for him. Kelly looked distinctly relieved.

They walked together down the corridor. "You ever been on a serial murder case before?" Sloan asked Kelly.

"No. I've worked homicides, of course, but I've never seen anything like this."

Sloan heard both fascination and awe in Kelly's voice and felt sorry for the younger man. The big cases were always awesome and exciting . . . when you were young. And at the beginning of the investigation. But when days went by without a capture, when another murder happened, maybe another and another, when your ass was so whipped from sleepless nights and sheer frustration you felt as if you'd been through a meat grinder, things became a lot less awesome and exciting.

Sloan had long since ceased to be either awed or excited about a case. He had come, instead, to dread each new example of man's capacity for brutality. He'd seen too much carnage. He had too frequent nightmares. He'd smoked too many cigarettes in his younger years, drunk too much whisky in his midlife. He'd accepted this case because it had been assigned to him. It was his job. But he wondered how effective he'd be this time. He was losing his edge, and he knew it.

If only he knew how to quit.

4

Music—hard, hot, and heavy—blasted into his mind, a mean, cruel, unrelenting rhythm that twisted through his brain.

Ka-thud. Ka-thud. Ka-thud.

The merciless beat hammered at him, battering him with violent force. He clenched his jaw and wrapped his arms tightly around himself, bracing for what was to come.

Ka-thud. Ka-thud. Ka-thud.

The rhythm became footsteps on the stairs.

His door opened, and he squeezed his eyes tight against the slash of light that stabbed into the darkness.

Darkness. His only protection.

The music grew louder.

Ka-thud. Ka-thud.

Fear burned sourly in his throat.

Like a horrible heartbeat, the rhythm pulsed, alive, savage, evil. It probed him with long hot fingers, lashed him with its stinging assault. He cried out, but no sound escaped his lips. No one heard his silent scream.

No one ever would . . .

The man shot straight up in bed, his body soaked with icy sweat. He trembled as if he'd been struck by lightning. The nightmare, as always, scrabbled away into the darkness like the evil, nameless creature it was, leaving him spent, tortured, wasted. His pulse raced with unspeakable fear for a few moments as he lay still, listening to the sound of his own breathing, feeling the rhythm of his heartbeat. Nausea followed, and then anger.

Rage bone-deep and as terrifying as the nightmare itself.

He slid out of bed and made his way on shaking legs to the bathroom. He flicked on the light and winced as it flooded his brain. A moment later, he peered through slitted eyelids into the mirror. His eyes were hollow, shadowed to match the dark stubble on his face. His skin was pale; it hadn't seen the sun in months. He looked like shit.

He had to do something. The nightmares, the headaches, the blackouts, all were coming more frequently now and were more intense. With each incident, a dark terror he couldn't define and didn't want to know crept steadily closer to his consciousness. It attacked at the most unexpected times, debilitating him with fear and anxiety.

Maybe he should see a shrink. He backed away from the mirror, pulling himself together by the sheer force of his will.

See a shrink.

Or not.

He was terrified somebody would learn what he already knew—that he was losing his mind. He couldn't let that happen. Not now. He had to hang on. He had to cope.

Taking a deep breath, he sought for the calm that seemed ever more elusive these days. He closed his eyes and breathed again, clutching the sink with an iron grip.

Grip.

Get a grip.

And then he felt something inside of him shift, subtly but surely, as if a mother's hand had moved him gently aside, away from the terror. A profound sense of relief washed through him, followed immediately by an almost painful craving for . . . ice cream. He blinked.

Ice cream?

He didn't particularly like ice cream.

Losing his mind. He was definitely losing his mind. After wiping his face with a towel, he nonetheless answered the

call for the frozen sweet and padded downstairs on bare feet
to the kitchen.

Irritably, he yanked open the freezer door. He probably
didn't even have any ice cream. The light from the freezer
compartment sliced through the dark kitchen, illuminating
the shelves inside. He stared at what he saw, his mind struggling to register that he not only had ice cream, he had *lots*
of ice cream. The shelves were lined with cartons in every
flavor imaginable.

Sweating again, he slammed the door and leaned back
against it, clutching his arms. Where in hell had all that ice
cream come from?

He didn't remember buying it. But then lately, there was
much he couldn't seem to remember.

Chunky Monkey.

The words popped into his head, reminding him of an old
rock 'n' roll song.

No, no, silly, that was "Funky Monkey," a playful voice
corrected him. A familiar, soothing voice.

He took another deep breath, and calm flooded him fully
at last, taking away the last shadows of the nightmare.

Ice cream.

What a great idea.

He opened the freezer again, and his hands went directly
to a carton of Ben & Jerry's "Chunky Monkey" ice cream.
He took it out and spooned a huge helping into a bowl. Then
he neatly replaced the carton in the freezer, pausing a moment to lovingly eye his frozen riches.

So much ice cream.

Carrying the bowl into the living room, he flicked on the
big-screen TV. He went to the entertainment cabinet and
searched through the extensive library of movies until he
came to the one he was seeking. He loved this movie.

He inserted the disc into the DVD player, then curled up
in a massive chair and took the ice cream in hand. As the
opening melody began, he reached for the remote control
and turned the volume up so the music would fill every dark
corner of the room. He nestled against the soft leather of the

chair and watched as a green frog sitting on a log in a make-believe swamp played a banjo and sang in a funny voice about being half-asleep and hearing voices calling his name. That too had been happening to him a lot lately.

5

Regan awoke long before Kat and Blair stirred. Her body clock, after all, was three hours ahead of theirs. Wide awake, she nonetheless snuggled beneath the comforter on the four-poster bed in Kat's guest room, feeling a strange but welcome sense of security.

Kat's entire house lent that feeling. Maybe because it was old. It had been built early in the century, just after the earthquake of 1906, in San Francisco's now fashionable Pacific Heights district. Or maybe it was because of the way Kat had so lovingly renovated it. Regan was amazed at Kat's domesticity, for she'd never known her sister to care much about their childhood home. But then, that probably had more to do with the childhood than the home, she mused.

A thin trickle of dawn seeped through the crack between the shade and the window, and Regan looked around at the tastefully decorated room, one of four large bedrooms in the fancifully painted Victorian house. Where had Kat learned to do this? Regan had thought her sister earned a living as a paralegal, which she did. But Kat had told her yesterday that she'd made her real money in renovating old properties in neighborhoods that were being revitalized. This was her fourth project in eight years, and, she claimed, her last. Her goal all along had been to be able to provide a decent house for herself and Blair, and this was it.

Imagine. Kat with goals. And reaching them. Kat, the one who'd always chased the wind, the child their parents had openly and frequently disparaged. Regan hoped the mean old man who was their father was looking down—or up as the case may be—and could see what Kat had made of her life. At the same time, she hoped he didn't see what she'd made of her own.

Regan rolled to one side and bunched a pillow into her arms, feeling hollow. It wasn't too late to make something of her life. Was it?

Later, when Kat and Blair were up, the three prepared a breakfast of coffee, fruit, and muffins which they took into the "snuggery," Kat's term for the small, cosy room off the kitchen where she and Blair often cocooned themselves to watch television or read the newspaper.

Although she loved the whole house, Regan was especially taken by this room's warmth and appeal. Her sister seemed to have a magical touch when it came to decorating, although the furnishings were eclectic, to say the least. In this room, an abstract painting dominated the main wall, a low Art Deco table held their coffee and muffins. Blair sprawled on a quaint Victorian-style fainting couch, and classical music emanated from a 1940s upright radio cabinet in the corner. Regan and Kat sat at opposite ends of a traditional-style sofa covered in a bright blue and white striped canvas. Tin buckets of silk irises, daffodils, tulips, and hydrangea brought the early springtime into the room.

It was a mishmash of color and style, and yet it all worked happily together. Regan would never have dared such a combination. Adam had liked everything to match. She scowled. *Screw Adam.*

"Can I see the classifieds?" she asked as Kat began to divvy up the newspaper. "Might as well start looking for a job. I can't mooch off you two forever." Regan had a financial cushion from her divorce, but it wasn't substantial, and besides, she didn't want to live on Adam's money. She wanted to make her own.

"What's your hurry?" Kat asked. "You just got here yesterday."

Regan exhaled, and her breath caught on an unexpected lump in her throat. "I've wasted fourteen years of my life. I can't afford to lose any more."

Kat glanced up at Regan. "It wasn't wasted, sis. Everything counts. Slow down now. Take some time to find out who you are. You can stay here as long as you want."

"Yeah, like forever. It's totally cool you're here." Blair handed her aunt the requested classified section, then bounced down into a chair next to Regan. "I'm in a recital next Saturday," she said, excitement lacing her voice. "Can you come?"

At Blair's unrestrained enthusiasm, Regan rebounded from her moment of gloom. "Recital? Of course I'll come." She was amazed by her niece's apparently unequivocal acceptance of a stranger into her life. Weren't teenagers supposed to be sullen and standoffish? "What kind of recital?"

"Ballet." She popped off the chair and did a little pirouette.

"Blair wants to be a professional ballet dancer," Kat explained. "She's really good, and she works hard at it. We're hoping she'll get accepted next fall at the special high school that focuses on the arts."

"You're lucky, you know," Regan said to Blair with a wistful smile. "You're talented, and . . . you have a supportive mother." Her mind tripped back over the years, to times when she and Kat were Blair's age and had entertained dreams of their own.

"Remember when you wanted to be a movie star?" she murmured to Kat.

Kat snorted. "Fat chance there was of that. Mama and Dad wouldn't even let me try out for the school play."

Regan heard the edge of anger in her sister's voice. So she hadn't gotten over it, after all.

"I wanted to be an astronaut," Regan said, recalling her supportive science teacher in school, whose anger had been almost as great as Regan's when John Bowen, Regan and Kat's father, had refused to allow Regan to enter the science fair, claiming that science was "the work of the devil."

"Why didn't you become an astronaut?" Blair's question interrupted Regan's bitter memories.

Regan gave an unhappy laugh and picked at the sweater she wore. "Dad didn't think it was 'ladylike,' and Mama wanted me to be just like her."

"What was she like, your mom?" her niece asked with unabashed curiosity.

Regan eyed her for a long moment. Hadn't Kat ever told Blair about the lovely, perfect, totally dysfunctional Bowen family? She glanced at her sister, and Kat shrugged, giving Regan permission to dive into the subject if she wanted to.

Regan hesitated, considering Blair's question. What *had* their mother been like? When trying to describe Eliza Jane Bowen, the word "doormat" came immediately to Regan's mind. And then . . .

Mama wanted me to be just like her.

"Your grandmother was . . . quiet. Pious. Industrious." Regan groped for positive images, but there were few in her memory bank. The only thing she could unequivocally thank her mother for was naming her Regan, after Eliza Jane's family. John had always hated Regan's name, thinking it too unusual and exotic. Regan had always liked it, for the same reasons.

"Narrow-minded, judgmental, submissive to her over-bearing husband." Kat took a bite of her muffin and added with a wicked smile, "Come on, Regan, you don't have to be nice around us. That's part of your problem. You're too damned nice."

Regan gave a nervous laugh, but she couldn't bring herself to speak ill of their mother in spite of her mixed feelings about the woman. Regan was, in fact, only just starting to understand Eliza Jane, or at least to suspect that their mother's quietly spoken but cutting criticisms of her children and others might have stemmed from deep-seated anger at her lot in life. Eliza Jane had allowed herself to become dominated by a man who, although not unloving, was strongly opinionated, strict, and judgmental.

Mama wanted me to be just like her.

It occurred to Regan that in one way at least, she had become like her mother—she'd married Adam at a young age, controlling, opinionated, dominating Adam. Someone very like her father.

Uncomfortable with that thought, she quickly buried it
and answered Kat. "You're probably right," she said. "It's a
habit I'll have to break, being nice."

Blair laughed. "Mom's only kidding, Regan. She's nice.
She just likes to scandalize people."

"I am not nice and don't you ever call me that again."
Kat threw a sofa pillow at her daughter, and the pair of them
howled with giggles.

Regan marveled at the ease between mother and daughter,
for she and Kat had certainly never known any such warmth
or camaraderie with either of their parents. Apparently when
Kat left the Bowen household, she'd left a lot of old baggage
behind. Regan hoped she could do the same.

She opened the classified section and turned to the employment ads. Out of the corner of her eye, she saw Blair
pick up the comics. Kat studied the entertainment section. A
clock ticked loudly from the hallway, and a peaceful,
Sunday-morning sort of hush fell over the room.

Newspaper rustled, and moments later Kat exchanged entertainment for the main news. A minute later, she let out a
small cry. "Oh, my God."

Regan lowered her paper and saw Blair look up sharply.
"What's wrong?" Regan asked.

Kat's face had gone white, and she was staring at the front
page, her eyes wide and her mouth slightly twisted where
she was biting her lip. "This can't be true."

"What?" Blair asked.

Kat raised her head, and Regan could see there were tears
in her sister's eyes. "She . . . she was a friend of mine," Kat
said, her words sounding choked. "I haven't seen her in a
while, but . . ."

Blair scooted across the couch and took the paper from
her mother. Regan heard the girl's sharp intake of breath,
and a lump of fear formed in her stomach.

"That's Darlene Dickerson, isn't it?" Blair asked. "The
woman you worked with a couple of years ago? Geez, how
creepy."

Regan couldn't stand it any longer. "What happened?
What's going on?"

Kat handed her the newspaper. "Darlene . . . she's been
. . . murdered."

6

Sam Sloan sat on a bench at the far end of Pier 7, staring at but not really seeing Yerba Buena Island in the distance. In his hands he held a half-empty carton of popcorn, kernels of which he distributed absently from time to time to seagulls and pigeons who came begging for their breakfast. Folded and lying on the bench next to him was this morning's newspaper. He'd read the lead story earlier:

> Two joggers found the battered body of a woman beneath a pier south of the ferry building early Saturday morning. The victim, who apparently died of strangulation but who had also been brutally beaten, has been identified as Darlene Dickerson, 32, of San Francisco. She is the third woman found murdered in a similar manner in the Bay Area since late February, and police now believe the murders are the work of a serial killer. Residents, especially women, are warned to take extra precautions to insure their safety. See related story, page 7.

One paragraph on the front page, cut, dried, and neatly wrapped up with a little warning, couldn't begin to describe the horror Sloan had seen when he'd viewed the victim's body. Newspaper readers couldn't possibly understand the enormity of this crime from this short, curt piece. No one except maybe the joggers who saw the carnage for them-

selves. How distanced we are, he thought, from the brutal
reality.

And then he thought, it was a good thing, that distance.
It kept the world sane. He, on the other hand, who seemed
unble to keep his distance, felt as if he were losing a little
of his mind, maybe part of his soul, with each case that came
his way. And yet, he seemed unable to get out of the business. He'd been in law enforcement for twenty years, at
Quantico for the last eight. He didn't know anything else.

Sam rubbed his eyes, which felt as if they were made of
sandpaper. His muscles were still stiff from the long airplane
journey from D.C. the day before. Maybe it was just his age
getting to him. Although most people didn't consider forty-
one old, maybe it was too old to be in this business.

He leaned against the hard bench and let his head fall
back. The age thing was a crock, and he knew it. There were
good agents, lots of them, older than he. His problems with
the job had nothing to do with age. They had everything to
do with the nightmares, the daymares for that matter. Even
now, behind closed eyes, the battered image of Darlene
Dickerson loomed. And Sam dreaded what was to come. The
interviews with her family, her friends, the delving into her
private life to find clues that would lead him to a suspect.
The image of the haunted, tear-filled eyes of Darlene's
friends and family joined the image of the murdered woman.

This was his problem with the job. And there wasn't a
damned thing he could do about it, because all of this *was*
his job.

You could quit.

It wasn't a new thought. He'd considered getting out of
the service, becoming a gumshoe or something. But somehow, taking photos of unfaithful spouses seemed demeaning
in comparison to taking psychopathic murderers off the
streets.

Pride. Sam allowed himself a small, ironic laugh as he
realized he was proud of what he did. Even as much as he
was beginning to hate his work, he believed it was important
work, and he'd been good at it. But recently, he'd begun to
doubt his competence. Things seemed to move slower for
him than they used to. His intuition had failed him in a

couple of instances. He didn't seem as sharp as he'd once been.

Sam looked at his watch. It was Sunday, but in his world, it didn't matter. He had work to do, and he knew he was stalling. A killer roamed these crowded, crooked streets, and like it or not, it was his job to find him.

Slowly he rose to his feet, tossed the empty popcorn container into a trash bin, and headed down the pier toward the city.

He had to pull himself together one more time, find this bastard and put him away, or more innocent women would die. He knew he could do it. What would happen after that . . . ? Sloan didn't know and didn't want to think about it.

7

Regan read the newspaper story about Darlene Dickerson's murder, and the lump of fear seemed to spread from her stomach through her entire nervous system. "This is awful, Kat," she said, for lack of something more meaningful. "I'm ... really sorry. It says here that two other women have been killed in the same way recently. Did you know about that?"

Kat hugged her knees to her chest, her face chalky, haunted. "Yeah, I read about them. But stories like that don't hit home until it happens to someone you know." She wiped unshed tears from her eyes. "Darlene was a good kid. Always joking, laughing. It makes you wonder, why her? Why did that awful person kill Darlene?"

The three sat in silence a moment, contemplating the unanswerable question. Then Kat said, "You know, this town gets scarier and scarier. Maybe we ought to move someplace where this kind of thing doesn't happen . . ."

Regan's eyes widened. The way Kat had been going on about this city and her life here, she'd thought nothing short of a devastating earthquake would shake her sister out of San Francisco. "What do you mean?"

"I mean, if it could happen to Darlene, it could happen to any of us."

An involuntary chill shuddered through Regan. What would she do if someone she loved—Kat, or Blair—died?

And such a horrible death. Regan had only just reclaimed her family. She wouldn't be able to stand it if something bad happened to either of them.

Kat interrupted her grim thoughts when she jumped up from the couch and strode to the front door. Regan heard the sound of the dead bolt being secured. Then Kat went to the back of the house and locked that door. When she returned, her expression was both thoughtful and troubled. "I've been a little lax lately in making sure the doors are locked. I've always considered this a safe neighborhood. I know that killer probably isn't lurking at the corner, but let's just all be sure and keep the doors locked."

"You sound like Mrs. Donovan," Blair said with a groan.

Kat turned to Blair, her gaze consuming her daughter. Regan could tell that despite her sister's breezy, casual relationship with Blair, deep down Kat Bowen was ferociously maternal. "I'm sure there's nothing to be worried about, but oh, baby, please don't take any chances. Maybe I ought to start driving you to school."

Blair let the comics section she'd been holding drop to the floor. "Don't even go there, Mom. I like riding the subway. All my friends are on it. Nothing's going to happen in the middle of the day on a BART train, for God's sake. Besides, they say she was found under a pier near the ferries. It's not exactly our backyard."

Kat gave her daughter a tight smile. "Up here," she said, pointing to her head, "I know you're right. But in here"— she indicated her heart—"it worries me. I'd die if anything like that happened to you."

Blair darted her mother an impish grin. "So would I."

Later that night, Regan stood in her darkened room, looking out the window. Fog had drifted in across the Golden Gate Bridge, diffusing the light from the street lamps, obscuring the details and stealing away the color, but she could make out the solid forms of the row of "painted ladies" that shouldered their way up the hill across the street. She was already growing to love these quaint, old Victorian houses with their gingerbread trim carefully painted every color of the rainbow.

Regan knew how much Kat loved her own painted lady, and she wondered if her sister had been serious about moving someplace safer. Living in a big city had its dangerous side, Regan supposed. People you knew could get murdered. But surely Kat's talk of leaving town was an overreaction.

Regan tried to imagine a serial killer stalking the streets of sleepy little Middleton, Virginia, and couldn't. If Kat wanted to move somewhere safe, Middleton was just the place. But the thought of her sister living in that stifling, plastic, phony community made her laugh.

And the thought of herself ever returning to that suffocating little town, or anyplace like it, made her want to throw up. These streets might be more dangerous, she thought, dropping the lace curtain back into place, but she'd rather take her chances here than ever go back to a life like the one she'd left behind.

8

Kevin Carrington parked in his assigned slot in the company garage, gathered his laptop and cell phone, adjusted a sweat-stained black and orange San Francisco Giants ball cap over his hair, and was about to get out of the car when he was startled by a sharp rap on the window. He looked up to see a grown man in steel-rimmed glasses gawking at him and waving childishly. A reporter? Probably not. More likely a groupie. He'd never known geeks could have groupies.

Kevin was still unusued to his celebrity status even though several years had passed since he'd taken his software company public and become one of the richest men in Silicon Valley. His computer games had become hot commodities, and he'd become an all-American hero when he'd amassed a fortune virtually overnight. Shy to the point of being antisocial, however, he'd found it difficult, painful even, to face the press and the public who were hungry to learn the secret to his youthful success.

He grimaced and got out of the car. *If they only knew that to me, it's just a game. It's all just a game.*

The geek groupie approached him, and Kevin affably signed an autograph for him, making a mental note to find out how the man had gotten past the security guard at the gate. Nobody like that was allowed on the grounds of

HomeRun, Inc., a sprawling complex in Palo Alto, the heart of Silicon Valley.

Kevin regarded the building before going inside. It was the architecturally unpretentious yet technically complex home of the company he'd started unknowingly when he was still a teenager, when he'd developed his first computer game while still at boarding school. He'd never meant it to become a business; it had been simply a pastime, a means of staving off the loneliness. He'd been surprised by the phenomenal popularity of the game among his schoolmates, who until they'd discovered his invention had shunned him as the introverted loner that he was.

One of the boys' fathers, Ed Johnson, had seen the potential in the game and had provided enough financial backing for a marginal launch at a computer show, where it had caught the attention of a major manufacturer of electronic games. They'd sold the rights, retained some royalties, and both walked away stunned at their unexpected success, their "home run," as the investor called it.

Kevin went to work for the manufacturer but didn't last long. He didn't work well with others. He also didn't like being pressured to create other computer products predesigned for "marketability."

Well-funded from his first success, he'd set up an awesome computer lab in his apartment and went not to work for himself, but to play. Even though Ed Johnson kept urging him to, he didn't care about coming up with another game and another and another to sell as he'd sold his first. He cared about amusing himself, challenging his substantial intellect, and creating worlds that would keep the real world at bay.

But in the years that had passed since, he'd discovered that others were hungry for his kind of amusement, challenge, and distraction. He'd never meant to become rich, but almost without his knowing how, he had.

"Good morning, Mr. Carrington." Richard Beatty, his ever-eager assistant, greeted him brightly as Kevin pushed through the glass doors of the executive suite. "I'm so glad to see you. I have a thousand things I need to go over with you." He paused, giving Kevin an appraising look, as if he found something lacking in his boss's appearance. "After you've had your coffee, of course."

Kevin looked down at his faded jeans and sneakers. He again adjusted his ball cap, then rubbed the growth of whiskers on his cheeks. He must look pretty bad to this dapper little man who wouldn't dream of stepping out of the house unshaven or wearing clothes that hadn't been starched and pressed. Kevin knew Richard wished he'd try harder to conform to the image of the successful entrepreneur, but Kevin didn't give a flip what he looked like.

All he cared about was the challenge that lay inside his computer. And he was eager to get to it without further delay.

"Coffee is good," he said, and headed to the sanctuary of his office.

For a multimillionaire, Kevin's personal workspace was surprisingly unpretentious. While his managers and support staff had taken full advantage of the fortune generated by the successful public offering to furnish lavish offices and conference rooms, Kevin had insisted that his remain the way he liked it. Simple.

He knew Richard disliked that about him, as well.

Kevin wasn't sure there was anything about him Richard did like, except his money.

He gave a quiet laugh and placed his laptop on the eight-foot Formica-topped table that served as his desk. He didn't care whether Richard liked him or not. Richard was good at his job. That's all that mattered. Kevin Carrington didn't want people to care about him. People who got too close frightened him.

Richard presented Kevin's morning coffee—a triple skinny latte—on a handcrafted pottery tray in a matching mug as big as a soup bowl. Kevin's one indulgence had been to hire an executive chef to oversee the growing corporation's internal food service system. To his delight, he'd discovered the man made a killer latte.

Next to the latte was a steaming bran muffin, a bowl of fresh fruit, and a cup of yogurt. Richard did this to him every morning, and every morning Kevin sent the food back untouched. He'd never told Richard about his daily stops at

McDonald's for sausage biscuits. Why ruin the guy's day?

Richard gave him twenty minutes then knocked sharply at the door. "Ready for business?"

Kevin was already deep into the project that had captured his imagination and was annoyed at being interrupted.

"What do you want, Richard?"

Without speaking, the assistant plonked down a pile of paperwork nearly two feet high on the table. "I know you don't like to deal with it, but since you're the top dog around here, you have to. Just go through this with me, tell me how you want to handle things, and I'll take it from there."

That was the real reason Kevin kept Richard around.

Kevin looked at the enomous stack of letters, faxes, and hard copies of e-mail. "All that's come in over the weekend?"

Richard didn't answer, and Kevin glanced up at him. "What's the matter?"

"Ah, well, sir, you've been gone since last Monday. This is last week's correspondence."

His patronizing attitude grated on Kevin. Didn't the guy get it? He couldn't concentrate in this madhouse. He often worked at home.

But he'd been gone a week? It was possible, he supposed. Kevin was used to big chunks of time slipping away as he sat totally engrossed in front of his computer. "Well, let's get it over with," he said irritably. "I don't have all day. I have to get back to my work. My real work," he added pointedly, nodding his head toward his laptop.

"Yes, sir. I understand, sir."

9

"What computer skills do you have?"

Regan moistened her lips and gave the young man who sat behind his desk her most confident smile, although inside she was trembling. A friend of Kat's had lined up this interview, and she didn't want to blow it. According to what she'd been told, *Pro.Com* was the hottest computer industry magazine on the market, and its owner and publisher, Jeff Roundtree, was looking for an administrative assistant who could run the show in the office while he was out hustling.

"Most any word-processing program," she lied, "but WordPerfect in particular." She'd used the software at her antiques store.

"Spreadsheet?"

"Excel."

"PageMaker? Photoshop? Quark?"

Oops. A drop of sweat trickled down her spine. Still, she refused to be daunted. "Mr. Roundtree, I can assure you that although I'm not skilled at the last three, I'm fast on the keyboard and an even faster study. And," she added, feeling her way to more solid ground, "I'm organized. As you can see from my résumé, I've been running my own business for years. I can run this office for you. No problem." Regan gazed at Roundtree and didn't blink. She had only rudimentary computer skills, but she *was* organized. And she wanted this job desperately. *Needed* this job.

Jeff Roundtree eyed her for a long moment, then allowed a slow grin to ease onto his lips. He was about her age, maybe a little older, with thinning brown hair and the beginning of a bulge around the middle. He wore a conservative suit and tie, and looked at her out of gold-rimmed glasses. "If I may ask, why are you not still running your own business?"

Regan was unprepared for the emotional jolt that slammed through her at his question. It felt as if he'd shot her through the heart.

"It's called a divorce," she replied, forcing strength into her voice, although her lip quivered slightly. "I . . . we had to close the store to make the property settlement work."

Regan had never hated anyone as badly as she hated Adam McKinney at the moment. Here was his ghost again, about to ruin something else for her.

"I see," Roundtree replied quietly and looked at the résumé again. When he looked up, he smiled, and Regan thought she saw a hint of compassion in his eyes. Maybe he too had gone through a divorce. "Well, I like your confidence," he said. "Maybe we ought to give it a shot."

Regan wasn't sure she'd heard him correctly. "You mean . . . you want to hire me?"

He laughed and leaned forward on his forearms. "Why not? On a probationary basis. If you're as good as you say you are, you're just what I need. If you're not, you're out of here. Fair?"

Regan smiled at him, liking his honesty. "More than fair. When do you want me to start?"

"Tomorrow?"

Regan was certain her feet weren't touching the pavement as she hurried out of the building after the interview. Equally elated and terrified, she almost ran the few blocks to the building where Kat worked as a paralegal. She flew into her sister's office and collapsed, breathless, into a chair.

Kat jumped up and ran to her. "Regan, what's wrong?"

Regan looked up into Kat's worried face, and a giggle

bubbled up. "I . . . got the job," she managed between breaths.

Kat grabbed her by both hands and pulled her out of the chair again and into her arms. "Way to go! I knew you could do it." She released Regan, who was now altogether quite breathless.

"The fact is, I'm scared spitless, Kat. What if I can't do the job?"

"You told him you could," Kat replied after Regan related the gist of the interview. "If you said it, something inside of you must have meant it. You can always go to night school to learn those software programs if you have to."

Regan looked at Kat thoughtfully. "I was telling the truth about being organized. And about being fast on a keyboard. And, yeah, there's a part of me that believes I can do this . . . if Jeff Roundtree is a patient man."

Kat made a wry face. "He's not known for that, but who knows, maybe he's different with his employees than with his corporate attorneys. He's known around here for being as aggressive as a bulldog. I know one thing, he's ambitious as hell. You make him look good, help him reach his goals, and you'll be his for life."

"Kat, I start tomorrow. It occurs to me that other than this"—she looked down at the conservative navy dress she wore—"I don't have many clothes that are suitable for that job. I mostly wore denim things at the store. Country-style, you know?"

Kat raised an eyebrow. "Are we talking shopping trip?"

10

Five hours, four stores, and too many dollars later, Regan and Kat piled into Kat's Acura laden with boxes and bags from her sister's favorite boutiques. After a few false starts, they'd finally agreed on a new look for Regan. Chic but not trendy, tailored but not staid. She had purchased dresses, jackets, slacks, blouses, scarves, underwear, shoes, and the pièce de résistance, a cocktail dress she doubted she'd ever wear, but so hot and perfect she couldn't resist buying it.

She felt a little guilty about how much money she'd spent, but it gave her a perverse sense of pleasure to know that it was Adam's money she'd squandered. He'd have had a fit if he knew what she'd just done. Regan laughed. Maybe she should have spent more, just to spite the SOB.

It was nearly ten o'clock when they got home after picking up Blair at a friend's house. Kat threw a frozen pizza in the oven, and Regan hauled her loot up to her bedroom, Blair dancing excitedly at her heels.

"I can't wait to see what you bought!" the young girl cried eagerly.

In a few minutes, Kat joined them, bringing the adults each a glass of red wine and a soft drink for Blair. Regan was efficiently hanging everything in the closet, trying to decide which outfit to wear for her first day at work when she came upon the cocktail dress. She held it against her and looked in the mirror, listening with pure pleasure as Blair and Kat both exclaimed over it.

It was made from an exotic fabric that at first glance appeared to be deep purple but which in a certain light glinted both ruby-red and bronze.

"Oh, cool. Try it on!" Blair insisted. She didn't have to ask twice. Regan slipped the dress on and Blair fastened the zipper in back, and all three of them stared at the image reflected in the mirror.

"Awesome," Blair uttered.

"Drop-dead gorgeous," Kat murmured.

Regan was speechless. It had been a knockout in the store, but at home, under softer light, it was even more stunning. "If I just had someplace to wear it."

"We'll find someplace. You're gonna break some hearts with that number, sis."

Regan had no interest in breaking hearts.

"It's a man-magnet," Blair declared, as if she knew all about men.

"I don't want a man." Regan hadn't meant for her words to sound harsh but realized they had.

"Maybe you don't," Kat said softly, "but I do."

Regan whirled and stared at her sister. "You've got to be kidding. Why? Why on earth would you ever want a man? I mean, you have everything, Kat. A beautiful home. A great job. You've done it all by yourself. You don't need a man."

Kat turned abruptly to her daughter and tousled her hair. "Bedtime, young lady. Tomorrow's a school day."

"Oh, Mom," Blair protested, "this was just getting interesting." But in the end, she obeyed her mother. Kat left to retrieve the pizza, and Regan changed into her pajamas and robe. When her sister returned, Regan reached for a slice of pizza and munched hungrily.

"Want to pick up where we left off?" she asked. Regan was determined to talk Kat out of making the Big Mistake.

"We can if you want."

"I want. It's important. You've got a great life. I'd hate to see you go and spoil it. I repeat, you don't need a man, Kat."

Her sister piled into the middle of the bed and sat cross-legged with the pizza in front of her. "I know I don't *need* a man, Regan. But I want one. I'm not the superwoman you seem to think I am. I never meant to live alone or to raise Blair as a single parent."

Regan was astounded . . . and disillusioned. She'd thought Kat was stronger than this.

"Trust me, Kat. You don't want a man."

"You've never been lonely, have you, sis?"

Kat's question caught Regan by surprise. No, now that she considered it, she never *had* been lonely. Empty maybe, but not lonely. There'd always been someone around she could call on. "No, I suppose not. But I think I'd rather be lonely than owned."

"You didn't have to be owned. You let yourself be. Like Mama." Kat's words, although not spoken in malice, stung nonetheless.

"I think men view ownership as part of the marriage contract," Regan replied bitterly.

"So, you've become a man-hater?"

"Well, no . . . it's just—"

"Don't hate men, Regan. Just because you made a bad choice in Adam . . ." Her voice trailed off, and she gave her sister an apologetic look. "I'm sorry. I shouldn't have said that."

Regan lifted one side of her mouth in a mirthless grin. "Don't worry. You didn't offend me. I did make a mistake in marrying Adam."

"You fell into the patriarchal trap Dad and Mama set for us. You were always the good girl, and you simply did what you were told. But that was then and this is now. You'll find somebody else."

"I'm not looking."

Kat took a sip of wine, and when she spoke again, there was an edge in her voice. "The swinging single life isn't all it's cracked up to be, Regan. It's tough. It's lonely when there's no one to share your life, no one to help you through the everyday ups and downs, no one there for you on your birthday or Christmas. Independence is fine, to a point. But I wouldn't mind having a partner to help pay the bills or"— she gestured at the walls—"to keep up this place. Besides," she added with a sigh, "I'm tired of sleeping alone."

Regan stared at her sister, stunned. "Then why haven't you gotten married?"

Kat shrugged and sat back on the bed. "I've never met anyone I wanted to marry."

"Even Blair's father?"

Kat smirked. "That was teenage lust. I never considered marrying him, even if he'd stayed around. Blair was a happy accident. But I do think she's missed something by not having a father in her life."

Kat's words shocked Regan. She was almost angry at her sister, as if Kat had let her down. But at the same time, Regan heard the longing in Kat's voice, felt the pain behind her words. It must not have been easy for Kat all these years, in spite of all she'd accomplished. And it must not have been easy for her strong-willed sister to admit it. Regan's heart softened, and she sat next to Kat on the bed.

"So, how're you going to go about meeting Mr. Perfect?"

Kat squeezed Regan's fingers and laughed. "No Mr. Perfect exists. I'm not setting myself up for that disappointment. But Mr. Nice Guy, Mr. Goodfather, Mr. Responsible, Mr. Great Lover, or all of the above would do." She let out a long breath. "Finding him is the hard part."

When Regan had run away to California, it had been to the sanctuary offered by her sister, a safe place where she could lick her wounds, find herself, and get a new start. It had been all about Regan. It had never occurred to her that Kat might need her, as well. She was suddenly ashamed she'd been so self-absorbed. "How can I help?"

Kat exhaled a little laugh. "I don't know. I'm out of practice when it comes to looking for a guy. I haven't dated in a long time."

"I find that hard to believe. I figured you must have men lined up to go out with you."

"Not. I go to work, I go to the grocery store, the hardware store, Blair's school. Most of the men I meet are already married or else not very interesting."

Regan tilted her head and looked at Kat. "What kind of man would you find interesting?"

Kat pursed her lips, thinking. "Someone who's as not-normal as I."

"A not-normal guy? Give me a break. That's just asking for it."

"I don't mean a psycho," Kat protested. "I just mean someone who's also been an outsider, who marches to the proverbial different drummer. Someone who's a bit of a free spirit."

Regan tried to visualize such a man. "You looking for an old hippie? I somehow can't see you tooling around in a rainbow-painted VW van with a guy who smells like patchouli."

Kat fell onto her back with laughter. "No. Oh, God, no. I . . . I just want a guy who loves life, who knows how to laugh. I'd really like to meet a guy who likes to dance, go on long walks, and who doesn't like tofu."

Regan grinned. "That's quite a laundry list." She hesitated, thinking, then added, "Seems to me if you want to meet a guy who likes to dance, you should go dancing."

Kat looked up sharply and matched Regan's grin. "What a concept, sis." She sat upright, went to the closet and pulled out the purple cocktail dress. "That's exactly what we're going to do."

I I

The man sat at a table in the dining room at HomeRun, Inc., the *San Francisco Examiner* spread out before him and a cup of coffee in hand. A few other employees chatted and brainstormed over breakfast at the dark mahogany tables. He glanced around the room. How pretentious it all was. The tablecloths. The soft lighting. And especially, he thought with disdain, the corporate chef, although the man had to admit the chef's talents kept the employees happy. He found it ridiculous, however, that the company was paying big bucks to the guy when all Kevin Carrington, the big cheese around here, ever tasted were his lattes.

But then, the little dweeb was rich enough to do whatever he damned well pleased, he thought bitterly.

He turned his attention to the newspaper and only when he read a particular story did his resentment against Kevin Carrington subside. A smile crawled slowly across his lips. The cops up in San Francisco seemed to be scratching their heads about all those dead women. They'd even brought the FBI in on the case, and a special agent, a profiler from Quantico had been assigned.

The man chuckled, feeling almost gleeful. He laid the paper on the table and wiped his flushed brow with a napkin. His heart pounded with excitement and his nerves sang with tension. Neither the police nor the FBI would ever catch this guy. They might pin the murders on somebody, but it wouldn't be the real killer, for he was far too clever, too adept at disguise, to ever get caught.

The man turned the page.

Another article caught his eye in the business section. The story wasn't long. Just a little snippet reporting the record earnings of HomeRun, Inc., and lauding the genius of the company's founder, Kevin Carrington. The man rolled his eyes.

Kevin Carrington would be nowhere right now if it hadn't been for him.

His earlier resentment returned and brought with it a deep-seated rage. Why did Kevin get all the glory? He hadn't done any of the work. Kevin didn't even care about going public. All he'd wanted was money to buy more computer shit so he could run away into his virtual worlds and hide from reality. But because of the hard work of others, Kevin had ended up hitting the jackpot with one of the most successful IPOs a high-tech company had ever engineered and become an overnight hero to greedy entrepreneurs everywhere.

At least Kevin hadn't turned to his father for the money, the man was forced to concede as he thought about it. God knew Michael Carrington was loaded, but he'd never done anything for his son except ignore him. The man admitted grudging respect for Kevin's having had the balls to stay away from that asshole. But Kevin's sustained arrogance and indifference to those who'd made him what he was infuriated the man. After all he'd done for Carrington, the silly twit treated him as if he didn't exist. He appreciated nothing. He never said thanks. In fact, he rarely even spoke to him.

The man slammed the newspaper shut on the table and became aware that others were staring at him. He didn't care, about them, or Carrington, or HomeRun, Inc. He was sick to death of them all, but most especially of Kevin. Sick of kissing his ass, and of saving it, as well. Carrington didn't give a shit about him or anybody else. His boss stayed lost in his crazy little cyberworld; nothing and nobody else was important to him.

What am I doing here? the man wondered suddenly. Why

do I stick around? What do I care what happens to Kevin Carrington? At the moment, he hated Carrington so much he wished the geeky kid would die. And then an idea came to him. The man straightened his back, smiled at the people who kept glancing at him uneasily, and stood up. He slung his brown overcoat over his shoulder and headed for the door.

He'd had enough, and soon he would be free.

12

Sam Sloan entered the Golden Gate nightclub in the area of San Francisco known as "South of Market," or SOMA to the locals. He stood just inside the door, allowing his eyes to adjust to the dim atmosphere. Once inhabited by the homeless and the drug addicted, SOMA had in recent years become gentrified, as a plethora of dot-coms and other information-technology companies had taken up residence here during the boom times. Technostocks had taken a nose-dive, and a lot of those companies were now out of business, but clubs like this that had grown up to serve that clientele had survived. The Golden Gate was reputed to be one of the hottest heterosexual nightspots in the city. It was a place, Sloan suspected, where the killer might come in search of prey.

Music blared from a monster sound system, and garish klieg lights flashed in time to the throbbing beat. Dancers crowded the floor, a few of them appearing to know something about the Latin dance that was in progress, the rest just gyrating in time to the music. The atmosphere reeked of booze and anticipated sex.

Sloan despised places like this. They made him feel as if he'd descended into a corner of hell. He'd made the rounds of these kinds of meat markets earlier in his life, when his wife had left him and he'd been desperate for something to stave off the loneliness and guilt. But he'd quickly discovered that for all the action and noise, these places were empty, devoid of honesty and truth and beauty in any form. People came for one reason—to forget about honesty, truth, and beauty. They came to lose themselves in sensation, to drink, dance, and if they were lucky, to get laid afterward.

Jesus, Sloan thought suddenly, I sound like a preacher. He didn't give a damn what these people did and certainly had no right to be judgmental. Still, places like this bred the darkest of crimes—rape, assault, and even murder.

And that's why he was here.

Sloan gazed around the room, wondering if the killer was here, too, watching, surveying the women, selecting his next victim. After studying the victimology of the three women who'd been murdered recently, Sloan believed that the killer was a dancer, or at least, that he chose his victims by coming to places like this. Relatives and friends of all three women reported the victims were last seen getting ready for a night on the town. All three were found the following mornings, brutalized, their bodies lying at the water's edge in San Francisco Bay like so much driftwood.

There were lots of places like this in the Bay Area. The killer could be frequenting any or all of them. But Sloan hadn't come here to make an arrest. He had no idea yet whom he was looking for. He'd come here to *get* an idea. To try to put himself into the head of the murderer. To figure out what made him tick, and what made him kill. Was it just because the women who gathered in these places were an easy mark? This seemed the obvious answer. But from experience, Sloan knew that serial killers worked in strange ways. There was usually something more, something deeply psychological about their choice of venue. And about their choice of victims.

In this case, the killer had a thing against redheads, Sloan was certain. He pressed his way through the throng of patrons, his eyes roaming the crowd, picking out women with red hair. He wanted to go up to them and warn them of the danger lurking nearby but knew they'd think he was a lunatic if he did. His gaze suddenly caught on a pair of attractive young women seated at a small table, both looking distinctly uncomfortable.

First-timers, he thought.

Redheads, he noted.

One of them, the one with longer hair, must have felt his gaze on her, because she looked up and their eyes met. She was probably in her mid-thirties, with a pretty face and a dress that clung seductively to the kind of body men fantasized about. *Get her out of here,* he thought. This woman and her companion were sitting ducks for a madman like the one he was after.

Sloan nodded to the woman, but she looked away. He made no move toward her table. Instead, he turned and deliberately lost himself in the crowd, but when he felt he'd become sufficiently invisible, he found her again and kept his eye on her.

The two women didn't stay long. He saw the one who'd caught his eye lean across and shout something to the other, as conversation was impossible in this thundering din. The other woman gave the first a disdainful look, but both stood up, took their wraps from the backs of their chairs, and headed for the front door. Sloan followed, oddly relieved that they were leaving but wondering if they were simply getting ready to hit another club. Barflies, headed into the spider's web?

He watched them get into a Luxor cab, and then they were gone. A feeling of helplessness swept over him. Even if he wanted to, he couldn't save these women, or any of the others who were vulnerable to this madman. All he could do was his job, and if he was lucky, he'd find the son of a bitch before another woman died. He headed down Eleventh Street, deep into the heart of SOMA, observing the fashionable and not-so-fashionable late-night revelers coming and going from the numerous clubs and restaurants. He was stalking an elusive chimera of the murderer, and with each step, his frustration mounted.

13

"Did you see that guy staring at us?" Regan said, looking over her shoulder out of the back window of the cab as it swept past the nightclubs on Broadway and into the Broadway Tunnel. "He really gave me the creeps."

"I thought he was pretty cute." Kat's voice held an edge of irritation, and Regan knew she hadn't wanted to leave the club so quickly. They'd been there less than an hour, and Kat had been looking forward to a night on the town. But Regan's head was pounding from the music, and tension knotted her shoulder muscles. Maybe Kat was having fun, but Regan was miserable. She'd felt naked and exposed in her skimpy purple cocktail dress, and she'd been downright frightened when the tall, ruggedly good-looking man had caught her eye.

What would she have done if he'd approached her? Other than Adam, she hadn't been with a man, even to dance, in the last fourteen years, and the thought of a strange man's hands on her body was terrifying.

She glanced at Kat, who stared silently out of the window, and felt guilty. They'd come because Kat wanted to pursue a social life, and instead Regan had acted like a perfect ninny and run away. Gloomily, she realized how asinine her behavior was. So what if the man had asked her to dance? Isn't that what they'd come for? What was there to be afraid of? She regretted her insistence that they leave.

"I'm sorry, Kat. Want to go back?"

"No." Her sister offered nothing more than that one terse word, and Regan knew the evening was ruined. They rode in silence the short distance to the old Victorian house in Pacific Heights. Regan paid the driver and followed Kat up the steps, hoping to find some way to make amends, but Kat simply bade her good night and went to her room.

14

The man stood beside the bay, his hands in his pockets, his head tilted back. He gazed at the moon, watching mesmerized as filmy clouds scuttled over its silvery face, creating an interesting tapestry of shadow and light. He drew in a deep breath, inhaling peace along with the damp, salty air. Then he turned. He still had work to do.

He went to his vehicle that was parked nearby, opened the rear door, and with an effort, hauled the woman's body out by the arms. This one was heftier than the others had been. But then, Briana had been hefty, too.

Careful not to stain his clothes with blood, the man dragged the body to the water's edge and dropped it into the bay, where it made more of a squish than a splash when it hit the mud.

Had his brother's body made a sound when they'd thrown it in the ocean? he wondered. The man's throat tightened, and he glared down at the dead woman. Damn her, he thought, feeling the rage return. Damn her to eternal hell . . .

15

Regan arose early and had breakfast ready for Kat and Blair when they finally trundled down the stairs after sleeping in. She'd brought in the newspaper, scanned it looking for a specific kind of ad, and had it ready to show Kat when the time was right. She was desperate to make up for her foolish behavior of the night before.

When she came into the kitchen, if Kat was angry, it didn't show, and Regan remembered with gratitude that her sister rarely carried grudges. Still, she felt an urgency to make things right. After they'd finished the eggs, toast and fruit compote Regan had prepared and were discussing plans for the day, Regan brought out the newspaper.

"I was thinking," she began hesitantly, choosing her words carefully, hoping she'd say the right thing. "I mean . . . I think I freaked last night because it was all just too much, too soon. Besides, I don't even know how to dance."

"You don't have to explain," Kat said.

"Yes I do." She laid her hand on Kat's arm. "I ruined your evening, acting like a frightened adolescent." She turned to Blair with a small smile. "Sorry. Don't take that personally."

Blair just shrugged, but she was obviously intrigued. "What'd you do?"

Regan explained what had happened. "And I bolted like a scared rabbit."

"We'll know not to do that again," Kat laughed ruefully.

"No. We *will* do that again. You're right, Kat. I need to put what happened with Adam behind me and get on with my life, and that includes finding some way not to hate men, not to be afraid of them. You want a social life. You want to meet a man who likes to dance, but frankly, it was so crazy and noisy in that place, I don't know how you'd ever meet anyone you'd take seriously."

Kat picked an orange from a bowl on the kitchen table and began to peel it. "Maybe you're right. So what's your suggestion?"

Regan laid the newspaper in front of her sister. She'd circled an ad with a red marker: "Sterling Pace School of Dance. Change your life. Make new friends. Learn to dance." A list of exotic-sounding dances followed, as well as a photo of a couple obviously having a great time dancing in each other's arms.

"Let's take some lessons. It'd be a way to ease into the scene instead of jumping into the deep end, like we did last night."

Kat stared up at her, aghast. "Good grief, Regan, that's for bluehairs."

Regan's cheeks burned, but she didn't budge. "Maybe not. There's bound to be other people our age who want the same thing you want—to meet others who like to dance but who don't particularly like to go clubbing."

"Mom, you're so out of it," Blair blurted, turning to straddle her chair. "Dancing like Regan's talking about is all the rage. Lots of people from my ballet class take those kinds of lessons." She jumped up, took the chair in her arms like a dance partner, and paraded around the kitchen in a dramatic imitation of some exotic tango. "See? Pretty sexy, huh?"

Regan and Kat laughed at Blair's antics, but Regan could see her sister still wasn't convinced. "Come on, just try it once. It says here the first lesson is free. If it's an old folks' home, we'll leave. What have we got to lose?"

"Go on, Mom, do it. Don't be so stodgy."

"Stodgy? Where'd you learn that word? And who says I'm stodgy?"

Neither Regan nor Blair answered that one. Then Blair set the chair down and put her arms around her mother's shoulders. "Go once, Mom. If you don't like it, you don't have to go back."

Regan heard the longing behind Blair's encouragement and realized that her niece desperately wanted her mother to meet a man who might at long last become her father. What had been an effort at compromise between going out to dance clubs and doing nothing at all took on new significance, and Regan stiffened her resolve.

"That's right. One time. That's all I'm asking."

16

The Sterling Pace School of Dance was on the corner of a busy intersection in North Beach. It occupied nearly an entire city block and was lit up like a Christmas tree with splashes of vibrant neon color, looking for all the world like another, although very large, dance club. Regan swore beneath her breath. Was this really any better than going to a nightspot?

Kat didn't turn off the engine, but sat staring up at the brightly lit marquee that announced various events and contests. "You sure you want to do this, sis?"

Regan watched people going from the parking lot into the building. They were fresh faced and eager, all dressed to the nines. "I don't see a single bluehair," Regan remarked, encouraged. "Come on. Let's go in. If it's awful, we'll just leave." Maybe it would be awful, like the club she'd fled on Friday night. Or maybe, she forced a hopeful thought into her mind, it would be fun. Maybe Kat *would* meet someone who liked to dance, someone nice who was learning to dance, too. Regan wasn't interested in meeting a man, but it wouldn't hurt if she learned a few dance steps in the process. She pulled the handle and opened the car door, not giving her sister another chance to change her mind.

They were greeted at a reception desk by a woman with big, blond hair and a friendly smile. Her name was Wanda.

"You're newcomers, aren't you? Haven't seen you here before."

"Yes," Regan replied, for once being the spokesperson for the sisters. "We . . . uh . . . read the ad in the paper, and—"

"You're here for a free introductory lesson," Wanda finished for her with an easy, understanding smile. "Here, sign this register, and we'll get you started."

Wanda must have seen the skepticism on Kat's face, because she looked right at her and said, "Don't worry. It's a lot of fun."

The studio differed from the dance club in that it was not only larger, but much better lit. Regan noted gratefully that it was smoke-free, as well. The main ballroom consisted of what appeared to be three round stages upon which couples danced, perhaps at varying stages of skill, Regan guessed. On one platform, she saw a man with thick, silvery hair moving alongside one couple, swaying with their movements, obviously coaching them.

"That's Sterling," Wanda said when she saw Regan watching him. "He's the best. He's been teaching people to dance for nearly forty years." The admiration in her voice was clear, and Regan took heart that she was going to learn to dance from a man so . . . unthreatening.

"What do we do for partners?" Kat asked, seemingly warming to the idea.

"We have several teachers for you to dance with. Most of those guys on the floor are teachers. We teach a lot more women than men, you see."

Regan studied the men. None of them fit her image of dancing instructors. No too-tight black pants, no slicked-back hair. These guys looked . . . nice. They were well dressed in suits and ties. Some wore more casual attire, but all seemed like the kind of men Kat would be safe in meeting. "How do we get started?"

"I'll introduce you to Sterling," Wanda said, steering them in his direction. "He likes to greet newcomers personally."

In a few moments, the number ended, and the couples took a break. The older man approached them.

"I see some new faces here," he said heartily, holding out his hands. "Welcome, ladies. I'm Sterling Pace. Are you ready to change your life and learn to dance?"

Regan stifled a laugh. "Yes, we are," she replied. "I think," she added, darting a quick, doubtful look at Kat.

"Well, come on. Let's show you how much fun this is." He took a remote control from his pocket, pressed several buttons, and music filled the room. As the others looked on, Sterling Pace took Regan in his arms, and before she knew what was happening, he began to whirl her around the dance floor. He was strong and sure, and following his lead was easy. They returned to where Kat and Wanda stood watching them, and Pace released Regan and took Kat for a spin.

"He's quite a good dancer," Regan said, rather flustered but suddenly excited about the prospect of learning to dance.

"He's probably won more contests than anyone in the Western world," Wanda said.

"Contests?" Regan hadn't thought about dance being some kind of sport.

"Oh, honey, there're contests everywhere. A lot of his students go on to be top competitive dancers. You'll see."

Regan wasn't interested in dancing competitively. "I . . . we . . . just want to brush up on a few steps." *And my sister wants to meet a man who likes to dance.* At that thought, Regan let her gaze wander around the room again. Were any of these men likely candidates to become her new brother-in-law?

"Well, you've come to the right place. And your timing is great. There's Peter Smith coming in now. He's chronically late, which aggravates Sterling to no end, but he's also the best instructor by far we have on staff. Want to meet him?"

Regan saw a tall man in a navy sport coat coming into the ballroom. He had light brown hair and a nice-looking face, although she thought him just short of handsome. He walked with an easy grace, and his smile was warm as he stopped to greet the other dancers. He reminded Regan of Hugh Grant. To her surprise, she felt her pulse quicken.

Wait a minute. This is Kat's gig.

"Maybe you should introduce him to my sister first. She's

. . . the one who really wants to learn to dance. I'm just here to support her."

Wanda gave her an odd look, as if she were crazy not to want to meet Peter Smith. "Suit yourself, but it looks to me as if your sister is in good hands with Sterling."

Kat indeed appeared to be in good hands. Regan noted with relief that her sister was actually talking and laughing with the dance instructor. She couldn't imagine Kat having a romantic interest in a man so much older than she, but still, Regan was relieved to see Kat getting into the spirit of things.

When she returned her attention to Wanda, Regan discovered that she had no option but to meet Peter Smith, as he was headed directly for them.

"Hello, Wanda. You're looking fine tonight." His smile could charm the socks off a dragon, Regan thought, feeling an unwanted glimmer of attraction toward him. He turned to greet her and extended his hand. She either had to take it or appear rude. "Peter Smith," he said, his eyes riveting hers.

His skin was warm, his blue-eyed gaze disconcerting. She felt her heart skip a beat or two. Uh-oh. What was going on here? "R-Regan," she stammered, "Regan McKinney."

"Well, Regan McKinney," he said with a mischievous grin. He cast an amused glance in the direction of Sterling Pace. "Are you ready to change your life and learn to dance?"

Cocky. Peter Smith was cute, but cocky. Regan didn't know quite what to do with a cocky man. "I—I'm here because of my sister, actually." Why was she stammering again? And why was she making excuses not to dance with Peter Smith? She straightened and tilted her head to the side slightly. She wasn't about to let this man get under her skin. "But I suppose I could learn a step or two while I'm here."

17

Peter Smith normally paid only cursory attention to the women at the studio. They were his students, and it was his job to charm them while he taught them the steps of the dance, but he'd never found any of them particularly interesting on a personal level. That's why his reaction to this one took him by such surprise.

He'd spotted her standing next to Wanda the moment he'd reached the door to the ballroom, and something inside of him had shifted. He felt almost magnetically drawn to her. As he'd observed her from the shadows of the doorway, something about her seemed oddly familiar, strangely compelling, but he couldn't put his finger on what it was. He didn't think he'd seen her before.

She appeared to be about his age, young enough to have a youthful sparkle about her but old enough to show a certain maturity. She had shoulder-length hair, strawberry-blond in color and styled in a manner that allowed it to swing breezily when she turned her head. She was pretty rather than beautiful, with a freshness about her he found captivating. She was dressed rather conservatively for a dance class. Most female students wore clothing that tended toward the flashy—party dresses and showy jewelry—but this woman wore a simple pair of black slacks and a white silk blouse.

On her, however, the simplicity looked elegant. Intrigued, he made his way toward her.

Up close, she was as appealing as he'd found her from a distance. He could tell she was ill at ease, however, and it didn't surprise him. Most newcomers were. Some got cold feet before they ever made it to the dance floor.

Peter suddenly, urgently, hoped she wouldn't leave, and the power behind his feelings unsettled him. She was just another student, he reminded himself. At the same time, he also remembered why he must keep her, like all the rest, at arm's length. "What kind of dance are you interested in learning?" he asked, sticking to his professional approach, although her green eyes lured him. "Rhythm? Smooth? American style? International?"

He saw her flush and suddenly wondered if she was feeling something for him, as well. Unlikely. Dear God, he hoped not.

"I don't know," she replied. "Just the basics, I guess. Nothing fancy. I just want to be able to fend for myself on a dance floor."

"Then let's give this a try," he said, indicating the peppery Latin music that was playing. "It's an easy one to learn." It was also one dance that didn't require partners to get too close.

Peter showed her the basics and gave her a strong lead with his right arm when he twirled her around and guided her through the fast footsteps. At one point, however, she stumbled and withdrew her hand from his.

"I'm hopeless," she said, sounding miserable.

She wasn't hopeless. She was quite good, in fact, to have been keeping up as well as she had. Peter realized that he was demanding far more of her than he did most beginners. It was almost as if he wanted to run her off.

"You're doing fine," he said, then added, "for someone with two left feet."

Peter didn't know where that nasty little comment had come from, and he was appalled at his rude behavior. He gave her one of his smiles that he knew charmed most women, but he saw that his words had stung. "I'm only joking," he said. "You really are doing fine. I'm pushing you a little hard, I guess. I promise, I'll take it easier."

She appeared to be a good sport about it, and Peter relented as promised. He hoped Regan wouldn't mention the incident to Sterling, whose cardinal rule was that students be made to feel good about themselves. He liked this job, and he wanted to keep it. It was about the only time he could relax and enjoy himself. Perhaps that was why he'd always kept his distance from his students. He didn't want personal complications to interfere with his enjoyment of the short time he had in the studio.

Personal complications. Regan McKinney? What was it about her that was different? And why did he find her so threatening?

The number ended, but to his consternation, Peter found he didn't want to let her go. He ought to excuse himself and find a partner who was just another face, but instead, he heard himself asking if she'd like to take her trial lesson in one of the smaller rooms, where he could show her the steps without interrupting the class that was about to resume its session.

Before she could reply, Sterling Pace and the woman he'd been dancing with joined them. "Evening, Smith," the older man said, looking pointedly at the clock on the wall. "Glad you decided to make it."

Peter knew he was late. He was always late. Time was a difficult concept for him, it seemed, but he didn't care. He was here, and he knew he'd give Pace his money's worth.

"Traffic." It was always a good excuse, since everybody who lived or worked here had experienced the city's notorious gridlocks from time to time, traffic snarls that turned San Francisco into one giant parking lot.

Pace grunted. "I want you to work with these ladies, if you don't mind. Give them an hour of your brilliance in Studio Two, and I'll bet they sign up." He took the hand of his partner, bowed and kissed the air above her fingers. "It was my pleasure, Ms. Bowen. I hope you'll decide to join us." He nodded at Regan. "The same to you. Have fun." With that, he rejoined the class he'd been leading, leaving Peter with both women.

He didn't mind. It was safer this way. He took each

woman by an elbow and escorted them to the smaller class-room, trying like hell to behave normally, even though his pulse was racing.

"So, what'll it be?" he asked, closing the door behind him. "How about a little traditional ballroom, a little night-club stuff, and something more unusual . . . a sampler, so to speak?"

He was speaking to both women, but his eyes were on Regan. She shrugged and glanced at the other woman. "I . . . I guess that's okay. This is my sister, by the way, Kat Bowen." Kat was an attractive woman, but her hair was too short, too dramatic for Peter's taste, and she was too thin and angular. He went for women with more curves. Like Regan.

God help him.

18

"Well?" Regan asked two hours later when she and Kat returned to the car. She couldn't speak for her sister, but Regan's knees were a little weak, not only from the unaccustomed exercise, but also from the electric attraction she'd felt toward Peter Smith, in spite of his remark about her having two left feet. Regan was inexperienced with men, but all evening she'd gotten the feeling that Peter might have been attracted to her, too, although he'd kept up his teasing manner. Maybe he was a professional flirt, as well as a dancer. Maybe Kat felt the same way, that Peter was attracted to her. Regan frowned slightly at the thought.

"It was fun," Kat admitted. "And Sterling was kind of cute."

"Sterling? Isn't he a little old for you?"

Kat gave Regan a sour look. "I didn't say he was the guy I've been looking for, although if he were fifteen years younger, he might be. Imagine, a man who's made his living dancing. Now that's marching to a different drummer."

"But what about Peter? He's more your age. I think he liked you."

Kat didn't answer right away. "Peter's cute, but he's not my type. And besides, he sure seemed smitten by you."

Regan's cheeks burned. "Smitten? You've got to be kidding. He's a charmer, all right, but I'm sure he flirts with all the women. We signed up for classes, didn't we?"

They had indeed decided to enroll in lessons. For the next four Monday evenings, they would attend "Dance Basics." The studio also sponsored parties, according to Peter, and although they hadn't committed to attending any, Regan felt such social gatherings were bound to be better than the club scene she'd found so threatening. She wondered if Peter went to the parties.

The phone was ringing when they walked in the front door, and Blair picked it up. She turned to Regan with a curious look on her face. "It's for you."

Who could be calling her? Regan wondered, going to the phone. "Hello?"

There was a slight hesitation, then a man's voice inquired, "Regan McKinney?"

"Yes?"

"This is Peter Smith. We met earlier at the Sterling Pace Studios."

As if she'd forgotten. "Yes, Peter. Thanks for the lesson. It was great." She glanced at Kat, who hid a gleeful grin behind her hand.

"I said something tonight I didn't mean, and I'm afraid I offended you," he said. "I'm calling to apologize."

"Something about my having two left feet?"

"Uh, yeah. I don't know why I said that. You're really quite a natural on the dance floor."

What was he up to? Regan wondered. Was he afraid she would complain to his boss? "Well, it's very sweet of you to call, Peter, but it wasn't necessary. Maybe I do have two left feet."

There was a long silence on the line, then, "I was wondering if you'd consider going out with me this weekend."

His invitation took Regan completely by surprise. She also didn't know how to respond. She wasn't ready for this sort of thing.

"Out? Where?" Her divorce was too recent, the wounds still too raw. She didn't know herself, and she needed time. But Peter's face loomed in her mind's eye, his easy grin and twinkling eyes seducing her.

"I don't know. Since you're new to the Bay Area, I thought maybe I could show you around a little on Saturday. There's a lot to see. We could do downtown, you know, the cable car thing, Fisherman's Wharf, or go out to the Presidio, maybe over to Sausalito. The weather's supposed to be nice. It'd be a good day to be outside."

A day in San Francisco's golden sunshine with a good-looking man showing her the sights? Tempting. Regan glanced uncertainly at Kat, who was nodding vigorously.

"Go," Kat whispered.

"Go," Blair echoed, doing a little dance on the stairway.

Regan hesitated, then heard herself say, "I . . . I guess that would be all right. What time?"

"I'll pick you up at ten, unless that's too early."

"No, that's fine. I'll see you Saturday."

Regan replaced the receiver on its cradle and turned in stunned dismay to her sister and niece. "What have I just done?"

Kat hugged her. "You've just made a date with a really nice guy, it seems to me."

"How do you know he's a nice guy? We don't know anything about him except he's a great dancer. And you're the one who was looking for a man who likes to dance, not me."

"But you're the one he asked out. Besides, I told you, he's not my type."

"Did *you* meet anyone, Mom?" Blair asked hopefully.

Kat fluffed her daughter's hair. "Yeah, actually, I did, but he's too old for us."

19

The body of Chloe Martin was discovered early Wednesday morning in the shallow waters of the bay near Candlestick Point, on the far southeastern side of San Francisco, near Candlestick Park Stadium. Her emerald sequined dress was as shredded as her body, and her bloated face was no longer recognizable. The coroner estimated she'd been dead several days.

Sam Sloan shook his head. "What kind of bludgeon is he using?"

"There're wood splinters everywhere. My guess it's a bat of some kind."

"Like a baseball bat?"

"Maybe."

There'd been wood splinters imbedded in the remains of the other victims, as well, adding one more similarity to the murders.

Sloan's gut knotted. Like the other victims, this woman looked as if she'd been dressed for a night on the town. Had she been at one of the clubs he'd visited last Friday night? Had he seen her with the killer? Could he have saved her?

Detach. Don't let it get to you. There's nothing you could have done to save her. He heard his inner voice speaking, but he wasn't convinced it spoke the truth. Grimly clenching his jaw, Sloan left the coroner to his examination and sought out Brad Kelly. His office was on the fifth floor of the Hall of Justice on Bryant Street.

"I want to go to the media," Sloan told him. "There's enough evidence now that he's after a certain type, in a certain environment. Even though we don't know what he looks like, we can issue a warning to women with red hair not to frequent any Frisco dance clubs at the moment, and certainly not to leave with a stranger."

The media was one of Sloan's favorite tools for the apprehension of killers, and he knew how to work the reporters. Even though many of them were no longer true journalists but rather "infotainers," whose job it was to titillate and entertain rather than inform, Sloan approached them with respect. He needed their help, whether he liked their style or not. He appealed to their humanity, spoke of the victims as if they could have been sisters or wives of those writing the stories. Sloan remained positive, always positive, even when he despaired of ever laying hands on the murderer.

"We must let the public know this guy is out there, and that he's going to kill again," he told the small gathering of reporters later at police headquarters.

"Any idea who he is?" one female reporter wanted to know.

Sloan gave the reporters what he could, the profile his team had managed to compile so far. "We believe he's a Caucasian male in his late twenties to mid-thirties. He's probably employed and makes decent money. He likely drives a late-model car, one big enough to transport the bodies. Most importantly, we believe he likes to dance, or at least he frequents the clubs in the Bay Area. Each of the victims was last seen alive in these places."

"Any similarities among the victims?"

Sloan nodded. "He goes for women in their twenties and early thirties, attractive women with red hair. They were all wearing dressy, flashy clothing. They were strangled, then their bodies were beaten and thrown into the bay." He ran his hands through his hair. "I implore you, warn the public. This guy is a monster, a mentally disturbed man who will kill and kill again until we stop him. It's not safe for women, especially those with red hair, to go to dance clubs right now. And though he may be doing redheads now, he could easily switch to blondes or brunettes later. Sometimes these guys change their MO or their signature. So warn every woman in the Bay Area."

Sloan let out a heavy breath before continuing. "And for God's sake, if women of this description do go to a club, warn them against leaving with a stranger. This guy could be anybody. Killers like this look like every other ordinary Joe on the street. Sometimes they can be very attractive and charming. They don't have horns and a tail, they don't have fangs, they don't look like Dracula. The fact is, they are often masters of blending in." He looked around at the solemn faces of the journalists. "I need your help. We're getting closer to learning his identity, but in the meantime, your stories could save someone's life."

A murmur buzzed around the room as the reporters prepared to leave. "Don't you know anything else about this guy?" asked a particularly persistent woman. Her features were hard, her voice raspy. Her press badge identified her as a reporter for the *Chronicle*.

Sloan looked up at her and replied grimly, "Yeah. He might be into baseball, too."

20

"He's here!"

Regan heard Blair's announcement all the way upstairs and cringed. She hoped Peter Smith hadn't heard it from the street. She'd die if he got the idea she was eager. She was so nervous her stomach was in a knot.

The doorbell rang, and the knot tightened.

Why had she agreed to go out with him? She wasn't ready to date. Regan wasn't sure she'd ever be ready to date. She glanced in the mirror and saw she hadn't put on any lipstick. Quickly, she applied a light pink. She looked at herself in the full-length mirror. Maybe she ought to change clothes. Kat and Blair had talked her into wearing her new, crisply pressed, rather tight-fitting jeans. Were they too tight?

The open collar of her starched blue and white striped cotton shirt revealed the scoop neckline of a gold tank beneath. Was it too scooped?

Regan inhaled and tried to calm down. She looked just fine. In fact, with the weight she'd lost in the last six months, she looked great. She just wasn't accustomed to looking so . . . well . . . so sleek.

Footsteps sounded on the stairs, and Blair burst into the room. "Come on! He's waiting!" She took Regan by the arm and dragged her to the door. "Omigosh, he's so cute! I know you're going to have a wonderful time."

Regan wished she was as confident as Blair.

Peter Smith was as appealing as he'd been at the dance studio. He too wore jeans, topped with a light blue polo shirt that almost matched his eyes. Those eyes lit when he saw her. "You look great."

Regan shrugged, embarrassed. Adam had rarely complimented her during their fourteen years together, never in recent memory. Probably because she hadn't looked so great. She was suddenly glad Kat had insisted on the jeans. "Thanks," she managed at last. *You don't look so bad yourself.*

"Ready?"

"Do I need anything else?" she asked, picking up her shoulder bag and a small camera in case they went somewhere scenic.

"You might want to take a sweater. This is San Francisco. Hot one minute, cold the next. I have an umbrella in the car, just in case."

The car was a vintage Jag convertible, low-slung, sort of a pewter color and polished to a sheen. It seemed obvious to Regan that it was Peter's pride and joy. What, she wondered, did this man do for a living besides teach dance lessons? Surely he couldn't afford an automobile like this on what he made at Pace's studio.

She studied him as he put the car in gear and eased it down the steep hill. He was good-looking, but not what she'd call handsome. His features were regular—no chiseled jaw, no aquiline nose. His hair was light brown, his eyes blue, his build medium. Average in every way, and yet when taken as a whole, not average at all. Her decided attraction to him frightened her, and she looked away.

"So, where do you want to go, Lefty?" Peter asked, and shot her a grin so devastating she couldn't be mad at him.

"I thought you wanted to apologize for that."

"I do. That's why I wanted to take you out today, to make it up to you if I hurt your feelings."

"But you just made fun of me again."

That grin again. "No I didn't. I said it this time as a— what do you call it?—a term of endearment."

Endearment. Oh, dear.

Regan left that one alone. "Do you really think it could rain?" she asked, peering up at the pale blue sky laced with wispy white clouds, acting like Winnie-the-Pooh, trying to be nonchalant when in fact her nerves were wired.

"Maybe. Maybe not." He came to a stop at the bottom of the hill, then turned to her again. "So, where's it going to be?"

Regan shrugged. "You decide. I don't know the area at all."

"Then how about breakfast in Sausalito for starters? I know this great little place right on the bay."

"Sounds good to me."

As they approached the famous landmark Golden Gate Bridge, Regan caught her breath sharply. A shroud of fog had descended just at the bridge entrance, rendering the giant metallic structure totally invisible. Cars exiting the bridge appeared to be coming out of nowhere, and as Peter drove onto it, she felt as if they were entering some kind of strange and spooky surrealistic world. "This is weird," she remarked, unsettled, as she peered through the windshield at the thick, wet soup.

"Just give it a minute," Peter said, tossing her a grin. "We'll drive out of it before we get to the other side. It happens a lot. Fog will obscure the south side, and it'll be clear as a bell on the north. As for it being weird, you should see it at night, with all the amber and orange lights. You'd think you were on another planet."

Regan's nerves, which had begun to relax, tightened again until at last, as promised, they emerged into brilliant sunshine. It was as if they'd passed through some kind of magic portal.

"I think the weather around here is going to take some getting used to," she remarked. Looking down from the dizzying height to the water below, she asked, "How far down is it?"

"Over two hundred feet, give or take, depending on the tide," Peter answered. "It's a favorite jumping-off place, you know."

"Jumping-off place? You mean . . . ?"

"Over twelve hundred suicides since the bridge was built

in 1937. San Francisco, in fact, is the suicide capital of the United States."

He spoke without emotion, as if he were a tour guide ticking off statistics, but his words gave Regan the creeps. She recalled the recent murders in the area. San Francisco, for all its polish and international flair, certainly had its dark side.

She chose not to comment further, and they rode in silence through the winding streets of Sausalito.

It *was* a great little place, Regan thought when they entered the small restaurant that overlooked the shimmering waters of the bay. The café was in an old house that had been lovingly restored. Outside, its clapboards were painted yellow and white, and inside, each room was decorated in variations on the yellow and white theme. Different wallpapers and hues of paint brought the sunshine in even on dreary days, Regan surmised.

They were served on old-fashioned blue willow china, and when her platter of seafood crepes topped with hollandaise arrived, to her relief, Regan found she was ravenous. Peter had ordered a more traditional breakfast of eggs, sausage, and biscuits.

"How'd you find this place?" she asked between bites. "It doesn't seem exactly on the beaten path."

She was startled to see a shadow of a frown cross his forehead, as if her question, which she'd asked just to make conversation, had somehow upset him. "Sometimes I get restless," he told her curtly, "and I just get in the car and drive. I was out cruising one day last year and got hungry and accidentally happened into the place."

He offered nothing more, and an awkward silence fell between them. Maybe he didn't like small talk. Distinctly uncomfortable, Regan decided not to push him by asking some other mundane question. Moments later, however, Peter spoke, and when he did, there was no trace of annoyance in his voice or words. Maybe she was imagining things.

"Did I tell you, you look great?" His tone was back to normal, teasing, flirtatious.

Caught off guard, Regan felt herself blush. "Yes. Thank you."

"Thanks for coming today." He toyed with his fork, dragging the tines through the residue on his plate. She realized suddenly that he was nervous, which made her feel a little better.

"Thanks for asking."

He raised his head to look directly at her. "I, uh, I'm not very good at this," he said. "I don't go out with many women. I hope I didn't put you off calling you Lefty again."

Peter's unaffected style touched her heart, and she was grateful for his honesty. She felt safe with him and was glad he hadn't turned out to be more sophisticated and experienced with women. She felt as if they were on common ground.

"I'm not very good at it, either, Peter. And as long as you're not making fun of me, you can call me Lefty."

They laughed, and Regan's spirits soared. When had she last laughed with Adam?

"You know," Peter said, "it's kind of strange, but when I met you the other night, I felt like . . . well, I don't know, kind of like I've met you before."

Pickup line or sincerity?

Regan chose to believe Peter was being sincere, since he'd already picked her up. She too had experienced an instant attraction to him, although she didn't exactly share the same feelings of having known him before. He was still very much a stranger to her, a mysterious stranger at that. And she was still nervous, wary of him, of any man.

She took a sip of coffee and smiled at him. "That's a nice thing to say, I think, but I can assure you we haven't met before. I've never been to California."

"Did you move here, or are you just visiting?"

Regan felt herself grow edgy. She didn't want to talk about her life. "Moved. A couple of weeks ago."

"From where?"

"Virginia."

When she didn't offer anything further, she hoped he'd drop his questions. He waited for only a few seconds, however, then asked, "Why'd you move?"

A part of her was irritated with Peter for poking into her life, but another part understood that he was just trying to get to know her better. Wasn't that what a date was all about? Still, Regan found she had to clear her throat to speak.

"My sister lives here, and I . . ." Her throat tightened a notch, and she cleared it again, determined to get this over with. "Peter, I've just been through a bad divorce. I came out here . . . to start over." The moment the words were out of her mouth, she felt better. This was her truth, and it was nothing to be ashamed of.

"I'm sorry," he said and reached for her hand. "In a way." He squeezed gently. "And in a way not. You're single, and you're here. Your loss is my gain."

Regan didn't know exactly how to take that. She'd never met anyone who laid his cards so openly on the table. Not knowing how to respond, she gave him a rueful smile, removed her hand from his and took another sip of her coffee.

"How can I help you?" he asked after a moment. "You need a job?"

"I've just found one, actually, but I'm on probabationary status. The boss wants to make sure I can cut it."

She told him about *Pro.Com* magazine and Jeff Roundtree, then somehow the conversation turned to her antiques business and what had happened to it, and the shadows of her recent past closed out the sunshine of the moment.

As if he sensed her pain, Peter dropped his questions and signaled the waitress for the check. "Let's go before the day gets away from us."

Outside, the sunshine was brilliant and had dissipated the last vestiges of fog on the bay. The waters glistened and sparkled in the light, and Regan's spirits brightened once again. If nothing else, Peter Smith was a sensitive, thoughtful man, and she was grateful.

They walked to the end of a dock and watched the Sausalito ferry wend its way among a legion of sailboats into a mooring. Peter pointed out landmarks on the San Francisco skyline that were visible across the water on this clear day— the ferry building, the Transamerica Pyramid, the Palace of Fine Arts with its neoclassical dome and Corinthian pillars.

Regan snapped a few pictures of the city from a distance and had Peter pose in front of the restaurant for another.

"How long have you lived in San Francisco?" she asked, raising her face to the warmth of the sun as they returned to the car.

"Oh, I don't live in the City." He opened the car door for her, and she took her seat. "I have a place down the coast," he said, gesturing toward the Pacific Ocean as he rounded the car to his side.

"Is it far?"

"No place in the Bay Area is very far. It's just that the roads are congested. They call it 'L.A. North,' " he added with a laugh, settling into the driver's seat. "It's a nightmare. It takes me about an hour to get to Sterling's even though it's not far. Now," he said, turning to her and draping his arm across the back of her seat, "what would Milady like to do and see on this fine, fresh day?"

He sounded old-fashioned, but for some reason, she didn't find him corny. She had to admit she rather liked being treated like a lady. Kat would die if she knew that, but Regan had lived all her life in the South, where the rules were different, and women were supposed to be respected and treated well by their Southern gentlemen.

Except that she hadn't been.

In an epiphany, Regan suddenly realized how cruel Adam had been to her, how domineering, how patriarchal. He'd never hit her or physically abused her, but his verbal abuse had been acerbic and frequent. Why hadn't she seen it for what it was?

But Regan already knew the answer. Adam was in many ways just like her father, John Bowen. Regan had grown up with parents who criticized and condemned. She didn't know anything else. Sitting here in the sunshine next to Peter, she thought for a moment she might cry, not from sorrow, but from sheer joy at knowing there was another, better world for her than the one she'd left behind.

She raised her eyes to meet his gaze and again felt that inexplicable tug of attraction. *Be careful. Go slowly. You don't know this man.*

It struck her how incredibly vulnerable she was at the

moment. She was hungry for acceptance, starved for affection, in deep need of validation of her worth. She'd better go really, really slowly with Peter Smith. He seemed like a nice, sweet, sensitive kind of guy, and yet . . . he also seemed to have his little strange moments.

Be careful. Go slowly. You don't know this man.

She also didn't know the area. "You decide," she said, again letting him guide the day. "I don't know much about San Francisco. Kat's taken me to the Museum of Modern Art and the Yerba Buena Gardens, but I've been so busy, I haven't seen much else."

He started the car. "Are you the outdoors type?"

She considered that a moment. She'd never thought about what "type" she was. "I like being outdoors," she answered at last. "I played tennis back home . . ." She broke off.

Back home.

She had to quit saying that.

"I'm thinking it's such a great day, maybe we should go to the Presidio," Peter suggested. "If we have time afterward, we'll go into the City and ride the cable cars. What do you say?"

The sun glinted off his hair, turning the light brown golden. His smile was radiant, his eyes inviting. Even though she had her defenses on alert, Regan was glad she'd come out with him. "Sounds good to me."

The Presidio, he explained as they drove back across the Golden Gate toward the city, was once an army fort, a garrison that dated from the Civil War era. When the army left in 1994, the land became part of the Golden Gate National Recreation Area. "There's a golf course, hiking trails, bike paths, quiet beaches and hideaways. It's almost like being in the country even though it's right in the City."

A short time later, Regan walked beside Peter on a narrow trail through towering, fragrant eucalyptus trees. The sounds of the city, so nearby, were hushed, sometimes not even audible. An occasional foghorn blared a warning from time to time as ships entered and left the Golden Gate. They were alone on the path, the only two people on the earth, it seemed at the moment.

Suddenly and for no apparent reason, Regan shuddered.

Her mind flashed to the recent newspaper articles about the women who'd been murdered in the Bay Area. To the warnings issued by the FBI: women, especially redheads, were warned not to go out with strangers. And yet here she was, alone in the woods with a man she barely knew. Unsettled, she glanced at Peter, who caught her gaze and gave her that sexy smile to which she was growing very attached. Regan released the tension that had tightened her jaw and cursed her overactive imagination. Peter Smith was no serial killer, she reassured herself, although it seemed he very well might make off with her heart.

"Smells great, doesn't it?" Peter inhaled, raising his head slightly as he sniffed the salty marine air and the eucalyptus trees.

She took in a deep breath, too, and the sharp scent of eucalyptus, pine, and cypress tingled in her nostrils. She heard a bird call from somewhere in the woods. Sunlight slanted through the trees, giving her the feeling that they were lost in an enchanted fairy-tale forest. It had been a long time since she'd been aware of the beauty of nature. She was happy that Peter had brought her here, had wanted to share this special place. Regan's misgivings vanished in a heartbeat, and she breathed deeply again of the crisp air, feeling more alive than she could ever remember.

21

Peter Smith was still blown away that he'd invited Regan on a date. Although he liked women, he always kept his distance, in his dance classes and in his emotions. He wasn't very good at relationships. Occasionally, a niggling little voice inside suggested he might even be *afraid* of getting involved with a woman.

That was ridiculous, of course. But still, he had to admit it was a little strange that although he was solidly heterosexual, he'd never once in his thirty-five years had a serious affair. He glanced at the pretty woman striding along beside him.

Maybe it had nothing to do with being afraid of relationships with women. Maybe he just hadn't met the right woman.

Until now.

Even as he thought it, a small warning shot through him. *Don't get involved.* He didn't know where the thought came from, and he didn't want to hear it, so he shook it off. There was no reason to be alarmed. He was just inexperienced with women, he told himself, and nervous about today.

He'd invited Regan to spend the day with him, but he wasn't quite sure what to do with her. At the studio, he knew what to do with and for the women who came partly for dance lessons and partly for male companionship. With them, conversation came easily, because they were safe. They were his job. And they would leave without him when the evening was over.

Regan McKinney, on the other hand, seemed to be a different matter altogether. He didn't want to like her, but he did. There was something about her, something he couldn't explain, that seemed to draw him like the proverbial moth to the flame. He looked at her again and felt his heart skip a beat. The sunlight burnished her coppery hair that swung like a curtain of fire with each step she took.

You know what happens when you play with fire . . .

Although his inner voice troubled him, again Peter chose to ignore it.

They reached a fork in the road, and suddenly Peter was anxious to get back to where there were other people around. Being alone with her seemed too intimate. "This leads back to Fort Point," he said, indicating one of the paths. "Do you want to keep going, or head back?"

"Are you reading my mind?" she replied, smiling but breathing hard. She tucked a strand of hair behind her ears. "I can't believe I'm so out of shape."

Peter hoped his relief didn't show. They turned down the path that led past the National Military Cemetery and back to the redbrick building that once served as the headquarters of the army post. Their arms brushed occasionally as they walked, heightening Peter's inexplicable anxiety.

"So, did you enjoy your dance lessons the other night?" he asked, seeking safe ground.

"Yeah, that was great."

Peter could almost feel her in his arms, and he had to work not to think about it.

"It's good exercise."

She laughed. "Obviously, I need it. But that's not why we came to the studio."

"Why *did* you come?"

Why did you have to come into my life? Peter felt an edge of irritation. Until he'd laid eyes on Regan, his life had been well ordered, under control. But now, everything seemed different. Was this what it was like to be in love? The very notion made him even more nervous, and he picked up his pace.

"For my sister, actually," Regan said, and it took Peter a moment to remember what they'd been talking about. Distracting. She was so damned distracting. Not to mention beautiful.

"What about your sister?" He remembered the sister, the tall, skinny one.

"Could you slow down a bit? I told you I was out of shape."

Peter hadn't realized he'd begun walking so fast. "Sorry," he said and slowed down again. He felt his heart pounding hard in his chest, and blood sang in his ears. What was wrong with him?

"Kat mentioned that she'd like to meet a man who likes to dance. She dragged me to this dance club the other night, and it was really awful. So I suggested we take dance lessons instead. I think it's a lot safer than those clubs."

Peter had to force himself to focus on what she was saying. "I've always hated dance clubs myself," he said, managing to pick up a thread of the conversation. "Too crowded and noisy, and nobody really dances."

"Not to mention a serial killer on the loose, apparently haunting those places in search of his victims," Regan commented. "I guess you've read about that in the papers?"

Peter came to a dead stop, and it took Regan a few steps to realize he wasn't keeping up. She halted and turned around. "What's the matter?"

He thought of Regan at one of those dives, at risk, exposed to the murderer, and his blood ran cold. He hurriedly closed the space between them and took her by one arm. "Promise me you won't go to places like that again."

He had a sudden, terrible urge to kiss her, as if that would somehow make her promise not to put herself in harm's way. His face eased slowly downward, moving closer to hers. He could see the tiny beads of perspiration on her brow and just above her lips. He noted the pale freckles on her nose.

And then he stopped. What the hell was he thinking? He barely knew this woman, yet he was acting as if she were his possession or something, like he had the right to dictate what she did with her life. He saw the confusion in her eyes, and he released her arm. "Sorry. I didn't mean to . . ."

"Mean to what?" she asked with a shake of her head. A slight frown creased her forehead.

"Uh, to scare you."

She gave him a dubious grin and rubbed her arm where he'd clutched it. "You didn't scare me, Peter, but don't worry. I can assure you, wild horses couldn't drag me back to that place."

He stood gazing at her, wanting her, wanting to be far away from her. "Well, then," he said after a moment. "Good. Let's go."

Back at Fort Point, Regan went to the ladies' room and Peter stepped in line at an ice-cream vendor's kiosk. He was still shaken by his behavior moments before, alarmed by his unfamiliar and runaway feelings. Out of the corner of his eye, he thought he saw a young boy watching him as he selected their ice cream. The child seemed familiar, but when Peter turned to get a better look, the boy was gone.

Regan had asked for a single scoop of pistachio, and he ordered a double cone, chocolate over butternut. He didn't wait for her before taking a bite of his. He desperately needed something to cool the unfamiliar fire in his belly.

22

"I was getting worried about you," Kat fussed when Regan let herself in the door after saying goodbye to Peter. It was nearly dark, and she'd been gone for hours.

Blair bounded down the stairs. "Did he kiss you?" Her teenage eyes were wide and eager.

She wished. "No. He didn't kiss me. Nice girls don't kiss on the first date. Don't you know that?"

Blair groaned. "Give me a break."

Regan hung her handbag over the back of a kitchen chair and took a bottle of water from the fridge. When she turned, she saw both Kat and Blair staring at her. "What?"

"So, did you have a good time?" Kat asked, turning back to her cooking project.

Regan plopped into a chair, physically and emotionally exhausted. "Yeah. I had a great time."

And she had. After the tour of the Presidio, Peter had taken her into the City where, as promised, they'd ridden the cable cars. They'd had a late lunch in Chinatown, and then strolled by the waterfront. It couldn't have been more perfect, except . . .

There was something she couldn't quite put her finger on. Peter had asked a few questions about her life, but when she'd tried to find out about his, it was as if a door shut between them. He'd been sweet and solicitous, but at times moody. She wasn't quite sure how to take him.

She gave her sister and niece a blow-by-blow of the day's activities, avoiding any mention of her feelings about Peter. Kat spotted the hole immediately and jumped in. "But what about him? What's he like? Did you like him? What does he do?"

Regan had made little inroad when she'd questioned Peter about that. "I don't know exactly," she admitted. "Something to do with the stock market, I think. He told me he makes his own trades on-line, and he seems to know a lot about high-tech companies. He thinks Jeff Roundtree is going to have a hard time taking *Pro.Com* public because of the dot-com bust on Wall Street. Stuff like that makes me think he knows what he's talking about. Maybe he's a stockbroker, I don't know." She took a sip of water, thinking about Peter's evasiveness. Did he have something to hide?

"Is he rich?" Blair asked, straddling a chair.

Regan shrugged. "He drives an expensive car."

"That could mean nothing except that he's got a large credit line," Kat remarked dryly, dishing up supper and placing plates on the table.

"True." Regan took no offense at Kat's skepticism. She was skeptical, too. "He didn't come right out and say it, but I suspect he lost money on some of his investments recently."

"Are you going to see him again?" Kat wanted to know.

For that, Regan had no answer. "Who knows? He didn't ask for another date."

"Bummer," Blair said.

Regan turned to her niece. "Maybe not. I told both of you I wasn't interesting in dating for a while. We had a nice time, but if I don't see him again, that's okay."

But later that night, as she climbed beneath the comforter and snuggled into the pillows, Regan admitted to herself that that was a lie. She *wanted* to see Peter again. He hadn't told her a lot about his personal life, but then, neither had he demanded that she give away too much about her own. He'd admitted that he wasn't used to going out with women, and

Regan suspected that he was as wary as she of becoming too involved. And that made him safe.

Would she see Peter again? She closed her eyes. Time would tell.

23

*Someone was in his room. He knew it. He could smell some-
body there. It was the man. Although the darkness was too
thick for him to see, he knew the man was getting closer,
closer. The boy cowered beneath his covers, too frightened
to run, too terrified to breathe. He willed himself to be invisible. He couldn't take it, he couldn't stand the feel of the
man's greasy, smoke-stained hands on him again.*

*"Where are you, you little fag?" The man's voice was
angry as he pulled away the covers.*

*The boy held his eyes shut tight. He was invisible. He'd
dematerialized. As long as he kept his eyes closed, the man
couldn't see him. "Where are you? When I find you I'm
going to beat the shit out of you. You know what happened
to your brother. You do what I say, or it's gonna happen to
you."*

Invisible. Stay invisible.

*The man couldn't see him, but oddly, he could see the
man, even with his eyes closed. He watched as the light came
on in the room, and the man approached a figure in the bed.
Who was that in his bed? the boy wondered.*

*He shivered in the cold, nowhere space where he hid and
watched without feeling what the man did to the boy. He
watched the boy's pajamas being ripped away. He saw the
man fondle the boy's genitals until the undeveloped penis*

became hard. *He watched the man take his own penis out and force it into the boy's mouth.*

Who was that boy?

That boy who didn't scream, or cry, or in any way resist the man's assault. He must be brave, that boy. Or dead. But the boy looking on saw that the other child wasn't dead. He also sensed he didn't feel anything. He must be magical, that boy. It didn't hurt, what the man was doing to him now. It had hurt the onlooker and humiliated him, but this boy was able to take it. He felt sorry for this boy, but grateful that the boy was the victim, instead of himself.

When the man was finished, he turned, and to the horror of the onlooker, the evil fiend grinned right in his face. He could smell the sickening sweet odor of whiskey on the man's breath and see his yellow stained teeth.

"You just thought you were invisible," the man said, taking him by the neck and shaking him until his brains hurt. "You little cocksucker! You coward!"

The man's eyes bulged, and his face contorted with rage. "Wait until she hears what you've done. She isn't going to like this, not at all, bugger-nose."

She.

The boy knew exactly who the man was talking about. She. The demon of the night. The boy's fear turned to fiery ice. The man's torture was nothing compared to hers.

The woman was summoned, and suddenly the boy was in a courtroom of some kind. She was the judge, and the man was the jailer. He held the boy tightly by the arms, rendering him helpless. Loud music played, music with a hard, heavy, hot beat.

Ka-thud. Ka-thud. Ka-thud.

"Guilty!" the woman cried over the music and slammed a gavel so hard on the bench that it burst into shards.

Ka-thud.

"Guilty!" she cried again. She approached the boy, and he could see that instead of a gavel, she held his brother's baseball bat in her hands. "Guilty," she hissed a third time, and she raised the bat. "It's your fault that your brother is dead."

And then suddenly, he was his brother. He screamed and

covered his head with his arms, but nothing could protect him. He felt the bat strike him hard across the face. Once. Twice.

Ka-thud. Ka-thud.

The boy heard his bones crack, felt a searing pain where the bat struck his flesh. He wrenched his body, trying to get away, but the man held him fast. Another blow cut away his ear.

Ka-thud.

He screamed, but there was no sound.

He cried out for help, but knew no one was there to help him.

The boy jerked around and looked at the man, beseeching his mercy, but the man's face suddenly morphed into that of someone the boy thought he knew, and yet didn't recognize. The familiar face was not a friendly face, however. It wasn't that of someone who had come to save him. This Whoever-It-Was had come for some other reason.

The new face turned toward the woman, and the boy felt himself being released. He watched as the man with the new face took the bat away from the woman and flung it into the darkness. The man took the woman by the neck and squeezed and shook and shook and squeezed until her eyes bulged and her face turned blue. The boy knew he ought to help her, but he stood frozen, a part of him filled with righteous rage and wanting to see her die. He watched in fascination, thrilling to the violence, the power, the vengeance wreaked by this familiar stranger.

The man with the new face dropped her body and stood over it, hatred burning in his eyes. He retrieved the ball bat from the darkness and held it above the woman's body.

Suddenly the boy was *the man. It was he who stood over the woman, wielding the bat. It was he who brought the stick smashing down across her face, he who now heard her bones splinter.*

Ka-thud.

She didn't cry out, because she was already dead. Why had the man killed her first? The boy wanted her to feel the pain. He wanted her to hurt, to suffer the torture.

The music pumped obscenely in his ears, and rage filled his belly.

He hit her again and again and again. Her blood spurted over him with each stroke until the bat became slick in his hands.

Ka-thud. Ka-thud. Ka-thud.

She would never hurt him again.

24

Regan arrived at her office early Monday morning, hoping to get her desk straightened and her act together before Jeff showed up. Last week, her first on the job, had been stressful, and even though she'd managed to stay ahead of Roundtree's not insignificant volume of correspondence, by late Friday afternoon, there were still a few things left hanging.

Although catering wasn't included in her job description, Regan made a pot of coffee, mainly because she wanted a cup. This zany town seemed to run on caffeine, and she was already hooked on the dark, rich blend of French roast coffee available on virtually every corner. Jeff had told her he bought fresh-ground coffee for the office from a nearby coffee seller, and Regan guessed that Jeff, like the other up-and-comers with dreams of corporate riches, wouldn't be caught dead serving a pedestrian brand like Folgers. It just wasn't part of the scene.

As the aroma of the French roast filled the small office, Regan turned on her computer. She'd caught on quickly to the various software packages Roundtree used, including the programs for page layout. She was encouraged by her natural, instinctive ability to understand and use computers.

"You have mail," a disembodied computer voice informed her. She wondered what junk mail was coming at her. She hadn't given her e-mail address to anyone, so she wasn't expecting any personal messages. She sat down in her chair and clicked the retrieve icon. Might as well clear the e-mail clutter away before she got started with her day.

But there was only a single message, the subject of which was simply "Hello." Curious, she clicked it open, and when she saw it was from Peter, she smiled and her heart melted. It melted even more when she read the message. It was a poem about the day they'd spent together, followed by a brief note:

"Thanks for a great day. I hope we can do it again soon. See you in class. Peter."

She wondered where Peter had gotten her e-mail address, but she supposed it didn't matter. Although she was ambivalent about her feelings for him, she'd been disappointed he hadn't called her yesterday, and she had to admit she was glad he'd sent the e-mail.

She'd almost forgotten about their Monday-night dance class. Suddenly and for no reason, she felt nervous about seeing Peter again. She was determined not to let this thing, whatever it was, get out of hand. Maybe she just shouldn't go. If she didn't see Peter again, it wouldn't get out of hand. Simple. And not. Before she had time to consider it further, Jeff Roundtree bustled through the front door.

"I see you came back."

She smiled a little uncertainly. "I hope you wanted me to."

He came closer to her desk and gave her a long, slow, appraising look that disconcerted her just a little. His gaze roamed from her face to mid-torso, which was all he could see as she sat behind the desk, and returned to her eyes. It was probably nothing, her imagination combined with her troubling concerns about Peter, but his survey seemed a bit too intimate. Inwardly, Regan grimaced and prayed that Jeff Roundtree wasn't planning to come on to her. She liked him as a boss, but she wouldn't be able to handle it if he tried to transform it into any other kind of relationship.

"You did real well last week," he said at last. "I think you're going to work out fine. I was especially impressed with those letters you wrote."

Regan had almost forgotten she'd written the letters. He'd

given her the gist of what he wanted to say and asked if she'd compose them for him. It had been easy, and she'd thought nothing more about them. Now, she wondered if that had been some sort of test.

"Thank you."

"I didn't hire you on as a writer, but you seem to have a knack for it. Would you be interested in writing an article for the magazine from time to time?"

Regan could hardly believe it. "I . . . well, I don't know if I'm good enough."

"I'll be the judge of that." Roundtree headed for his office. "I see that you've already made some coffee," he called over his shoulder. "Please throw it out and use this." He wagged a bag of freshly ground coffee from the nearby Coit Tower coffee vendor in the air before plopping it onto the counter next to the coffeemaker and heading into his office, never breaking stride.

Regan glared after him, not sure whether to be annoyed or amused. She was so surprised and flattered at his compliment about her work, however, that she decided she could live with his affectations about coffee.

When she'd made a fresh pot, she returned to her computer and tried to decide how, or whether, to answer Peter's message. She poised her fingers on the keyboard, but couldn't decide what to say, so instead, she closed the program. She'd get to it later, after she'd had time to sort out her feelings.

She'd spent the entire day on Sunday trying to do just that, but to no avail. She'd jumped each time the phone had rung, hoping it was Peter, but he hadn't called. By nightfall, she'd managed to convince herself that even if he did call eventually, it was premature to date him, or anybody else. Now, she found that just receiving his e-mail shook that resolve.

During the morning, Regan answered numerous phone calls, typed correspondence, sent some faxes, made another pot of coffee, barely finding time to catch her breath in between. She was quickly learning that Jeff Roundtree kept a furious pace and expected those around him to do so, as well. He was a young man on the rise, ambitious, hard-working, and determined. Regan could admire those qualities, but she hoped he didn't miss out on life along the way, as Adam had. Ironically, after her day with Peter, Regan felt a twinge of pity for Adam. She couldn't remember a single time when he'd enjoyed a thing in life other than vanquishing an opponent in the courtroom.

She also felt strangely sorry for the young woman who'd stepped into her shoes, Adam's new wife. Would she allow Adam to dominate her the way Regan had? She cringed at the thought, but then put it aside. Why should she feel sorry for either of them? She should be grateful instead. And she was. They deserved Middleton and each other, and Regan was ecstatically glad to be free. In retrospect, the divorce was the best thing that had ever happened to her, she decided.

It was around three o'clock in the afternoon when Jeff finally took a break and came into the front office where Regan sat. "I've got an assignment for you," he announced.

Regan cocked her head slightly to one side, curious. "Assignment?"

"Yeah. You know this morning, I mentioned your writing an article from time to time for *Pro.Com*. Well, I want you to see if you can get an interview with Kevin Carrington and write us a piece about him. See if you can dig out his secrets. How did he do it? What kind of game plan did he have? Did he have any inside help? See if you can get some names, some sources for me."

"Who's Kevin Carrington?"

Roundtree looked at Regan as if she'd just stepped off an alien space ship. Then his expression reflected disappointment. "You're kidding me. You don't know about Kevin Carrington, the boy wonder of Silicon Valley? Self-made multimillionaire by the time he was twenty-seven?"

"I'm new here, remember?" Regan defended her ignorance, refusing to allow Roundtree to bully her. "Maybe you'd better assign the story to someone else. Or do it yourself."

"I'm not a writer," he told her. "I'm a deal-maker. All my regular freelancers seem to be tied up. Besides, I don't think Carrington would see me. He avoids the press like the plague."

"What makes you think he would see me?"

"You're a woman. He seems to be more open to talking to women than men, but he's real shy, I understand. It won't be easy. Carrington's got a prissy little pit bull for an assistant, a guy named Richard Beatty who's very efficient at fending off the press for his boss. I wouldn't even make an appointment, if I were you, because I don't think they'd give you one. I'd just go to the headquarters of HomeRun, Inc., and take my chances. The offices are near Palo Alto. Carrington's quirky. Perhaps if you camp out on his doorstep, he'll give you an interview."

The whole idea was daunting to Regan, but at the same time, challenging. She knew she could do more for *Pro.Com* than answer phones. But this? "When do you want this story?"

"When can you give it to me?"

"I don't know. I need to do some research on Carrington before I try to see him. I don't want to seem ignorant."

Roundtree nodded his head toward her computer. "All the background you need is on the Internet. The facts about him and his public offering have been out there a long time. It's the inside scoop, the human-interest story, the private life, that I'm after." He examined his nails and added, "I also want to know how he did it. I want to know his contacts, his money sources, his advisers."

"Why?"

Again that look of disbelief at her naïveté. "Because, like I've told you, in spite of the present bust in Internet business, I've got plans to take *Pro.Com* public. Timing is everything. I missed the first boom, but there'll be another, and when conditions are ripe, I want to be ready."

25

"What a geek," Blair said, staring at the likeness of Kevin Carrington that Regan had pulled off the Internet before she'd left the office. Regan had to agree. One of the world's richest entrepreneurs looked back at them from a pencil sketch an artist had drawn of him, appearing for the world to be the poster boy for the media's stereotype of the ulti-mate computer nerd. Regan figured the sketch was several years old.

Kevin Carrington appeared to be in his late twenties at the time the sketch was drawn, with brown hair barely show-ing beneath a San Francisco Giants baseball cap. The bill of the cap was pulled low over his forehead, shadowing what appeared to be a rather flaccid, boyish mien. He wore John Lennon–style wire-rimmed glasses, and his cheeks were stubbled with an incipient beard. His overall appearance could only be described as scruffy. The artist had drawn him wearing a red and black plaid flannel shirt, complete with pocket protector and calculator.

"Who's *that*?" Kat asked contemptuously when she saw the illustration.

"A guy named Kevin Carrington. My boss has asked me to do an article about him." Regan could hardly keep the excitement out of her voice. "I didn't have much time this afternoon, but I managed to download this from the Internet, just to get started."

Kat looked over Blair's shoulder at the picture. *"That's* Kevin Carrington? Somehow I thought he'd look different. Richer, or older . . . or . . . something."

"You've heard of him?" Regan laid the rest of the pages about Carrington on the kitchen table and headed for the refrigerator.

"Of course I've heard of him," Kat replied. "Everybody around here's heard of him. But I can't remember ever seeing a photo of him."

"Apparently there aren't any," Regan told her. She opened a bottle of Safeway peach-flavored select soda and drank deeply. "He's a hermit, from what I've read, and he refuses to have his picture taken."

"I have one of his first computer games," Blair said. "Want to see it? I think it's the one that got him started."

Regan turned to her. "You do? Of course I want to see it. Can you show me how to play it?"

"Sure. But you'll have to come to my room. It's sort of old-fashioned by now, and it only works on my desktop."

Blair had both a desktop and a laptop, not to mention a handheld electronic reader, a Game Boy, a PlayStation 2 and myriad other game equipment. She was one of those kids who took computers for granted as an everyday tool of life, and Kat had indulged her with whatever computer equipment she could afford. "It's the future, sis," she'd explained, justifying her purchase of yet another box of software Blair wanted. "I want her to be on top of things when she gets out of high school. I want her to be more than . . . a paralegal."

"Nothing wrong with being a paralegal," Regan had argued, but she knew what her sister meant. She would like to be more than a secretary, too. Her short stint at *Pro.Com* had made her believer that the world of computers, in spite of its present slump in the financial markets, was indeed the world of the future.

"The game will have to wait until later," Kat said. "Dance lessons tonight, remember?"

Regan remembered. But she hedged. "Maybe we shouldn't go," she suggested nervously.

"What?" Blair and Kat exclaimed in unison.

"I mean . . . maybe it was a mistake to sign up. I'm not sure I can afford it." But this was BS and she knew it. So did the others.

"You're not backing out on me now," Kat insisted. "You're the one who started this, and you're going to finish it." She touched Regan's arm gently. "I know what it is. You haven't heard from Peter, have you?"

Regan sat on a kitchen chair and sipped at her soda. "Yeah, I heard from him. He sent me an e-mail today."

"Cool," Blair said.

Regan sighed. "Or not. I don't know, guys. He's nice, but . . . the truth is, I'm terrified. I didn't count on meeting someone like Peter. I don't even want to get involved with a man right now. I'm too new at all this. I want to get my feet under me, make my own way for a change."

Kat took the seat next to her. "You don't have to get involved with him. Just dance with him, if he's your teacher. You don't have to go out with him again."

"That's the problem," Regan said miserably. "I want to."

26

Regan searched the packed parking lot at the Sterling Pace
Dance Studio for a space, finally locating one in a far corner,
and Kat wheeled in just as someone else headed for the slot.
Blair was staying with a neighbor for the two hours Kat and
Regan would be gone, although she'd pitched a fit at not
being able to stay home alone. "I'm fourteen years old, Kat,"
she'd argued. "I can baby-sit myself. I baby-sit for other
people, remember?"

But Kat was adamant. "Not right now, sweetie. I'm sorry.
It's not that I don't trust you. But with that creep loose on
the streets, I'm not taking any chances."

"That creep" continued to garner headlines, and the police
were getting nowhere in their search for him. According to
the newspapers and TV anchors, the SFPD and the FBI were
pulling in manpower from surrounding cities and counties
and working around the clock to find and capture the killer,
but so far, they had found little to go on.

Regan and Kat hurried from the parking lot into the
brightly lit studios where a smartly dressed throng of people
mingled and chatted. Regan's skin felt warm, and her heart
was beating a little too fast. She looked around, realizing
how anxious she was to see Peter. When she didn't find him
among the crowd, she was deeply disappointed. And then
she caught herself. *Wait a minute, chicky. You keep saying*

you don't want a relationship. You're getting exactly what you're asking for, so don't complain.

Wanda spotted Regan and Kat and pointed them in the direction of their classroom. There were nine other people in the room awaiting the instructor, four couples and another single woman. They chatted easily, as if they were at a cocktail party, and Regan wondered if they'd been together for a while as a class. In a few moments, an attractive man in his mid-thirties hurried into the room, looking distinctly annoyed.

"Good evening, ladies and gentlemen," he said, and with that, his face lost its impatient expression and he smiled broadly.

"Good grief," Kat whispered to Regan. "That's Sterling Pace, thirty years younger."

"I'm Cameron Pace, heir to this wonderful kingdom of dance," he said with a laugh as he gestured expansively. His hair was thick and wavy like his father's, black instead of silver, with just a hint of things to come along his temples. He wasn't a tall man, but was well built and muscular. He was handsome, as well, animated and charismatic like his father.

"I'll be your instructor tonight, as our regular teacher hasn't yet arrived," Pace announced. "Shall we get started, then?"

The regular teacher.

Peter Smith.

Peter wasn't coming. In spite of her intellectual conviction that it was better not to see him again, Regan could feel the surge of disappointment clear to her fingertips. Why hadn't he come? Was he angry with her for not returning his e-mail? Had something bad happened to him?

She tried to focus her attention on Cameron Pace and the lesson he was giving, but her heart wasn't in it. When a man approached and asked if she'd like him to be her partner for the class, she demurred at first, but then changed her mind, realizing she needed a partner if she was going to learn the dance steps properly.

Cameron Pace zeroed in on Kat like a fly attracted to honey, and he stuck with her for most of the evening. Regan watched them together and saw Kat actually flirting with the man. She was happy for her sister, even though she herself was feeling let down and dispirited. *Get over it*, she told herself. Their whole point in coming here was for Kat—*not Regan*—to meet a man who liked to dance.

27

His plea to the public for help in locating the killer had netted Sam Sloan nearly six thousand phone calls and letters, most of them worthless. A lot of the informants fingered suspicious neighbors, others suspected husbands, boyfriends, or bosses. Many of the calls were clearly the work of crackpots, others blatant attempts at revenge, but Sloan's team sifted through them one by one. Somewhere in the haystack there might be the proverbial needle.

It was tedious, tiresome work, and they'd been at it around the clock for longer than a week when the investigators got their first break in the case. It came in the form of a homeless bum who was arrested for vagrancy. He'd been asleep in South Park, not far from the row of nightclubs Sloan had cased in SOMA.

A young mother with a baby in a stroller had alerted police to the presence of the bum, and when they'd found him passed out in a copse of budding bushes, they'd also found a splintered baseball bat next to him, soaked in blood.

"This your toy?" Sloan asked the dazed bum who, he surmised, must be suffering from the Hangover from Hell. The man was wearing a ratty brown overcoat that was still dirty from his night on the ground in the park. His watery, bloodshot eyes and foul breath bespoke the dinner of whiskey he'd consumed the night before.

"I don't know what you mean." The bum squinted at Sloan, then slowly turned his focus to the bloody bat that lay on a table before them. "You talkin' 'bout that?" "Yes, I'm talking about that. The baseball bat. The one with the blood all over it. Is it yours?" Sloan knew it wasn't, but he wanted to find out if the bum had found it somewhere other than the park and in his drunken stupor, moved it.

The bum shook his head slowly, and Sloan could almost feel the pain behind his eyes. "Never shaw that there bazeball bat before," he mumbled. He leaned closer and reached out to touch the bat, but Sloan caught his arm.

"You don't want your fingerprints on that, buddy, trust me," Sloan said gently. He nodded to the uniformed officer who stood nearby. "Book him and lock him up. He needs to sleep it off before we talk again." Then he turned to Brad Kelly, who sat across the table from him. Between them lay the bat, and both knew they'd found at least one of the murder weapons.

"Forensics is ready to take a look at it," Kelly said. Because of the serial murders, the bat and the bum had been brought directly to Sloan before either had been processed through the system. The bat hadn't yet been examined for fingerprints. Sloan doubted that Forensics would find any, but he was eager for them to try. He also wanted the crime lab to compare the blood on the bat to that of the victims. Had the killer used this weapon on more than one woman, or did he give each of them a brand-new bat?

Sloan stood up. "Good. Let's go."

Outside the room, two uniformed officers from the SFPD stood talking in low voices. One of them, Patrolman Jack Mahoney, had found the bum. "We'll ride with you," Sloan told him, and the four men strode toward the parking lot and Mahoney's black-and-white squad car.

The small park was now cordoned off with yellow crime-scene tape, and several uniformed cops stood guard. A crowd had gathered, and a news team from one of the local TV stations, KRON, was taping an on-the-scene story. The reporter recognized Sloan from the earlier press conference and came at a gallop.

"Special Agent Sloan!" The woman shouted his name in

a peremptory tone. "Can you tell us what's going on here? I understand the police have found the murder weapon used by the serial killer."

"It's premature to say that," Sloan growled. He was used to handling the media and dealing with aggressive reporters like this, but at times, he hated them. They were like vultures, circling around any rotten carrion they could find to titillate their viewers. Worse than ambulance-chasing lawyers, the infotainers often distorted the facts they reported. Sloan didn't need that to happen now.

"You can tell your audience that a baseball bat was found here, and that it is being examined to learn if it was connected to any of the recent murders."

"What about the guy the cops arrested? Is he the killer?"

Sloan shook his head. "Nope. Just a bum who had the misfortune to wander into this particular part of South Park before he passed out." With that, he turned away from the reporter.

The bat had been found at the base of a large clump of forsythia bushes that were planted in a circle, leaving a protected space in the center. "A perfect little bashatorium," Kelly joked grimly when they peered into the center where the bum had been sleeping. "Do you suppose he brought them all here, killed them, then drove the bodies to various places on the bay for disposal?"

"I guess we'll know soon." Already, forensic investigators were on the scene, taking soil samples in hopes of finding blood and other human fluid and tissue that might point them to the killer. Sloan was particularly hoping they'd find tissue that could be used in a DNA search for the murderer.

"There's definitely blood here," one of the forensic men said, recognizing Sloan and coming toward him. "Lots of blood soaked into the ground. Shards of the bat, shards of bone, skin, fabric, a real treasure trove."

"Good." Sloan then walked around the perimeter of the circle of bushes, taking long strides, measuring, thinking, studying, speculating. If his killer had used this place as his "bashatorium," as Kelly so crassly called it, then he wasn't as organized as Sloan had first thought. This was a little too risky, too exposed. Still, it wasn't totally out in the open, as was the middle of the park. Sloan had pictured the man killing in a closed area, such as a house, warehouse, or garage. Maybe he'd done that before. Maybe this site indicated that the killer was becoming more frenzied, less careful. Or maybe he'd killed in other places like this and simply been lucky that no one had seen him in action.

"Get some of your people on all the other parks in the City," he suggested to Kelly. "Let's see if our boy's done this in the great outdoors before."

When they were finished at the park, Sloan declined a ride back to police headquarters. He needed to walk, to think. To get away from the stink of rotten blood.

He stopped into a café for a sandwich and a cup of coffee, something to settle his nerves. This case was getting to him, even though he'd only been on it a couple of weeks. He lifted the cup of hot coffee, but his hand was shaking so badly he had to set it back down on the table.

Shit.

He didn't need coffee. He needed a drink.

Sam Sloan had entered law enforcement a bright-eyed and idealistic twenty-year-old. His commitment was to righting all the wrongs of the world, and he'd been certain he could do it if he just worked hard enough.

He'd worked hard. Damned hard. So hard his young wife had given up on their marriage, complaining that he was never home and that he cared more about being a cop than a husband. But his commitment to public service had never faltered. After all, losing Sarah had been a high price to pay for saving the world. He couldn't stop now.

But the world, it seemed, wouldn't be saved, no matter how hard he worked. Deciding he'd be more effective somewhere other than local law enforcement, he'd left the Detroit PD and had applied to the FBI academy. He'd worked hard again, making his way swiftly up the ranks, at last attaining his ultimate goal of being accepted into the Behavioral Science Unit at Quantico.

He'd thought at last he had a chance to really make a difference.

That had been five years ago. Had he made a difference? He ate part of his sandwich without tasting it. No. He couldn't say he had, even though he'd solved some major cases. It seemed that as soon as one badass was taken off the streets, there were two or three more to replace them.

What was wrong with this world? he wondered. What are we doing to create these monsters? It was at times like these, when he waxed philosophical, that he became the most depressed. Once, a couple of years before, that depression had sent him to the bottom of the bottle and had nearly cost him his career. He'd managed, with the help of his immediate supervisor, who was also his best friend, to pull out of it, but there were times when the darkness was dangerously inviting. When he'd gone into the darkness, days went missing, but he didn't care. When he was in that dark place, he was protected from the horror that seemed to consume his life.

A car passed outside, glinting a slash of sunlight into Sloan's eyes and bringing him back to the moment. Jesus, he swore, realizing where he'd let his thoughts roam. Brooding and self-pity weren't his style, nor would they help him find the killer. Abruptly, he shoved his half-eaten sandwich away and stood up. He paid for his meal and stepped outside, squinting in the intense sunshine. Cursing his weakness, he began the short walk back to the Hall of Justice.

28

Kevin Carrington awoke with a monumental migraine headache, the kind that made him sick sometimes for days. He
lay very still on his bed, eyes closed, sweating, breathing
heavily, willing the pain to go away. His stomach roiled, and
tears burned his eyes. Christ, when was this going to end?

He ought to go see a doctor, but he was afraid. Afraid a
doctor would find something terrible was wrong with him.
Maybe he had a malignant brain tumor. Maybe he was going
to die. Well, if he was, he wished his body would hurry up.
At least then the pain would go away.

He eased his head to one side and opened an eye wide
enough to see the numbers on the digital clock by the bed.
Ten past ten. Day or night? He didn't know. Except for the
thin light of the clock, the room was dark, shuttered by
blinds designed to keep the light out, no matter what. He'd
always had trouble sleeping unless it was totally dark. The
darkness was his friend, his protector, his shield.

He rolled over and pulled a pillow around his head. Darkness. He needed the darkness.

He lay there, trying to figure out where he was. The place
was familiar, and yet it wasn't his home. And then the fog
lifted and he remembered.

Santa Barbara. Three hundred miles down the coast from
Palo Alto.

He was in Santa Barbara. He forced himself up on one elbow as a sense of urgency swept over him. He had to get up. He had things to do. It was slowly coming back to him now—where he was and why he was here. He swung his feet over the side of the bed and eased himself out. Slowly, he shuffled into the next room where screen-savers on several computer monitors winked and bubbled at him. In one corner, a video camera was mounted on a tripod, and the lens was aimed at a canvas-backed director's chair.

Carrington let out a long breath. He clicked on the light and winced at the pain behind his eyes. His head felt as if it might explode at any moment. His shaking hand rested on the switch. It would be so easy to turn it off again and return to the safety of the darkness.

Instead, Kevin Carrington stepped up to one of the computers and woke it up. He had work to do. This project was different from the others, far more dangerous, far more painful, but a journey he had to take. He didn't understand it, but he knew he must do it . . . or he would go insane.

29

More than a week had passed, and Regan hadn't heard from Peter. He hadn't been at the studio for her lessons on Monday, and no one there seemed to have heard from him. She was worried about him more than anything, although she was also deeply disappointed as well that he seemed uninterested in contacting her again. She had stewed about him all day Tuesday until finally she could stand it no longer and had placed calls to several hospitals in the area. None had a patient named Peter Smith.

To keep her mind occupied, Regan buried herself in her work, and in between administrative assignments, managed to work on ideas for the Carrington story. Jeff was anxious to have it finished, but she hadn't found an angle she thought would work. Most of the items she'd read on the Net and in old newspaper files told the same old story: Kevin Carrington had developed his first computer game while still a schoolboy, and with the encouragement and financial aid of a classmate's father, Ed Johnson, had sold it to one of the largest manufacturers of electronic entertainment equipment and software in the world.

Later, he'd written more software for games, formed a company, and eventually gone public to raise money for still more software development. Kevin Carrington was undoubtedly king of the computer-game hill.

I wonder whatever happened to his backer, Ed Johnson?
The thought hit her like a bolt of lightning. It seemed
logical that if Johnson had made money on Carrington's boy-
hood venture, he would have stuck around to see what the
kid would come up with next. Jeff had asked her to try to
find out how Carrington had pulled off his wildly successful
public offering. Maybe Johnson was the answer. Surely the
man who'd known Carrington as a boy would be able to
give her more information than she was getting from the
Internet. But where the hell was Ed Johnson?

It was an impulsive move and a real long shot, but Regan
picked up the phone and dialed the number in Palo Alto for
HomeRun, Inc. "Ed Johnson, please," she said to the receptionist.

"One minute."

The receptionist put Regan on hold. Suddenly she froze.
Dear God, could it really have been that easy to find Carrington's mentor? Instantly, she panicked. What was she going to say to Ed Johnson? She had no questions prepared,
no script in front of her, and she'd never been very good at
winging things.

Before she had a chance to hang up, a man's gruff, husky
voice answered the phone. "Johnson here."

"Uh, hello, Mr. Johnson." Regan felt as if her mouth were
full of cotton. "My name is Regan . . . Regan McKinney. I'm
with *Pro.Com* magazine."

She paused, half expecting him to hang up, but he didn't.
"Yes, Ms. McKinney. How can I help you?"

She had no choice now but to go on. She'd given out her
name and the company name.

"I'm writing a story about Kevin Carrington for our magazine, and—"

He cut her off with a sharp laugh. "Good luck. Kevin
doesn't talk to reporters."

"I've heard that. That's why I called you, actually. I read
your name in some of the articles that were published when
HomeRun went public, and I learned that you had been his
original backer. I figured if you were in on his initial venture,
you might have been involved in his public offering, as
well."

He laughed again, and this time it sounded friendlier. "Well, you nailed that one. But how'd you find me? I try to keep a low profile, too."

"I called the company and asked for you."

"Oh."

It had been too incredibly simple. Apparently Ed Johnson thought so, too. Regan smiled, a little proud of herself. It gave her courage to go on.

"Mr. Johnson, my assignment is to write a story about Mr. Carrington, the man, not about the business. Of course, I'm learning that it's hard to separate one from the other."

"That's true. Kevin eats, sleeps, and breathes computers."

Regan was encouraged that Ed Johnson seemed cooperative. "Well, that's what I'm looking for in my story. What makes Mr. Carrington tick? I'm looking for the human angle of the story, the warm, fuzzy side to it."

Johnson huffed. "There's nothing warm and fuzzy about Kevin Carrington." He sounded bitter.

"Why is that?" The question tripped eagerly off her tongue, and Regan tucked the phone between her head and shoulder and reached for a yellow legal pad to take notes. This might be the only chance she'd have to interview Johnson, and she didn't trust her memory.

"I don't know his whole background, but from what I can tell, Kevin was a pretty lonely little boy, a kid stuck in a boarding school by his famous father who never came to see him," Johnson said matter-of-factly.

"Famous father? Who was he?"

"Michael Carrington, the movie star. Maybe you're too young to remember him. He hasn't made a movie in two decades."

"I've heard of him. *He's* Kevin's father?" Why hadn't any of the articles mentioned that rather big detail? Regan scribbled as fast as she could.

"Actually, Kevin doesn't want that spread around," Johnson added quickly. "I shouldn't have mentioned it."

Why had he, then? Regan wondered fleetingly if Ed Johnson didn't feel somewhat fatherly to the boy he'd befriended years ago. Had he let Kevin's secret slip because he resented Michael Carrington? Or was the earlier bitterness she'd heard in his voice aimed at Kevin? Had Johnson lost faith in his boy wonder? Had they had a falling-out?

"Why doesn't Kevin want the world to know who his father is?" she asked.

"He and his father . . . haven't spoken in many years. I don't know exactly why, but he doesn't want to have anything to do with Michael Carrington. Look, Ms. McKinney, if you print this, he'll have my head. I don't know why I said anything . . ."

"I can't promise I won't print what you've told me, but if you wish to remain anonymous, I can arrange that. Please, help me, Mr. Johnson."

"I'm sorry. I've said too much already. If you want facts about the IPO, I'll be happy to oblige, but I can't give you personal details about Kevin."

Disappointed, Regan relented. "I understand. Then, if you have a moment, I would like to ask a few questions about the public offering."

Jeff had asked her to find out the secrets to Carrington's success, as well as what drove the young entrepreneur emotionally. He wanted names, contacts, money sources, all of which Ed Johnson freely gave her.

But by the time they reached the end of the interview, she knew the real reason why Kevin had made it to the big time.

Ed Johnson had made it happen for him.

Ed Johnson cared about Kevin Carrington, cared deeply. He was Carrington's "secret weapon," and even if Jeff could convince him to go to work on *Pro.Com*'s behalf, she doubted Johnson would put the same effort and love into an IPO for Jeff Roundtree.

Regan took a break, went into the ladies' room and found she was shaking. She also felt strangely sorry for Kevin Carrington. There was something about the way Ed Johnson had spoken about the boy stuck away in a boarding school that pulled at her heartstrings.

She must find out more about that lonely little boy.

"Did you know that Kevin Carrington is the son of Michael Carrington, the movie star?" she asked Jeff Roundtree moments later.

He looked up from the work that held his concentration, and it took a moment for her question to register. "What?"

"I just found out that Kevin Carrington, the darling of Silicon Valley, is the son of Michael Carrington, darling of the silver screen a long time ago."

Jeff's jaw visibly dropped. Then he gave her a slow, appreciative smile. "I knew you could do it. That's a scoop, as far as I know. I've never read that anywhere. You sure it's true?"

"I intend to find out."

"What else did you dig up?"

She laid a list of names on his desk. "Here's your contacts. My source said to feel free to talk to any of them."

He scanned the list. "Nothing earthshaking here. I know about all these guys." He looked up at her again. "Who's your source?"

Regan shook her head. "Can't say. That was part of the deal."

Jeff Roundtree stared at her. "You ought to be a reporter, not an admin assistant."

Regan thrilled to his praise. Nobody had ever made her feel this validated. Nobody, that is, except Peter.

"Is that an offer?" she asked.

"I can't afford a full-time reporter. That's why I use freelancers. But I'll pay you extra money for any story you write. You'll get what the others get. Besides, I can't afford to let you off that front desk right now, either."

"What're you going to do when I make my run to Palo Alto to try to talk to Carrington? Answer your own phones?" Regan was so lighthearted she felt giddy, and she couldn't wait to try to get in to see the computer genius now.

"I'll hire a temp," replied Jeff. "When're you going?"

30

Ed Johnson hung up the phone, deeply disturbed by what he'd just done. He should never have mentioned Kevin's father to that reporter. For whatever reason, and Johnson had never known the details, Kevin had made it clear he wanted nothing to do with Michael Carrington. He'd disowned his father, if that was possible, at least emotionally. It was as if Michael Carrington were dead, and Kevin was glad of it.

It was one of the dark secrets that surrounded the young genius, and to Ed's knowledge, no one but Kevin knew the depth of his hatred toward his father. The times he'd tried to broach the subject, Kevin had cut him short. His demeanor had turned dark, and his fury had been almost frightening in its intensity, so Ed had let it go. It was, after all, none of his business.

But Kevin would indeed have his head if he found out Ed had spilled the secret to this reporter. Johnson looked around at the posh office in which he worked, in which he'd made a fortune for himself and for Kevin Carrington. If Kevin found out what he'd done, he could kiss this all good-bye.

31

Peter Smith pulled the Jag into the parking lot at the Sterling Pace Studio and looked at his watch. For once, he was going to be on time. It was Monday night, and he was eager to see Regan again, although it troubled him that she hadn't answered his e-mail. Maybe he shouldn't have sent it. Maybe she didn't get it. He could have sent it to the wrong address, he supposed. Maybe she didn't like his poem.

He was as edgy as a schoolboy as he walked briskly to the back door.

Inside, he saw Sterling Pace in the small office, toiling at the paperwork Peter knew the dancer hated. Pace looked up, spotted Peter, and scowled. He stood and came to the door of the office.

"You're fired, Smith," he said curtly.

Peter stared at him, not believing he'd heard right. "What?"

"I said, you're fired. You don't show up for over a week, don't call, and just waltz in here like nothing's happened? You're good, kid, but not that good. I need reliable help, and you ain't it."

Peter was astounded. "But I did call, Sterling. I had to go out of town on business. I called and spoke with Wanda, and she said she'd give you the message. That was our agreement when I came to work here, that my time would be flexible to accommodate my other schedule. You know how my job is."

"Wanda didn't tell me or anyone else," Pace said, "and I specifically asked her if you'd called in. We've been short-handed for days. Sorry, I've already hired someone to take your place. Clear your locker and don't come back." The older man turned his back to Peter and went into his office, slamming the door behind him.

Peter stared at the closed door. This couldn't be happening. He'd worked hard for Sterling Pace. He loved the man. He loved the whole business of dance. Pace himself had told him he was the best instructor in the studio. It didn't make sense that he was being dismissed. He started to knock on the door, and then stepped away, a shadow of a doubt crossing his mind. He *had* called Wanda, hadn't he?

There must be some mistake, he thought, looking around for the receptionist. Of course he'd called Wanda. He pushed his way past the students who stood milling about in the lobby and approached Wanda, the mountain of a woman who sat behind the reception desk.

Wanda looked up, and her omnipresent smile, a professional prop in the dance business, suddenly dropped from her face. "Well, well, look who finally decided to grace us with his presence," she said, not unkindly but with an unmistakable edge of sarcasm.

"What's wrong with you people?" Peter snapped. "I called and told you I would be out last week. You know that's how my business is."

Wanda shook her head. "Didn't call *me*, sugar. Who'd you talk to?"

Peter's heart was pounding as his confusion turned to anger. He knew he'd called this woman. Why was she lying? He'd always thought Wanda was his ally.

"Never mind," he said and turned away, clenching his fists to keep his temper under control. He mustn't lose his cool. He took a deep breath. He didn't know why Wanda had betrayed him, but he wasn't going to waste energy being angry with her. This was surely just a misunderstanding, and they were totally overreacting. If they wouldn't give him a chance to set it right, it was just as well he was leaving. He didn't have time for people like this.

But he did have time for Regan McKinney, and he desperately wanted to see her, especially now that he wouldn't be teaching her dance class anymore. He maneuvered through the crowd, stopping to speak to a few people who greeted him, but when he reached the classroom, he saw that neither Regan nor her sister was there. In fact, this wasn't a beginner class at all, but rather an advanced rhythm group gathered in that particular classroom. What was going on here?

He looked at his watch. The time was just after seven P.M. The date read: Wed. March 27.

Wednesday.

Peter's head began to throb, and he left the room, stunned by his mistake. No wonder Pace was so pissed off at him. He was supposed to have been back on Monday, the twenty-fifth. But he'd thought today was Monday, and he hadn't called in. Today was Wednesday, not Monday.

Woodenly, Peter went to the locker room and removed the few personal items from his locker. He wished he could quit his damned day job. Those responsibilities, and his schedule, really screwed up his perception of time. He'd stayed out of a sense of duty, but his real love was here, in the dance studio. Here was one of the few places where he was genuinely happy, where he was free to be himself.

As he walked out into the chilly San Francisco night, he reflected that at least one good thing had come of his tenure at the Sterling Pace Studios—he'd met Regan. His heart lightened at the thought of her. He had to call her and let her know he was back in town. He wondered if she'd missed him.

32

"Listen to this." Regan sat at Blair's desktop computer later that evening, reading an article she'd unearthed on an Internet site featuring studies of old movie stars.

"Michael Carrington's last film was *Thunder in the Sky,* a war flick that bombed, if you'll pardon the pun, in 1967. That was the same year Kevin Carrington was born," she said, checking her legal pad that was quickly being filled with her notes. "Michael apparently was heavily into alcohol and drugs back then, as was his wife, Kevin's mother, Liliane, and he didn't make another film until the mid-seventies."

"Was Liliane a movie star, too? I don't remember her." Kat was sprawled across Blair's bed working a crossword while Regan searched the Net on her niece's computer to learn more about Kevin Carrington's father. Blair sat cross-legged on the floor playing a handheld computer game. Both Kat and Blair were intrigued with Regan's assignment and were hovering to see what she came up with.

"Her name was Liliane LaRue, it says here. She was a starlet, but her career never got off the ground. She died of an overdose of drugs when Kevin was only six. No note was found, but it says here her death was possibly a suicide."

"How awful," Blair said. "Poor Kevin."

Then Regan came across something that was even worse. "Oh, my God," she murmured.

"What?" Kat glanced up sharply.

Regan read directly from the article. " 'Friends of the family say she became despondent over the death of her oldest son, Darrin, who was drowned near the family's Santa Barbara home in 1972. The Carringtons were out of the country at the time, on location in Africa where Michael was filming his latest movie. Sources say that Liliane blamed herself for her son's death and had a nervous breakdown. Apparently she never recovered from it.' "

"How sad." Blair put her game aside and came to peer into the computer screen over her aunt's shoulder. "How old was Kevin when his brother died?"

Regan figured it out in her head. "He must have been about five. Poor kid," she murmured, "losing first his brother, then his mother, all before he was seven years old. Estranged from his father. No wonder Kevin's not exactly a warm, fuzzy kind of guy."

Regan continued her search, looking for more information about Michael Carrington. There were no obits, so apparently he was still alive. But where was he? she wondered.

The phone rang, and Blair dashed to answer it. "Kat, it's for you," she yelled from the hallway. Blair returned to her room, and Kat went for the phone. A few moments later, she returned, grinning widely.

"That was Cameron. He's asked me out."

"Who's Cameron?" Blair asked, frowning.

"Our dance instructor," Regan replied, happy for Kat, although her feelings were shadowed by her own disappointment that she hadn't heard from Peter.

"I thought Peter Smith was your teacher," Blair said. "By the way, whatever happened to him?"

Regan's cheeks burned, but she returned nonchalantly to the computer. "I guess he didn't have as good a time as I thought."

"Why don't you call him?" The teenager was tenacious.

"I'm not going to call him. I don't know his number, and even if I did, I wouldn't. Girls don't call boys."

"I can't believe you're so old-fashioned. Girls can call

boys just as well as boys can call girls, right, Mom?"

But Kat wasn't listening. "He said he had to get special permission from his dad to get involved with a student."

Blair made a face. "A daddy's boy? How old is this guy?"

Kat gave her a sharp warning look. "He's not a daddy's boy, and I don't know how old he is. I suppose if you're in that sort of business, you have to keep your distance from your customers. If it got around that the instructors were lechers, it'd ruin the company."

Blair laughed. "Maybe the instructors *are* lechers. Both of you got asked out by them in spite of the rules."

Regan and Kat exchanged glances. Blair had a way of telling it like it was. She was right. Maybe the instructors only paid lip service to ethics. Maybe they were really there to meet women. Maybe Peter met some other woman . . . or women. Regan cut that thought short. "When is your date?"

Kat looked at her watch. "Tonight. He's picking me up at nine."

"But it's a school night," Blair objected.

"Not for me. I'm a grown-up, remember? Besides, we won't be out late. You and Regan can wait up if you want and interrogate me when I get home."

"Where're you going?" Regan asked, astounded that her sister would accept a date on such short notice.

"Dancing, where else?" She giggled girlishly and headed toward her room. "Gotta get ready."

A jolt of alarm shot through Regan, and she followed her sister down the hall. "Dancing? Where?"

"To one of those places you hate. La Habanera. It's a Latino dance club in the Mission District."

Regan stood in Kat's doorway, fear lacing through her. "Don't do it, Kat. You don't know anything about Cameron Pace. The police are telling everybody, especially us red-heads"—she glanced pointedly at her sister's color-enhanced red hair—"to stay away from those clubs until they catch this killer."

Kat went to her closet and pulled out a bright yellow spaghetti-strapped, bare-backed cocktail dress with a full skirt that flared at mid-thigh. "Looks a little south-of-the-border, don't you think?"

Regan didn't answer, and Kat looked up. "You think Cameron Pace is the serial killer?" she said. "Get real, Regan. You're being paranoid."

"I think you're taking an unnecessary chance."

Kat turned to her sister, an exasperated look on her face. "Look, Regan, I know you mean well, but I've lived in this city for a lot of years. I know my way around. I understand your being uncomfortable in a nightclub, but . . . I'm not you, sis. I've been wanting a night on the town, you know that. I really like Cameron, and I know I'll be safe with him. The killer's after single women, not someone with an escort."

Cameron Pace arrived at nine P.M. on the dot. Regan had to admit he was handsome in sport coat, slacks, and open-necked shirt, and he greeted Regan warmly. But when Kat came down the stairs, dressed in her stunning yellow "cha-cha" outfit, as she called it, it was clear in which sister his interest lay.

After they'd left, Regan closed the door and locked it, then leaned against it, deeply troubled. She knew she was probably being paranoid, as Kat had accused, but she couldn't shake her strange premonition that *something terrible* was going to happen tonight.

33

Regan stood in the doorway to Blair's room, watching her niece whose attention was once again absorbed by her computer game. Blair looked up, and when she saw Regan, she asked, her voice sounding worried, "She's going to be all right, isn't she?"

"I'm sure she'll be fine," Regan answered after a slight hesitation. "Your mom has done what she said she wanted to do. She's met a nice man she really likes, and they both enjoy dancing. I'm just being a fraidy cat because I'm not used to being a city girl."

"But that killer—"

"Isn't going to touch her," Regan interjected. "Your mom is right, she's with an escort. Nobody's going to hurt her." Regan bit her lower lip, praying that her words sounded braver than she felt. "Don't worry about anything. I'm here if you need me."

Downstairs, Regan scoured the kitchen until it gleamed. She turned on the television but there wasn't anything of interest to her. She picked up a book, but couldn't concentrate. She kept imagining Cameron Pace's big, thick hands closing in like a vise around Kat's thin neck. *The killer likes to dance.* Why couldn't Pace be the killer? It'd be a natural for a killer who likes to dance to teach at a studio. Maybe that's how he worked—he met someone at the studio, asked her out for a date, and the trusting victim went with him, thinking herself safe with an escort.

Regan knew her imagination was raging out of control, but she couldn't help it. She tried to think of what to do. Should she call the police? Her better judgment warned her against it. Cameron Pace could be the killer, but most likely he wasn't. If she called the police, she'd make a fool of herself, embarrass Kat, probably ruin her sister's chances with Cameron forever, and for what? Her paranoia?

Still, Regan felt compelled to do something to make sure her sister would return home safe and sound, and a plan gradually came to her mind. Going to the front window, she raised a slat in the miniblinds and looked across the street. Mrs. Donovan's light was still on. She picked up the phone.

"Hello, Mrs. Donovan? This is Regan, Kat's sister . . . I'm fine, how are you? . . . That's good. I know it's late, but I was wondering if I could ask a favor . . ."

Twenty minutes later, Mrs. Donovan was settled in front of the television, and Regan was nearly ready to go. She wore the only dress that was appropriate for La Habanera, the sexy purple minidress she'd sworn she'd never wear again, just as she'd sworn she'd never again traipse through the door of a dance club.

But tonight she couldn't *not* go.

34

Regan paid the cab driver and stepped out onto the curb in front of La Habanera, a rather seedy-looking Mexican nightclub at Twenty-ninth and Mission Streets. Music blasted from inside the club, a hot, heavy Latin beat that both menaced and enticed. Her heart was beating loudly, too. She could hear the pulse pounding in her ears. She drew in a deep breath, calling herself every kind of fool for coming here and knowing Kat was going to be furious with her for showing up to chaperone. She glanced over her shoulder, ready to stop the cab and get back in it, but it had already gone.

She was aware of eyes on her, the stares of the men, mostly dark-skinned Latinos, some wearing cowboy boots and hats, who loitered outside. One man, cruising by in a fifty-eight Cadillac, called out to her in Spanish. She didn't understand what he said, but she got the drift from his lurid gesture of insinuation. She saw a man openly hawking what she presumed to be dope from behind a telephone pole. With a shudder, Regan pulled the scarf that matched the dress tighter about her shoulders. Summoning her flagging courage, she went inside and prepared to pay the cover charge.

"No charge, señorita," the man at the door told her. He was large and overweight. His grin revealed a gold front tooth. "Wednesday is ladies' night."

She edged nervously through the doorway, wondering if she'd find her sister in this sleaze hole. The mostly Latino crowd swayed to the rhythm of the music, and the air was redolent with the sweet smell of marijuana. She was surprised Kat would come to such a place. She also wondered if Cameron Pace was a cheapskate. Did he take all his dates out on ladies' night because it was free? She tried to recall whether any of the baseball-bat murders had taken place on Wednesday nights, but couldn't be sure.

She had to stop this . . . this Cameron-bashing. What was wrong with her? And then it hit her that maybe she was just a little jealous. Maybe she was angry with Kat for finding a man when Peter had dumped Regan after only one date. Regan didn't like to think she was so shallow, but maybe she was. But right now, it didn't matter. She'd come to insert herself into Kat's date, wanted or not, to make sure Kat wasn't alone with Cameron Pace. The killer hadn't committed any double murders, had he?

Once Regan's eyes adjusted to the dimly lit club, it wasn't hard to spot Kat. She and Cameron were the center of attention as they performed what appeared to Regan to be some kind of exotic mating dance beneath the spotlights on the dance floor. Where had her sister learned to dance like that? Her skirt was pushed above her thighs, and Pace swung her around like a rag doll, then leaned over her as if in mock coitus. The crowd chanted *baile!* and *chi-chis!* as the music thundered.

Then Regan groaned at her naïveté. When was she going to get it? Kat already knew how to dance; she was just going to the studio to placate Regan's fears. Still, taking lessons had accomplished the objective—Kat had met a man who seemed to fulfill at least part of her wish list. He was perfect, if he wasn't a killer.

Regan brushed off the advances of several men who approached her and waited until the couple left the floor and went to their table before she approached them. "Hi," she said nonchalantly, as if it were the most normal encounter in the world. "Mind if I join you?"

Other than being clearly stunned at her sister's arrival,

Kat didn't appear to be upset. "Of course you can join us. My God, I never thought I'd see the day."

Cameron Pace stood there poker-faced, but he smiled when Kat invited her to share their table. He brought a chair from the next table and seated her with every gentlemanly courtesy.

Regan felt like a complete idiot. "I . . . if I'm intruding, just say so, and I'll leave," she stammered. "I got Mrs. Donovan to come over."

Kat grinned slyly. "So, are you on watchdog duty tonight, sis?"

"No." Her reply was too sharp, too fast, to be believable. "I mean, yes. Maybe," she corrected herself.

Kat laughed and shook her head. She glanced quickly across the table and winked at Cameron. "She thinks you're the serial killer."

Regan wanted to go through the floor, she was so embarrassed. She couldn't believe Kat would say that, and yet, wasn't it the truth? Didn't a small part of her believe it was possible? Regan deserved to be humiliated, she supposed. She had humiliated her sister and Cameron Pace, as well.

Pace grinned and raised an eyebrow. "The serial killer? The one who likes to dance?"

Regan lowered her head and bit her lip. Her suspicions sounded so ridiculous. She owed this man, and her sister, an apology. "Look, I'm sorry. I know I'm being foolish. But the FBI and the police and everybody who's looking for that guy are warning women with red hair to avoid places like this."

"You have red hair," Pace pointed out.

"Yes, and that makes two of us at this table."

"Safety in numbers?" he asked.

She glanced at Kat, who seemed highly amused at her sister's discomfort. "Maybe," she replied nervously to Pace.

The music picked up again, and Regan saw Cameron lean over and whisper something in Kat's ear. Her sister nodded, and Cameron leaned toward Regan. "May I have this dance?"

Regan glared at Kat. This was the ultimate humiliation, making her dance with Cameron Pace. Not only did she not know how to perform the steps, she also knew Pace must despise her for her distrust. But he seemed unfazed as he stood up, took her hand and led her to the dance floor.

His lead was as easy to follow as Peter's had been, and he was gentle with her, not forcing her to do anything tricky. She began to relax, and by the time the number was over, Regan found she'd actually enjoyed the dance. They returned to the table where drinks had been served. Kat had ordered red wine for herself, a Dos Equis beer for Cameron, and something golden and bubbly for Regan.

"Ginger ale," her sister said, nodding at Regan's drink. "Nothing strong for the chaperone," she added wryly.

Regan had thought the drink was champagne. How mad was Kat?

"You're a good dancer," Cameron told her. "You and your sister have a natural rhythm. I'll get you out of those beginner classes and into something more challenging soon."

His kindness made her feel even worse. "Look, maybe I ought to go. This was a stupid idea. I'm really sorry for barging in." Regan reached for her small evening bag.

"Oh, no you don't," Kat said, slapping her hand away from the purse. "Didn't you like that dance?"

"Well, yes, but—"

"Cameron, can you handle escorting two women tonight?"

His eyes lit up in amusement. "It'd be my pleasure. And," he added with a twinkle, "I'll make sure the bogeyman doesn't get either of you."

35

The killer hadn't struck in nearly two weeks, and Special Agent Sam Sloan had begun to wonder if the murderer had moved on. Serial killers often "worked an area," then moved someplace else, covered their tracks and waited for a while until police investigations calmed down. Then they suddenly went back to work. Sometimes they used the same MO, the same signature, sometimes not.

However, Sloan was pretty sure this killer wasn't a transient. He believed the murderer was from the Bay Area or had lived here a long time. His profile was that of a single white male, twenty-five to thirty-five, a professional person in a white-collar job, affluent, who had a vendetta against a woman with red hair. He killed that redhead over and over again in effigy. Only his victims weren't dummies. They were women who reminded him of the original redhead he hated. He couldn't kill the real target—maybe she was already dead, or maybe he couldn't bring himself emotionally to murder her, so he substituted random strangers whom he picked up at dance clubs.

He was fairly organized as far as serial killers go. Although Forensics had found no identifiable fingerprints on the bat, the blood matched that of Chloe Martin, the latest victim. Sloan believed the killer had planned where he would murder the woman and placed the bat in the bushes before bringing his victim to the park. He'd chosen the place well even if the public park was somewhat risky. The time of death was estimated around two A.M., when the park was generally deserted except for the likes of Toby Hankins, the homeless drunk they'd brought in. Hankins had nothing to do with the murders, but Sloan wondered what the killer would have done if the old man had wandered into his bashatorium.

Sloan was pouring himself another cup of foul-tasting coffee when Inspector Brad Kelly came into his office, grim-faced.

"They've found another one."

This victim, Anna Maria Chavez, was a little older than the others and was Latino rather than Anglo, as the rest had been. Her mane of red hair had probably cost a lot to dye in some salon, and had cost her her life, Sam thought sadly as he looked down at the corpse in the morgue. Other than the age and race of the victim, this murder followed the killer's pattern. She'd been strangled before being battered, and her body had been left beneath Pier 80, near Candlestick Point, not far from where the body of Chloe Martin had been discovered. Unlike the Martin woman, however, whose body hadn't been found for several days after her murder, this victim was fresh. Lividity had barely set in, and the coroner surmised she hadn't been dead for even twenty-four hours.

Upstairs in Kelly's office, Sloan looked out the film-streaked window. The waters of the bay lay before him, beyond the freeway and the skyscrapers, sparkling in the morning sun. The city hummed with life and vitality. San Franciscans had done a swell job of renovating their city after the Loma Prieta earthquake of 1989. But Sloan wasn't doing such a swell job of finding the killer who prowled their streets, stalking women with red hair.

He cursed beneath his breath, frustration, rage even, surging through every cell in his body.

36

Regan poured herself a cup of high-test coffee, glad now for Jeff's obsession with freshness in his java. She was groggy and dragging this morning, even though Cameron had brought the sisters home by midnight. Instead of using good sense and going to bed, however, the two women had sat up for another hour, indulging in a glass of wine and girl talk.

Although her sister wasn't angry with her for barging in on her date with Cameron, Regan had another reason to regret having gone to the dance club the night before. When she'd returned, she'd found a note pinned to her pillow, written in an adolescent, loopy style: "Peter called. No message. Love, Blair."

Well, she thought, disappointed, maybe he'll try again.

She returned to her desk just as a "Silver Bullet" messenger entered the front door of the office suite, carrying a huge bouquet of yellow roses.

"Are you Regan McKinney?" the delivery woman asked with a smile. Delivering flowers must be the world's greatest job, Regan thought as she nodded and accepted the heavy vase. Flowers made everyone happy. "Yes, thanks," she mumbled.

Her hands trembled slightly as she placed the vase on her desk. She couldn't imagine who might be sending her flowers. Her fingers shook as she fumbled among the fragrant blooms for the gift card.

The words leaped out at her: "Please forgive me for not being there on Monday. Something came up. I'll call later today. Peter."

So. He hadn't dumped her after all. Was that a good thing or a bad thing?

For the rest of the day, every time the phone rang, Regan's heart did a little lurch. Apparently her heart thought Peter's attentions were a good thing, even while her mind kept warning her away.

It was nearly five o'clock before he called. She recognized his voice instantly. "Peter, hi. I got the flowers. They're beautiful. Thank you."

"I hope you like yellow roses. Would you rather have had red ones?"

How could she not like two dozen gorgeous yellow roses? "They're perfect."

A silence stretched between them for a long moment, then Peter said, "I'm sorry I didn't make it to class. I should have called. I had to go out of town on business. Did you get my e-mail?"

Regan felt her skin begin to tingle. "Yes," she said. *Over a week ago.* "How'd you know my address?"

Peter laughed, and the sound brought the image of his sexy smile to her mind. "That was a no-brainer. It took a couple of guesses, but Regan@procom.com made sense."

"I see." Of course. It really was a no-brainer.

"Do you have dinner plans this evening?"

Regan thought a moment, her emotions vacillating. Then without hesitation, she blurted, "Nothing I can't change." The moment she spoke, she regretted acting so eager. Why'd she done that?

Because, she answered herself, she *was* eager to see Peter again.

"How about some seafood? I know this great little place . . ."

It was Regan's turn to laugh. "You seem to know a lot of 'great little places.' "

"So I don't like to cook." He paused. "Will you come?"

37

A little over an hour later, Regan entered Oscar's, an unpretentious establishment most tourists would never happen upon. She'd agreed to meet Peter after work, rather than have him pick her up at home, since the restaurant was only a short cable-car ride from her office.

Peter was already seated, waiting for her, and when she saw him, something inside of her started a slow meltdown. He wore a yellow crew-neck sweater over a button-down collared shirt, and the color made his eyes seem bluer than she remembered. Kat preferred men like Cameron who dressed in higher fashion, but Regan had always gone for the more conservative look. Land's End and L.L. Bean were her favorite catalogs.

He stood when he saw her approach, and his smile seemed like pure sunshine. "Hi," he said, taking her hand.

Regan's heart was pounding, and she felt light-headed. She hadn't remembered him being this good-looking.

"Hi. Sorry. Am I late?" She looked at her watch.

"Nope. Right on time. For once, I was early."

She sat opposite him at a small table at the back of the restaurant. The light was subdued, but not dim. The tables were covered with linen. The chairs were upholstered. Around them, the other early diners appeared to be mostly an after-work crowd of businessmen and -women. It was comfortable, inviting. Peter did seem to know how to choose good places. She suspected the food would be excellent here.

But she hadn't exactly come for the food.

When they were settled and the waiter had taken her drink order, she looked across at Peter. "Thanks again for the roses. They're beautiful."

"I . . . I'm glad you liked them. I'm really sorry I haven't called in a while."

"Don't worry about it. I'd hoped to see you at class, but I learned some steps anyway." She smiled and lowered her eyes slightly. "Either I do have two left feet, or my partner wasn't as good as you. I seemed to stumble a lot."

"Well, next week—" Peter started, then cut himself short, looking upset. He took a sip of water and wiped his mouth with his napkin.

"Next week what?" Regan asked, feeling a niggle of anxiety.

"I started to say I'd be your partner again next week, but . . ." He hesitated, then said, "The truth is, I won't be going back to Sterling's. I . . . got fired."

Regan stared at him, stunned. "Fired? For what? Wanda told us you were the best instructor there."

He drummed his fingers lightly on the tablecloth. "The operational word is 'there.' I wasn't there. I . . . well, I have to travel a lot with my day job, and I had an agreement with them that I'd let them know when I couldn't make it. I thought I'd called and let them know I'd be out a few days, but apparently . . . I forgot."

"Oh, Peter, I'm so sorry. Surely they'd forgive you just this once. I imagine good instructors are hard to come by."

His demeanor darkened. "It's not the first time, Regan. I try, I really try, to keep all the balls in the air, but my life is so hectic that sometimes I drop one occasionally. Unfortunately, I dropped one too many at the studio. I don't blame Sterling for canning me, but I'm going to miss it."

Regan reached for his hand. Peter's honesty about something that was obviously very painful to him made her want to comfort him. "I'll miss it, too," she said. "I don't think I'll be going back. It just wouldn't be the same without you. Besides," she added with a short laugh, "we accomplished what we went there for. Kat and Cameron Pace seem to have a thing going now, and she didn't tell me, but she already knows how to dance quite well."

"Kat and Cameron?" Peter looked puzzled. Then he smiled and shook his head. "Well, I'll be damned."

"What do you mean?"

"Oh, nothing. It's just that I've never known Cameron to become involved with any of the women students. It's against the rules, you know."

"That's what he told Kat, that he had to get special permission from Sterling to ask her out. But, then, you broke the rules, too. Look at us."

His gaze suddenly seemed to bore into hers. "What about us, Regan?"

Her face grew hot with embarrassment. "I . . . I don't know, Peter. What about us? I'm not sure there is an 'us.' "

"I hope there is."

She chewed her lower lip. She actually hoped so, too, but she said, "I never meant to become involved with anyone so soon after my divorce."

As she spoke the last two words, she realized she'd said them without the acid anger she'd felt only a short time ago. Without the bitterness, and the hopelessness. Somehow, since she'd met Peter, she'd forgotten the anger. The only thought she'd had, in fact, about Adam and all that she'd experienced in Middleton, was gratitude that she was free and away from his terrible control and domination.

"I suppose I shouldn't become involved with anyone, either," Peter said, surprising her.

"Why not?" *Oh, dear God, don't let him be married.*

But before he could answer, her wine arrived, and Peter ordered another for himself. They attended to the business of ordering their meals, and the waiter left.

Regan waited anxiously for Peter's answer. Maybe he wasn't married, but what other reason would he have for saying that he shouldn't get involved with her? But he just returned his gaze to her and smiled. "Did I tell you, you look great?" he asked.

Flustered, Regan wiped one cheek with the back of her fingers. Her skin was still searing. "Not today," she replied lightly. "But you said it twice on Saturday, so now you're one ahead of the game." She was making a joke, but he looked as if she might have offended him.

"I can't say it often enough," he murmured after a moment. "Regan, you're the most beautiful, fascinating woman I've ever met. I'm sorry if I seem a little . . . adolescent to you. Like I told you, I'm not practiced at this. Please bear with me."

The internal meltdown intensified. Good-looking, sincere, funny, not Mr. Perfect, but perhaps Mr. Wonderful. She'd thought she wasn't ready to become involved with a man, but Peter seemed to have a way of healing the wounds Adam had left in her soul. Here he was, sitting across from her, not only buying her dinner, but also enriching her destitute emotions, stroking her bruised ego, feeding her hungry heart. The caution signs were still up, but way down deep inside, the barriers were beginning to tumble.

38

Looking across at Regan, Peter realized for the first time how lonely he'd been all his life. In spite of his hectic days, his enormous obligations, his life up until now seemed suddenly empty. Perhaps that was his own fault, for he'd never allowed himself a personal life. He was dedicated to the job he'd vowed to do, to those who depended on him. What was it about Regan McKinney that had so easily caught his attention and changed the habits of a lifetime?

She was indeed the most beautiful and fascinating woman he'd ever met. But there was more to it than that. Something in her eyes, something about her demeanor, reminded him of someone, but he couldn't remember who. All he knew was that she sparked a happiness in him he'd never known. She engendered a feeling of comfort and security. Crazy, but there it was.

"Peter," she said, bringing his attention back to the moment, "just before the waiter came, you said that you probably shouldn't get involved with anyone, either. What did you mean?" He saw a crease in her brow.

Peter thought a moment. How to answer her . . . ?

"It's about my time," he said at last. "The time I have to give to . . . a relationship . . . is limited. I have some demanding commitments I can't neglect. It's why I got fired from Pace's studio."

"What kind of commitments? What do you do, Peter?"

Peter felt the pulse beat harder at his neck. "I have sort of a . . . home, I guess you'd call it, for some at-risk kids. They need me pretty badly sometimes." He saw the surprise on her face, then it softened into a smile.

"Kids? Oh, Peter, that's wonderful. Where is this home? Can I help you with them?"

He gave a small laugh to hide his unease and shook his head. "No. I'm the only one they'll have anything to do with." He saw the waiter approaching. "Here comes dinner. If you don't mind, I don't want to talk about the kids tonight. I so rarely get a break from them."

Peter's heart was thrumming. What had made him tell her about the kids? He'd never shared that with any outsider. It was his private, personal life, a commitment few could understand. But it seemed Regan McKinney was quickly becoming something to him other than an outsider. She was beginning to mean something to him, to mean a lot, in fact, and the very thought scared the bejesus out of him.

Get out before it goes any further.

He heard the warning, he knew it was the right thing to do, and yet . . .

The waiter arrived with steaming platters of seafood and pasta. "Bon apétit," he said with an engaging smile.

Peter suddenly realized that Regan had grown quiet. The smile had vanished from her face. "What's wrong? Are you okay? Is your food okay?"

"Fine," she answered, sounding curt. She picked up her fork. "I'm fine." He watched as she tasted her fish, which swam in a sea of baby vegetables, freshly harvested from the rich farmlands in California's interior. The fish and vegetables were served on a bed of angel hair pasta, cooked perfectly *al dente.* "The food is delicious."

Uncertain what he'd said to put her off, but certain that he had, Peter said no more, but went to work on his own plate. A ball of anxiety formed in his stomach, however, stealing away his appetite.

Get out before it goes any further.

Or before Regan decides I'm a complete bozo, Peter thought gloomily.

39

Regan knew she probably shouldn't take Peter's reluctance
to tell her about the children he worked with personally. It
was probably a matter of client privilege or some such. But
it was the way he'd cut her short that bothered her. Like
slamming a door in her face.

They ate in awkward silence, and when the waiter asked
if they'd like dessert, neither was interested. It was as if they
had an unspoken agreement to get out of there as quickly as
possible.

"Just bring the check, please," Peter said, reaching into
his back pocket. The waiter left, and Regan saw Peter frown
slightly. He felt the other back pocket, then picked up his
jacket that he'd taken off before she'd arrived. He groped
inside, looking for something, but came up empty-handed.

"This is terrible," he said, looking distressed.

"What's wrong?"

"My wallet. I seem to have lost my wallet."

"Oh, dear. Do you suppose someone stole it?"

Peter gazed at her, and she perceived a shadow of doubt
mingling with the embarrassment in his expression. "I don't
know. Sometimes I get in such a hurry, I forget things. Regan, I'm sorry . . ."

She reached for her purse. "Don't be. These things happen. I have my credit card." She produced her newly ac-

quired Optima card from her neatly organized wallet.

"I'll pay you back . . ."

"Not necessary." Regan gave the card to the waiter, then turned to Peter. "Look, don't worry about it. I'm actually glad to have a chance to reciprocate for Saturday." And she was, even though she was beginning to find Peter just a little on the irresponsible side. But she was willing to give him the benefit of the doubt. After all, he'd told her he was taking care of a bunch of high-risk kids. That was enough to distract anyone, she decided.

They left the restaurant just as dusk began to set the city lights atwinkle. Regan drew her jacket tighter around her and turned to Peter. "I enjoyed our dinner, but I think I'd better head on home now."

"I'm so embarrassed," Peter said in that honest, schoolboy tone that seemed to go straight to her heart. "Please forgive me."

"Peter," she said, almost exasperated, "there's nothing to forgive." She shrugged and smiled. "It was my pleasure. I'll see you later."

She turned and began to walk up the hill. Kat's house wasn't far, and she decided the exercise would do her good, not because she'd overeaten, but because she needed to sort out her feelings for Peter.

Regan heard footsteps behind her. "You're walking home?" Peter called, catching up with her.

"It's not far."

"Since I can't pay for a cab, would you at least let me walk with you? The streets aren't so safe after dark."

Regan didn't want Peter to walk her home, but he had a point about safety. "Suit yourself."

They strode together in silence for several blocks, and with each step, Regan's curiosity about him grew. Kids. He worked with at-risk kids. Delinquents? Special-needs kids? In spite of his quirky ways, her heart went out to him for helping disadvantaged children. She wished he'd tell her more about them. Let her into his life a little more. She'd actually like to help him, if he'd let her. After all, she'd never have children of her own.

They reached Kat's house, and Regan unlatched the front

gate. "Well," she said, turning to him, her breath rather short from going up and down the hills. "Thanks."

"Regan," he said, touching her cheek. "I can't tell you how mortified I am about not having my wallet. I'm not that kind of guy. You have to believe me. Listen, I can understand if you don't want to, but . . . would you give me another chance? Go dancing with me Saturday night?"

"To one of those clubs? No way."

"No. To the Fairmont, on Nob Hill. They have a couple of five-star restaurants, and there's an orchestra scheduled in one of their ballrooms on Saturday night." He took her hand. "I promise I'll bring my wallet," he added with a grin.

Regan stared up at him, unsure. This man was driving her crazy. Still, there was something about him she couldn't resist. He was also batting a thousand when it came to knowing "great places."

"Promise?" she replied, lifting the edges of her mouth. "I don't know if my credit card can support a five-star restaurant."

"Touché," he said. "I'll call you and let you know what time I can get reservations."

"Fine. See you Saturday." She started to go, but he took her by the arm and turned her to face him again. He said nothing, just lowered his mouth to hers. Regan could have sworn lightning sizzled through her when she felt his lips on hers. Peter Smith might be boyish in manner at times, but there was nothing boyish or inexperienced in his kiss. Nothing tentative, either. He kissed her with a passion unlike anything she'd ever known, which in turn ignited a fire in her that left her knees weak and her heart thundering.

At last he drew away, leaving her wanting more. "See you Saturday," he uttered, then turned and strode down the steep hill.

She stared after him, shaking her head.

Peter Smith, Peter Smith. Who the hell are you, Peter Smith?

40

The cost of the dress was worth the expression on Peter's face when he picked her up on Saturday night.

"He must have money somewhere," Kat had said, informing Regan that the Fairmont was strictly top-drawer, patronized by movie stars, wealthy international jet-setters, and business people. Panicked, Regan had called to inquire as to the appropriate dress for the evening. The concierge had told her that guests tended toward the formal, although of course, Madame could wear whatever she pleased, denim and bare feet excepted.

After her first spending spree, Regan wasn't sure she wanted to spring for the white sequined and beaded dress she'd admired in the window of the Ralph Lauren boutique, but Kat insisted that she buy it. "It's perfect," she assured her sister. Gazing at her image in the fitting room mirror, Regan had to agree. The dress was both sexy and demure, covering everything and yet clinging provocatively to Regan's curves from shoulder to ankle. Apparently Peter, who'd arrived in a tux, was knocked out by it, as well.

"You don't look just great this time," he said, that sexy grin easing onto his lips. "You look stunning." His gaze traveled slowly down her body and back again. When it met her eyes once more, he said, "Where have you been all my life?"

Regan shivered. She'd never felt more beautiful, more wanted, or appreciated. "Thank you, Peter," she murmured. Blair made them pose for a snapshot on her digital camera, and then they were off. "Don't wait up," Regan whispered to Kat.

Peter opened the car door for her, helped her to adjust the hem of her dress so it wouldn't get caught when he closed the door, and went around to his side. He slid into the driver's seat, but before he started the engine, he took something out of his pocket and handed it to her. It was his wallet.

"Just wanted you to know I came prepared tonight."

"Are you sure there's money in here?" she quipped. "I didn't bring very much myself."

He took the wallet back and placed it in a pocket inside his jacket. "Don't worry. We're covered." He started the car, and out of the corner of her eye, Regan saw him grin. She believed him. She knew the incident at dinner had bothered him a lot, enough that he'd couriered a certified check to her office the next day to cover the cost of the meals she'd put on her credit card. When he'd called later to tell her when he'd pick her up, she'd tried to tell him it wasn't necessary to repay her, but he'd convinced her his male ego would be really bruised if she didn't take his check.

As advertised, the Fairmont was first-rate. A caravan of stretch limos were parked in front of the hotel, making Regan wonder briefly if it was prom night. An army of doormen escorted guests into the hotel while valets parked their cars. Inside, elegantly dressed men and women in tuxedos and evening gowns paraded through the splendid lobby and corridors. Regan was glad she'd bought the white number and didn't mind that eyes turned in their direction when they entered.

Peter had requested a table in a prime location with an excellent view of the bay and the City's night lights. The City glimmered like fine jewelry against the night sky.

"Champagne?" he asked.

"Sure."

Peter ordered a brand Regan hadn't heard of, something the wine steward assured him was better than Dom Pérignon.

"An excellent choice, sir," the steward said with a nod and hurried off.

Regan knew the champagne was going to be expensive, and she hoped Peter could afford it. Social workers generally didn't make a lot of money. But she sensed Peter wasn't any ordinary social worker, and from his conversation about the stock market on Saturday, she suspected he was a private investor who'd made quite a bit of money. Perhaps his work with the kids was a philanthropic involvement.

She hoped that before the night was out, she'd know more about the kind, gentle, slightly erratic, and very enigmatic Mr. Smith.

But the night went by in a blur of exquisite food, delicious champagne, and dancing that left her breathless. She tried a few times to go into Peter's personal life, but each time he managed to spin the conversation elsewhere. Finally, she just gave up and surrendered to the magic of the evening.

It ended far too soon. When the conductor announced the final set, like Cinderella, Regan was surprised it had grown so late. She didn't want this night to end. The final dance was a slow number, and Peter held her closer than he had all night. She felt him kiss her hair. She raised her face, inviting him to kiss her lips.

He lowered his head ever so slowly, took her lips in a gentle kiss, and they forgot the rest of the world.

"Stay with me tonight," he murmured.

The desire for him that was already raging through her burned hotter. "Where?"

"Here. I have a room."

She gave him a sardonic smile. "Wasn't that a little presumptuous?"

"I didn't plan to ask you to stay. I reserved a room because I didn't want to make the drive home after having drinks." He pulled her close to him again, and they danced in silence. The door had been left open; it was her decision.

Regan's heart pounded. She shouldn't stay. What would Kat think? And Blair. But in the end, the heat of Peter's body and the intensity of her desire won out over her sense of propriety. She was her own woman now. She could do whatever she wanted. When the dance ended, she looked into his eyes. "Yes, Peter," she whispered. "I'll stay with you."

41

When the dancing was over, they walked hand in hand down the long, red-carpeted hallway, passing scenes of framed photos of the 1906 earthquake. Peter felt like an earthquake was passing through him, and he trembled in anticpation as they entered the elevator. What had he done? He desired Regan McKinney, but he was afraid. What if something went wrong?

Don't be a coward, a voice inside him reprimanded. *Go on, do it! Live your dream, for a change.*

Peter swallowed. He'd set this scenario up, he'd invited her to his room, and she'd accepted. He'd look like a complete fool if he didn't go through with it now. *Go on, do it!*

They reached the forty-third floor, and the bell on the elevator interrupted his uneasy thoughts. He took Regan's elbow as they stepped into the hallway.

The penthouse suite he'd reserved was as sumptuous as the rest of the hotel. A king-sized bed was crowned with pillows piled high and dressed in white linen. The maid had turned back the covers, and candy kisses lay upon the pillows. Soft lamplight illuminated the room, which was furnished both tastefully and luxuriously.

"Oh, it's lovely," Regan exclaimed, turning to him, obviously delighted. He took her gently by the shoulders.

"Are you sure about this?" he asked. "If you want to

change your mind, I won't take it personally."

Her reply was to kick off her shoes, stand on tiptoe and encircle his neck with her arms. She pressed her lips against his and opened them slightly. His skin began to burn, and his groin stirred. There was no going back now.

He kissed her mouth hungrily, tasting the sweetness, devouring the sensation. He heard a little moan escape her throat, and it turned him on even more. He felt for the zipper at the back of her dress and slowly edged it downward, his lips never leaving hers. As the beaded fabric peeled away, his hands roamed the flesh of her back, exploring her skin from the curve of her neckline to the curve of her bottom. She wore no underwear.

It was his turn to moan.

He felt her hands loosening the bow tie from around his neck, and he reluctantly ceased his sensual exploration long enough to help her rid him of his jacket and shirt. When she moved away from him, her dress fell to the floor, and he pulled her against his bare chest and kissed her again and again. He couldn't get enough of her.

"Oh, my God, Regan, and I thought you were beautiful before," he murmured, his hands moving ravenously over her naked body. He felt hers on him, as well, stroking his back, drawing him closer. Then her fingers were at his waist, unfastening, unbuttoning, unzipping. He led her toward the bed and together they fell across the crisp white sheets.

His lips trailed kisses down her neck and over her breasts, and she arched toward him. He suckled at her nipples, encircling their rosy peaks with his tongue, feeling them harden beneath his touch.

Another moan, but he wasn't sure which of them had made the sound.

His cock was so hard and heavy that he thought he would burst, but he didn't want to ruin the moment. *Wait, wait. Not yet.* He pulled away, breathing hard. And then she touched him, encircled his erection with smooth fingers.

"You'd . . . better not do that," he stammered. "I'm on the edge as it is."

"We have all night," she whispered and stroked him gently anyway. He moved over her and slid inside her hot, moist darkness, all the while looking into her eyes, searching for any sign that he wasn't welcome there. He saw none. Instead, she returned his gaze, and her own was filled with passion and longing. He saw her bite her lower lip.

"Am I hurting you?"

"Oh, God, no. I've never felt anything so delicious in my life."

She began to slowly undulate beneath him, and this time, he followed her lead in their lovers' dance. She moved faster and closed her eyes. With each thrust, Peter thought he would come, but somehow he managed to hold on until he felt her contract around him in a series of tiny spasms and heard her cry out in pleasure. Only then did he allow himself the release that satiated his own passion. It seemed as if it lasted forever.

42

Regan lay nude in Peter's arms and felt his heart beating hard against her own. He was still inside her, and she never wanted him to leave. She had never experienced such sexual delight before. She knew Peter had held back to give her pleasure before taking his own, unlike Adam, who'd never bothered to consider her needs. Adam had been a selfish lover, if she could call him a lover at all. Their intimacy, she realized, had been mechanical, functional, practical. They'd had sex to make a baby, not to show their love for one another.

Make a baby. Regan bit her lip. She wasn't afraid of becoming pregnant, but she and Peter had not practiced safe sex. She knew very little about him. What if he had AIDS? she thought suddenly. After all, this was San Francisco. God, when was she going to quit being so naïve and trusting?

"Peter?" she said, shifting in his arms.

"Uh-mm?"

She hesitated, ashamed that she would think for one minute that Peter wouldn't protect her if he had some dreaded sexually tranmitted disease. Still, her fearful self had to ask. "Are you . . . healthy?"

He laughed softly. "Yes. Are you?"

Regan hadn't considered that the concern went both ways. Her cheeks burned. "Yes."

"We shouldn't have done that," he admitted. "I hadn't
planned on this or I would have brought something."

The cold, clinical reality of what they were discussing
chilled any residual ardor, and to her great disappointment,
Peter rolled away from her. When he was no longer inside
her, she felt suddenly alone, insecure. And she missed his
warmth.

"Don't worry. I can't get pregnant," she told him. Might
as well get this part of it over with. If he had any intentions
of pursuing a relationship with her, and if he wanted children, they might as well stop things before they went any
further. "I'm infertile," she added.

He leaned on one elbow and looked down at her. With
his free arm, he stroked her cheek. "I don't care about that.
I just want to know you're okay with . . . what we did, are
doing."

She reached up and drew his head toward hers and kissed
him with the richness of her spent passion. "I've never been
so okay in my life." She thought she might cry with the
tender emotions that welled up within her, and she suddenly
wondered if what she was feeling for Peter was love. She'd
thought she'd been in love with Adam, but she'd never felt
anything like this before. Did he feel the same way? "Are
. . . you okay with it, Peter?"

He drew away slightly, but only to gaze more directly
into her eyes. "Yes. I'm just not used to . . . to feeling this
way toward anyone."

She took his hand and laid it across her pounding heart.
"Feel that?" He pressed his palm against her skin and nodded. "I'm not used to this, either," she murmured. Then she
smiled in invitation. "But I'd like to get used to it."

His hand slid from her collarbone to her breast, and he
slung one leg across her torso. "Maybe we ought to practice
some more."

Their lovemaking was slower this time; tender, explora-
tory, but the end was just as explosive as before. When at
last they cuddled together beneath the comforter, Regan
sighed. She tried to feel guilty for what they'd done, but
didn't. This was the most honest she'd ever been with a man,
and with herself. And the truth was, she wanted more. Did

Peter? She wished he'd say something, but his breathing grew even, and she realized he'd fallen asleep. She draped an arm around him, and in his sleep, he nestled closer to her body. Regan smiled. Peter didn't have to say anything. The very intimacy of their embrace said it all.

43

In the dream, Peter and Regan were walking in a park some-place, maybe the Presidio, when suddenly a creature he knew was inherently evil lurched from the shadows of the forest and began to pursue them. Peter turned to face the beast, but it wasn't Peter the horrid creature wanted. It vaulted after Regan. Peter went after it, trying to save Regan, but the brute snagged her tender skin with its talons. Blood spilled through the dream, mingling with Regan's screams.

Peter jerked awake, a scream of his own lodged in his throat. He was soaked in a cold sweat. His heart thundered, and he was shaking. It had only been a dream, but it had been so incredibly real. Someone, or rather some*thing,* had been trying to harm Regan, a beast so evil it must kill to survive. He lay still, breathing hard, trying to calm down.

It was only a dream.

Suddenly he became aware of Regan sleeping by his side, and the events of the evening flooded his mind. The dinner, the dancing, the look in her eyes when she'd agreed to stay the night with him. And sometime during the night, they'd become lovers. The memories should have filled him with joy, but instead, a sick terror ebbed into his soul. The evil force in the dream seemed to reinvent itself in his imagina-tion, and Peter was seized with the irrational but powerful notion that if he didn't leave her immediately, something terrible would happen to her.

His heart slammed against his chest as he eased his body out of bed. He prayed she wouldn't wake up before he left her. He didn't know what would happen if she did.

Gathering his clothing that was scattered about the floor, he hurried into the bathroom. Moments later, fully dressed, he tiptoed to her side of the bed. She was so beautiful in her sleep, and he didn't want to leave her. But fear for her safety enshrouded him like a hideous spiderweb.

She'd said she hadn't brought much money, so he placed cab fare for her on the dresser. He crept quietly to the door and opened it, then paused. Glancing over his shoulder, he shook his head in disbelief that he was doing this. But even as he stood there, ambivalent and filled with despair, the inexplicable sense of danger grew stronger and more threatening. He had to leave her. And he had to do it *now*.

44

Regan awoke feeling unusually contented and strangely lan-
guid, but she quickly remembered what had happened the
night before and knew why she was feeling so special. She
reached out for Peter, hoping to take the night's activities
into morning, but the bed was empty. Regan sat up.

"Peter?"

She got out of bed. "Peter? Are you in the bath?" She
went to see, but no one was there. Maybe he'd gone out for
a walk, or downstairs for breakfast. She didn't know if he
was an early riser or not.

She checked the closet. He'd said he'd anticipated staying
at the hotel. He must have an overnight bag or something.
But the closet was empty, as well.

And then she spotted the twenty-dollar bill on the dresser.
What on earth?

She picked up the money and stared at it in disbelief.
This couldn't be. And yet the sick feeling in her stomach
told her it was true. Peter had left sometime in the night,
sneaking out like a coward, leaving her some "compensa-
tion" on the dresser. Appalled and humiliated, Regan wad-
ded the bill and threw it across the room. "Goddamn him,"
she swore, and then glanced at the bill on the floor. She
would have laughed if it hadn't been so horrible. Was that
all her services had been worth to Peter Smith?

She wanted to cry, but she was too angry. At him. At herself. How could she have been such a fool? How could she have let her libido lead her into the bed of a man she didn't know, and obviously, couldn't trust? She wondered if he'd been telling the truth about being healthy. Hell, she might have contracted AIDS from him for all she knew.

Miserable and shaking with rage, Regan glanced at the white sequined gown that lay on the floor, mocking her. What a tramp she would appear, sneaking home in last night's clothes. What a slut she was! How could she face Kat and Blair?

Chagrined, she donned the dress, as her only option was to go home naked. Before fleeing the scene of her degradation, she picked up the twenty, carefully smoothed out the wrinkles, and laid it back on the dresser. The maid, at least, would appreciate it.

She crept out of the hotel, taking a service elevator that deposited her on Sacramento Street, the servants' entrance to the posh hotel. Face burning with shame, she flagged a taxi. She tried unsuccessfully to ignore the knowing looks the cab driver shot her from time to time in his rearview mirror on the short trip to Kat's house. He probably took her for some high-priced call girl. She laughed bitterly to herself. She'd acted like a call girl, all right, but he'd paid her like a cheap whore.

Thankfully, neither Kat nor Blair was up yet when she sneaked into the house like a burglar and tiptoed up the stairs. She was too ashamed to face them. She also felt dirty. Going into the private bath that adjoined her bedroom, she stripped out of the dress and stepped under the shower, turning up the water temperature to high, as hot as she could bear. The scalding water punished her body as she washed her hair and let the rich sudsy shampoo slide down her body. Her mind filled with images of Peter's hands on her body, and her eyes filled with tears.

Why did he have to be such a jerk? Why were all men so cruel? And why in God's name had she set herself up like that?

Regan wiped the suds away and scrubbed her body furiously with a net pouf. She rubbed and rubbed until her skin turned red, as if by doing so she could scrape away what she'd done. The water temperature began to cool, and Regan realized she must have drained the hot water heater's capacity. How long had she been in the shower? Half an hour? An hour? Whatever, it wasn't long enough. She still felt defiled as she stepped into the steamy atmosphere of the bathroom.

Feeling unlovely, Regan dressed in the most unlovely thing she could find—baggy old jeans and a shabby sweatshirt. The day was cool, and the rain that had been forecast began to fall. The weather seemed as miserable as she was. Regan hung up the white ball gown, which she now despised, rumpled her bed to look as if she'd slept in it, and headed down the stairs. Might as well face the music, she thought, wondering if she could lie to her sister.

45

Every muscle in his body seemed to ache when Peter awoke again. He looked around his room, disoriented and confused. What was he doing here? And how did he get here? He'd thought he was with Regan, at the Fairmont. They'd dined, and danced, and made love until at last they'd fallen asleep in each other's arms.

Hadn't they?

Or had it all been just a dream? He let out a heavy sigh. If it was, it had been the most wonderful, sensual dream he'd ever had. He smiled at the images of intimacy with Regan that lingered in his mind. Then he rolled over and saw his tuxedo hanging over the back of a nearby chair.

Not a dream.

Peter bolted upright in bed and stared at the clothing. Oh, sweet Jesus.

And then he remembered everything. They *had* dined. And danced. And made love. And sometime during the night, he'd left her. But *why*?

That, he could not remember.

He closed his eyes, the agony of regret shooting through every nerve. Why? Why had he done such a cruel and crazy thing? But even as he questioned his motives, an echo of the fear that had assailed him in the dark of the night in the hotel room shuddered through him. Not fear for himself, but fear for her.

He remembered he'd had a nightmare that had left him shaken, almost debilitated, and that he'd felt in his guts that if he didn't leave her, something terrible would happen to her. Now, by the light of day, that seemed ludicrous. Yet the fear lingered, and it was real. But, he wondered suddenly, was he afraid *for* her, or afraid *of* her?

Deeply troubled, Peter got out of bed and dressed without being aware of what he put on. He wandered into the kitchen and made a pot of coffee. Loading his coffee with sugar, he stepped out onto the glass-enclosed deck that overlooked the ocean. Beyond the protective glass, a storm battered the Pacific. Wind howled in gales, churning the waves to a frothy gray-green, and rain pelted heavily on the beach far below. His house shuddered from rooftop to floor and seemed on the verge of being blown over the cliff and into the ocean.

Inside his soul, an equally fierce storm raged. It was completely unthinkable that he could be afraid of Regan McKinney. Peter had never been afraid of anything, certainly never of a woman. But then, there'd never been a woman like Regan. He'd never experienced feelings like those he had for her.

But to be afraid of her? Give me a break, he muttered to himself, swearing again under his breath.

And it made no sense for him to fear *for* her. He would never harm her. She was perfectly safe lying in his arms in a penthouse in one of San Francisco's most prestigious hotels. And yet, he couldn't shake the feeling of impending danger.

He sipped his coffee and wondered what Regan must have thought when she awoke to find him gone. It was a despicable thing to do, whatever his reasons, and he doubted she would ever speak to him again.

The notion deepened his gloom. He'd never wanted anything or anybody the way he wanted Regan. She filled him with joy and hope and sunshine, made him realize for the first time how much of life he'd missed.

Was he going to let some ridiculous, unnamed fear ruin his chances for a happier life? Was he so ignoble that he'd just walk out on Regan like that, without giving her any reason or explanation?

Peter paced the floor, edgy and uncertain. Should he call her or not? He didn't know. If he did, would she hang up in his ear? Probably. Would she understand his explanation? Never. He didn't understand it himself.

But he had to try.

Heart pounding, he went inside and picked up the phone. His heartbeat thrummed even harder when he heard the phone ringing on the other end. He almost hung up. He thought of Regan's face, serene in sleep, and then of how hurt she must have been. No. He owed it to her to try to apologize. He didn't expect her to let him into her life again, but he couldn't leave her in such cowardly disgrace.

46

Kat was making breakfast when Regan came into the kitchen. "Have fun?" Kat asked.

"Yeah," Regan replied unenthusiastically. "You were right. The Fairmont was spectacular."

"So why don't I hear a glow in your voice or see stars in your eyes?"

Regan had hoped she could remain nonchalant and act as if what had happened was no big deal, but she couldn't. Instead, she sank into a kitchen chair and put her head in her hands. "Oh, cripes, Kat, I'm the world's biggest fool. He . . . he was so wonderful. He treated me like a queen, and . . . and when he asked if I'd stay the night with him, I did."

"So? You going to feel guilty like Mama would want you to?" Kat took two mugs from the cabinet and poured them each a cup of coffee. "Blair's not here. She went to a friend's house last night after you left. So it's just you and me, sis. You can talk freely. If you want to."

Regan gratefully accepted the coffee. "Thanks." But she offered nothing more, and a long silence stretched between them as she slowly sipped the scalding brown liquid.

At last, Kat sat down opposite Regan. "So, was he good in bed?"

Her blunt question brought blood to Regan's cheeks. Kat had never been one to mince words, but this was embarrassing, and it made Regan angry. "Yes," she replied sharply. "He was very good in bed. Better than you can imagine." Her mounting anger made her brave, and she blurted, "I came twice in a matter of minutes. I didn't know women could do that. Did you? I mean, I thought we needed some recovery time."

Kat sputtered coffee all over the table. "For God's sake, Regan. TMI. Too much information. I just wanted to know, you know, in general . . ."

Regan eyed her sister and laughed harshly. "Can't believe I got you." But her funk returned. "But don't get too excited. I closed my eyes thinking I'd met Prince Charming, and when I opened them again this morning, he was gone."

"Oh," was all her sister said. Another silence hung between them. Regan's throat tightened and tears threatened again. She blinked them away and sipped her coffee.

"He didn't bother to wake me to say goodbye, or leave a note. But there was a twenty-dollar bill on the dresser. I guess he thought that was sufficient. After all, I did enjoy myself."

For once, Kat seemed at a loss for words. "I'm sure that wasn't it, Regan. I'm sure there was a good reason why he left."

"Yeah, like maybe he's married and had to go home." The ugly thought had just occurred to her. "It could be. I don't know squat about that man."

"Did you use a condom?"

Regan's humiliation grew worse. She shook her head, and the tears spilled at last.

"Oh, boy," Kat said, blowing her breath upward into her bangs. "We'd better get you checked out."

"I know."

The telephone rang, startling both women. Kat answered it, then without speaking, handed the receiver across the table to Regan.

"Hello?" Her voice was shaky, and she didn't want to talk to anyone.

"Regan, it's Peter."

She didn't reply.

"Listen, I called . . . to say I'm sorry—"

"You sure are, mister," and she hung up.

Moments later, the phone rang again. Regan looked at Kat. Her sister shrugged. "It's your choice. Don't answer it, and you'll never know why he left."

Regan pushed the button. "Hello." Her voice sounded harsh and angry to her ears.

"Please don't hang up. I . . . I need to talk to you."

Regan thought she heard a note of desperation in his voice, but she didn't relent. "Talk fast."

"Can I come over? I . . . want to talk to you in person."

"Are you married, Peter?"

A hesitation, then a bitter laugh. "No. I'm not married. Please, may I come?"

Regan didn't know what to say. She was hurt and furious with him, but she also held undeniable feelings for him. What if he had a good reason for leaving their bed? "I might be busy today."

"Please," he begged again. "It's important." He paused, then added, "It may be the most important thing I've ever done in my life."

47

The man was furious. Somebody was fucking with him. Somebody was taunting him, flaunting her right in his face. He could see her in his mind's eye, head thrown back, dancing, laughing, mocking. Asking for it.

Ka-thud.

The single knell reverberated in his brain, clearing his rage and focusing his thoughts. Somebody was trying to stop him. Somebody kept getting in the way.

Well, he wouldn't be stopped. And he wouldn't waste any more time. He'd planned to take it easy, go slow, enjoy the ride, so to speak, but now, he felt an urgency to complete his mission. He had to finish his work, and nothing, nobody would stand in his way.

48

Regan had agreed to let Peter come to Kat's house later that afternoon. She wanted time to pull herself together before she faced him again. Kat offered to take Blair to the skating rink to give Regan privacy, but Regan didn't want to be alone with Peter Smith.

"I don't trust myself," she admitted. "When I'm around him, I'm not normal. I do stupid things."

"I think you're in love," her sister stated.

"Not." But Regan feared that Kat was right. Last night she'd thought she was in love, and when she'd heard his voice on the phone, her feelings for him roared to the surface in spite of her anger. People couldn't turn love off and on like a water faucet, could they? Was she in love with Peter, or wasn't she?

He arrived at four P.M., bringing with him a gallon of French chocolate ice cream. "A peace offering?" He handed the carton to her.

Regan worked hard at holding on to her anger, for it was her only defense, but Peter's sexy smile, the one that blazed in his blue eyes and lit his entire face, unglued her. She was glad he hadn't brought flowers or an expensive gift, as she'd feared he might. Flowers were trite, and a gift would have been inappropriate. But ice cream she could accept. "Okay." She took the carton. "Want some?" She gestured him inside.

"Sure."

Her heart was beating too hard as Regan led Peter into the kitchen where Kat was busying herself creating some concoction for their dinner. Kat always cooked when she was nervous, and apparently, she was nervous about Peter's visit, because the kitchen was a wreck. Kat turned and greeted their guest.

"Hello, Peter."

"Hi."

Small greetings from people ill at ease. "Peter's brought chocolate ice cream. Want some?"

"You bet. And dish up a bowl for Blair, too." Blair had been relegated to her room for the time Peter would be there. Regan hated to ask her to stay out of sight, but she didn't want Blair to know about her misadventures the night before. Regan wasn't proud of them.

Regan scooped the ice cream into four bowls. Kat carried Blair's upstairs, and Regan and Peter took theirs into the front parlor. The serving of the ice cream had been ceremonial, a means of postponing the difficult emotional encounter that lay ahead between them.

Regan turned on the gas logs and took a seat opposite Peter on the matching sofas. She gazed down at the bowl of chocolate ice cream in her hands, not knowing where to go from here. She raised her chin and challenged him with her eyes. "So, okay. You called this meeting . . ."

Peter placed his bowl on the coffee table between them, the ice cream untouched. He leaned forward, his forearms resting on his long thighs. He bowed his head slightly, and she saw him rub his temples as if he had a headache. There was small satisfaction in knowing this was hard for him. "Thanks for seeing me," he began.

"You're welcome." Regan's throat tightened with emotion. Her angry self wanted to make this difficult for him, but there was another side of her who'd already forgiven him.

"I don't exactly know where to begin, or what to say, except that I'm sorry I left last night."

Regan clenched her jaw and remained silent, waiting,

dreading whatever he had to say. It must be something really
big, and really bad.

"You see, I had a nightmare sometime just before dawn,"
he proceeded. "In it, you were in terrible danger." She waited
for more, but that seemed to be it.

Regan looked at him, incredulous. "You left because you
had a bad dream?"

He opened his mouth as if to reply, then took in a breath
instead. He shook his head. "It was more than that. I know
this sounds crazy, because it is, but I had this really intense
feeling that if I didn't leave right then, something bad was
going to happen to you."

She exhaled a huff of a breath. "Well, yes, that certainly
sounds crazy," she said lightly. She gazed directly at him.
"*Are* you crazy, Peter?"

Peter leaned back against the sofa and gave a short laugh.
"I don't know. I went home and went back to bed, and when
I woke up, I couldn't believe what I'd done. It seems so
foolish now, but in the night . . ." His words drifted away,
and Regan shuddered involuntarily. Peter's face was haggard
and drawn. The nightmare, whatever it had been, had deeply
frightened him.

"Do you have these nightmares often?"

He shook his head. "No. I don't even dream very much."

"So what do you think it was?"

Peter leaned forward again and looked at her, his expression both earnest and pleading. "I'm embarrassed to say this,
because it's not a very 'manly-man' thing. But I'm not good
at lying, either. I think . . . my dream, the nightmare, was my
psyche showing me how afraid I am of becoming involved
with you."

Regan wasn't sure what to say to that. "Afraid?"

Peter looked away. "I told you I've never had a serious
relationship with a woman before."

A suspicion hit Regan. "Are you trying to tell me you're
gay, Peter?"

His head jerked around in surprise. "No. I'm not gay.
How could you think that after last night?"

"I didn't think that until you told me you were afraid of
having a relationship with me."

Peter held out his hands, palms up, then took her hands in his. "I know it's hard to believe that I've been such a workaholic all my life that I just never made time for a personal life, but it's true. Now, I think I want to change that. But it isn't easy. I'm rather set in my ways. I have a lot of obligations that demand my time. I'm not used to having a woman around. I think part of my fear is that I'll offend you by my ineptness, or inadvertently ignore you when I don't mean to. I . . . I really care about you, Regan," he said, giving her fingers a squeeze. "I would never mean to hurt you. But I'm afraid I might, just from sheer selfishness and inexperience."

His words—and his ingenuous attitude—melted the last of Regan's reserve. She'd never met a man so honest, so apparently ego-free. "So . . . what are you saying? Where do you want to go from here?"

She saw him swallow. "If you can forgive me for taking off last night," he said, "and if you think you can put up with me until I get a little more used to all this, well, I'd like to keep seeing you. I can't say where it will lead. All I know is that I care for you, Regan. I care for you very much. Please, will you forgive me?"

How can a girl say no to that? Regan thought wryly. She drew Peter toward her across the coffee table, until their lips were almost touching. "I think I can forgive you," she said, kissing him lightly, "but I need to know one thing."

"What's that?"

"What were the twenty bucks for?"

49

The rain hung on to San Francisco, enveloping the city in a dreary miasma that set Regan's teeth on edge. Although she and Peter had made up the evening before, she was still unsettled by the events of the weekend. On Saturday, he'd been a fabulous lover. Last night, however, he'd seemed content to hang around the house with Kat and Blair, like he was a brother or something. Regan didn't know what she'd expected him to do, run out and rent a motel room so they could continue their sexual explorations? It was kind of nice, actually, she thought in retrospect, that he wanted to be around her family. Blair seemed particularly taken with him.

One thing was certain. Peter Smith had turned her world upside down, and she had to be very, very careful not to fall off. He was still very much an enigma, although admittedly, an intriguing one. Still, she needed an anchor to hold her steady during all this, and that anchor was her job. That's why she'd come into work early. She wanted some quiet time to think and get herself organized for the day.

Regan hung her umbrella on the coat tree and vigorously shook the rain from her all-weather coat. She made coffee and bustled around the office, trying to concern herself with the business at hand, but her thoughts kept returning to Peter, and a silly smile kept creeping onto her lips.

Regan turned on her computer, intending to finish her notes on the story about Kevin Carrington. When she had everything ready for the interview, she'd make her drop-in visit at HomeRun, Inc. Maybe today, if the rain let up.

"You have mail," the computer informed her, and her heart skipped a little beat. Was it from Peter?

There were several messages, and they took quite a while to download. Probably junk mail, she thought. When the messages were retrieved, she went through them, deleting the trash. The last message caught her eye; the subject line read:

Dance Till You Die.

Alarmed, but also curious, Regan double-clicked to open the file. All it contained was a hyperlink to a site on the Internet. She clicked on the link and watched in fascination at what unfolded on the screen.

First, music flooded the room, a hot, heavy-metal sound with a primitive beat. *Ka-thud, ka-thud, ka-thud* went the bass, so loud that it shook the very air around her. Regan fumbled with the keyboard, trying to find a way to turn the volume down. As she was doing so, Jeff Roundtree entered the office.

"What the hell's going on?" he demanded, shouting over the blaring noise.

Regan looked up at him and shouted back, "How do you turn the volume down on this thing?"

Jeff reached for the mouse, but before he could attempt to turn down the volume, a sound like a crack of thunder emanated from the speakers, and the screen split in half diagonally as if hit by a lightning bolt. Regan let out a startled scream.

The upper right half of the monitor became a brilliant yellow, while the lower left turned a dark, shadowy purple. A tiny figure started to move, dancing in time to the music, leaving the upper right-hand corner and making its way to the center of the screen. As it grew larger, Regan saw it was a woman, and as it approached the center of the screen, her blood ran cold. The woman, although a cartoon figure, was unmistakably her. The face was a caricature of her own. The hairstyle, the reddish hair color were hers. Most horrifying of all, the figure wore a dress Regan recognized instantly. It was her own purple cocktail dress. Regan covered her mouth with the back of her trembling hand. What the hell indeed was going on here?

Suddenly, the figure of a man stepped from the shadow side of the screen into the yellow backdrop. He was tall and well built but his clothing wasn't defined. He was just a solid, dark figure. He took the cartoon-woman in his arms, and the music shifted to a sedate waltz. Round and round the couple danced, faster and faster as again the music gained momentum. Then the man's hands moved from the dance position up to encircle the woman's neck. He lifted her as if she weighed nothing and began to shake her like a rag doll in time to the beat of the music, which shifted at this point back to the heavy-metal sound of the opening.

Moments later, the woman went limp, and the man dropped her. Her lifeless form lay against the bright yellow background.

"Good God," Roundtree uttered. "We'd better call the cops."

But neither he nor Regan moved as the next scene un-folded. They watched transfixed as the man reached into the shadow side of the picture and brought out a large baseball bat. The music intensified, and as they looked on in horror, he began to beat the woman's body in time to the angry rhythm.

Ka-thud.

Ka-thud.

Ka-thud.

With each blow to her head and increasingly mangled corpse, blood spurted across the screen and dripped down-ward in a chillingly realistic effect. Soon, the entire monitor turned bloodred. And then a message scrawled itself across the crimson screen: "The dancemaster is watching. He doesn't like your moves."

50

Sam Sloan felt his skin crawl as he viewed the murderous cartoon drama on the computer screen. He and Kelly had come immediately in response to Jeff Roundtree's nearly hysterical call to the SFPD. Sloan stared at the killer's carefully choreographed murder play. It fit in every detail with the previous murders—the dance, the strangulation, the postmortem mutilation. This was one sick, angry bastard. But he was also smart. A computer genius, it would seem.

Sloan took out his cell phone and dialed a number. "I've got a job for Carnivore," he told the man at the other end, and gave him the necessary details to get the FBI started on trying to trace the sender of the obscene video e-mail message. Although controversial, the FBI's Carnivore software had been highly effective in locating and identifying computer terrorists, the maniacs who created and distributed computer viruses that caused havoc in businesses and governments around the world. He wondered if the program could pinpoint this creep, as well.

Regan McKinney, he was certain, was targeted as the killer's next victim. But why? And why had he sent her this warning? Sloan didn't think the murderer had warned any of the other victims. So far, his investigation had shown that the other women had been random targets of opportunity.

But this time, the killer had pinpointed his intended victim ahead of time and issued a warning. Why? A killer this sharp surely knew that the FBI would be called when Ms. McKinney received such a horrifying e-mail. Was he ready to be caught? Or was he playing cat and mouse with them all?

And why Regan McKinney? Sloan turned to her. She seemed somehow familiar, although he was sure he'd never met her. The stricken expression on her face shot an emotional blow to his gut. He had to find this killer, and soon. He didn't want to see her bloodied body lying on a gurney in the morgue.

"Have you any idea who sent this to you?"

Regan McKinney looked up at him with large, frightened eyes. Her hair color was lighter than that of the other victims—strawberry-blond—but red enough to qualify. She shook her head, sending coppery tendrils flowing around her face.

"I don't know why anyone would send this to me," she replied, her choked voice barely above a whisper.

"Do you dance? Go out to the clubs?" Sloan knew the answer even as he asked the question. That's why she seemed familiar. He'd seen her a couple of weeks ago, the night he'd made the rounds of the clubs in SOMA.

"I . . . we've been taking dance lessons, my sister and I. She wanted to meet a man who likes to dance." She spoke without emotion, and Sloan knew that fear had deadened her nerves. She was in shock.

"Your sister. What's her name?"

"Kat. Katherine, actually. Katherine Bowen. She's a paralegal at a law office down on Montgomery Street."

"Does she have red hair?" Again, Sloan knew the answer. The woman Regan had been with at the club, probably the sister, had had red hair, as well, although he recalled hers as being much darker.

"Yes. Really red hair." Regan McKinney's eyes met his, and he palpably felt her terror.

"What dance studio are you going to?"

"Sterling Pace's."

Brad Kelly scribbled notes while Sloan asked the questions. The young officer didn't seem to mind letting Sloan lead this investigation. Sloan was glad. Sometimes eager cops got in the way, with their big egos and endless turf battles. "You know the place?" he asked Kelly. The policeman nodded.

"Who's the 'dancemaster'?" Sloan asked Regan. "Pace?" She thought about it a minute. "I suppose he is. He owns the place. But . . . he's an older guy, probably in his sixties. I thought you were looking for someone a lot younger."

"We are. What about his other instructors? Is there a second-in-command?"

He heard her sharp intake of breath. "Oh, my God," she uttered. "Cameron."

"Who's Cameron?"

"Cameron Pace, Sterling's son. He's in his mid-thirties, I'd say. He . . . he took over our lessons when another instructor didn't show up, and my sister . . . Oh, my God—"

"Your sister what?"

"She's fallen for him. In fact, she went out with him a few nights ago to a Latino dance club in the Mission District."

Sloan swore under his breath. Didn't anybody listen to his warnings? At least Katherine Bowen hadn't turned up dead . . . yet.

"Did anything unusual happen when she was with him?" he asked, trying to conceal his concern. "Did she mention anything out of the ordinary to you afterward?"

Regan gave him a tremulous smile. "No. Nothing happened. I know because . . . I barged in on their date. I got this really uneasy feeling about her going out to a dance club after the warnings that have been in the media. I got scared after she left and took a cab there myself. I figured she would be safer if we were together." Her smile faded. "I felt like a fool at the time, but now I'm really glad I did it. I'm not saying Cameron is the killer, but—"

Sloan helped her out. "You may have saved her life," he said quietly. Sloan had no evidence against Cameron Pace, but this was the first time he'd had a lead, a name, an identity to work with. He was itching to get his hands on this "dancemaster." But first, he had to make sure Regan and her sister were out of harm's way.

"I must warn you, Ms. McKinney, I believe you and your

sister are in grave danger," he said darkly. She nodded. Her face was pale, and he could see tiny beads of perspiration on her forehead. He wanted to reach out and wipe them away and take her fear along with it, but then, that was impossible. She had every reason to be afraid. "I'm going to order round-the-clock police protection for both of you."

"Police protection? What kind of police protection?"

"We'll post a twenty-four-hour surveillance team near your sister's house, and an officer will accompany you at all times."

Regan shook her head. "That means we're the ones being held prisoner. Kat'll never go for it, and I don't think it's necessary, especially if you arrest Cameron Pace."

He leveled with her. "We can't arrest Pace, at least not at the moment."

A frown creased her brow. "Why not?"

"We haven't a shred of evidence that he's the killer. We don't have probable cause to arrest him." He saw her shudder and knew that in spite of what she said to the contrary, she was convinced Cameron Pace was the man.

She stood up and rubbed her upper arms briskly. "Mr. Sloan, if there's any chance he is the killer, how can you let him roam free?" Her voice held a challenge alongside her fear.

He grimaced. "That's the American way. Innocent until proven guilty. We're not allowed to preventively detain a suspect just because we fear he may commit a crime in the future. But you can bet, Ms. McKinney, we'll be all over Cameron Pace the moment we leave here. We'll shadow him twenty-four/seven. If he is our boy, he'll have a hard time striking again. And maybe we'll get lucky and find hard evidence of his guilt. But," he added, looking directly into her eyes, "he might not be the killer. The killer could be any of the instructors at Pace's studio or any other dance studio. Or, maybe not an instructor at all, just a wacko who calls himself the 'dancemaster.' Now, I need to know one more thing. You said your sister went for Cameron Pace. What about you? Did you meet anybody who came on to you at your dance class or anytime you went out to a club?"

Regan shuddered. She felt suddenly light-headed, as if she would faint.

51

Regan heard Sloan's question, but she didn't reply right away. Instead, she stared out at the rain that was still coming down in sheets and wondered what her former friends were doing back in Middleton. She wondered if it was raining there. She wondered how her life had spun so far away from the safety and predictability of that little burg. Maybe she should flee this crazy city, Frisco, and return to the softer, safer South.

She turned to Sam Sloan and thought fleetingly that she'd seen him someplace before. Probably on television, she guessed. He appeared to be in his late thirties, maybe early forties, but he seemed to have a lifetime of worry etched into the lines of his craggy face. His hair was dark, but there was gray at his temples. She wondered if his eyes, a deep blue, had ever reflected humor. Sam Sloan wasn't smiling, looked as if he never smiled. His expression sent the term "mean cop" shivering through her.

What was she going to tell Sam Sloan? She couldn't lie, and yet she wanted to protect Peter from being interrogated. As unsure as she was about the future of their relationship at the moment, her feelings for him ran deep. Maybe she even loved him. One thing she knew for sure. Peter Smith was no serial killer, and Sloan would be wasting his time and the taxpayers' money chasing after him.

"I never met anyone at a dance club," she answered at last, only partially addressing his question. "I only went out twice, once with Kat, and last week with her and Cameron. I don't like those places. They're too sleazy."

She paused and waited, hoping that would be sufficient for Sloan. But of course it wasn't. He was an investigator for the FBI. A professional interrogator. A bulldog.

"What about at the dance studio? Did you meet anyone there?"

"Of course. They have partners for you when you go as a single. I danced with several guys, including Sterling and Cameron."

"Do you remember the names of the other instructors?"

Regan bit her lip. "Only one. Peter Smith."

In the silence that followed her answer, she heard the scratch of pencil on paper as the other policeman made notes.

"Did you see Smith only at the dance studio, or did you have anything else to do with him?"

Her mind flashed back to Saturday night, and the white sequined ball gown, and Peter's body against hers, on hers . . . in hers . . . Her skin burned.

"Actually, I had a couple of dates with him. He's a nice guy. Not your man, I assure you."

Sloan didn't seem assured. Nor did he give up. "When did you go out with him? And where did you go?"

Regan gave him minimal details. "I didn't get to know him very well," she explained. *Not very well at all.* It struck her that in spite of their intimacy, she had no idea where he lived or how to get in touch with him. Right now, that seemed like a good thing. She wouldn't have to lie.

"When are you going to see him again?"

She dropped her eyes and studied her fingernails. "I . . . don't know." Peter hadn't asked for another date when he'd left Kat's place the night before.

"When did you see him last?"

"Yesterday afternoon. He came over to Kat's house, where I'm living. He stayed for supper, then left."

"What time did he go?"

Regan was growing edgy at Sloan's persistent questioning. "I don't know. Around eight o'clock, I guess."

"Was he going home?"

She turned on him. "I don't know. For God's sake, Peter's not a killer. You're asking questions about the wrong man."

"Maybe. But we have to follow up every lead, Ms. McKinney. I'm sure you understand."

She did understand, but she didn't have to like it.

"What does Mr. Smith do, other than teach dance?" Sloan pressed on. "Or is that his full-time occupation?"

Regan shook her head, feeling miserable, as if she were somehow betraying Peter. "He has another job, but I don't know what it is. We've never talked much about it. It has something to do with some children, but I don't know in what capacity. He could be a social worker."

"What does he look like? What kind of car does he drive?"

Each question stabbed at her like a sharp knife. It embarrassed her that she knew so little about the man whose bed she'd shared and who, it seemed, had stolen her heart.

"He's not tall, about five eleven, I'd guess. He has brown hair, blue eyes, regular features. Nothing outstanding about his looks, really. Not handsome, but not bad-looking, either. Sort of . . . regular, I guess."

Regular. And yet not. Peter's package was really quite nicely put together.

"Do you know where he lives?"

"No."

"Phone number?"

She winced. "No."

Sloan asked again for a description of Peter's car, and she reluctantly gave it to him.

"He drives a Jag? On a social worker's pay?" Sloan remarked skeptically.

Regan shrugged, acutely uncomfortable, because she shared Sloan's sentiments. But she came to Peter's defense. "I think he has other income. He's mentioned the stock market."

When Sloan at last ceased peppering her with questions, she glared up at him. She knew he was only doing his job, but she had to convince him he was barking up the wrong tree.

"Peter isn't your killer, Mr. Sloan."

His eyes leveled on hers. "How do you know?"

She couldn't hold his gaze and looked away. "Because, he just isn't. I admit I don't know a lot about Peter Smith, but whenever I've been with him, I've found him to be kind, thoughtful, honest . . ." She thought about his admission that he was afraid of getting involved with her. He hadn't come right out and said it, but she suspected that his dedication to those children was part of the reason he'd never allowed himself a personal life. "He doesn't have a mean bone in his body, Mr. Sloan. His problem, it seems to me, is that he's too kind, too thoughtful, and I suspect he lets people take advantage of him."

Sloan nodded slowly, patronizingly, she thought.

"Maybe. But we have to check him out anyway. Somebody sent you a very graphic and pointed e-mail message, Ms. McKinney. Somebody who knows you. Who knows what you look like. Who saw you in that dress—"

"Peter never saw me in that dress."

She saw Sloan frown slightly. "When did you wear it?"

"When I went to the clubs. That's all." She didn't want to think that the killer had been at one of those places, maybe both, and had spotted her wearing that dress. She'd never in her life done anything to attract attention to herself, until she bought that dress. And now, it seemed, it had attracted plenty of attention, all right. The wrong kind of attention. She wanted to run home and burn the damned thing.

"So Peter Smith never saw you in that dress?" Sloan asked.

"That's correct."

"Then maybe he's not our boy." Sloan glanced up at Regan. "May we borrow it? The dress, I mean? I want to see how closely it resembles the one on the computer."

Because the FBI needed to work at her computer station, and had in fact rather taken over his office suite, Jeff gave her the rest of the day off. Regan saw his scowl as she donned her coat, and she didn't blame him for being upset.

"I'll be in at eight-thirty sharp tomorrow," she promised. "If the rain goes away, I'll go to Palo Alto."

Roundtree's face was inscrutable. "We'll see," he replied.

What did he mean by "We'll see"? she wondered as she walked slightly ahead of Sloan and the other officer out of the building. Had he changed his mind about letting her do the Carrington story?

Her spirits, already in the toilet, flushed on down.

52

Sloan and Kelly had confiscated Regan's party dress and left her under the watchful eye of two plainclothes cops in a car across the street from Kat Bowen's house. They were on their way to pay a visit to the Sterling Pace School of Dance when they got a call from headquarters.

The body of a woman named Jennifer Short, or what was left of it, had been found much farther south than the other victims, near Oyster Point, in South San Francisco. Kelly turned the car around and headed toward the morgue where the remains had been taken.

Half an hour later, Sloan gazed down at Jennifer Short's mangled, battered corpse and wondered if the killer was leaving the area. Was this victim a farewell present to the City by the bay? Or was the murderer just expanding his turf?

The woman's body had been found by early-morning fishermen, and the coroner estimated that she'd been dead only a few hours. Although this killing was similar to the earlier ones, the victim's body was not found at the water's edge, but rather higher up, in the dock area, close to a parking lot, in a fairly visible place. And although she was red-headed, the victim didn't have on a party dress. Instead, she wore jeans and a light blue blouse with tiny flowers printed on the gauzy material. As with the others, however, she'd been strangled, then beaten with a bludgeon of some kind.

Copycat? Sloan wondered. Or the real killer?

"Did he use a baseball bat?" Sloan asked the coroner.

"It was a blunt wooden instrument of some kind. Could be a baseball bat."

Sloan turned to Kelly. "What's Forensics got on the splinters of wood found in the bodies? Did they come from the same instrument? Was it a baseball bat?"

"I don't know. Haven't heard from them."

"Well, goddammit, get them on the phone." Sloan was impatient. He hoped he wasn't dealing with little bureaucrats in the San Francisco PD's Forensics Unit. He needed answers, and he needed them now. "They've had plenty of time."

Kelly left the room to make the phone call. When he returned, his expression was drawn. "Yeah, they think he's using a baseball bat. The splinters are the same kind of wood, and Forensics thinks they may have all come from Louisville Slugger baseball bats."

Sloan's head jerked up sharply. "That's more like it. Get some people on it, find out where he's buying them."

"Already done," Kelly replied defensively.

Sloan realized for the first time that the stress of the investigation was eating at Kelly, and he was sorry he'd barked at the officer. God knew, Sloan didn't need to put anyone under any more pressure than they were all already feeling, himself included.

"Good," he said more gently. "Then let's go meet Sterling Pace."

53

It was early afternoon by the time they finally arrived at the Sterling Pace School of Dance. The doors were unlocked, but the place was deserted. "Anybody home?" Sloan called out, but his voice echoed down the empty hallway. He and Kelly checked out the main ballroom on the first floor and the smaller classrooms, as well, but no one appeared to be around. "You'd think they'd have better security in a place with so much expensive sound equipment," Kelly remarked. They walked down the hall toward the back of the building and saw a light on in a small room near the end. A man with silver hair looked up in alarm when he heard their foot-steps.

"Sterling Pace?" Sloan asked.

"Yes. I'm sorry, but you startled me," the man said, coming toward them. A deep crease furrowed his brow. "Wasn't there someone at the front desk?"

"No, sir," Kelly said. "Must have gone to lunch." He presented his ID.

Sloan followed suit. "Special Agent Sloan. FBI."

The crease deepened. "FBI?"

"Yes, sir. We're investigating some murders that have happened in the Bay Area in the past few weeks, and we just want to ask you a few questions."

Pace hesitated, then invited them into his small office.

There were only two chairs. Sloan and Pace sat, Kelly leaned against the desk and took out his notebook.

"You may be aware, Mr. Pace," Sloan began, "that there have been a series of murders recently in which the victims appear to have been kidnapped or coerced away from dance clubs in the city."

Pace nodded, his mouth tightening. "Yes, I'm very aware of what's happened. It's really cut into my business. People are afraid to go dancing."

"They have good reason to be afraid," Sloan told him. "We believe the killer is a skilled dancer, and that he stalks his victims in dance clubs."

"Why are you here?" Pace leaned forward, elbows on thighs. "Do you think the killer took dance lessons from our studio?"

"Took lessons, or perhaps gave them."

Pace straightened abruptly. "Gave them? You mean one of my instructors . . . ?"

"We don't know. But one of your students received a very graphic, threatening message which we believe was sent by the killer. She gave us the names of two people she met here. Instructors. We want to talk to them." Sloan saw Sterling Pace's face go white.

"Who?"

"A man named Peter Smith, and . . . your son, Cameron Pace."

It seemed as if Sterling Pace aged before Sloan's eyes. The lines in his face seemed to deepen, and his shoulders lost their proud carriage.

"You can't be serious. My son's not a killer," he objected, but there was just enough doubt beneath the protest to intrigue Sloan. Did his father suspect Cameron had something to hide?

"We're not saying he's the killer. But he has gone out with the woman at least once, and he's taught her here at the studio."

Pace shook his head. "I've told him and told him not to get involved with the students," he growled. "Who is the woman?"

"Regan McKinney. Actually, Cameron dated her sister,

Kat, but ended up taking them both to La Habanera last Wednesday night."

"That doesn't make him a killer."

"No. But whoever sent the threatening message was familiar with a certain dress owned by Ms. McKinney, the same dress she wore that night. You see, Mr. Pace, the message was on the Internet. It was a cartoon of Ms. McKinney being murdered on a dance floor, in that dress."

"Good God."

"There was a message at the end of the video." Sloan indicated that Kelly should read the words from his notepad.

" 'The dancemaster is watching. He doesn't like your moves.' "

"The dancemaster? Who's the dancemaster?" Pace asked.

"I suppose some would say you're a dancemaster," Sloan replied pointedly. "You, or your son. You own this studio, you teach dance, you're a master of the art, and I understand Cameron is following in your footsteps, so to speak."

Sterling Pace covered his face with his hands. "It isn't Cameron. It couldn't be."

Kelly spoke up. "Mr. Pace, is your son into computers?"

Pace looked distressed, and it took a moment for him to answer. "He works for a chain of stores that sells computers," he admitted at last.

Sloan glanced at Kelly, then asked Pace, "Does he own a computer himself?"

"Sure, but who doesn't these days?"

"Do you know if he spends a lot of time on the Internet? Does he write programs? Things like that."

Their line of questioning finally angered Pace, and he scowled. "My son works in a computer store. He sells the damn things. But frankly, I don't think he knows much about them. He uses his computer to stay in touch with people using e-mail, that sort of thing, and he's put our accounting on computer here at the studio," he said with a nod at the machine on the desk. "But he's no hacker or anything like that."

"Where's Cameron right now?" Sloan asked.

The distraught father looked at his watch. "He should be

at work." Pace gave them the name and address of the company where Cameron was employed.

"Now what about this other instructor, Peter Smith?" Sloan saw a dark look cross Pace's face.

"Ex-instructor," Pace said. "I fired his ass last week."

"Why?"

"Unreliable. He's probably the best instructor we had, but you couldn't count on him, you know? We agreed when he came to work here that his hours could be flexible. Apparently he travels a lot with his 'real job,' as he calls it, and sometimes he doesn't know from one day to the next whether he's going to be in town or not. But," Pace added defensively, "he agreed to always give us a call, let us know when he couldn't make it, so we could make arrangements to bring in a substitute. And he didn't do it, one too many times."

"Do what?"

"He didn't call in. He was gone for over a week the last time, and we didn't know whether he was ever going to show up again. So when he did, I fired him."

Sloan crossed one leg on top of the other. "What kind of work does he do in his 'real job'?"

Pace shrugged. "I haven't got a clue. He never talked much about himself. It's a shame, you know, he's a damned good dancer. A wonderful instructor. The women love him. He's a natural with women. I hated to lose him, but I've got a business to run. And if it gets out you're questioning my instructors, especially my son, about those murders," he added grimly, "that business is down the tubes."

Sloan ignored the man's protest. One phrase repeated in his mind.

He's a natural with women.

"You got an address on Smith in your personnel files?" Kelly asked.

Pace went to a filing cabinet in one corner, rummaged through it for a moment, and drew out a manila folder. "Here's his job application. I don't know if the address is current or not. He's worked here for over a year."

He made a copy for the officers, and Sloan thanked him

before leaving. In the police car, Sloan handed the paper over to Kelly. "You know where this is?"

Kelly frowned. "Yes, but it's not exactly a residential neighborhood."

54

By midday, the rain had stopped, and although the sun wasn't out, at least the clouds had begun to dissipate. Regan peered out of the front windows of Kat's house and saw the nondescript gray automobile of the surveillance team parked across the street and down a couple of houses. She wondered what old Mrs. Donovan would say if she knew Kat's house was under surveillance because a killer might be lurking nearby.

The thought made her ill. And another even more so. Regan was putting her sister and her niece in jeopardy by remaining here. Sloan had told her she and her sister were in grave danger, but it was Regan the killer seemed to be after. She should move out. At least until this nightmare was over.

She'd already proposed as much to Kat when she'd called to tell her what had happened, but Kat, of course, wouldn't hear of it. Kat'd said it was sufficient that the police were assigning a man to escort her to and from work and wherever else she needed to go, and one to Blair, as well. She seemed to think it would only be for a few days.

Regan sincerely hoped so. She wasn't sure her nerves could stand this kind of terror for long. She regretted the necessity for such protection, but she was glad to have it, for herself and for the family she'd only recently reclaimed.

Sam Sloan seemed convinced that Regan was the killer's next intended victim, and she couldn't disagree. It was no accident that somebody had e-mailed her and directed her onto that site on the Internet. The killer must have seen her at one of those clubs. It gave her the creeps to think that he'd studied her well enough to be able to draw a cartoon character that looked like her, a character who wore her dress. She shuddered.

Who would want to kill her? And why?

Sloan had told her the guy was a madman, but that didn't explain why he'd apparently fixated on Regan. It had something to do with the way she looked, Sloan had said. He'd explained that psychologically, she must remind the killer of someone who'd harmed him in the past. Maybe his mother or his sister or even a grandmother or aunt who had abused him at some point in his youth. That woman probably had red hair, and she must have liked to dance, he'd told her.

Oddly, on some level Regan felt sorry for the man. No child deserved to be treated badly. Growing up was hard enough. She thought back to her own childhood. She'd never considered herself abused by her parents, but in a way, she supposed that her mother's constant criticism and her father's repressive domination, even in the name of righteousness, could constitute a form of abuse. It had certainly destroyed her self-confidence, and at times, like now, she wasn't sure if she'd ever totally get it back. But what she'd experienced was minor compared to what some children went through, she supposed. What kind of abuse had this killer suffered that had turned him into such an animal?

Regan looked at her watch. It was only half-past one. The afternoon stretched out in front of her like an endless highway to oblivion. She crossed her arms and paced the room, grinding her teeth until she became aware of what she was doing and relaxed her jaw.

She wanted to call Peter and tell him the FBI was going to question him, but she didn't have his phone number. She looked in the Bay Area directory and discovered there were lots of Peter Smiths and P. Smiths, and P-Something-Smiths. The process of sifting through them in hopes of reaching her Peter was too daunting. Surely he would call soon.

Where was he? she wondered. Would Sloan find him? If he did, what would he, the FBI investigator, learn about Peter Smith that she, the lover, could not? Even though she didn't like the thought of Sloan interrogating Peter, she hoped the FBI might at least get a few answers for her. Like what Peter did for a living, and who those children were.

As the minutes ticked by, Regan became more nervous, scared, and antsy, and a short time later, she decided there was no way she could stay cooped up in this house, held prisoner by her fear. She thought of Jeff's parting shot as she left the office: "We'll see." Was he was going to pull her off the story? Was he going to fire her?

"We'll see, indeed," she said, making a sudden decision.

She changed the recorded message on Kat's voice-mail service, adding, "Peter, please leave a number where I can reach you."

Then she took out her cell phone and with unsteady fingers dialed the officers across the street. "I'm sorry, boys, but I'm not going to stay locked up in this house. I have an appointment I have to keep in Palo Alto."

"But you can't—"

"Oh, yes I can. Now, you have a problem, and I have a problem. Your problem is to keep an eye on me, right?"

"Yeah," the officer said glumly.

Regan grinned in spite of the knot in her stomach. "Well, my problem is that I don't have any wheels. I say we solve each other's problems, and you drive me to my appointment."

After clearing it with headquarters, the two policemen agreed to take her to Palo Alto, the hub of Silicon Valley, about forty-five miles south of San Francisco. Their names were Bill Logan and Mike Forrester, and they were very young to be cops, Regan thought as she climbed into the back seat. She frowned. It bothered her that she was old enough to notice.

On the way to her "appointment," which of course didn't exist, Regan studied her notes, trying to find an angle that would get her in to see Carrington personally. Maybe she could claim she was a long-lost relative, but she immediately dismissed the idea. She imagined a lot of "long-lost relatives" tried to show up on the doorstep of a guy as rich and famous as Kevin Carrington.

Then she thought of Ed Johnson, Carrington's mentor, and her nervous stomach seemed to settle just a bit. She'd spoken with him on the phone, and he'd been helpful. He'd made her feel comfortable. Maybe she should ask to see Ed Johnson first. Maybe she could convince him to help her get an interview with Kevin Carrington.

It was a chicken's way in, she realized, but then, she'd never done anything quite this bold.

55

They drove down the Bayshore Freeway through traffic and smog, both of which seemed to get thicker the farther south they went. A relentless sun somehow managed to penetrate the foul atmosphere, simmering the air into a poisonous stew. The forty-mile drive took them over two hours. As they approached the sprawling, campuslike headquarters of HomeRun, Inc., Regan decided that Silicon Valley had the worst air she'd ever inhaled.

At first, the guard at the gate wouldn't let them pass. "Mr. Johnson says he has no appointment with you today."

Regan's pulse pounded in her ears. She wondered if the cops suspected that the guard spoke the truth—she had no appointment. But she was determined to get in to see Johnson, if not Carrington. "There . . . there must be some mistake. I'm certain he agreed to see me today."

Then to her surprise, Bill, the driver, took out his police ID and flashed it at the guard. "Please tell Mr. Johnson that Ms. McKinney needs to see him right away."

She held her breath, and moments later, they were ushered onto the grounds of HomeRun, Inc. "Was that legal?" she asked the young cop.

He shrugged. "I didn't say we were here on official business. I can't help it if he assumed that. Besides," he added, "I don't want to make this trip again. I hate that freeway."

Regan silently applauded his audacity, and his boldness bolstered her own flagging courage. "Thanks," she murmured.

They pulled into the parking lot, and to her consternation, Bill and Mike both got out of the car and started toward the door with her. "Wait a minute," she said, stopping in midstride. "You two can't go in there with me."

"Why not?" Bill said, an amused grin on his youthful lips. "He's expecting cops, remember? Besides, I've always wanted to see the inside of one of these high-tech places. I wonder if it's full of geeks running around in little white lab coats."

Regan was annoyed, but she refused to be angry. Okay, if she had to take "the boys," as she was beginning to think of them, with her, then so be it. She was here, Ed Johnson was here, and with any luck, Kevin Carrington would be here also. Her luck had held so far. She took a deep breath, relaxed her jaw, straighted her spine, and headed for the front door.

Inside, two athletic-looking, tanned, blond female receptionists were stationed behind large desks, one on either side of the lobby, like Xena-warrior watchdogs guarding the gate to the Inner Sanctum. In addition, an armed security officer built like a gorilla stood with his feet planted slightly apart in front of the double golden oak doors that sealed this entry foyer from the rest of the building. His arms were crossed, and he wasn't smiling.

Regan's heart beat heavily as she approached one of the receptionists to ask for Ed Johnson, but before she could introduce herself, a middle-aged man with thinning hair barreled through the doors, nearly toppling King Kong.

He glared at Regan, then looked uneasily at her two escorts. "What the hell is this all about, Ms. McKinney?"

Regan gulped and floundered for words. Her knees felt as rubbery as her courage, but she refused to cave in. She'd made it this far, and she intended to complete her mission. Forcing a bright smile, she approached Johnson resolutely, hand extended. "Thank you for seeing me on such short notice," she said, taking his hand with a firm grip. "I apologize if my . . . er . . . escorts have caused any trouble."

Ed Johnson scowled at her, then eyed the two young men suspiciously. "Escorts? The gate guard told me they were cops."

"It's a long story. Has to do with a serial killer stalking me."

She hadn't meant to say that, but it served to immediately snag Johnson's interest. "A serial killer? You're kidding?"

"I wish I were."

Johnson seemed befuddled, as if he didn't know quite what to do with this redheaded woman who'd brazenly barged into his territory accompanied by cops and talking about serial killers. Regan would have been amused if she hadn't been so terrified. "I didn't have an appointment with you on my calendar . . ." Johnson said, almost apologetically.

"I must have been mistaken," Regan broke in, "but it's such a long way to come. If I could speak to you for just a few minutes . . ."

Johnson heaved a sigh and looked at his watch. "I have a staff meeting in thirty minutes . . ."

Staff meeting. That meant that Kevin Carrington was probably in the building. "I won't take that much of your time. Please, Mr. Johnson."

He hesitated, vacillating. At last, he said, "Well, I suppose . . . Come with me."

The boys started to follow them through the double doors, but Regan turned and shook her head. "You guys wait in the lobby. I won't be long, and I'm sure I'm perfectly safe with Mr. Johnson."

Behind the doors, the building sprawled out horizontally, sheltering a maze of offices and cubicles in which people went about their jobs just as they would in any other large company. Regan made a mental note to tell Bill that they didn't wear lab coats, and they weren't all geeks. Johnson led her to an office, rather than a cubicle, and ushered her inside his well-appointed workspace. When she was seated, he sat behind his desk and regarded her with undisguised amusement.

"I have to hand it to you, Ms. McKinney, you've got chutzpah. No wonder your magazine assigned you this article. Very few reporters have ever made it past those doors."

Regan willed herself not to blush but knew she did. His words were manna for a hungry ego.

"I'm not a reporter actually," she told him, suddenly at ease with him now that his jets had cooled. "Jeff Roundtree is the editor and publisher of *Pro.Com* magazine, and I'm just his administrative assistant. I honestly don't know why he gave me this assignment."

Johnson's lips twitched upward. "I suspect Mr. Roundtree knows talent when he sees it. Now, why did you come to see me? I've told you everything I can about Mr. Carrington. I'm not at liberty to give you an interview concerning his personal life. I . . . ah . . . believe that's what you told me your story's focus was."

"Yes. That's what I'm supposed to write about. The personal side of Mr. Kevin Carrington."

Johnson leaned forward and pressed a button on an intercom. "Madge, would you please order us two lattes from the restaurant?" He cocked his head at Regan. "That okay with you?"

She shrugged, surprised at his sudden shift into hospitality. She also thought he looked distinctly nervous. "Sure." When he returned his attention to her, she continued. "Look, Mr. Johnson, I appreciate your time, but it wasn't necessary . . ."

"The least I can do is buy you a cup of coffee," Johnson said. "I'd hate to think that you made the long trip here for nothing."

Regan would hate that, too, and she didn't intend to let that happen. "Why do you think Mr. Carrington is so reclusive?" she asked quickly. "I promise, your name won't appear in the article. I'll even let you read it before I turn it in to Jeff."

Ed Johnson shook his head in resignation. "I'll have to write Roundtree a letter of recommendation for your tenacity, Ms. McKinney. If I tell you just a little, will you go away?" He laughed when he said it, but she could tell he wasn't joking. He didn't want to talk about Kevin Carrington.

"You can throw me out right now," she said with what

she hoped was a disarming smile. "But I'd rather have a little than nothing at all."

Johnson drew in a breath of resignation. "Kevin is reclusive because that's his nature. It's that simple. He's a quiet, shy, retiring kind of guy who lives in a world he creates on the computer. I suspect he was neglected as a kid, and having such an introverted personality, he withdrew into a world where he could invent his own playmates. Armchair psychology, to be sure, and just my own speculation."

"You like Kevin, don't you?"

Johnson thought for a minute. "Yes, I like Kevin. I'd even go so far as to say I'm fond of him, but at times, I'd like to strangle him."

An image of a woman being strangled in the frightening Internet cartoon flashed in Regan's mind, but vanished as quickly as it came. "Why is that?" she asked, disconcerted.

"Please don't print this, but the truth about Kevin is that he's totally unreliable." She heard the exasperation in Johnson's voice. He went on. "He's a typical genius, I suppose. Certainly the most creative person I've ever known. But try to pin him down for a meeting, or a deadline, or anything, and it's like trying to catch the wind."

"How does he manage to be so successful?"

Johnson scratched the side of his nose. "I don't want this to sound arrogant or egotistical, but frankly, I've made him successful. I don't want credit for it, so don't put it in your article. God knows, I've made my share of his fortune along the way and that's reward enough. Except . . ."

Regan waited. For a man who didn't want to grant an interview, Johnson was talking his head off. Why? It was almost as if talking to her were a catharsis for his frustrations. She might not be able to use it all, but he was giving her a lot of good background. "Except what?" she prodded.

"Except that I'd like to see the kid pull himself together, to live a more normal life. You know, like have a girlfriend, maybe get married someday, have kids. He's such a loner. I guess . . . I feel sorry for him," Johnson added wistfully. "You know, I hadn't thought about all this until you brought it up, but in a way, I feel a little like a father to Kevin, and yet to him, it's like I don't exist. I hardly ever see him, and when we're together, his mind is a million miles away."

Regan heard the hurt behind the words. "You don't see him? I thought he worked here."

He gave a short, almost bitter laugh. "Oh, he works here, when he chooses to come in. With what he does, he's not locked into coming to an office. He has the world's most sophisticated computer lab in his home over in Los Altos Hills."

Regan scribbled down the name of the town where Kevin Carrington lived, then asked, gesturing toward the hallway and the cubicles beyond, "But what about this? HomeRun, Inc. He has a business to run."

Johnson smiled patiently. "Besides being a computer wizard, Kevin is smart in other regards. He doesn't want anything to do with running the business, so he's surrounded himself with people to do it for him."

"Like you?"

Johnson nodded. "We take care of the real world for him, so he doesn't have to live in it."

There was a knock on the door, and a server dressed in white shirt, black slacks, and bow tie entered carrying a tray upon which two large white cups rested. Steam rose from the cups, bringing with it the tantalizing aroma of coffee. Regan's mouth watered in spite of herself.

"You can put it on the desk," Johnson told the man, indicating a clear space. "Thanks."

"You're welcome," the server said, glancing at Regan in open curiosity and giving her a quick smile before leaving.

"That's an example of Kevin's ability to surround himself with competent people," Johnson said when the server had gone. Taking one of the cups from the tray, he handed it to Regan. "HomeRun, Inc., has a top-notch restaurant, La Palma, probably better than any other one in Silicon Valley, maybe even the whole Bay Area, because Kevin hired a world-class chef to run it. It's one of the bennies that attracts top talent to HomeRun and keeps them here."

"Kevin, the recluse, hired a world-class chef?" Regan scribbled away, surprised that a person like Kevin would know or care about such bennies.

"Actually, it was Richard Beatty's idea."

"Who's Richard Beatty?"

"Kevin's right-hand man. A very efficient fellow."

Did she detect a note of jealousy here? "Jeff told me Kevin had an assistant who kept the press away. Would that be Beatty?"

"It would be. Richard is very possessive of Kevin's time and guards him like a bulldog."

"Pit bull is what Jeff called him," Regan said before she could stop herself. But Johnson just laughed.

"It's common knowledge. Nobody likes Richard, but everyone respects him. He's good at his job, and he's loyal as hell to Kevin."

Regan dared to ask a question that had been burning in her mind ever since Johnson had mentioned it in their first interview by telephone. "You told me Kevin is the son of Michael Carrington. I've researched Michael, but I can't seem to get anything current on him. Is he alive?"

"We're treading on thin ice here, Ms. McKinney."

"Please call me Regan. And I promise, I won't give it away that I learned about his father from you."

"Carrington is very much alive, although he's become as reclusive as Kevin. Maybe more so, because he's not forced into the limelight like Kevin is. Michael lives in an exclusive development south of Carmel."

"I read about Kevin's mother's death. Has Michael ever remarried?"

Johnson snorted. "Several times. But he's not married at the moment, I don't think, although he keeps a mistress nearby, a woman named Jones. She calls here from time to time for Kevin, but he won't talk to her. He won't talk to his father, for that matter."

"Does he hate his father?"

Johnson shook his head. "Who knows? I don't think Kevin has deep emotions like love or hate. It's kind of spooky sometimes. He's so detached he sometimes doesn't seem human, and yet I've seen him throw the damnedest temper tantrums." He looked embarrassed at having revealed this. "I'm sorry, Ms. McKinney, uh, Regan, that is, but you seem to have a way of getting me to say things I shouldn't." He looked at his watch, and added, "I'm also sorry that I'm going to have to ask you to drink up, because it's almost time for the meeting to start."

Regan was disappointed that she obviously wasn't going to meet Kevin Carrington this afternoon, but she wasn't going to push Ed Johnson any further. The man had been more than cooperative. He'd been gracious even. "Thanks, Mr. Johnson. I really appreciate your time. Please know you can trust me to keep your identity confidential." She drank about half the latte, but couldn't finish it in a hurry. "Delicious," she said, wiping a dash of froth from her lips. "Thanks."

She handed him a business card. "This is my office number at *Pro.Com,* just in case you want to get hold of me." As an afterthought, she scribbled her cell phone number on the card, as well, handed it to Johnson and shook his hand. "Thanks for seeing me."

Johnson escorted her to the lobby, where Bill and Mike both looked immensely relieved to see her. Ed Johnson said goodbye, turned to leave, then stopped and looked back. "I meant it about recommending you to Jeff Roundtree," he said with a grin. "That bit about being stalked by a serial killer was a brilliant way to get my interest. What's the real reason for the police?"

Regan's euphoria over the interview fled, and her stomach tightened once again. "I wish I were that brilliant, Mr. Johnson, but the bit about the serial killer was for real. You may have read about the guy up in San Francisco who's murdered a number of women. It's a long story, but the bottom line is that it seems he's taken a bead on me. That's why the cops."

Ed Johnson looked shocked, then genuinely stricken. "Good Lord. How do you know he's after you? Did he send you a threatening note or something?"

"He sent me an e-mail that linked to a site on the Internet, and . . . there, in cartoon, he murdered me."

She saw his face turn ashen and beads of perspiration break out on his high forehead that was getting higher by the day as his hairline receded. "Please," he mumbled, "take care of yourself."

His concern touched her, and she tried to pretend she wasn't afraid. "I'll be fine. How could I be in any danger with two of San Francisco's finest by my side?"

When they stepped outside, the sun had finally broken through, and Regan's spirits picked up. She hadn't exactly accomplished her mission, but she'd come close, and Johnson had given her some valuable insight. She might never get an interview with Kevin Carrington, but another possiblity had suddenly occurred to her.

One way or another, she *would* get Jeff his story.

They climbed into the unmarked car and were just outside the gates of the compound and headed back to San Francisco when a large dark-colored SUV came at them at high speed. Bill swore and swerved to the right to give the oncoming car road room.

Regan turned and looked out the back window. The vehicle barely paused at the gate, then sped down the drive and disappeared behind the large hedges that shielded the compound from public view. Recalling the close scrutiny of the guard when they'd arrived, Regan figured whoever was in the SUV must be somebody important, for the guard had signaled him right through. Maybe it was Richard Beatty, the trained pit bull, she thought with a laugh, late for the meeting. She turned to the boys.

"Hey, guys, anybody up for a trip to Carmel?"

56

Ed Johnson returned to his office, oddly shaken by the young woman's statement that she was being stalked by a serial killer. She seemed so calm about it, going about her business as if it were no big deal. He actually admired her for it, but as he took his seat again, he wondered what her real agenda was. She wasn't a reporter, although she had the natural ability to dig information from people, like him. He grinned and finished the remains of his latte.

Maybe she was a gold digger trying to get to Kevin, a woman after his millions. If so, he decided, she was both creative and resourceful. Kevin could stand to meet a woman like her.

For some reason, Ed Johnson liked Regan McKinney, in spite of her aggressiveness. There was something about her that seemed familiar, but he couldn't put his finger on it. She was attractive, although not beautiful. Her open expression and green eyes radiated girl-next-door innocence. If she was using this ploy of writing a story on Kevin to wangle her way into meeting him for other reasons, it didn't show.

Maybe that's why he'd talked so freely to her. He'd told her things today, and in their earlier phone interview, that could cost him his job. And yet he trusted her pledge that he would remain anonymous as her source. Maybe he was still hoping that someone would be able to help Kevin mend whatever fences stood between him and his father, and maybe he thought Regan McKinney might be the one for the job.

Or maybe he had a secret death wish. Maybe he was tired of playing to Kevin's every whim and eccentricity. Maybe deep down he wanted Kevin to give him the ax. Because if Kevin didn't set him free somehow, even some painful way like he was imagining, Ed knew he'd spend the rest of his life serving the strange man he'd come to know and love as a boy. He felt trapped.

Lost in reverie, he jumped when his secretary's voice came through the intercom. "Don't forget the meeting, Mr. Johnson. It's time."

57

By night, Cameron Pace taught dance at his father's studio. By day, he managed Electronica, Inc., a large retail outlet on West Portal Avenue that sold computers, software, electronic games and gadgets. Sam Sloan had no trouble recognizing the younger Pace, for just as Regan had told him, the son was a carbon copy of the father.

"Sam Sloan, FBI," he said, presenting his ID to Pace. A streetcar thundered by, lumbering along toward the Twin Peaks Tunnel, momentarily making conversation difficult. When it had passed, he added, "I need to ask you a few questions."

Sloan always watched carefully for a person's knee-jerk reactions to being confronted by an FBI agent, because sometimes that split second was enough to determine a person's guilt, or at least his involvement in a crime. But if Cameron Pace had anything to hide, it didn't show. His face registered no surprise, no alarm, no guilt.

"Fine. Would you like to go into my office?" His voice was cordial, and he gestured them politely ahead of him. This guy was slick, Sloan thought. He could imagine how he must charm the women on the dance floor.

Cameron's office was no larger than his father's, but decidedly more cluttered. Kelly followed Sloan into the room.

A window looked out at fog, a frequent visitor, Sloan was quickly learning, to this part of the world.

"Now, how can I help you?" Cameron asked.

"You can start by telling us where you were yesterday and last night."

Pace didn't bat an eye. "As I'm sure you know, the studio is closed on Sundays, and so is this store. It's my only day off, and I spent it at home, reading a book. Why do you ask?"

"Another woman was murdered last night," Kelly answered, "and this morning, one of your students, Regan McKinney, received a very threatening message that we have every reason to believe was sent by the killer."

Sloan watched Pace's composure slip. "Regan? My God. That's terrible."

"Yes, it is," Sloan said.

"But why are you questioning me?" Pace asked, his face suddenly turning pale.

"Because, Mr. Pace," Sloan replied, "in the message, this killer called himself 'the dancemaster.' We thought he picked out his victims at dance clubs, but a 'dancemaster' sounds more like an instructor of dance."

Pace grimaced. "I see."

Sloan observed the changes in the man's facial expression and body posture as he went on. "In his message, the murderer portrayed Ms. McKinney wearing a certain purple dress, the same dress she had on when she went to La Habanera with you and her sister. He said, 'The dancemaster is watching. He doesn't like your moves.' So the killer is someone who saw her at the club, someone who apparently didn't like the way she was dancing, or perhaps with whom she was dancing. Or," he paused for effect, "perhaps it was someone who danced with her."

Pace dropped into a chair, his eyes wide. "You . . . you think I'm the killer?"

Sloan leaned against the desk. "You got an alibi?"

"I told you I was at home all day."

"Where do you live."

"In Noe Valley. On Liberty."

Kelly made note of the address, and Sloan went on.

"What about last night?"

Pace hedged slightly, then repeated emphatically, "I was at home."

"Can you prove it?" Sloan knew intuitively he was lying. "Did you make any phone calls that would be charged to your bill that could prove at least that someone was at your house?"

Pace shook his head, looking distinctly uncomfortable. "No," he answered, then looked pleadingly at Sloan. "I can't prove I was at home, but I was. All day. All night. I came into work about seven-thirty this morning."

"That doesn't help you much. If no one can testify to your whereabouts, you have no alibi."

"But I'm not guilty!" Desperation laced the dance instructor's voice.

"There's another way to prove your innocence, Mr. Pace," Sloan said. "Would you be willing to provide a sample of blood for DNA testing? I can't force you to take it, but it would go a long way in engendering my trust that you're not our man."

Sloan saw Pace swallow hard. If Pace consented, he likely could be discounted as a suspect, although some killers were egotistical enough to think they could somehow fool Mother Nature. Sloan waited. Another streetcar rumbled by outside, clanging its bell.

"I'll take whatever test you want," Pace said at last, sounding defeated. He gave Sloan a strange look. "I may be a lot of things, Mr. Sloan, but I'm not a killer."

Sloan wondered what he meant by "I may be a lot of things." Was Pace involved in some other shady activity? Was he embezzling money from the store? From his father? Was he a gigolo? All of the above were possible, but they were none of Sloan's concern. His job was to stop a killer.

"We need you to come downtown with us," Sloan told him firmly.

"Now?"

Sloan nodded.

Pace let out a sigh. "Well, my shift's almost over anyway. Let me get someone to cover me for the last few minutes."

He left the office, and Sloan nodded for Kelly to follow him. It was possible Pace would bolt.

While he waited for them to return, Sloan took the opportunity to look around Pace's office. There were the usual accoutrements—desk, computer, file cabinet, phone, fax machine—and one not so usual. Standing in the corner was an exercise machine like those he'd seen advertised on television, the kind that was designed to build huge biceps and chest muscles.

Huge biceps.

The better to strangle you with, my dear?

Sloan eased the top desk drawer open and rummaged through the clutter inside, but found nothing of particular interest. The second drawer proved more intriguing, however. It was a large file drawer, and as his fingers walked over the few files it held, they came to one that contained pornographic photos—of men with men.

Sloan closed his eyes and quietly shut the drawer.

I may be a lot of things . . .

58

The man sat through the interminable meeting, watching the others with eyes that felt as if they were on fire. His head began to pound with one of those infernal headaches, and nausea twisted his stomach. He ought to get up and leave. He didn't need to be here. He already knew everything that was being presented to the staff. But he didn't want to draw attention to himself. Too much was at stake right now. Too many important decisions to make, actions to take.

He must lie low and wait until his plan began to unfold.

He drew in a deep, calming breath, willing the pain to leave his head, and oddly, moments later, it did. The man frowned and looked around, suddenly aware that all eyes were on him. He was being asked questions. But who were these people? Where was he? Why was he here? His heart began to hammer a thousand beats a minute.

Control. Stay in control.

Help! Somebody help me!

He stood up, and to his amazement, he found the words to respond to the question that had been directed at him. He, in fact, heard himself delivering a cogent speech to those gathered in the room. The man knew the words were coming from his mouth, and yet he had no idea who was speaking. It wasn't him.

And then he knew who'd dared to step onstage and usurp

his power. Take away his authority. Send him to the back.

Rage boiled in his chest. He was sick of this, always living in the shadows of someone else, never knowing when he was in control. He hated his life. He hated the wimp who controlled his life. He hated his life so intensely, in fact, that he was willing to die to set himself free, if that was the only way out.

But if he died, he wouldn't be the only one to go.

59

As much as he'd loved his job as dance instructor, Peter Smith was glad he didn't have to report to the Sterling Pace studios tonight. He had his hands full. The children had been very naughty today, and he was exhausted. One of them especially concerned him. The boy had been hiding a lot lately, and today, Peter hadn't been able to find him anywhere. He was the dark one of the bunch, the most wounded, the angriest. The one Peter worried about most.

Normally Peter was able to hold the wacky, willful brood together. He knew just how to soothe the ones who were troubled, make others laugh, and he guided them as best he could along their precarious paths. It wasn't an easy job, and God knew, it was a thankless one. But he had no choice in the matter. He'd been handed the responsibility years ago, and he'd agreed to honor it forever.

Only recently had he begun to question that decision. Only since he'd met Regan McKinney. Even then, he hadn't meant for things to go so far, or so fast, between them. In fact, he'd never meant to get involved with her, or anyone else for that matter. But there'd been something about her, her smile, her eyes, even her body movements, that drew him to her the moment he first saw her. She seemed familiar somehow, and when he'd first danced with her, his longing had overcome his senses.

Since they'd become lovers, that longing had grown steadily stronger. Anxiety knotted his stomach. Was it fair to her to continue on, or should he stop seeing her before it went any further?

Even as he thought it, he knew he couldn't stop seeing Regan McKinney. Peter had never been in love, indeed didn't really know what love was, but his feelings for Regan came as close to his perception of love as any he'd ever known. He was tired, he'd had a huge, difficult day, and his reward would be to hear her voice on the phone. He picked up the receiver and dialed the number he'd memorized.

60

Regan returned home, tired but encouraged. All the way back from Palo Alto, her mind had been busily exploring ways she might get in to see Michael Carrington. She'd also been anxious to learn if Peter had called and left his number. She bade goodbye to "the boys," left them to their surveillance vehicle, and bounded up the steps.

"I'm home," she called, hearing noises coming from the kitchen. She was looking forward to sharing her adventure with Kat. But when she rounded the corner and went into the kitchen, the look on Kat's face stopped her cold. "What's wrong?"

Her sister had been rolling out homemade pasta, and her face was grim beneath a dusting of flour. Fear laced her voice. "Blair hasn't come home yet."

Regan glanced at the clock on the wall, and her heart dropped to the pit of her stomach. "I thought a police officer was supposed to be assigned to her."

The fear in Kat's voice turned to anger. "I thought so, too, damn it. But school's been out four hours, and she hasn't shown up yet."

"Have you called the police?" *Oh, sweet heavens, don't let anything have happened to Blair.*

"Of course I've called the police. All they knew was that she'd been assigned an officer for personal protection, and that he'd last reported in when he arrived at her school. I've called the school, her ballet studio, her friends. She's . . ." Kat's eyes welled. "She's none of those places. Oh, Regan, what if . . ."

"I knew I should have moved out," Regan said, her legs giving out from under her. She plopped into a chair and hung her head in her hands. "It's all my fault."

"Fault isn't the issue here," Kat snapped. "If anyone's at fault for Blair being missing, it's the cops. They . . . they promised to protect her."

"Where's your bodyguard?" Regan asked.

Kat nodded toward the back door. "Went outside for a smoke. And speaking of bodyguards, where are the two who're supposed to be keeping watch over you? And where, by the way, have you been?" Kat's voice pitched higher with each sentence. "I've been worried sick about both of you."

Regan was sorry she hadn't left Kat a note. "I had the boys drive me down to Palo Alto. Sloan's guys needed to work at my computer to try to trace the sender of that horrible message, and I more or less got sent home from work. As I left the office, I got the impression that Jeff wasn't too happy about the FBI showing up and commandeering his offices. I was afraid he was going to fire me when I came in tomorrow, so I figured if I could get that Carrington interview, maybe it'd save my job."

"Did you get it? Did you talk to Carrington?"

Regan shook her head. "Not exactly. But I did get some good stuff from the man who's been his mentor and financial guide from the beginning."

With Blair missing and a killer on the loose, the afternoon's interview seemed suddenly unimportant, and Regan realized she'd gone to Palo Alto as much to run away from her fears and troubles as she had to get the interview. She shouldn't have gone. Maybe if she'd stayed home, Blair wouldn't be missing. That was totally illogical, she knew, but she blamed herself for the danger that surrounded them all.

The phone rang. The sisters exchanged glances, and Regan reached for the receiver, thinking it might be Peter.

"Hello?"

The voice on the line was female, young, and excited. "Hi, Regan. It's me. Can you ask Mom if I can stay at the mall and eat at the food court?"

Relief washed through Regan at the sound of her niece's voice. "You'd better talk to your mom," she said and handed Kat the receiver.

"The mall?" Kat nearly screeched. "Where the hell have you been, young lady? I've been scared to death. And where's your police protection?" She pressed the speaker phone button so Regan could hear.

Blair sounded puzzled. "He's right here. Why are you freaking? I left a message on the voice mail. I didn't have any homework and nothing to do after school, and Todd agreed to take me to see that new Chinese film at the Metreon theaters."

"Todd? Who's Todd?"

"The policeman." Blair clearly thought her mother was being dense.

"I'm going to kill him," Kat breathed. "That policeman was supposed to bring you home, not take you to the movies. How old is he, anyway?"

"Mom, calm down. You're acting like he's done something wrong."

"He has. Let me talk to him this minute."

A low, masculine voice came on the line. "Officer Todd Chambers."

"What the hell do you think you're doing taking my daughter to the movies?"

"It's where she wanted to go, ma'am. I wasn't instructed to bring her straight home. My orders were to keep her in sight at all times. She was determined to see this movie, and since we couldn't get hold of you to get permission, I had no choice but to go along with her. I'm sorry if it's caused you any inconvenience. I made her call you, both at work and at home, but you weren't available."

Regan could almost hear Kat seething.

"Well, it has, and I want you to bring her home right now."

"Yes, ma'am. We'll be there directly."

Kat slammed down the phone and collapsed into a nearby

chair. "Christ, I'm a terrible mother," Kat sobbed. "First, I wasn't available to get her messages, and second, when I came in, I didn't even think to check the voice mail. Blair usually takes care of that."

Regan touched Kat's hand gently. "You're not a bad mother. You're a great mother. This isn't your fault, none of it. I'm the one who's brought all this on you."

Kat looked up at Regan, tears in her eyes but anger on her face. "You brought nothing on us. It's not your fault some crazy sicko zeroed in on you at the dance club."

Regan let the subject drop and was about to go to the phone to retrieve the voice-mail messages when the doorbell rang. "I'll get it," she said. Peering out of the lace curtains that fell across the cut-glass oval in the door, she saw Agent Sloan on the porch. Next to him was Cameron Pace. Astonished, she unlocked the door with fumbling fingers.

"Come in."

The investigator wore a dark, all-weather coat over the same suit and tie he'd had on earlier in the day when he'd come to the offices of *Pro.Com* magazine. He looked slightly rumpled, and his face showed the strain of his job. He stepped into the hallway. Cameron Pace, looking distinctly distraught, followed him.

"Is your sister here?" Sloan asked.

Regan nodded and called out, "Kat. It's for you."

Kat came through the door from the kitchen and stopped short when she saw the two men.

"This is Sam Sloan," Regan said, wondering wildly what he was doing here with Cameron. "FBI."

Kat sniffed and cleared her throat, then took a step toward the men. "Cameron?" she asked, frowning. "What's this all about?"

"I . . . need to speak with you. In private, if we could."

Kat shot Regan a troubled glance, then gestured Cameron toward the parlor. Sloan took Regan's elbow.

"Maybe you could find a cup of coffee for me in the kitchen."

61

Kat's bodyguard, Kyle Aronson, had returned to the kitchen, and Regan made coffee for both men, her curiosity raging. When the water began to pass through the filter, she couldn't stand it any longer and turned to Sloan.

"Okay, so what's going on?"

"I'm sure your sister will tell you."

"Tell me? Tell me what? That Cameron Pace is the murderer? You've left her alone with a killer?" Now she was the one who was freaking.

"He's not the killer." Sloan's voice was low but self-assured.

Regan eyed him skeptically. "How can you say that? He fits the profile, doesn't he? A single, white male in his twenties or thirties, a man who likes to dance. In fact, he's a 'dancemaster,' wouldn't you say?" Regan thought back to the misgivings that had led her to catch up with Kat and Cameron at La Habanera the previous Wednesday and didn't share Sloan's optimism about Cameron's innocence.

"You're right about all of the above," Sloan conceded. "But two things have me convinced he's not our man. First, he volunteered for DNA testing. He gave blood today to be sent to a lab for DNA analysis. We've found foreign hair and skin cells on the victims that we can use to compare it with. If his matches, he's our man. If not, it's definitive that he's innocent. But I don't think he's the killer."

"Why not?"

"Because he didn't blink when we suggested he volunteer to be tested. If he were guilty, he'd have objected."

Maybe that was enough for Sloan, but Regan needed more. "You said there were two things . . ."

"Yes. He has an alibi, at least for last night's murder."

Regan began to breathe a little easier. She didn't really want to suspect Cameron Pace—after all, Kat was crazy about him.

"What's his alibi?"

"At first he told us he'd been home alone all day yesterday and all night last night. But it turns out that's not exactly the truth."

"Why would he lie and make up such a crummy alibi?"

Sloan stared into his coffee. At last he looked up at Regan. "Even though he's not a murderer, Cameron has been hiding something for his whole life. Ironically, if he continued to keep it a secret, he might have been arrested for murder. When he realized the gravity of his situation, he told us where he really was yesterday. A lot of folks have confirmed his alibi."

Sloan wasn't making any sense. "Where was he?" Regan asked, getting impatient. Why was Sloan hedging like this?

"At a place called the Cockpit in the Castro district, his favorite gay bar. He was there all evening with his steady boyfriend."

Regan's jaw dropped. "Cameron Pace is gay? That can't be. I mean, he flirts with all the women at the studio, he invited Kat out for a date, I mean—"

She was interrupted when Cameron came to the kitchen door. "I'm ready to go," he said to Sloan. He wouldn't meet Regan's eyes.

Sloan downed the last of his coffee, stood, and looked at Regan. "Take care of your sister tonight. She's going to need it. By the way," he added, "have you heard from Peter Smith?"

Since she hadn't yet checked the voice mail, her reply was truthful. "No. I'll let you know."

"Thanks. Take care."

Numbly, Regan ushered them to the front door, and when they left, she went into the living room where Kat sat staring into nothingness. Her face was ashen, her breathing shallow. Regan sat down beside her and took her hands, not knowing exactly what to say. "Kat, I'm so sorry."

Kat didn't reply.

"Sloan told me about . . . Cameron's alibi," she tried again.

Again nothing.

So Regan shut up. Sometimes if you didn't know what to say, the best thing was to say nothing at all. She just sat quietly stroking the back of Kat's hands.

Outside, raindrops began to patter against the window-panes again. The clock in the hall struck seven forty-five. Regan heard Kyle Aronson in the kitchen. It sounded as if he were washing up the coffee cups.

Regan wanted desperately to comfort her sister. "Look, it's not the worst thing in the world if a guy's gay. Cameron is a nice person. He . . . he just wasn't real honest with you . . . with us."

"He's not just gay," Kat said hoarsely. Regan had never heard her sound so desolate.

"What do you mean?"

"He gave blood for a test to prove by DNA he's not the killer."

"That's what Sloan told me."

"With his permission, they did another test on his blood while they were at it, and it showed that Cameron . . . is HIV positive."

62

Sloan dropped Cameron Pace off at his apartment. "Don't leave town," he said. "We may need to talk some more."

As he got out of the car, Pace indicated that he'd heard Sloan, but as he walked up the steep steps to his apartment building, he looked defeated. Sloan regretted what had happened, but maybe it would in the end save Pace's life. He couldn't believe the man hadn't been tested for AIDS, considering his lifestyle.

Sloan felt sorry for Cameron Pace, and not just because of the results of the blood test. In this day and time when most homosexuals had long since dropped the cloak of secrecy surrounding their sexual preferences, Cameron had chosen to remain in the closet, hiding the truth about this aspect of his life. He'd told Sloan the real reason for his secrecy was his father, and the dance studio. "I know when my father finds out about me, he'll disown me." Pace's voice had broken at that point. "I'll lose the only family I have, and I'll lose my inheritance, as well."

Depressed and discouraged, Sloan headed back to police headquarters. Would Papa Pace really disown Sonny Pace? That, he supposed, was not the real issue. The real problem for Sterling was Cameron's blood test. Even if Sterling didn't turn his back on Cameron, would the customers of the Sterling Pace School of Dance quit coming if they found out an instructor was HIV positive? It was illogical, because dancing didn't spread the virus, but people were pretty ignorant of the truth. Many still believed the AIDS virus could be spread in the air and by touching.

The complex and emotionally charged problems about to hit Sterling Pace didn't really concern Sloan, but they saddened him. In fact, the world in which he moved—the shadow side of life—saddened him. He felt despair coil in his belly as he maneuvered the hilly streets of San Francisco and wondered if he would ever be free of the constant melancholy that accompanied him day and night.

Not in this job.

The answer depressed him even more. He had to get out of this line of work, but before he could think about that, he had to finish what he came here for. He thought about Kat Bowen and Regan McKinney. How could he protect them from this psychopath? The man was a genius and slippery as an eel. Sloan's people had told him that the Carnivore system had been able to trace the e-mail message to a server in the Bay Area, but they couldn't get past that to find the point of origin. Everyone, it seemed, was frustrated by this killer.

At headquarters, Sloan caught up with a haggard-looking Kelly. "Anything on Peter Smith?"

The pair had decided to split up after they brought Cameron Pace in for testing. Kelly and two of his people went to check out Peter Smith at the address they'd taken from Sterling Pace.

"It doesn't exist," Kelly told him.

"What?"

"There's no such address, and even if there were, there are no houses in that part of town. It's in a seedy warehouse section of the city, on Potrero Hill."

"Swell."

Peter Smith had given Pace a phony address. Why? Sloan's gut tightened as the pieces began to fall into place. This person calling himself Peter Smith had dated Regan. If he'd been watching her house, he could easily have followed her to La Habanera, seen her in that dress. On the two dates she'd told him about, Smith had obviously charmed Regan, who didn't believe he was the killer, which made her even more vulnerable.

When, he wondered with a shudder of cold premonition, would Peter Smith try to kill her?

Sloan had to stop him. But first he had to find him.

Fatigue suddenly washed away every ounce of his energy, and Sloan realized he hadn't eaten in hours. The coffee he'd consumed at Kat Bowen's house grumbled in his stomach. "Want to grab a bite?" he asked Kelly.

The younger man looked utterly grateful. "I could use it."

Over thick steaks, steaming mashed potatoes, and other comfort food, Sloan and Kelly took the case apart, bit by bit, turning everything over and looking at it from different directions, but everything pointed to the same conclusion: the most likely suspect at this moment was the man who called himself Peter Smith.

He took out his cell phone and dialed Kat Bowen's number. "May I speak to Regan?" he asked when a girl answered the phone.

"Hello?" Regan said a few moments later.

"Regan, it's Sloan. Have you heard from Peter?"

He heard the hesitation in her voice. Would she lie to him?

"He called just before Kat got home," she told him. "He left a short message on her voice mail, said he'd call again, but I don't know when."

"Didn't he leave a number?"

"No." Her reply was swift, brittle, edgy.

"Don't you find it a little odd," he pushed, "that he's supposedly crazy about you, yet he's given you no way to get in touch with him?"

"Maybe he's just old-fashioned," she snapped. "I told you I'd let you know when I heard from him, but I didn't consider that short message exactly important."

"Any communication from him is important," Sloan said. "You think he'll call again?"

"He said he would," she replied impatiently.

"Let me speak to your sister."

When Kat picked up the phone, Sloan explained to her that he wanted to tap her line. "Every lead, and all my instincts, are pointing to Peter Smith," he said gravely. "We have to find him, and fast. Please help us."

63

Tuesday morning, Regan was escorted to work by a different officer, this one in a marked police vehicle. Bill and Mike, or their replacements, remained on duty in front of Kat's house. Inside, a team of technoexperts had set up a device to intercept and trace all incoming calls. When Kat had told her what Sloan wanted, Regan had initially been furious, knowing it was Peter's incoming call he was after. But when she thought about it, it didn't matter what gyrations he went through to get to Peter, in the end Sloan would find out it was all for nothing, because Peter wasn't the killer. Regan hoped Peter would call soon. When Sloan was able to talk to him, he'd get the answers he was after, and that would be the end of it.

When she got to work, Jeff Roundtree was distinctly unhappy with the presence of her uniformed escort in his office. "My God, Regan," he growled behind closed doors where the cop couldn't hear, "we had the FBI in here all day yesterday, and now the cops? What if the other media get wind about what's happening around here? It could queer everything I've worked so hard for."

Regan understood. She was a liability to Jeff just as she was a danger to Kat.

"It's okay if you fire me," she said, her voice unsteady. "I'll understand."

Jeff sat down heavily and swiveled his chair to look out at the gray San Francisco morning. "I'm not going to fire you," he said at last. "I'm sorry I sound like such a selfish bastard when you're the one whose life is in jeopardy."

Regan took a seat in another chair. "I like this job, Jeff, and I like you. But if you have to give me a leave of absence—"

He turned sharply again in his chair. "I'm not asking you to take a leave of absence." He ran his hands through his thin, straight hair. "Damn it, Regan, I care about you."

His comment took her by surprise. What did that mean? They stared at each other across his desk. She didn't reply, because she didn't know what to say.

Finally, he spoke again. "You're the best . . . employee I've had come down the pike since I started this business," he said, sounding embarrassed that he'd let his emotions show, "and I don't want to lose you. Especially to some kind of nutcase like this guy. It's okay," he said quietly, "about the cop. Just ask him to keep a low profile, okay?"

Regan nodded, but deliberately turned the conversation in another, less personal, direction.

"I went to Palo Alto yesterday."

Jeff's head jerked up. "You did what?"

She smiled, gratified that she'd surprised him. "I had my escorts take me to HomeRun, Inc."

Jeff stood up, a grin replacing his early consternation. "Did you get to see Carrington?"

"No."

He sat back down, but leaned forward on his elbows. "So, what happened?"

She told him about her interview with Ed Johnson, and what she'd learned about Kevin Carrington's life and personality. "I don't have enough yet to build a complete story, and I don't hold out a lot of hope that I'll ever get an interview with Kevin Carrington, but I'm thinking about trying to see his father, Michael."

The grin did a slow waltz across Roundtree's face. "Regan McKinney, you are a piece of work."

She shifted in her chair, and heat blazed on her cheeks. "What exactly does that mean?"

"It means you've got more guts than I do. Here you are the target of a madman, and yet you're going about your business like nothing was wrong."

She decided that was a compliment and was pleased. However, he was mistaken if he thought she was being courageous. She was only trying to cope with the surreal by clinging to the mundane.

"I didn't say I'd figured out how to get in to see Michael Carrington, but I wanted you to know my plans."

Jeff Roundtree's expression sobered. "Look, Regan, your job is secure. I want that story, but it can wait until this . . . other . . . is cleared up. Please don't take any chances."

She decided to accept his warning as sincere and not a come-on. "I won't," she assured him, standing. She headed for the door. "And I'll try to keep the cops out of sight."

64

Sloan and Kelly walked briskly through the lobby of the resplendent Fairmont Hotel. Kelly looked around, gawking openly at the luxurious surroundings, making noises about wanting to be rich enough someday to bring his wife here, but Sloan didn't care whether it was a palace or a flophouse. He wanted information about the man who'd rented the penthouse last Saturday night.

The slim Asian manager was cordial but wary when Sloan told him he needed information about a guest. "I'm sorry, sir, but our policy forbids us to give out anything about our guests," the manager told them. "It's a privacy thing, I'm sure you understand."

With a sigh, Sloan presented his ID. He must be tired. He should have done that in the first place. When he was younger, he'd never have made such a mistake.

"On the other hand," the manager responded with a gratuitous smile, "we wish to cooperate fully with the law. What is it you want to know?"

"You had a guest in the hotel this past Saturday. A Peter Smith. Could I please see his registration information?"

The manager went to the computer behind the gleaming marble registration counter and tapped in his request. He looked up at Sloan.

"I'm sorry, but there was no Peter Smith registered in the

hotel last Saturday. Are you talking about the thirtieth? Or did you mean the week before?"

"The thirtieth." Why wasn't he surprised? "Who had the penthouse suite?"

"Which one? We have several."

Sloan cursed beneath his breath and took out his cell phone. He dialed the number for *Pro.Com* magazine. Regan answered on the second ring.

"Agent Sloan here," he said. "I hate to bother you at work, but we're trying to get a line on Peter Smith."

"I'm well aware of that," she replied dryly. "Nobody told me, or my boss, that you were going to tap this phone, too. Jeff's furious, and I'll probably lose my job."

He heard the anger in her voice, and even though he understood why, her inability to understand the danger she was in pissed him off. She must really be in love with this psycho.

"Listen, Regan," he said with considerable effort to control his temper. "You may think Smith is the greatest person in the world, but the fact is, he's a liar. We checked out the address he gave on his employment application at Sterling Pace's, and the place doesn't exist. Now the manager at the Fairmont tells us no one by that name was registered here last Saturday night."

There was silence on the line. Then Regan said in a faltering voice, "There's some mistake. I can guarantee you, Peter and I stayed in a penthouse there on Saturday night."

"Can you remember the room number?"

She gave it to him. He thanked her and hung up. But he'd heard the pain in her voice and knew she must be both embarrassed and unhinged at the moment. He hated that he'd had to drop Peter Smith's deception on her like that, rather than telling her in person. Just another nasty aspect of his job. Hurting people.

He turned to the manager and gave him the number. "If Peter Smith wasn't registered in the hotel, who occupied that room this past Saturday night?"

The man found the computer record quickly. Sloan could tell he was nervous. "It was registered in the name of Mr. Adrian Pierce."

Kelly made note of the alias. "What address did he use?"

Sloan wasn't surprised that it was the same nonexistent address Peter Smith had given Sterling Pace. "Did he pay with a credit card?"

"Cash."

"Cash? How much does a penthouse go for here?"

"That room is two thousand for a weekend night."

Kelly whistled, and Sloan raised his brows. "This guy, Pierce, forked over two grand in cash?" he asked. "Don't you require something other than his signature when somebody pays in cash? I mean, what if he trashed the place? How would you find him, if he gave a phony address?"

The small man looked indignant. "This is the Fairmont, sir. Our clientele is . . . above that, shall we say?"

Sloan let out a heavy breath. Obviously, this place was out of his league. "Has anyone occupied the room since then?"

"Two different parties, one on Sunday, another last night. It's a very popular suite."

So it would be covered with all kinds of fingerprints, those that hadn't been wiped clean by a maid's dust cloth. Still, it was possible they might find something they could use. "I'm sorry, but we're going to have to take that room out of circulation for a while," Sloan told the obviously dismayed manager. "This Adrian Pierce is a suspect in the murder of a number of women in the area. We need to check the room for prints and anything else we might find."

The manager's eyes widened. "You mean he's that serial killer?"

Sloan shrugged. "Maybe. Will you help us find out, or will we have to get a warrant?"

65

The rest of Regan's day passed without event. The policeman had been content to keep an eye on her from a small, inconspicuous office, which pleased Jeff. She went about her business as Jeff's administrative assistant, making the coffee and answering the phones. She welcomed the normalness of it all, because Sloan's call had deeply disturbed her, and she didn't want to think about the maelstrom of danger that swirled around her.

Why had Peter given his employer a phony address? And how could it be that he wasn't registered at the Fairmont? They didn't just hand over the key to a penthouse to someone who wasn't registered there. There was something definitely wrong with this picture. Although she didn't know Peter well, she knew instinctively that he wasn't a liar. These prevarications hadn't been Peter's doing.

But if not Peter, then who? Was someone trying to set him up? A chill shivered through her. Why would anyone want to set him up? A nice man like Peter—*about whom she knew very little*. Doubts began to assail her. Maybe he was involved with the Mafia or something. Maybe his "day job" had nothing to do with children. Maybe he dealt drugs . . . Maybe . . .

Regan's imagination shot into high gear, filling her mind

with all kinds of terrible suspicions. If Peter didn't call soon, she thought she'd explode.

But Peter never called.

By five o'clock, Regan was a basket case. Still seeking normalcy by following routine, she called Kat and offered to do the shopping for the evening meal. They planned their meal, and Regan made a list. She nodded to her bodyguard. "Mind stopping by the supermarket on the way home?"

He grinned. "Even cops have to eat."

Regan said good night to Jeff and left the office, trying her damnedest to look, act, and feel as if nothing extraordinary were taking place in her life, but as she exited the protection of the office building, she found herself glancing in all directions. What, or rather, who was she looking for? Did she expect to see some thuglike character lurking nearby? Or was it Peter she was hoping to encounter?

The uniformed officer accompanied her to the supermarket, and Regan felt as if all eyes were on them. That was crazy, of course. Her overactive imagination at work again. After all, didn't cops have families? Didn't they go to the grocery store like everyone else? Like he'd said, even cops have to eat. She decided she was being paranoid. Nobody was staring at her. It was all in her mind.

She was about to enter the checkout line when she remembered that she'd left some pictures at the photo counter to be developed. She hesitated. Maybe she didn't want to pick up those pictures. They were the ones she'd made on her outing with Peter to Sausalito and the Presidio.

Peter.

There he was again. Regan's heart contracted. This couldn't be happening. It was all a mistake. A terrible nightmare.

She found the claim tab for the photos in her purse and picked them up, but she slipped them into her handbag without looking at them. She paid for the groceries, and the policeman walked her back to the cruiser. Now she really felt conspicuous.

Anger suddenly coursed through her. Why was this happening to her? She'd come to San Francisco to start a new life. A normal life. A fulfilling life. She'd found a great job and, she'd thought, a new friend in Peter Smith.

But now, everything seemed to be crumbling beneath her, leaving her alone and more afraid than she'd ever been in her life. She shivered as she got into the car.

66

The man knew the bitch was being watched. He'd seen the same gray car parked outside the house for several days. Two men sat inside. A surveillance team. What a boring job that must be, he thought.

She was under escort, as well. As he stood in the doorway of a small market down the street, he saw a marked police car pull up to the front of the house where she was living. She got out and went directly into the house, and behind her, a cop carried in two sacks of groceries. Our taxpayers' money at work, he thought dryly.

The man fingered the fabric in his coat pocket, and a thrill of excitement laced through him. He knew he was taking an unnecessary risk, but it had to be done. This woman threatened his plan. She'd slipped in without him seeing her, and if he wasn't careful, she could ruin everything.

He wasn't afraid of her, because he could easily take her out, but he wanted to punish her for what she'd done. He wanted her to know he was pissed, and that he was coming after her. The Internet message was only the beginning of what he had planned for her.

The man smiled in anticipation. He looked forward to methodically terrorizing her. She deserved it. And then when he'd had his fun, he'd kill her and clear the way for the grand finale.

67

Sam Sloan hesitated before pressing the doorbell on the fancifully painted Victorian house where Regan McKinney lived with her sister. He hated to interrupt Regan's life any more than necessary, but he'd reached the point where he had to talk to her again, quiz her at greater length, learn certain things about her that might fill in some blanks in his profile of the killer. At least she was alive and would be able to answer his questions. Usually, he thought grimly, ringing the bell, his victimology study was postmortem.

He was greeted by a pretty teenager in jeans and a sweatshirt. Kat Bowen's daughter, he surmised, smiling at the girl. "I'm Special Agent Sloan," he said, offering her his ID. "FBI."

The girl's eyes widened. "Wow!" she said. "Cool!"

"I need to speak with your aunt, Regan McKinney. Is she available?"

He saw doubt flicker in her eyes, and she hesitated. "I don't mean to seem rude," she told him, "but could you wait on the porch? They warned me not to let any strangers in the house, no matter what."

Sloan took a step backward. "They were right. I'll wait here." The door shut, and he heard the lock click into place. Smart kid, he thought.

Moments later, Regan peered out, and seeing it was him,

unlocked the door again and invited him into the house.

"I'm glad your niece was so cautious," he told Regan.

She looked down at her hands as if examining her nails. "We're all a bit . . . nervous around here these days. Please come in." She gestured toward the living area to the right of the entry hall. "May I take your coat?"

He handed her the all-weather coat he'd found invaluable in the unpredictable climate of San Francisco. She hung it on the hall tree, and they went into the comfortably appointed room.

"Have . . . you found Peter?" she said, turning to him with anxious eyes.

He shook his head. She took a seat in a large armchair, and he sat down on the sofa, filled with dread at what he was about to do. Had to do, if he were to do his job. He hated seeing the anxiety, the fear, the grief in the eyes of those he questioned, victims and families of victims of the darkest crimes. Victims—and potential victims. He swallowed. "No, we haven't found him. We're certain, however, that his name's not Peter Smith. He registered at the Fairmont as Adrian Pierce. There's no telling how many aliases he may be using."

Regan's face paled, and her brow furrowed. "Adrian Pierce?" she repeated, incredulous.

Sloan's heart went out to her. Apparently, she really cared for the man she called Peter Smith. Maybe she'd even fallen in love with him. How devastating to learn the depths of his deception. Sloan forced himself to continue.

"Adrian Pierce was the name on the registration form for the penthouse suite you identified as being where you stayed on Saturday night. I'm certain there's no mistake, because the address he used was the same phony one he'd given Sterling Pace."

He heard Regan let out a heavy breath and saw her chew on her bottom lip as she considered this new information. He waited, but when she didn't say anything, he went on.

"I know this is difficult, Ms. McKinney, but I need your help. You're the only one we've found so far who's been with this man and lived to tell about it."

She wheeled on him, fire in her eyes. "How can you say

that? What makes you so damned sure that Peter is the killer? I agree, it's weird that he's made up this name, and that he gave a phony address, but there must be some explanation for it."

Sloan dipped his head slightly in marginal agreement. "You're right, of course, there could be some other explanation. That's why I came by tonight, to see if there's anything else you can tell me that would help us find him and give him the chance to clear his name."

She looked away but didn't reply.

"Please, Ms. McKinney . . ."

"My name's Regan." Her voice was brittle.

"What else do you know about Peter Smith that would help us find him?"

She shrugged, looking miserable, and regret again slammed through Sam Sloan. He waited, and finally she spoke.

"I've already given you a description of his car. I have no idea of the license number." Her words were heavy. She was trying, but it hurt, he could tell.

"The SFPD's on the lookout for Jags like the one you described. Trouble is, this town is loaded with expensive cars like that. The other trouble is, he may not live here."

"He doesn't."

It was Sloan's turn to frown. "What? How do you know?"

"I just remembered. He told me he didn't live in the City." She gave him an apologetic look. "I'm sorry," she said with a shrug. "I forgot. He said he had a place down the coast, that it took him about an hour to get to the dance studio."

"Down the coast? Did he mean south?"

Again she shrugged. "I would assume 'down' meant 'south.'"

Sloan leaned forward, encouraged. "Is there anything else he told you that would help us?"

"I'm not doing this to help you," she snapped. "I'm doing it to help Peter. I know if you met him and talked to him, you'd find out he couldn't possibly be the killer."

Sloan winced at her naïveté. And her vulnerability. She didn't believe Smith or Pierce or whatever the hell his name was could be the killer, and that put her squarely in harm's way.

"There's nothing I'd like better, I can assure you. Help me find him. So far, the man's a ghost. We don't even know what he looks like, except for your description. 'Regular,' I think is how you depicted him. Can you come up with anything more specific, identifying marks, scars, anything that would give us a better ID?"

She paused a minute, then nodded slightly. "Wait here." She left the room and returned moments later with a packet of photos processed at a supermarket chain. "I took these the day Peter and I spent together in Sausalito and the Presidio." She handed them to him without opening the package.

Sloan's heartbeat picked up slightly. Photos. This could be the break they needed. Earlier, he'd given Regan's minimal description to a police artist, who'd told him it just wasn't enough to go on. He opened the envelope and withdrew the pictures.

Regan had been right on two counts—there was nothing remarkable about Peter Smith. He was, indeed, rather "regular." He also didn't look like a killer. In one shot, which showed him up closer than most of the others, his smile reached deeply into his eyes. He not only looked benign, he looked kind, caring, rather like Sloan thought a priest or a guru ought to look. He appeared to be what Regan perceived him to be, a nice, regular sort of guy.

But things weren't always as they seemed, and killers didn't have to look menacing to be deadly. "May I keep these?" he asked.

Regan nodded. "If you'll leave me the negatives."

The smell of something burning wafted past him, and Regan sniffed the air. "Uh-oh," she uttered and jumped from the chair. Sloan followed her into the kitchen at the back of the house where she was frantically retrieving a large casserole dish from the oven.

"I'm on kitchen duty tonight," she said breathlessly, "and I nearly burned dinner."

"Where's your sister?"

Regan placed the steaming dish on the cool rings of the

electric stovetop and closed the oven door. "Had a late meeting. She should be home soon."

The aroma of pungent spices sluiced through the kitchen, and Sloan's mouth watered in spite of the fact he'd eaten a large meal in the middle of the afternoon. Home-cooked food was a commodity he rarely encountered. He went to the stove and examined the casserole. Other than some slightly charred places on the top layer of the pasta, the dish looked fine. "Looks okay to me," he commented, suddenly aware of how close he stood to Regan. He stepped back slightly.

She turned to him. "I made a big casserole on purpose," she said. "Thought I'd ask the bodyguards if they'd like to have some. If you'd like, you could join us."

68

Now why had she done that? Regan asked herself. Special Agent Sam Sloan made her nervous, and he certainly was no friend of Peter's. And yet, there was something about the sadness in his eyes, the lines in his face, that made her feel somehow sorry for him. He had a tough job, and she knew he was only trying to protect her and her sister and Blair with his questioning.

"I wouldn't be intruding?" he asked.

"I wouldn't have invited you if you were."

He gave her a small smile, the most smile she'd seen from him since they'd met yesterday. "Then, yes, I'd like that."

"Why don't you sit in here?" Regan suggested, indicating the kitchen table. "I have to make the salad and put the bread in the oven."

Sloan did as she suggested, and as Regan dug the salad makings from the refrigerator, she again questioned her motives for inviting him to dinner. She felt somehow traitorous to Peter, and yet a part of her wanted Sloan to find the enigmatic man who'd obviously stolen her heart. She wanted answers as badly as Sloan did. Just to different questions.

"So what are you going to do with the pictures?" she asked.

"Take them to the media. Or at least take this one, the close-up."

Regan dropped the knife she'd just retrieved from the drawer, and it clattered onto the tile floor. "The media? You're not going to put his picture in the newspaper, are you?"

"And on television. Everywhere I can until he comes forward."

She picked up the knife and turned toward Sloan. "Is that really necessary?" she demanded. "I mean, why not give him a few days? Maybe he'll call me. Maybe he'll show up—"

"Maybe he'll kill another woman."

Sloan's words stopped her cold. "You really believe that, don't you?" Regan said.

He regarded her steadily. "I believe he might. And I believe that woman might be you. Or he could go for your sister or your niece first, just to make it worse for you. You want to take that chance?"

Regan's blood turned to ice at the mention of her family. "You said it's me he's after. Why would he kill Kat or Blair?"

"This man wants his ultimate victim, whoever that is, to suffer. If what we saw on the Internet is his real MO, and I have every forensic reason to believe it is, he plays with his victims, scares the living bejesus out of them before he kills them. He wants to see them suffer. He wants to terrorize them. It's all part of it, maybe the most important part."

The delicious scent of the casserole suddenly nauseated her. "Am I his ultimate victim?"

Sloan clasped his hands together and templed his arms on the tabletop. "Maybe. He's certainly treating you differently than his earlier victims." He paused, apparently deep in thought. Then he said, "For argument's sake, let's say that it's not Peter, that instead it's somebody you know, somebody you've abused in the past. Anybody come to mind?"

Regan stared at him, astounded and more than a little offended. "Somebody I know? Somebody I abused? I've never abused anyone."

"An old boyfriend you might have scorned? Some weird kid on your block you might have made fun of? These sickos often don't need much of a snub to turn sour."

Her mind raced back over her thirty-four years, frantically

searching for memories of childhood encounters, teenage troubles, but found nothing. "I can't think of anyone or any incident that could set someone off like this."

"What's your ex-husband like?"

This surprised Regan even more. "Adam? Adam wouldn't do this. He's not a real nice guy, but he's not a murderer. And besides, he lives a continent away, with a new little wife and maybe a new baby by now." She couldn't conceal the bitterness she still felt toward Adam. But she couldn't imagine him being a serial killer.

"I'll have our people check on him anyway. And if you think of anybody who might want to harm you like this, please let me know right away."

Sloan's suggestion that she might have offended a psychopath somewhere along the way chilled Regan. She'd never willingly hurt anyone, but could she have inadvertently slighted some mentally ill person whose rage had built over the years until now he was going to kill her? It was too much, over-the-top unbelievable.

But then, there was one of the FBI's top profilers sitting at her kitchen table, telling her she could be this killer's ultimate victim. It made her feel more than vulnerable. It made her feel hollow, cold. Terrified.

Just what the killer wanted.

"I'm not his ultimate victim," she managed over a thick, dry tongue. She reached for a glass from the shelf, poured if full of water, and drank deeply. "I don't know why he's doing this to me. I never hurt anybody. Are you sure he didn't send that same message to the other victims to scare them, as well?"

"We can't be sure, of course, because they can't tell us. They're dead. But my interviews with their families have shown that most of the victims either didn't have computers, or didn't use them much. No, I think this is a shift in his MO. You may not be his ultimate victim, but for some reason, he's chosen you to experience the next level of his cruelty."

Regan leaned back against the kitchen counter. She set the knife down and put her hand to her throat. "But why?" she asked in a quavering voice. "Why me?"

"Other than that you must physically resemble the true target of his rage?" Sloan pressed his lips together into a tight line and shook his head. "You were probably just in the wrong place at the wrong time."

69

Regan had not slept well, and she got up early to bring in the newspaper. She was anxious to see if Peter's picture had made the front page. Her eyes felt fuzzy and scratchy as she squinted and scanned the porch for the paper, but the carrier had obviously missed . . . again. She went down the steps to the front walk and spied the paper nestled beneath a hedge. As she bent to pick it up, she saw something out of the corner of her eye. A fabric of some kind was snagged on the branches of the shrub and seemed to wave at her in the light breeze.

She started to reach for it, thinking it a piece of trash that had been blown from someone's garbage, when she suddenly froze. The fabric was light blue, gauzy, and it appeared to be stained heavily . . . with blood.

A scream rose in her throat but died as pure terror tightened around the muscles there. Adrenaline sent her heart rate soaring. She glanced around and saw the surveillance team watching her, and she began to gesture wildly to them. Bill and Mike were back on duty, and they hit the pavement running.

"What's the matter?"

Still rendered speechless with fear, Regan could only point at the fabric.

Bill approached it cautiously. "Oh, Jesus!" he uttered under his breath. He took out his cell phone, punched in some numbers and waited, his eyes glued to the fabric, which fluttered in the wind like a macabre ghost.

"Sloan? Logan here. You'd better get over here fast. I think our man has left Ms. McKinney another little present."

Regan was shivering uncontrollably when she returned to the warmth of the house, but it wasn't because she was cold. The blood. All that blood. Parts of the scarf were still light blue, but much of it was stained an ugly dark brown, and it didn't take a genius to know what caused that stain.

She went into the snuggery, sat on the sofa and pulled a knitted afghan tightly around her. Kat found her there a few moments later, staring into space, seeing nothing but the blood.

"What's the matter?" Kat asked. "Are you sick?"

Regan shook her head. "Just cold." She told her sister what she'd found outside, and Kat went to the front door.

"There're cops all over the place," she said.

"That's fine with me," Regan replied. "But a fat lot of good they'll do if this wacko really wants to get at us. He must have crept up to the house right in front of whoever was supposed to be keeping an eye on it. Doesn't give me much faith that we're being protected."

Her eyes stung with tears, but she batted them away furiously. She patted the sofa, indicating for her sister to sit beside her. Regan leaned forward and grabbed both of Kat's hands in a fierce grip. "Kat, listen, you've got to take Blair and get the hell out of town until they catch this creep. I didn't want to tell you, but yesterday Sloan indicated that he . . . the killer, I mean, might kill you and Blair both just to hurt me. I'm scared, Kat. Scared for you and Blair and me . . . Nobody's safe until they catch him."

Regan was scared. She could feel her fear oozing from her pores along with a cold sweat. But Kat shook her head.

"I'm not going anywhere. I'd never leave you, especially not with all this going on." She gave Regan a reassuring grin. "Nobody's going to kill us, Regan. Not with all these cops around. They're bound to get him soon."

Regan wasn't reassured. "That killer could have broken

into this house last night and the cops wouldn't have known it."

The doorbell rang, and Kat went to answer it, leaving Regan still huddled under the afghan. Moments later, Sloan came into the snuggery.

"Are you all right?"

She glared up at him. "Hell, no, I'm not all right. I thought your people were supposed to be protecting us. That creep got so close he might as well have just walked in the front door." She knew it wasn't Sloan's fault, but she needed a target for the anger that seemed to be quickly replacing her fear. She paused, feeling somewhat mollified. "So what do you think? Was that another present from the killer, or is my imagination running away with me?" Regan knew the killer had planted the scarf, but suddenly she wanted wildly to believe that the wind had whipped the filmy fabric into the yard, and that it was muddy, not bloody.

Sloan's next words dashed any such possibility. "It was the killer. We'll have it tested, but I'm certain the scarf is made of the same fabric as the blouse the last victim was wearing. He must have kept it as a souvenir."

The chill returned to Regan's bones. "Oh, dear God," she murmured. She began to tremble again, and Sloan sat down next to her.

"Because of certain circumstances surrounding Sunday's murder, I thought we might have a copycat killer on our hands, you know, someone who tries to re-create the work of the killer who's getting all the headlines. But if he's a copycat, he also knows a lot about the killer, including his fixation on you."

"So he's not a copycat," she said.

"No. I think he's our man." Sloan drummed his fingers on the coffee table, and silence fell between them. "This should never have happened, Regan," he said at last, "but it did. Which shows just how clever this guy is. But we can't take any more chances. I want you and your sister and niece to go to a safe house."

Regan looked up to see Kat and Blair standing together in the doorway. Kat's expression was strained, and Blair was chewing her lower lip.

"What good's a safe house if this guy's watching where we go?" Kat asked. "I'd rather stay here and let the cops increase the surveillance."

"I can't let you take that risk," Sloan told her. "We have places where you'll be safe. He won't be able to find you, not unless he's God."

70

Clad in robe and pajamas, Peter Smith poured himself a cup
of coffee and opened the morning paper that lay on the table.
He took a sip, and then nearly choked. He blinked in disbelief as he stared at the front page. "What the hell?" A
picture of him stared back, a photo he'd never seen before.
Shocked and horrified, he picked up the paper with trembling
hands and sank into a chair. With growing disbelief, he read
the article:

> Police are searching for this man in their investigation of the
> rash of recent murders in the Bay Area. He goes by the names
> of Peter Smith and Adrian Pierce, but other aliases are possible.
> Anyone seeing this man should consider him armed and danger-
> ous. Do not approach him, but call the police immediately.

Peter's mouth went dry, and his nerves tingled. What was
going on? He hadn't killed anyone. Where had the police
obtained that picture of him? He'd never seen it, couldn't
remember where it could possibly have been taken, or by
whom. And who was Adrian Pierce?

He reached for the phone. This was a terrible mistake. He
had to call the authorities immediately and set it straight.

No. Put the phone down.

The voice inside him was so loud the message reverberated in his mind for a long moment. Peter knew that voice, and dread poured into him. Then panic edged in, mingling with the dread. What should he do?

Get away! Get as far away from here as you can. Run!

This voice was young, terrified. Peter knew this voice, too.

Two sides to his nature went to war—should he stand and fight, or run for his life?

He hesitated, his hand still on the telephone, his heart pounding. What would happen if he called the police? He hadn't killed anyone. They wouldn't throw him in jail. Would they? He thought about the others, the children he was reponsible for. What would they do if he went to jail?

A dark shadow settled over him, and a feeling of unrest and rage trickled through him. Why him? Why were they looking for him? He hadn't done anything wrong.

And then he thought about Regan. What must she be thinking? He looked again at his photo in the paper and suddenly realized who had taken the picture. Regan had made it the day they went to Sausalito. A deep pain of grief and disappointment cut through him. Why had she given that photo to the police? Did she think he was a killer?

He stood stock-still, his heart thundering, his mind racing madly for an answer, some explanation for this terrible mistake. The only thing that made sense was that someone was framing him. But who?

Whoever it was, Peter wouldn't let him get away with it. And even though Regan had betrayed him by giving that photo to the police, he couldn't bear the thought that she suspected he was a killer. Dear God, how could this have happened? He must call her. He had to make her understand he was being set up.

Even as these thoughts raced through his panicked mind, an odd notion assailed him—there was something he had to do, something he had to finish. An inexplicable sense of urgency sent him into his bedroom where he went to the closet for a duffel bag. There was someplace he had to go.

He reached for the bag which was on the top shelf, but when he glanced down, his eyes lit on something on the floor at the back of the closet. He jumped, startled, thinking at first it was a small animal of some kind hunkering in the corner, but then he saw it was a coat, a dark brown wool coat folded, or rather rolled, into a lumpy form on the closet floor.

Peter frowned. He didn't own a dark brown wool coat.

Carefully, he lifted the garment from the floor. He unrolled it as he brought it into the bedroom. Where the hell had this come from? He'd never seen it before in his life. Who had put it in his closet, and why?

The coat was expensive. Cashmere. Lightweight but heavy enough for Bay Area winters. He held it up to the light coming in through the sliding doors that led to the deck. There was something on the coat. Something crusty and foul-smelling. It was brown, but darker than the coat, and it was smeared on the wool in several spots. Peter raised the coat to his nose, then dropped it suddenly as he recognized the odor.

Blood.

He jumped away from the coat as if it were a rattlesnake. His mind reeled, grasping for an explanation. He felt as if the world was falling out from under him. Why was his picture in the paper? Why were they calling him a killer? And what was that bloody coat doing in his closet?

Fear and panic tightened his gut. Somebody had planted that coat. Somebody was setting him up big-time.

Run!

Hastily, Peter grabbed a few items of clothing and stuffed them into the duffel. He didn't know where he was going, only that he must leave now. He donned a pair of jeans and a flannel shirt that were draped over the back of a chair. He put on sneakers that were parked just beneath the edge of the bed and drew on a ball cap. Running down the stairs, he grabbed the keys to his car, and then he stopped.

Regan.

He couldn't leave without calling Regan. He had to convince her that he wasn't the killer, no matter what the paper was saying. He had to make her believe him. He couldn't stand that she'd think such a horrible thing about him. If he knew she believed in him, he would find a way to sort through this mess and prove to them all they were making a monstrous mistake. But he needed her to believe him.

Peter picked up the phone that was mounted on the wall in the entry hall just inside the garage. He dialed the number at Regan's sister's house. His heart hammered.

"Hello?"

It was a man's voice. Peter hung up. Wrong number? He dialed again. This time a woman answered. But it wasn't Regan. Maybe she was having a party. Friends answering her phone when she couldn't get to it. At eight-thirty in the morning?

"I'm calling for Regan McKinney."

There was a slight hesitation on the line, then the woman said, "This is Ms. McKinney's residence, but she's not here at the moment. Who's calling, please?"

Peter looked at his watch. What had he been thinking? Of course she wouldn't be at home. She'd be at her office.

"Never mind. I'll try her later."

Slamming down the receiver, he tried to remember her office number but couldn't. He ran back upstairs to get his day planner, and with shaking fingers, managed to find the number for *Pro.Com* magazine. The line rang three times, and Peter almost hung up. If she wasn't there, he'd have to leave without speaking to her. He hated to do it, because he didn't know when, or if, he'd ever see her again. But the clock was ticking, and he had to get out of there.

"Pro.Com Magazine. How may I help you?" The sound of Regan's voice was like balm to a wound, and it soothed Peter's nerves instantly.

"Regan, it's me, Peter."

"Peter! Where are you? Have you seen the newspaper today?"

He heard fear in her voice, and a trace of hysteria. "That's why I'm calling. What the hell's going on? Why'd you give that picture to the police? You can't possibly believe I'm that serial killer?"

He heard a little snuffle, as if she were crying. "Oh, Peter, please come and talk to the police. No, I don't believe you're the killer, but . . . but there are some things, questions, they have about you that I can't answer."

His earlier fear and panic knotted in his gut. "Questions? What kind of questions?"

"Peter, why did you give a phony address on your job application at Sterling Pace's? The address you gave doesn't even exist."

Oh, that.

"I can explain. It's no big deal. I've told you that I have a demanding job, but I probably haven't mentioned that it's very confidential in nature. I never give my address out to anyone."

"What *do* you do, Peter?" she asked, sounding both aggravated and frightened. "It's time you told me the truth. Listen," she added with increasing desperation, "this is serious, Peter. There are cops all over looking for you. You've got to come in and explain all this to them. You can't be evasive anymore. Your life might depend on it."

"Regan, I . . . I can't. Not just yet, anyway. There's something I have to do first. Something I have to finish. But you have to believe me, I'm not a killer. Somebody is setting me up." He thought about the bloody coat in his closet, and suddenly he had a suspicion of who might be trying to frame him. His skin turned clammy.

"Something you have to do?" Regan's shrill voice tore his mind away from the sickening suspicion. "What could be more important than clearing your name?"

His breathing was shallow and his heart raced. "Regan, do you believe I'm innocent or not? Tell me."

There was a long pause, then she said in a small, quavering voice, "I do, Peter."

There was something else he had to know. "Do you love me, Regan? I have to know where I stand with you."

Another pause. "I do love you, Peter. But I don't understand—"

"I can't explain things right now, but when this is all behind us, I promise, I'll tell you everything. But for now, know that I love you, too. I have to go."

"Wait, Peter. How can I get in touch with you?"

"You can't."

Her voice became quiet; she spoke barely above a whisper. "Listen, Peter, this phone is tapped. Don't call here again, or Kat's house, either. Write this number down. It's my cell phone." She gave him the number, which he scribbled on a scrap of paper he fumbled from his wallet. He doubted he'd call her, but it reassured him that she'd wanted to maintain contact.

"I've got to go now," he said, then added, "Regan, things are going to work out. Just trust me."

71

"We got him," the technician said. He, Sloan, and Brad Kelly were cramped in a communications van, hovering over equipment that was monitoring incoming calls both to Regan's house and her office. The first call had been too short to trace, but they'd been able to track Peter Smith's call to the office, because Regan had done a good job of keeping him on the line. But why the hell had she given him her cell phone number? Sloan was both furious and appalled. Apparently, despite all his warnings, she still believed Peter Smith's claim of innocence.

"Where is he?" Sloan asked the tech.

"The number's in an area quite a bit to the south of here," one of the technicians told him. "Somewhere in San Mateo County, maybe in Pacifica or farther south, along the coast. I'll have the address in just a minute."

Sloan didn't want to waste another minute. He turned to Kelly. "Let's go." The two investigators got into an unmarked vehicle and told the driver to head toward Pacifica until they received better directions.

The car jerked away from the curb, and Sloan took out his cell phone. He called the tech in the communications van. "What'd you come up with?"

"The number is unlisted, but the phone company has it recorded as belonging to somebody named Ed Johnson."

Ed Johnson. Another alias?

"Got an address yet?" He wrote it down as the tech read it to him. Then he asked for the number of the sheriff's headquarters in Redwood City. Sloan punched it into the cell phone moments later and spoke with Sheriff Tommy Lee.

"That's a really posh subdivision," Lee told him when Sloan gave him the address. "Gated community. Million-dollar villas overlooking the Pacific. Killer or not, this guy's a rich son of a bitch."

"How fast can you get a search warrant?"

"When do you need it?"

"I should be there in a little over an hour. Can you send some people over there? Just post them outside the gate and wait, unless he tries to leave. Detain him if that happens."

"You know for sure he's in there?"

"He made a phone call from there a few minutes ago. He could have left right after that. Probably did, considering what's going on. We think he's driving a silver- or pewter-colored Jag, an older model. We don't have a license number. Could you check your records and see if you can find it? It could be registered to a Peter Smith, Adrian Pierce, or perhaps Ed Johnson." Or none of the above, Sloan thought sourly. How many aliases did this guy have? "If you find the info on it, put an APB out for it down there, will you? Oh," he added almost as an afterthought, "you have a crime-scene unit, I assume?"

"One of the best in the state."

"Bring them along, if you will. I'm going to need some help."

Sloan pressed the button to disconnect the call, then dialed the van again. "Get me the number for the Mateo County Clerk's office."

The deed to the property at the address on the telephone records was also registered in the name of Ed Johnson.

Sloan continued his sleuthing from the backseat of the police car as it sped south on the scenic Cabrillo Highway. He was oblivious to anything but catching Peter Smith/ Adrian Pierce/Ed Johnson.

Rich men could be killers as well as poor ones.

72

Peter Smith tossed the duffel bag onto the passenger seat of the Jag and pressed the garage door opener. He jerked the car backward down the steep driveway to where he could turn it around at the base of his property, then wheeled into the narrow, winding street that led through the exclusive community. Peter ignored the guard at the gate, who attempted to greet him. He pressed the accelerator and his tires squealed. The urgency of his mission mounted, as did the horror of his suspicion.

When he reached Highway 1, he turned south and drove as fast as the winding road would allow, unaware of the steep mountains on one side and the broad ocean on the other. In his mind's eye, he saw only one thing—Regan McKinney.

73

The man was furious. How had things gotten so screwed up? He'd just wanted to give the bitch another scare. Planting the scarf in her front garden had been surprisingly easy, considering the surveillance team across the street and the bodyguards inside the house. He'd simply made his way up the hill from the little market, crouching behind the protection offered by the picket fences that stood in front of most of the houses on the street. His only exposure had been when he'd had to climb over dividing fences, but some of the yards, including Regan McKinney's sister's, didn't have fenced separations between them. When he'd reached Regan's place, he'd simply thrust his hand through the large shrub that served to divide the properties, snagged the scarf on a branch, and left the way he came.

He had other surprises planned for her, but now he wasn't sure he'd be able to pull them off. Dark rage surged through him. He should have just killed her when he'd had the chance.

Now, he'd have to wait. Bide his time. Rethink his plan. It didn't matter, he supposed, attempting to cool his rage, how much time it took. What mattered was that they died.

Regan McKinney.

And one more. The final one, the one who'd caused it all.

74

Regan, Kat, and Blair sat at the round Formica table in the small breakfast area of the safe house in Burlingame where they'd been taken shortly after Peter's phone call had been intercepted. None were happy about having their lives interrupted, being locked away in this place that smelled slightly of Pine-Sol and fried onions, but Sloan had been adamant. Apparently, they'd successfully located Peter's house from the phone tap, and Sloan was on his way to find him.

In a way, Regan was relieved. Once Sloan talked to Peter, once everything was explained, there would be no need for evasiveness or secrets, and the damned cop could start looking for the real killer.

The safe house was a typical suburban California-style house, stucco with a red tile roof, a Mediterranean wanna-be. It nestled inconspicuously among its look-alike neighbors in this upscale bedroom community not far from the airport. If anybody wanted to hide out, this was an excellent place. Everything here looked the same.

The cop assigned to stay with them flipped on the television. A popular game show was in progress. Regan gritted her teeth. She hated daytime TV, game shows and talk shows, soaps and sitcoms. Canned laughter grated on her nerves.

"I've got to do something, or I'm going to lose my mind,"

she said, dumping the last of her now-cold coffee into the sink. "Blair, can I borrow your laptop?"

Blair scooted away from the table and retrieved a slim portable computer from the room she'd been assigned. "Here," she said, handing the laptop to Regan. "What're you going to do?"

"Work on my article about Kevin Carrington."

"Can I help?"

"Sure. You can show me how to work this thing, for starters."

"I wish I'd thought to bring something to work on," Kat grumbled. "This is going to be a real bore."

"There're movies in the coat closet," the cop offered, pointing to a door just off the entry hall.

"Thanks, but it's a little early to do movies. I brought a book. Think I'll go into my room and hide."

Regan watched her sister leave the room and again felt a deep regret for all that had happened. They could, she supposed, treat this unexpected interlude at the safe house something like a snow day—a little holiday forced upon them. That's how Blair was taking it. But Kat had not asked for this holiday, and she clearly didn't want it. She was making the best of it, but Regan knew Kat wanted to be at work instead of here. Hell, she'd rather be at work, too.

Please, God, let this be over soon.

At the last minute before leaving Kat's house, Regan remembered her briefcase containing all the research she'd done on Kevin Carrington, and she was glad now she'd had the good sense to bring it with her. She dug out the printouts from the Internet and read over them again, passing each page along to Blair as she went. Her niece was in some ways still a child, but in many others, she was like a little adult. Blair was creative and intelligent, and like her mother, always spoke her mind. Regan enjoyed being around her and found her take on life rather refreshing.

"So, what do you think we ought to say about Mr. Kevin Carrington?" she asked with forced brightness when they'd both read all the pages. She refused to think about the possibility that anything they wrote might be in vain, that Roundtree might lose his patience and fire her after all.

"I feel sorry for him," Blair said. "I know he's rich and all that, but it doesn't sound like he's had a very happy life."

Regan felt the same way. It was hard to connect emotionally with a man she'd never met, and yet the pieces of his story, as she'd managed to assemble them, revealed a lifetime of loneliness and overcompensation. "I wonder what his mother was like?" she remarked.

"Have you looked her up on the Net?" Blair asked.

Regan shook her head. "I only read about her in that one article we pulled up on Michael Carrington. You suppose we could find out more?"

"We could try, or . . ."—she glanced sardonically at the blaring TV—"we could watch game shows all day."

They plugged Blair's computer into a telephone outlet, and moments later, the young girl's deft fingers were calling up information out of the ether.

"Liliane La Rue," she typed into the search engine.

Regan watched as the computer sorted and reached and dialed and finally brought up what they were looking for. There wasn't much, except for one Web site apparently established by a fan of Liliane's, "Lili.com." "Let's go there," Regan said, and Blair clicked on the link.

The Web site was a little slow in loading, as it included both graphics and music, but when the picture of the young actress scrolled onto the screen, Regan took in a sharp breath.

She could have been looking at herself.

75

Sam Sloan met up with Sheriff Tommy Lee and his people at the gate of Spyglass Hill, an exclusive community where Ed Johnson, aka Peter Smith, lived. After brief introductions, Sloan approached the man inside the guardhouse.

"What's going on?" the guard asked warily. "The cops have been sitting here for more than an hour. The owners won't like it."

Sloan took out his badge. "They'd like it even less if they knew what I know."

"FBI?" His expression darkened. "Well, what *do* you know?"

Sloan didn't answer. Instead, he took out the photograph of Peter Smith that Regan had given him. "You know this man?"

The guard glanced at the picture. "Sure. That's Mr. Pierce. Lives at the top of the hill."

Pierce.

"Adrian Pierce?"

"That's right. What's he done?" The man's curiosity could have glowed in the dark.

Again, Sloan ignored his question. "What about Ed Johnson? Does he live there, too?"

"Never heard of him. No, Mr. Pierce lives alone. Keeps odd hours. I don't see him much."

"Seen him lately?"

"Yeah. He drove out of here about nine o'clock. Seemed like he was in kind of a hurry. Let me check to make sure of the time." He picked up a clipboard. "Nine-eleven, to be exact."

Sloan looked at his watch and cursed. Smith or Pierce or Johnson or whoever-the-hell-he-was must've decided to hightail it while he still could. But why had he risked making those calls to Regan? Surely he must have known the cops would be tracing incoming calls. Even though Sloan believed Peter Smith to be the killer, he had to admit his pleas of innocence to Regan had sounded convincing. He'd told Regan there was something he had to do before he could explain things. What? Sloan wondered. Another murder?

"Any idea where he might have been headed?" Sloan asked the guard.

The man shook his head. "Not a clue."

"Where does he work?"

The security man laughed. "Work? You think people who can afford to live in these kinds of places have to work?"

Sloan was getting impatient. "What was he driving?"

"His Jag, of course."

"Does he have any other vehicles?"

"I've seen him in a black Lincoln Navigator once in a while. Big son of a bitch."

Big enough to transport a body?

Sloan went back to where Tommy Lee and the others waited. "You get that warrant?" he asked Lee.

The sheriff handed him the papers. "Is he inside?"

"No. He split a little after nine. Did you put out that APB?"

"I'm a very efficient man, Mr. Sloan," Lee said with a grin. "Especially when I'm after a perp like this. By the way, the car is registered to—"

"Don't tell me, let me guess . . . Ed Johnson?"

The gate guard glanced cursorily at the warrant, gave Sloan directions, and waved the police cars through.

The house was a three-story ultracontemporary affair made of redwood and glass. From the foot of the hill, it looked like a modern-day castle, soaring into the blue California sky.

Sloan and Brad Kelly, who'd remained a silent observer for much of the morning, got out of their car and removed their guns from their holsters. The other officers did the same and surrounded the house. Sloan approached a door on the first floor, next to the garage, and flattened his body against the outside wall. He pressed the doorbell and heard it ring, but no footsteps responded to the summons. Not that he'd expected anyone to be here, but the guard at the gate could have been wrong. Smith might not always live alone.

After a short wait, Sloan signaled to one of Lee's men to break the lock and disable the security alarm. The man had them inside in less than thirty seconds. "Don't touch anything," Sloan reminded everyone. Tommy Lee nodded to one of his men, who took out a packet of thin rubber gloves from his uniform and distributed them to the team. Sloan was impressed by the professionalism of these officers. If they were lucky enough to find evidence against Peter Smith in this house, he was reassured that it likely wouldn't be contaminated by their search.

Before going upstairs, Sloan peered into the garage, but it was empty. No Jag, no black Lincoln Navigator. Slowly, cautiously, the team made their way through the house and determined at last that it was unoccupied. "Okay, now people," Sloan directed, "let's see what we can find. Who's doing the fingerprints?"

Two officers, a man and a woman, stepped forward. "Where do you want us to start?"

"The telephones. We know he used the telephone here this morning."

Sloan and Kelly started their search of the premises in the main living area, while Lee and two other officers went to other parts of the house.

There was nothing unusual about the living area; it was a large, open room with glass doors that led out onto a deck. Beyond was a steep cliff and, below, the Pacific Ocean. The room was furnished with large, dark leather chairs and sofas, very masculine in style. In one corner stood a big-screen TV and a complex sound system.

Kelly opened a door to one of the built-in cabinets and let out a low whistle. "Look at this." He'd discovered an extensive library of movies on tape and DVD. "He could open a movie rental joint."

"Porn flicks?" Sloan asked.

Kelly riffled through the selection, then shook his head. "Not on these shelves. Lots of Disney stuff, some Jackie Chan, the Muppets. Looks like you could safely turn a kid loose in here."

Sloan recalled Regan telling him that Peter Smith had some kind of obligation to children. Did kids live here with him? He looked around, but other than the movie collection, there was no sign of youthful occupants.

He went into the kitchen. The coffeemaker was on. Dishes were stacked in the sink. Then he saw the newspaper lying open on the kitchen table, and Peter Smith's face smiled up at him.

Peter Smith had seen the paper and taken off in a hurry.

But where the hell had he gone? Sloan was infinitely relieved that Regan and Kat and Blair were safely tucked away where Smith couldn't get his hands on them, especially since he didn't trust Regan not to do something foolish. He'd tried to get her to give him her cell phone, but she'd refused, and he had no way to force her to give it over. He had, however, warned the cops who were assigned to the safe house to be on the alert if she received any calls on it.

In the meantime, he hoped he could apprehend Smith before he ever got a chance to call Regan again. He was counting on the APB to enable law enforcement officials in the area to find the car soon. That kind of car wouldn't be hard to spot. For the first time in weeks, Sam Sloan felt hopeful that this case was about to be resolved, that one more sicko would soon be taken off the streets, and that he could then, at last, get out of this business for good.

Tommy Lee appeared in the doorway. "I think you'd better come see what we found in the bedroom, Agent Sloan."

76

Kevin Carrington entered the darkened house and shuddered, although it was not cold. A storm had come in off the Pacific, and rain drenched the California mountainsides, sending torrents flooding into the valleys, surging into ravines and overflowing onto the streets and roads. Kevin didn't like the rain. Something about rain filled him with melancholy, and often when it rained he took refuge behind closed curtains, curled up beneath his covers like a little kid.

He felt like doing that now, but fought the urge. He wasn't a little kid anymore, and there were things he had to get done. He turned on the lights and proceeded down the hallway into the big room. He pressed a button on the wall, and a mechanism slowly drew the heavy draperies away from the floor-to-ceiling windows. Outside, beyond the deck, a sodden gray sky emptied itself into a gray-green ocean that flailed spray skyward in its turmoil.

That ocean. That sky. The murkiness of the wet sand. He couldn't bear to look at them, so he pressed the button again and retreated behind the curtains once more. There was only so much he could take.

Kevin hated this place. So many memories lurked here. His brother's death. His mother's. His father's desertion. And all the rest.

He hadn't been here in years, and although he owned the

house, he'd never expected to return to it. Then, a few months ago, an idea came to him. A new project had called to him. A different kind of project than his computer games, a deeper work, a more personal endeavor than he'd ever undertaken. He hadn't planned this project. It just appeared one day, and he knew he couldn't ignore it. Nor could he ignore the setting the project demanded. This house.

Now, it was almost complete. Today, maybe tomorrow, he would finish the work, and he was glad. It had been difficult to produce with everything else he had going on in his life. He hadn't had the time he would have liked to devote to it. But still, he'd done it, and soon . . .

Soon he prayed he would be free. Free of the demons that chased him through his dreams. Free of his fear that he was going mad. They say confession is good for the soul, and he hoped that by telling his story on videotape, he might avoid the psychiatrist's couch.

If he could stand the pain of the telling.

He placed the small bag he carried on a chair and went directly to the room he'd set up as his studio. He took a seat in front of a bank of recording machines, flipped switches and turned dials until he had everything set the way he wanted. He placed a particular CD into the player and turned the volume on high, wincing as the sound filled the room. The music was hard. Hot. Heavy. The bass reverberated off the walls and sent chills up his spine.

Ka-thud. Ka-thud. Ka-thud.

Trembling violently, he took his seat in the director's chair in front of the camera, pressed a remote control button to begin recording, and summoning every ounce of courage in his soul, faced the final chapter of his tale. He was unaware that as he spoke, he began to cry.

77

The roar of a jet thundered overhead, as had dozens of others during the day. How could anyone live in a place with so much noise? Regan wondered as she pushed the laptop away and ran her hands through her hair. Her head throbbed. She'd been trying to write her story for a couple of hours, but it was so hard to concentrate with all the jets booming into the sky nearby. She was also dubious of her skills as a writer. Why had she ever thought she could undertake a story like this? She had no training as a writer, and other than having managed to glean some interesting information from Ed Johnson and getting old facts off the Internet, she was way short on her research. She was making things up out of thin air, for God's sake!

But it wasn't the noise of the jets, or her inexperience as a writer that kept distracting Regan. It was Peter Smith. Thoughts of him kept creeping into her mind, and questions assailed her until she thought she might scream. She gave up at last, closed the laptop and went into the kitchen for a drink. In the pocket of her slacks, she felt the weight of her cell phone.

She knew Sloan was angry with her for giving her number to Peter, and even more so for not turning the phone over to Sloan, but Regan couldn't cut Peter off like that. Peter didn't have many friends in the world right now, it seemed, and although she didn't understand his actions, Regan believed with all her heart that he was being framed. Peter, gentle Peter, was not a killer. She wanted desperately for him to come forward and clear his name, but until he did, she wanted him to know she was his friend.

"Finished with your story?" Blair asked, coming into the kitchen.

"Hardly. I don't have enough to go on at this point. Not until I get to talk to Carrington, or at least his father. But that isn't going to happen until they let us out of this cage," Regan said, feeling suddenly trapped and housebound.

"Yeah, this is a bummer," Blair agreed, "but at least they stocked it with good stuff," she added, taking a soda from the fridge.

Regan went into the living room, away from the prattle of a TV talk show in the den, and flopped onto the sofa. Blair was right behind her.

"What's the matter, Regan?" she asked, sitting cross-legged on the floor near her aunt.

"Oh, nothing. A killer's after me, maybe after my family, as well, my friend Peter is accused of the crimes and has disappeared off the face of the earth. We're locked in this little house with nonstop television and jet plane noise in our ears, Kat and I can't go to work, you can't go to school, but really, nothing's wrong."

They were silent a moment, then Blair said, "You really love Peter, don't you?"

Unbidden tears rose in Regan's eyes, and her throat tightened. "Oh, honey, I don't know," she started, but she knew she wasn't telling the truth. "That's not true. I do know. Yes, I love Peter. I don't know how a person can feel this way about someone they don't know very well, but . . . Peter's just so . . . special, so different. He's wacky and unpredictable, but also tender and caring. He . . . makes me feel like a worthwhile person, like I have a brain and value in this world. Adam treated me like dirt. Maybe I'm just overreacting to being treated nice for a change, but . . . no, it's more than that."

"It's okay, Regan. I'm glad you love Peter, and I'll be glad when this is over so you two can be together."

"Me, too," Regan added, feeling miserable, wondering if she'd ever see Peter again.

78

Back in San Francisco's Hall of Justice, Sam Sloan and Brad Kelly drank bad coffee and waited. Forensics was testing samples from the bloody coat they'd found at Ed Johnson's villa. Law enforcement agencies throughout the state were looking for the Jag. But Peter Smith, aka Adrian Pierce, aka Ed Johnson seemed to have vanished into thin air.

They did have one answer waiting for them when they got back, however. The lab had confirmed that the material the scarf was made from was the same as that of the blouse worn by the latest victim, and the blood matched hers, as well. Small victory, Sloan thought. He hadn't needed a lab test to know that.

He wondered how Regan and her sister and the girl were faring at the safe house. None of them had wanted to go. He'd practically had to force them into it. Only the threat against her sister and niece had convinced Regan McKinney to take the offered protection. She was one stubborn woman, Sloan thought, not without admiration. She was courageous, as well, and because she was both stubborn and courageous, she could easily put herself at risk.

He took out his cell phone and dialed the number at the safe house. The cop on duty answered, then turned the phone over to Regan.

"How's it going?" Sloan asked.

"It's the pits, what d'you think? Kat's hibernating, hiding behind a book, Blair's bored but doing better than her mother, and I'm about to go out of my frigging mind," Regan snapped. "What's going on? Did you find Peter?"

He wished. "No. He'd left the house before we got there."

"Are you sure it's Peter's house?"

"His name's not Peter. And it's not Adrian Pierce, either, although that's the name the guard at the gate knows him by."

"So who is he really?"

"The house, the car, and his phone are all registered in the name of Ed Johnson."

"Ed Johnson! You can't be serious."

Sloan frowned. "You know Ed Johnson?"

"I've met someone named Ed Johnson, and I can assure you, he's not Peter."

Ed Johnson was a common name, of course, but it was too much of a coincidence that Regan, the killer's target, knew an Ed Johnson. "How'd you meet this Ed Johson?"

"I'm doing a story for our magazine on Kevin Carrington. He's something of a local hero, a guy who made a bundle when he took his company public a few years back."

"What kind of company?"

"Apparently, he's something of a wizard at creating computer games."

Computer games.

Dance Till You Die?

"What does that have to do with Ed Johnson?" Sloan's heart picked up several beats.

"Johnson is one of the top men in Carrington's company, HomeRun, Inc. It's located in Palo Alto. Johnson was Carrington's first financial backer, and he's stayed with him over the years. I interviewed him on Monday, and I can tell you again, he's not Peter Smith."

HomeRun, Inc.

Louisville Sluggers?

Was Kevin Carrington a baseball fan?

Sloan's mind was furiously processing what she was telling him. Palo Alto wasn't far from the villa they'd raided this morning. Even though the security guard at the gated community said he'd never heard of Ed Johnson, was it possible that Johnson supported the man who Sloan decided for simplicity's sake to call Peter Smith? Could Johnson be Peter's father? Maybe "Peter Smith" was really Ed Johnson, Jr. Or maybe Ed Johnson was a half-brother or some other relation. Maybe even Peter's lover. All of the above could be possible.

"I've got to talk to this guy. How can I get hold of him?"

Regan gave him the phone number at HomeRun, Inc. He thanked her, hung up, and dialed the number, but it was answered by a recording device giving daytime office hours and taking messages.

"Shit."

"What's going on?" Kelly asked, leaning forward eagerly.

"Regan says she knows someone named Ed Johnson." He filled Kelly in on the conversation. "It's too late to catch him at work. I wonder where he lives?"

"Maybe Tommy Lee could look him up."

Sloan agreed, and Kelly placed a call to Lee. But two hours later, the efficient sheriff had been unable to locate an address for Johnson. He hung up with a promise to keep trying, but Sloan suspected they'd have to wait until morning to catch Johnson at work. *If* he was at work. But if he was the man they were after, he'd be as missing as his Jag.

79

Ed Johnson mixed a scotch and soda and sank wearily into an overstuffed chair. It had been one bitch of a day. He hadn't even had time to read the newspaper. He'd been tied up in emergency meetings all day. What a time for Kevin to pull one of his disappearing acts. HomeRun's stock was falling, investors were bailing, and Kevin was nowhere to be found to reassure them. That was the trouble with HomeRun, Inc. Everything depended on Kevin's genius. Without the boy wonder, they had nothing. He was the spider who controlled the web.

Johnson had been worried about Kevin for a long time. The young man had never seemed very stable to Ed, but in the past few months, he'd seemed even odder, more distracted, scattered. He knew this time of year was always hard for Kevin, for this was the time, early spring, when his brother had died, and a year later his mother had committed suicide on the same date, April 4. Tomorrow was April 4, he noted absently.

Maybe he should encourage Kevin to seek some help. He knew the young Carrington would resist. He was the most private person Johnson had ever met. But if they were to survive as a public company, Kevin must get his act straight. He had to deal with whatever was needling him and get over it.

The phone rang, and Johnson set his glass down. "Hello?"

At first, no one answered, but Johnson thought he heard the sound of someone weeping. "Hello? Who is this?"

"Ed. It's me. I need help."

A chill ran down Johnson's spine. "Kevin. Where are you? Are you all right?"

"Something . . . terrible's happening to me, Ed. I'm . . . afraid . . ."

"Where are you?" Ed asked again.

"At the Santa Barbara house. I've locked myself in, but of course, I can always get out, can't I?" He laughed wildly, unhappily. "I mustn't leave here, Ed. I'm afraid of what will happen. Please come."

"Of course I'll come. But let me get some help over there right now. Let me call someone to come and stay with you until I get there."

"No!" Kevin shouted, sounding suddenly angry. "No one can know about this. Except . . ." He paused, and when he spoke, Ed heard his voice again shift tone. It was softer, thoughtful. "Yes, there is someone. Yes, I need you to bring her. Maybe she can stop him . . ."

Her? Stop *him*? What was he talking about? Was there someone else there, someone who might harm Kevin? "Kevin, has somebody kidnapped you? What's going on?"

"Kidnapped?" Johnson heard Kevin exhale a sardonic, mirthless laugh. "No. And yes, you might say that. Or maybe 'hijacked' would be a better word for it. I don't know. Just bring her. Tell her Peter needs her. It's a matter of life or death. She has to come."

"Who's Peter?"

"Don't ask." Kevin's voice shifted back to the angry, brusque, demanding tone. "Just call her. Her name's Regan McKinney. She lives with her sister in San Francisco, but don't call her there. Use this number. It's her cell phone." He read off a number, but Johnson, too stunned to think, didn't write it down. After all, he had her card.

"How do you know Regan McKinney?" Johnson managed at last.

"Just bring her," Kevin barked, "and get here fast. Take the company plane." Ed Johnson heard a click, and the line went dead. He stared at the receiver, then slowly replaced it on the cradle.

His biggest fear had come true. Kevin had gone mad. He'd said he'd been kidnapped, or rather hijacked, but something about that didn't ring true. If he'd been kidnapped, he wouldn't have locked himself in, his captor would have. Maybe, Johnson thought with a shudder, in his demented mind, Kevin had kidnapped himself. Whatever, Johnson was dead certain that if he didn't get to him soon, the younger Carrington would hurt himself. He considered calling the Santa Barbara police, but when he envisioned Kevin opening the door to the police, all he saw was the image of Kevin putting a gun to his head.

No, he couldn't call the police.

Maybe he should call Michael Carrington. Johnson had never known why Kevin hated his father so, but maybe he blamed Michael for the deaths of his brother and mother. If Kevin was on a mental precipice, Michael should know about it. But then, if he got involved before Kevin was safe, he might send his son over the edge.

Ed Johnson was shaking as he went to his briefcase and drew out Regan McKinney's card. He had no idea how Kevin knew Regan. Or why she hadn't been honest with him. She'd tried hard to get an interview with Kevin, but apparently she already knew him. Were they lovers? Had they had a quarrel? Was her claim that she was writing a story on him for a magazine just a cover to try to get to him?

And who the hell was Peter?

Filled with questions, fear and dread, Ed Johnson dialed Regan's cell phone number.

80

Regan was in the bathtub when her cell phone rang. Blair, who was hanging out in her aunt's small bedroom, heard it, answered it, and smuggled it into the bathroom. "It's a Mr. Johnson," she whispered, cocking her head curiously at Regan.

"Hang on," Regan said, "let me get out of the water."

Regan stepped from the steaming bubble bath and wrapped herself in a towel. Her heart was pounding when she reached for the phone.

"Hello?"

"Regan, this is Ed Johnson." He sounded upset.

"What's wrong? What's happened?"

"Why didn't you tell me you know Kevin?"

Regan frowned and took a seat on the commode. "I don't know Kevin."

"Don't play with me. This is serious. Something's going on with him. He just called from his family's home in Santa Barbara. He was very upset, a little incoherent even, but he asked me to bring you there. He said, 'I need you to bring her. Maybe she can stop him . . .' Do you have any idea what he's talking about? Who could you stop, and from doing what?"

Regan's eyes widened in shock and disbelief. "He asked you to bring me to Santa Barbara? I can't imagine why. Like

I said, I don't even know him. And as for who I can stop
... Ed, I don't have a clue what's going on here."

"He said to tell you that Peter needs you. That it's a
matter of life or death."

Regan's heart dropped to the pit of her stomach. Dear
Jesus God, what *was* going on here? "Ed, I promise. I don't
know Kevin. But I do know someone named Peter."

"Well, who the hell is he? And why would Kevin say
such a thing?"

Regan waved Blair out of the bathroom, putting her finger
to her lips, warning her niece not to say anything. Blair nodded conspiratorially and left, shutting the door quietly behind
her. When she was gone, Regan lowered her voice.

"Ed, I have a good friend named Peter Smith. A very ...
special friend. It might not be the same Peter, but it's too
coincidental that Kevin said Peter needed me."

"Where is your friend Peter?"

"I ... don't know. You see, he ... Peter's in some trouble."

"What kind of trouble?"

Regan grimaced. She didn't want to tell Ed Johnson, but
she had to. This was too macabre, too scary. She had to learn
what was going on. "Remember I told you that a serial killer
was after me? Well, the police think Peter's the killer."

She heard Johnson swear softly on his end of the line.

"Kevin indicated he might have been kidnapped. Maybe
this Peter Smith kidnapped him and is going to murder him."

"Peter is neither a kidnapper nor a killer," Regan insisted.
"And besides, the serial killer doesn't go after men. He's
after women, redheads in particular."

"Like you."

Johnson's statement hit her hard. "Yeah, like me."

"Suppose Smith is the killer, and that he's using Kevin
as bait to get at you?" Johnson asked, verbalizing Regan's
own sudden doubts.

"Except I've never met Kevin. Why would Peter, if he's
the killer, which he's not, use Kevin to get to me? Why not
just call me up and make a date?"

It struck her at that moment that if Peter Smith had any
intention of killing her, he would have done so. He'd had

ample opportunity. He'd said he was being framed for the murders, that someone was setting him up. Who? Kevin Carrington? Was Carrington the murderer? She continued her line of thinking with growing horror. Maybe Kevin *was* the murderer. Maybe Kevin knew Peter had been dating her, and for some reason had decided to kill her, maybe to spite Peter.

"I know he doesn't have any living siblings, but does Kevin have any cousins or friends?" she asked Johnson. "Could Peter Smith be a friend or relation?"

"I've never heard of any cousins or known Kevin to have any close friends," Johnson told her. "Of course, I don't follow his every step. I suppose he could know somebody by that name."

Regan's mind was racing even as her stomach knotted. If she went with Johnson, she could be walking into a death trap. But if she didn't go, something bad might happen to Peter.

"Did Kevin ask me to come, or did Peter?" she asked Johnson, wondering suddenly if Kevin had already murdered Peter.

"Kevin said to bring you. That you might be able to stop 'him,' whoever 'him' is. He seemed to be speaking of a third party. He said to tell you that Peter needed you. That it was a matter of life or death," he repeated.

Life or death.

Whose? Peter's? Or hers?

And who was "him"?

She hedged, considering her options. She probably ought to call Sloan and let him take it from there.

"Look, Regan," Johnson said. "I need to know, are you going with me or not? I've got a terrible feeling that Kevin's gone off the deep end, and that he might commit suicide if I don't get to him soon."

Suicide? Or murder? Or both?

"Why not let the police handle this, Ed? I mean, they're trained to deal with things like this."

"I would, except I'm afraid that if the cops were to show up, Kevin might kill himself before we could get to him. Please, I beg you, don't call the police, not until we see what the situation is. I promise you, when we get there, if we need to, we'll bring in the proper authorities."

Damn straight, Regan thought. In her mind's eye she saw Kevin Carrington, a madman holed up in a house in Santa Barbara, holding Peter hostage at gunpoint. What would happen if she called Sloan, and his people made a raid on the house? She closed her eyes, saw gunfire, saw Peter fall, then saw the indistinguishable figure of the shooter turn the gun on himself.

No one would win in that scenario.

Regan made a sudden and irrational decision. If Peter needed her, she would go to him. But not without taking precautions. A plan began to form in her mind.

"I want to go with you, Ed. Can you pick me up?"

"Where are you?"

"In a safe house, in a town called Burlingame. Do you know it?"

"Yes, it's not far. What's the address?"

"I don't know. I'll have to find out where we are and call you back. I'll go with you, Ed, but if you don't want the police and the FBI on our tail, this has to be secret. I can't let anyone here know when I duck out, or else they'll be right behind us."

Regan hung up, blood singing in her ears. Was she doing the right thing? Could she pull this off?

Would she end up dead?

Her skin clammy, she donned her robe and slipped the small telephone into the pocket. She wrapped a towel around her hair and left the bathroom as if nothing had happened. Blair, of course, was waiting in the hall, obviously about to burst with curiosity. Regan signaled her to come into the bedroom and shut the door behind them.

"You've got to cool it, or you're going to blow everything," Regan said, as much to herself as her niece. "So calm down."

Regan hesitated to involve her niece, but she didn't want to head out on what could be an extemely dangerous journey without someone knowing where she was going. She'd take her cell phone, of course, but if something happened so that she wasn't able to call for help herself, at least Blair would be able to tell Sloan where to find her body.

She told Blair about Ed's call, and her decision to go to Santa Barbara.

"You think Kevin Carrington is going to kill Peter?" Blair said in anguish.

Regan drew her close and gave her a hug. She knew her niece had fallen a little bit in love with Peter, too. "I don't know what to think at this point. But I feel in my heart that I have to go. And I have to do it, at least at first, on Ed Johnson's terms, that we don't tell the police."

"But how're you going to get there?"

"That's where I need your help. Johnson will come for me, but I have to find out where we are. Then, we'll need to disarm the security system. I'll sneak out later after everyone's asleep. Most of all," she said, touching Blair's hair, "I'll need you to keep your mouth shut until I call and let you know it's okay to tell where I am. I mean, you can't even tell your mother. Can I trust you?"

Blair nodded, her face flushed with excitement. "I'll pretend I didn't know anything about this."

"Can you wangle your way into the confidence of our guardian out there and find out this address?"

"I can try."

"Then see if you can get him to show you how the alarm system works. You're a kid. You're curious. Maybe he'll show you the code if you play it right."

"But when they wake up and find you gone, they'll know I had a hand in it."

Regan frowned. Blair was right. And it wasn't fair to ask her niece to go this far for her. "You're right. Never mind. I'll handle the questions. Just don't tell anyone where I went, okay?"

The aunt and the niece did a high five. "Now, skedaddle and let me get dressed."

81

Regan made good her escape more easily than she'd thought possible. The guard had disarmed the alarm system earlier in the day when a delivery of groceries had been made, and he'd forgotten to reset it. When she realized it, Regan waited until the guard, Kat, and Blair were engrossed in a movie, snuck out the front door and ran down the block, where she read the street name, Monte Vista, on the sign. There was no number on the safe house, but it was between two houses with numbers on their mailboxes out front, and it was easy to figure out the address. She called Ed Johnson on her cell phone, set the rendezvous time for 2:30 a.m., and returned to the house unnoticed.

She now stood at the corner of Monte Vista and the cross street, Granada, her heart pounding so hard she was nearly dizzy. Her skin was hot and damp, although the air was chilly. She saw headlights approaching and a sudden, sickening thought occurred to her.

What if Ed Johnson had made this all up? What if he, not Kevin, was the killer? What if she'd walked right into his trap?

Her mind was playing games with her, she knew, but nothing about the supposed conversation between Ed and Kevin Carrington made sense. Maybe it was Johnson's ploy to lure her away from the protection she'd been afforded by the police. Calling herself every kind of fool, she started to run back toward the house, but it was too late. Johnson pulled up next to her in a Lincoln Town Car and rolled down his window.

"Ready?"

"I . . . I don't know, Ed. This is all so . . . weird. Maybe we should tell the police."

He killed the engine and got out of the car. His face was puffy, and his expression distraught. She could see he'd been crying. "Maybe that would be the best thing," he said, leaning against the car door, looking forlorn and confused. "I swear, I don't know what to do. I've always protected Kevin, and I feel like I should protect him now. If word of this gets out, we're dead on the stock market. But that's not the important thing. It's Kevin I'm frightened for. I called him back to tell him I'd located you and that you'd agreed to come, and he sounded so . . . different. It was his voice, and yet it wasn't. I'm worried that he's strung out on drugs or something. His mother OD'd, you know."

"Yes, I know," Regan said softly. "On April fourth. That's today." Ed Johnson was a man who cared deeply about the mentally disturbed Kevin Carrington. And he was no serial killer. "Let's go."

82

Sam Sloan arrived at Kelly's office after a restless night. He couldn't shake the nagging feeling that he should have tried to find Ed Johnson last night instead of waiting for regular business hours. He poured himself a cup of coffee, looked at his watch, and willed the eight o'clock hour to come. According to the recording he'd heard the night before, HomeRun, Inc., opened its doors at eight A.M.

He tried the number five minutes early, but got the recording again. He dialed at eight o'clock. The recording greeted him. He dialed at 8:01.

"Good morning. HomeRun, Inc. How may I help you?"

"Ed Johnson, please."

"Mr. Johnson isn't in yet this morning. May I take a message?"

Damn. "Do you expect him in soon?"

"He's usually here by now, so I'm sure he'll be here shortly. May I tell him who called?"

"No, I'll try again later." Sloan hung up the phone and grabbed his coat. He turned to Kelly. "Let's go."

They were halfway to Palo Alto when his cell phone rang. It was Craig Watkins, the guard on duty at the safe house.

"Regan's gone."

Sloan swore a blue streak. "You sure? Maybe she slipped

out for a jog. She told me she likes to do that early in the morning."

"Her purse is missing. She wouldn't go jogging with her purse."

Sloan heard Kat Bowen's voice in the background, then she came on the line. "Sloan," she said, and she sounded hysterical, "how could you let this happen? Regan's been kidnapped."

Sloan felt his own creeping hysteria threaten his composure. "She wasn't kidnapped. She must have left of her own volition, since she took her purse."

"But . . . Peter must have gotten to her somehow. She wouldn't have done this unless she thought she could somehow help Peter."

Sloan had to agree, except . . . there wasn't any Peter. "You stay there. Promise me you won't leave. I'm checking on something that might help us find her. I'll get back to you when I know more. In the meantime, stay put in case she calls. And if she calls, you contact me immediately. Okay?"

He heard a small sob. "Okay," Kat said at last, then added, "Sloan, I'm so scared."

He was scared, too, but he couldn't let her know that. "We'll find her." He hoped he sounded more reassuring than he felt. "Please, just do as I ask. We don't need anything else to go wrong."

She hung up without further comment, and Sloan wondered if she was as strong-willed as her sister. Would Kat stay put? "Call your people," he barked at Kelly. "Get some more men over there. I don't care if the whole world sees the place surrounded by cops. At least it ought to keep this creep away from those two until we can nail his ass."

83

"I'm sorry, sir," the receptionist told Sloan after they'd managed to get by the security guard at the headquarters of HomeRun, Inc. "Mr. Johnson hasn't come in yet this morning. In fact," she said, glancing at the clock on the wall, "this is very unusual. I'm getting a little worried."

"Has anyone called his house?"

The woman looked uneasy. "Maybe I'd better let you talk to Mr. Beatty. He knows Mr. Johnson better than I do."

She rang a number and spoke into her headset briefly, then turned to Sloan. "Mr. Beatty will be out to see you momentarily."

"Who's Beatty?" Kelly wanted to know.

"He's Mr. Carrington's assistant," she told him.

"Who's Carrington?"

She looked at him as if he were an idiot. "Kevin Carrington? He's the reason any of us are here. He's the guy behind the products. The computer genius who comes up with all the games."

Sloan guessed he'd forgotten to mention Carrington's name to Kelly. "Regan was assigned to do a story on Carrington," he explained. "That's how she met Ed Johnson." Before he could say anything more, the door to the inner sanctum burst open, and a short, dapper man came at them. "What's going on here?" he demanded.

Sloan instinctively didn't like Richard Beatty. He was too pretty, and too sneery. He offered Beatty his ID. "We're looking for Ed Johnson."

Beatty glared at him. "What for?"

"We have some questions we want to ask him. Know where we might find him?"

Sloan suspected this arrogant little man knew where to find Johnson, but he guessed he wasn't about to tell. Not unless he was forced to. This was the kind of guy who savored and used whatever bit of power came his way.

"He hasn't come in yet," Beatty said.

"We know that. Want to give him a call at his house?"

Beatty eyed him with contempt. "Whatever you want of him, I can assure you, Mr. Sloan, that Ed Johnson is the most honest man on earth."

"Good. Then maybe he can answer our questions. Call him."

Beatty led them through the doors and into the privacy of his office, where he did as Sloan asked and dialed Johnson's home number. Or at least he dialed a number he claimed was Johnson's, but there was no answer. When the machine picked up, he left a terse message. "Johnson, it's Beatty. Call in." Then he hung up.

"What's this about, Mr. Sloan?"

"It's about murder, Mr. Beatty. And if you don't fully cooperate with us in this investigation, you could be charged with aiding and abetting."

The well-dressed man scowled. "Murder? You think Ed Johnson is a murderer?"

"He owns a villa south of Pacifica, down on the coast," Sloan said, sounding deliberately patronizing to annoy the little prick, "in which we found a coat. That coat was covered in blood. That blood matches the blood of a recent victim of a serial killer. I'd say that's reason enough for us to want to talk to Mr. Johnson."

Sloan took a piece of newspaper from his inside pocket, carefully unfolded it, and laid it in front of Beatty.

"Is this Johnson?" he asked pointing to the photo of Peter Smith from the front page article that had appeared the day before.

He saw the blood drain from Beatty's face as the small man eased into his desk chair. "No," he answered in a voice pitched a notch too high.

Sloan could see Beatty recognized the man in the photo. "If it's not Ed Johnson, then who is it?"

It took only a moment for Richard Beatty to recompose himself. "I have no idea. The face looks vaguely familiar, but it's certainly not Ed Johnson. Ed's older, balding . . ."

"Who is Peter Smith?" Sloan demanded, but Beatty looked up at him with an unwavering gaze. "I don't know anyone named Peter Smith."

Sloan uttered a low growl of exasperation. "Well, where can I find Johnson then? Does he live at that villa?"

"No. He has a place here in Palo Alto."

"What's the address?" Kelly asked, and wrote down the information Beatty gave them.

"Who lives at the villa?"

Sloan saw Beatty clench his jaw. "I have no idea," he replied. "I don't know anything about any villa."

Sloan knew he was lying, protecting someone. Peter Smith? "What about a vintage Jag? According to the records, Johnson owns one of those, too."

But Beatty remained unflappable. "No. He drives one of our company cars. A Lincoln Town Car. I've never seen him driving a Jag."

Sloan didn't bother to mention the phone being registered in Johnson's name, too. He knew Beatty wasn't telling everything he knew—his loyalty to Johnson, or Peter Smith, ran deep. Sloan decided to let it go for now. He gave Beatty a card. "Here's my number." He took the cell phone from his belt. "I'll answer it day or night. You call me if you see Johnson. Or better yet," he added, knowing it wasn't going to happen, "have Johnson give me a call."

84

THURSDAY, 8:55 A.M.

Regan ached clear down to her bones when she awoke. They'd been on the road nearly seven hours. Johnson had thought they'd be able to take HomeRun's corporate jet, but when they'd gotten to the airport, he'd learned that the pilot, who was always supposed to be on standby, was ill and unavailable. So they'd had to make the drive instead.

It had been pitch-black dark and raining when they'd headed south, but now the storm had passed, and a blazing, intense sun assaulted her eyes from the east. "Where are we?" she asked sleepily.

Ed Johnson had pulled his car in front of an imposing white stucco structure. It looked like a residence, but it was bigger than any house Regan had ever lived in. This one could have been a small hotel. "We're here," he said, turning off the engine.

And then the fog cleared from Regan's mind, and she remembered where they'd been headed, several hours ago.

Santa Barbara. This must be the Carrington mansion. Tall, stately palm trees lined the drive of the lushly landscaped estate.

Regan and Ed Johnson had not talked much on the long drive from Burlingame. She suspected they were both too scared and bewildered to try to make sense of this bizarre episode. She glanced at Ed and saw the exhaustion on his face and in his body as he slumped forward on the steering wheel and peered out the windshield at the mansion.

"You okay?" she asked, worried that he was having a heart attack or something.

Johnson let out a long breath. "Yeah. I'm okay. Just glad to be here." He unfastened his seat belt. "You stay here. Let me go first . . . in case . . . something's wrong."

Johnson got out of the car and walked beneath an imposing portico to the front door. She saw him ring the bell. Her heart was in her throat as she waited. After a long while, it seemed to her, the door was opened by someone she couldn't see, and Ed Johnson disappeared inside.

Now what? Regan wondered. She felt inside her purse and took out her cell phone. She pressed in the number Sloan had given her—his personal cell number, in case she needed to get hold of him—but she didn't punch the send button. Not just yet. Only in case something was wrong here.

A few minutes later, however, the door opened again and Johnson came back to the car.

"He's . . . okay," he said, but his eyes were troubled.

"Is Peter there? Is he okay?"

"I didn't see anyone but Kevin. But he says he wants to see you."

Regan opened the door and got out, shouldering her handbag, fingering the cell phone inside. This whole thing was too creepy.

She followed Johnson into the house, which was tightly shuttered against the outside sunlight. It took a moment for her eyes to adjust.

"In here," Johnson said and beckoned her farther into the interior of the cavernous mansion.

At first, she only saw his silhouette, a dark shadow against the lighter shadows of the drawn draperies. "Mr. Carrington?" she said, her voice sounding like a squeak in her ears.

He turned and stepped toward her, and Regan froze in shock and alarm. She opened her mouth to speak, but no words came.

Kevin Carrington moved closer, close enough for her to see he hadn't shaved in days. His clothing was rumpled, his

hair was disheveled, and his eyes seemed swollen and bloodshot. In spite of his unkempt appearance, she knew him instantly.

"Peter?"

85

"Peter isn't here." The man gave the bitch a smile of deep satisfaction. The plan had worked perfectly. "He sends his regards."

He saw Regan McKinney take a step backward even as Ed Johnson, that old fart, moved toward him.

"Kevin, what on earth's going on here?" Johnson demanded.

The man drew his hand from behind his back and aimed the gun he held at Johnson.

"Don't call me Kevin. I'm sick to death of Kevin. Kevin's gone now. He's never coming back. I'm in charge now."

The pair stood dumbstruck, staring at him, and the man began to laugh. "You never knew Kevin," he said at last to Ed Johnson. "You always thought you knew everything about him. But you didn't know jackshit."

"Kevin, let me get you some help," Johnson pleaded.

The man raised the gun ever so slightly. "I don't need your goddamned help. I don't need anybody's help, not even from Milquetoast Peter."

"But . . . you're Peter . . ." Regan whispered, still staring at him in shock.

Again the man laughed. He'd looked forward to this moment, but he hadn't expected it to be so much fun. "No, I'm

Adrian. Peter's gone out. I don't know when he'll be back. *If* he'll back."

"Are . . . you his . . . twin?" she asked.

The man snorted with contempt. "Twin? No. There's way more than two of us."

"What are you talking about?" Johnson said. "Who are you?"

"Shut up, old man, or I'll kill you right now," he said, grinning maliciously, "instead of in a few minutes." He turned his attention to the woman, and his eyes lost their focus slightly. Yes, it was her. Briana was back, here in this house. It was perfect. It was all so perfect.

Still holding his gun on Ed Johnson, the man went to the sound system that took up nearly one whole wall of the room. He pressed a button, and music roared into the room.

Music—hard, hot, and heavy—blasted into his mind, a mean, cruel, unrelenting rhythm that twisted through his brain.

Ka-thud. Ka-thud. Ka-thud.

It was that night again, and they'd come for him. Again.

But this time, it wouldn't happen. It would never happen again.

"Leave me alone." He turned to the man in the room who stood poised to grab him. "Go away. I won't do it."

He began to tremble and sweat, and he was unaware of anything except the fear that consumed him. He had to face these two. He had to get rid of them. They were monsters. They'd killed Darrin. They'd kill him, too, if he didn't kill them first.

He saw the man coming at him. Where was his bat? What could he use to stave off the attack? Sweat dripped into his eyes, further blurring his vision.

"Kevin, stop this," Ed Johnson said to him. "You're scaring me."

"I'm not Kevin!" the man screeched. "I'm Adrian. Don't come any closer . . ."

He heard a shot and felt his arm jolt upward as the casing ricocheted to the side, but he was unaware that he'd been holding a pistol. He looked at the gun in his hand. Where had that come from?

He looked at the man who slumped to the floor. From somewhere far away, he heard the woman scream. He saw her go to the man, but he wrenched her by the arm before she could help him.

"Let the bastard die," he growled, pulling her away. She was biting and kicking at him, screaming her head off. Good. He wanted her to scream. He wanted to hear her scream for a very long time. Just as Darrin had screamed. Right here in this house when Briana and her lover boy had killed him.

"Let me go," the woman yelled. "You're crazy."

Crazy.

No. He wasn't crazy. It was Kevin who was crazy, or who thought he was crazy. But he, Adrian Pierce, was in full command of his senses, and now he was in control of the others, as well. He'd sent them all away for now. He had a job to do, for them as well as for himself. When he'd finished, he would summon them, and they would all know that finally, they were safe. And that it was he, Adrian, and not Kevin or Peter, who'd protected them.

86

Regan stared in horror at the pool of blood that trickled from beneath Ed Johnson's body, which lay crumpled at her feet. Dear God, was he dead? She tried to go to him, but the madman had a visegrip on her arm. She looked at him and saw a sickening smile creep onto his lips.

"Come here!" he commanded, drawing her closer.

Her mind was numb with shock and terror. The music split her eardrums, a heavy-metal sound, horrible and hot and loud. Before she realized what was happening, the man tucked the gun in the waist of his jeans and took her by both arms.

"We're gonna have a little dance." His eyes looked glazed, and his face was contorted in a mask of rage.

His strength seemed superhuman. His fingers dug into her flesh, and he shook her to the rhythm of the intense beat. She tried to twist out of his arms, but he held her easily and played with her, as if she were a doll or a puppet. Around and around they went in a macabre sort of dance. Slowly, his arms moved upward, and just before they reached her neck, she suddenly recognized the grisly scenario. She was the figure in the cartoon she'd seen on the Internet. And this . . . monster . . . was the serial killer.

Sam Sloan had been right. Or almost right. Peter had been

involved in this somehow, but at that instant Regan doubted she'd ever know exactly how.

Because right now, this man . . . Kevin Carrington or Adrian Pierce or whoever he was . . . was going to kill her.

87

Peter struggled to surface, tasting danger in his mouth, feeling terror in every cell. He was being held down by Adrian, whom he'd always known was stronger but whom he'd been able to dominate by sheer wit and will. But now, Adrian was out there, and he was hurting the only person—other than the children—whom Peter had ever loved. If he didn't come forth, Regan McKinney would die.

With a herculean effort, he thrust upward, overcoming Adrian's strength, and when he did, he found himself with his hands around Regan's neck. He let go of her and stepped backward in shock. She stood before him, quaking, her hands at her neck, too terrorized to speak, even to scream.

"Oh, dear God, what's happened?" Peter said, breathless from the struggle. But in that instant, everything suddenly became clear. He understood all that had been going on with Adrian these past months. Adrian had learned to break free. Adrian, the one who carried the rage. Adrian, who knew no remorse. It was Adrian who'd been killing those women. And just now, he'd nearly taken Regan's life.

Peter was more afraid than he'd ever been in his life. Regan was in terrible danger. He was in danger, as well, and so were the children. They were all in danger. Somebody had to stop Adrian. But the only way to stop Adrian was to physically kill him, and if he died, they all would die. A sob jerked his body.

"Get out," he rasped at Regan. "Leave, now, before . . ."

But it was too late. Adrian was back with a vengeance. He whipped out the gun and pointed it at Regan.

"Don't listen to him. He's not in charge here," he said in a guttural tone.

It's not her, a voice screamed in Adrian's ear.

Adrian chose to ignore it. He glared at the cunt who stood eyes wide, paralyzed with fear. "So, you think your sweet little Peter can save you?" he sneered at her. "Don't count on it. Peter's weak, just like Kevin. I'm the only strong one in the bunch."

She's not Briana! The voice was even louder, more insistent.

Adrian hesitated and peered closely at the woman. Of course she was Briana. Looked just like her. Red hair, big breasts, same face. His rage boiled hotter.

No! She's not Briana! Don't kill the wrong woman! Find Briana!

Each short sentence resounded in his mind like the stroke of a baseball bat.

Ka-thud.

That bastard Peter was getting in his way. He must find a way to get rid of Peter like he had Kevin.

Find Briana!

Briana. The very name instilled both fear and fury. The man knew where Briana was. But Kevin had kept him from going there and taking care of this years ago, as he should have done. But Kevin was gone now. And the voice he was hearing was right—the time had come to find Briana and make her pay.

He stared at the woman who stood in the room with him. The voice had been right. This wasn't Briana. But he'd have to kill her anyway. She knew too much. But something inside, or someone inside, wouldn't let him do it. With a curse, he motioned her with the gun toward the garage.

"We're going to take a little ride, missy."

88

Regan gazed in disbelief at the man who'd nearly strangled her. It was Peter, she could swear it. For one brief moment, when he'd let her go, she'd looked up to see his facial features soften, his eyes lose their brittle madness, and in that moment, she'd seen Peter behind those eyes.

But in an instant he was gone, and the madman was back. And clearly this man was insane. He even spoke as if there were another person in the room with them, someone she couldn't see.

Astonishingly, she was alive. Her arms throbbed where he'd held her so brutally. She wasn't sure why he'd stopped before he tried to strangle her, because she knew he'd meant to. She had a reprieve. For now. Her mind raced, trying to think of a way to escape. "I . . . we can't leave him," she pleaded, pointing to Ed Johnson's inert form on the floor.

"He's not going anywhere." The man stared at the body of Ed Johnson, and Regan got the chilling sense that he was entirely detached from his grisly deed. As he must have been when he killed those women. As he would be when he decided to quit playing with her and get it over with.

He stalked over to her and gave her a rough shove toward the back of the house. "You'd better do as I say, now, before I change my mind."

With a last glance at Ed, Regan did as she was ordered.

They went through a kitchen big enough to serve a restaurant, then through a pantry and storage area, arriving at last at the door to the garage. "Open it," he commanded.

She did, and when she saw what was parked inside, her knees went even weaker, if that were possible. There in front of her was Peter's Jag. Her mind tried to wrap around the unthinkable, that this madman was indeed Peter Smith. He looked like Peter, but then again, not exactly. This man was scruffy, and his eyes bulged with rage. His voice wasn't Peter's voice, either. The man who called himself Adrian was neither Peter Smith nor Kevin Carrington, although Ed Johnson had thought he was Carrington.

Regan had never studied psychology, but a sudden notion struck her. Could this man *be* Peter, and Kevin, and Adrian? Could he be more than one personality? A multiple personality?

She had no time to consider the bizarre possibility. The man waved the gun at her and jerked his head toward the second vehicle that was parked in the garage, a huge, black Lincoln Navigator. She'd seen that vehicle before, she was certain of it, but at the moment she couldn't remember where.

"Get in," he snarled. "And don't try anything. I'm short on patience today."

He held the gun on her as she opened the passenger door, then he went quickly to the driver's side. In that moment when she was left unguarded, Regan slipped her hand inside her purse which was still dangling from her shoulder. She found the cell phone, into which she'd earlier entered Sloan's number. She didn't dare try to talk to Sloan, but she had to contact him. She pressed "send," dropped the phone and kicked it under Peter's Jag. She had no idea if Sloan could trace its location, but maybe he'd be able to. At least it might lead him to Ed Johnson, if he was still alive.

"What're you doing fooling around?" the man barked. "Get in."

Regan hoisted herself up into the leather seat, heart racing, all senses on overdrive. Maybe when they got into the mainstream of traffic, she could jump out at a stoplight and make a run for it. For some reason, the killer had spared her

from the fate his other victims had met. He'd held her in his
death dance, and then he'd let her go. She didn't know why,
but he'd bought her a little time, and she intended to find a
way to use it to escape.

A funky smell rose up to meet her as soon as she closed
the car door. It was a thick, metallic odor, cloying and sickening. She glanced over her shoulder and stifled yet another
scream. The back of the car, devoid of a seat, was covered
in blood. Red-brown stains were swashed over the tan floor
and sidewalls. Small chunks of matter that looked suspiciously biological in nature were scattered and spattered
everywhere, and along one side were lined several bloodied
baseball bats. Nausea rose and overwhelmed her. She
reached for the door handle, barely opening the door in time
to retch onto the garage floor.

"Shut the goddamned door," the man shouted at her, and
she felt the nuzzle of cold metal on her arm. He held the
gun on her as she righted herself once again, dizzy, terrified,
exhausted, and despairing of escape. If she'd had any doubt
that this man whom Ed thought was Kevin Carrington, who
called himself Adrian Pierce, and who she now feared was
also the Peter she loved, was the serial killer, those doubts
were out the window. Those were the baseball bats he'd used
to bludgeon the victims. This was the car he'd used to transport their bodies from wherever he'd killed them to where
he'd dumped them in the bay.

And now, she was the transportee.

89

Sloan and Kelly called ahead to alert the guards at the Burlingame safe house that they were approaching. When they turned the corner onto the street, Sloan was gratified to see a phalanx of police cars cordoning off the area. The SFPD would have to find another safe house for future needs, because the cover was blown on this one.

The carelessness of the guard on duty last night had cost the department a safe house, and might have cost Regan her life.

Sloan intended to have his ass for it.

Inside, Kat stood by the window, staring out at the nondescript backyard, rubbing her arms as if she were chilled. She turned and looked at him out of large, accusing eyes. "How could you let this happen?" she said, her voice low and husky. He could tell she'd been crying.

How, indeed, had he let Regan give them the slip? It was his fault for not taking the damned cell phone away from her. He'd known she'd do something foolish, and yet he'd let her keep the phone. He was losing it. Goddamned if he wasn't losing it. And because of his mistake, Regan would probably die.

He glanced at Blair, who was at the table hunkered over her computer. She looked up at Sloan, and something about the look on her face told him that she knew something about Regan's escape.

"It's my fault, Ms. Bowen," he said, feeling Kat's frustration and fear, "for not confiscating her cell phone. The guard on duty last night has been canned, at least for now, and there's an army of cops out there."

"Fat lot of good that's doing Regan."

Sloan went to Kat. He knew she was a strong woman. He'd seen how she'd taken the news about Cameron Pace—all of it—and how she'd stuck by him anyway. She'd also been there for her sister through this horrid ordeal. But this morning she seemed fragile, defeated. He wanted to reassure her, but he couldn't lie.

"Your sister must have left of her own volition," he said at last. "She wasn't kidnapped."

"She was in love with Peter Smith," Kat said. "She never believed he could be the killer. He must have called her on the cell phone and convinced her to see him."

"I was afraid of that," Sloan said, exhaling a defeated sigh. "Goddammit, why wouldn't she listen to me?"

"She's in love," Kat repeated. "She believes in Peter. If he called and asked her to help him, she'd do it in a heartbeat."

Sloan didn't comment further, but inwardly he cursed Regan's naïveté. She was in love with a murderer, and by going with him, had in essence likely signed her death warrant.

The keyboard was clacking loudly as Blair worked away at whatever computer game she was playing. Sloan moved toward her, and he saw her deliberately hit a button that cleared the screen.

"What're you working on?" he asked her.

"Nothing. Just playing a stupid kid's game."

He saw Kat turn her head sharply toward her daughter. She frowned but said nothing, and Sloan could guess her thoughts—this bright little cookie would never play a kid's game.

"Want to show me?"

"Oh, it's nothing you'd like." She popped out of her chair and went into the kitchen. "Want some coffee? It's not too old."

"No, thanks." He followed her into the kitchen and stood

behind her, placing his hands on her shoulders. "I want to see what you're doing on that computer." Slowly, gently but deliberately, he turned the girl to face him. "Tell me what you know."

He saw her press her lips together.

"You helped her, didn't you?"

Blair Bowen dropped her gaze from his, but held her silence. Her mother came into the room and stood beside Sloan, her eyes on her daughter.

"Blair, do you know something?"

"If you know where Regan went, please tell us," Sloan urged. "Your aunt is in terrible danger."

"Where is she, Blair?" Kat shrieked, taking her daughter fiercely by the arms. "Where did she go? Who did she go with?"

The young girl's eyes widened at her mother's wrath, and then they filled with tears.

"She . . . she went with Ed Johnson, to Santa Barbara, to Kevin Carrington's house . . . to . . . help Peter . . ."

Sloan closed his eyes and felt a knot form in his stomach. He'd already guessed that Regan had run to her lover, but the girl's confirmation made him almost ill. He wasn't exactly sure of the relationship between Ed Johnson, Peter Smith, Kevin Carrington, and Adrian Pierce, but they seemed to add up to a deadly combination. And Regan Mc-Kinney was right in the middle of it.

His cell phone rang, but it took him a moment to realize it. He pressed the button to receive. "Sloan here."

Nobody replied.

"Hello. Sloan here," he said again. But there seemed to be nothing but dead air on the line.

"Who is this?" he demanded, then looked at the digital printout on the caller ID. He swore under his breath as he recognized Regan's number. "Regan? Is that you? Hello, Regan? Talk to me."

Dead air.

Sloan knew instantly that Regan was in terrible trouble, but her incoming call gave him a ray of grim hope. At least she was still alive, or had been moments before when she dialed his number.

90

Ed Johnson awoke in darkness, and pain seared his body when he tried to move. His tongue was thick, and he couldn't think clearly. Something had happened to him. Something to do with Kevin.

And then it came back with sickening clarity. Kevin, the boy he'd loved, protected, and supported, had shot him.

Johnson lay back on the floor, the pain in his heart worse than the wound in his body.

"Why?" he murmured into the silence.

He thought he heard sounds nearby. Was Kevin still here? Where was Regan McKinney? Had he shot her, too? Before he had time to consider it further, the noises became louder.

"Cover me," he heard someone say.

Then footsteps sounded on the tile floor. Someone was coming in through the kitchen. The lights went on, and Johnson shut his eyes to the glare of the overhead tracks that beamed down on him like spotlights.

"Somebody's down," a voice shouted. The footsteps came closer.

"Careful. Check out the rest of the house. I'll see if he's alive."

Johnson opened his eyes to see a uniformed policeman kneeling beside him.

"Take it easy," the officer said. "It's going to be okay."

Ed Johnson knew nothing in his life was ever going to be okay again. At the moment, he didn't care if he lived or died. Everything he'd worked for in the past twenty years was gone, including the man he'd loved like a son, Kevin Carrington. He didn't know what had happened or why, but Kevin had gone off the deep end. Clearly, he was mad. And he was a murderer.

Johnson lay still while the paramedics gathered around him. He didn't care what they did to save him. He didn't particularly want to live. The only reason he must survive for a while was to help Regan McKinney. He was reponsible for bringing her here, and he'd placed her life in jeopardy. He had to do what he could to save her.

If she wasn't already dead.

91

Just short of an hour after receiving Regan's call, Sloan's cell phone rang again, and he grabbed for it. He'd been pacing and swearing silently, waiting for news. "Sloan here."

"We've got Johnson. He's been shot." It was Ron Perkins, chief of the Santa Barbara Police Department. Sloan had called them immediately after Blair confessed that Regan had gone with Ed Johnson to the Carrington mansion in Santa Barbara.

"Johnson's been shot? Is he alive?"

"Yes, but he's unconscious. They're taking him to the hospital as we speak."

The knot in Sloan's gut tightened. "Where's the woman?"

"No sign of her. There's a car in the garage. An older model Jag in mint condition. But it looks like another vehicle was parked there until recently."

Christ, he'd kidnapped her. Sloan didn't want to think about another possible scenario, that he'd already killed her and was taking her body to dump in the ocean somewhere. "Our perp has taken the woman," he managed from between clenched jaws. "What kind of car was it, do you know?"

"My people are checking the tire tracks now. It's something big, like some kind of heavy-duty SUV or something."

"Check for prints on the Jag, too," Sloan ordered, wishing like hell he could somehow transport himself to that garage in Santa Barbara, some three hundred miles to the south. He always appreciated the work of helpful law enforcement agencies, but these guys didn't have any idea the type of criminal they were dealing with here.

"Anything else?" He knew he sounded terse to the other officer, but he couldn't help it. His nerves were about to snap.

Ron Perkins hesitated slightly, then said, "Yes, there's . . . vomit on the garage floor near what would be the passenger side of the vehicle, if it was parked in the garage frontward."

"Vomit?"

"Yes. Looks like someone upchucked there fairly recently."

Sloan supposed that vomit was better than blood. Had Regan been that frightened that she'd thrown up when the killer forced her into the car? The thought set his teeth on edge, but at the same time offered a flicker of hope. If she'd vomited when she got into the car, that meant she was alive.

"You said Johnson was unconscious. Was he conscious at any time after you got there? Did anyone talk to him?"

"The paramedics told me he was conscious briefly just when they arrived, but then he passed out. He took a bullet through his shoulder and lost a lot of blood. He could have died if we hadn't shown up when we did. It's a good thing you called."

Sloan heard someone interrupt Perkins but couldn't make out what was being said. Then Perkins spoke to him again.

"My people just found a cell phone under the Jag. We'll try to trace the serial number and see if we can find out who the owner is."

But Sloan knew whose phone it was. Regan must have managed to dial his number and ditch the phone before being taken away in the SUV. At least at that point, she must have been unhurt and mentally alert, able to send some signal for help.

"Have your people check on automobiles registered to these names in your county—Kevin Carrington, Ed Johnson, Adrian Pierce, and Peter Smith—and get back to me right away. Regan McKinney's been kidnapped, probably at gunpoint since Johnson was shot. We've got to find her. This man's seriously deranged, Perkins. We think he's the serial killer we've been after up here in San Francisco."

Ron Perkins let out a low whistle. "What do you suppose he was doing at the Carrington mansion?"

"Good question. Who lives at the mansion?"

"Nobody. Place has been closed up for years." Perkins was interrupted again by his officers. "Look, I gotta go. I'll get back with you when we get the place checked out."

Sloan thanked the man and pressed the end button on his cell phone. He turned to Kat and Blair. "What do you know about Kevin Carrington other than that he's a computer genius who hit the big time?"

"He's the son of a movie star who was famous in the sixties," Blair offered, "and his mother looked just like Regan."

Sloan gritted his teeth. Why hadn't anyone bothered to mention any of this to him? "What do you mean, she looked like Regan?"

"Here, I can show you." Blair pressed a key to wake up her sleeping laptop computer, then accessed the Internet. She took Sloan directly to the site she and Regan had discovered earlier, "Lili.com," and there before his eyes, the image of Liliane LaRue opened his mind to a whole new set of possibilities.

"She does look like Regan, don't you think?" Blair said. "Only this woman's a lot thinner. Don't tell Regan I said that," she added.

Despite the difference in weight, the resemblance was remarkable. Sloan believed the serial murderer was killing women who reminded him of someone else. Kevin Carrington's mother looked like Regan. If his theory was correct, then Carrington had to be the killer, not Peter Smith. But where did Smith fit into the picture? And the elusive Adrian Pierce? And Ed Johnson, for that matter?

"Where is this woman?" he asked.

"Oh, she's dead. She died a long time ago, in fact, when Kevin Carrington was just a little boy."

Died a long time ago. Not available for killing now. So he has to make do with look-alikes. Sloan's mind was spinning.

"Does anybody know what Kevin Carrington looks like? Is there anything about him on there?" he asked, pointing to the computer.

"Oh, sure. Regan found lots." She manipulated the keyboard and brought up the image of Carrington wearing baseball cap and glasses, his face mostly shadowed by the bill of the cap. "It's hard to say what he really looks like," Blair told him, "because you can't see his face. And this isn't a photograph. It's just an artist's rendering."

Indeed, it looked like something a police artist might come up with. He studied the image, but physically, Kevin Carrington remained an enigma. "Is this the only picture you found?"

"Yeah. Ed Johnson told Regan that Kevin doesn't like to have his picture taken."

Murderers generally don't.

"Who's the famous movie-star father?" he asked, thinking there might be a family resemblance between father and son. He needed to get something out on the police network, an image of some sort so law enforcement officers would know who they were looking for.

"Michael Carrington. Want to see him?"

"Yes."

Michael Carrington's photos were numerous, mostly taken from tabloids and therefore a little murky, but Sloan recognized him even though he'd been just a kid in Michael Carrington's heyday. Unfortunately, father and son bore little resemblance, as far as he could tell. He wondered where Michael was now.

"Is he alive?" he asked the girl who seemed to know more than he about the killer.

"Yes. Regan said Johnson told her he was alive, but I don't know where he lives."

Sloan rubbed his eyes. "We'll find out. In the meantime I'd give my eyeteeth for a better picture of Kevin Carrington."

Blair fingered the keyboard. "I . . . uh, could show you something I've been working on. Maybe it would help."

Sloan stood on one side, Kat on the other, as Blair opened a file, the one, Sloan suspected, she'd attempted to hide from him earlier. Kevin Carrington's ball-capped image appeared on the screen.

"I got this off the Net," she said, a little proudly. "Now, watch this." She clicked the mouse, and a second image came on the screen. It was the same as the first, except in this one, there was no ball cap. "I took his hat off, electronically speaking," she said. "He looks kind of familiar, but I can't figure out why."

Kat leaned forward. "Well, I'll be damned," she murmured, studying the screen. "Can you take off his glasses and give him a shave, Blair?"

Using an eraser icon from the tool bar, Blair did as her mother asked, and as they watched, Kevin Carrington was transformed into a man Kat and Blair both knew.

"Peter Smith."

92

Regan was grossly uncomfortable, in addition to being scared witless by the man who drove the vehicle along the Pacific Coast Highway. She hadn't been able to use the bathroom in hours, and it was becoming critical that they stop somewhere soon. But she didn't know how to ask, or whom.

Because the man who drove the big black Lincoln Navigator didn't seem to be one person. Ed Johnson had believed he was Kevin Carrington. At one point, she'd thought he was Peter. This man called himself Adrian, and he mumbled and talked to himself as he drove, had entire conversations, in fact, with different imaginary characters in his mind. At times, his words were heavily accented, as if he were from a foreign country, but when he answered himself, his voice took on different sounds, accents, qualities, and intonations. Some of the responses were higher in pitch, like children talking. Once she was startled to hear a voice that sounded a lot like Peter's, but that conversation hadn't lasted but a sentence or two.

It was an amazing performance, brilliant even, if it hadn't been so terrifying. This man, this single person, seemed not only to be Kevin and Peter and Adrian, but a host of other personalities, as well. Regan had heard of the phenomenon called multiple personality disorder, but she'd taken stories like *The Three Faces of Eve* and *Sybil* to be more entertainment than reality. Now she fully believed they were true and that multiple personality disorder existed, because the madman behind the wheel was living, breathing proof.

Regan didn't know where they were headed, but the digital compass on the bloodstained luxury vehicle told her they were driving north, sometimes north-northwest. They went through a tunnel, and when they came out, the ocean had disappeared behind bare, brown mountains.

At last, her discomfort made her bold. "I need to go to the bathroom," she told him. "Could we please stop somewhere soon?"

The man looked at her as if she were the one who was crazy. His face was mottled, his skin red and blotchy, and his eyes bulged. He didn't answer, and he didn't stop.

"Please," Regan begged a little while later. They were on U.S. 101 now, a major highway that connected southern and northern California. Fast-food places and gas stations were everywhere, but she doubted he'd let her out of his sight. What did he care about her discomfort? Indeed, what was a little urine on his fancy car seats when blood was everywhere?

At San Luis Obispo, they left the main artery and headed up Route One, the coastal highway. When they passed Morro Bay and reached a less populated area near San Simeon, the man pulled the car over onto the shoulder of the road. He took the gun that had been resting in his lap for most of the trip, and he pointed it at her. Regan expected to die.

"Get out," he said.

She stared at him. Was he going to let her go? Or was he going to kill her here and drive on? She reached for the door handle and opened it. The sour taste in her mouth from having thrown up mingled with the fear that renewed its intensity.

"Get out," he yelled, and his eyes bulged even further. "You said you had to pee. Go do it, or shut up."

Regan jumped down from the vehicle and looked around for a bush or a tree, but there was nothing but a hillside rising steeply from the shoulder of the road. Terrified, humiliated, but in pain, she squatted beside the vehicle's large tire and relieved herself.

When she was finished, she thought about trying to make a run for it, but there was nowhere to run. The two-lane road was empty and open, and she'd be exposed, an easy target. She had no idea where they were headed, but the man had been talking to himself about "getting her at last," and "making him pay." It sounded as if he had a distinct destination in mind. Whatever mission he was on, he seemed to have lost his immediate interest in killing her.

"You about done?" His ragged voice came to her on the wind.

"Yes. Thank you." Regan snapped her jeans shut, glanced over her shoulder one last time at the empty road, and got back in the car.

The man seemed to forget about her after that. He drove holding the steering wheel in one hand, the gun in the other, but he paid no attention to her. She noticed he jiggled his leg as he drove and wondered why he hadn't taken advantage of their rest stop as she had. A few minutes later, he seemed to realize she was there after all and said, "Open the glove box and get out those CDs. I want some music."

Regan did as she was told. Anything to keep him happy until she could find a way to get away from him.

Inside the glove compartment was a small box that held half a dozen CDs. She took it out and opened it with trembling hands. There were five disks by artists she recognized—all acid rock from the seventies and eighties—and the soundtrack from the Muppet movie.

"What would you like to hear?"

The man turned to her, and his facial muscles relaxed into a radiant smile. "I love it when they let me drive," he said, sounding as if he were Blair's age. "Put on the Muppet movie."

93

The sudden shift in personalities nearly unhinged Regan all over again. At least this persona seemed less threatening. She slipped the disk into the player, and from the corner of her eye, saw the driver settle back against the seat as the familiar sound of Kermit the Frog's singing filled the car. Glancing at her captor, she saw that his eyes were no longer bulging, and his skin tone had gone pale. He was leaning back in a relaxed posture, looking only vaguely like the animal who'd kidnapped her.

He'd let the gun slide from his hand. It rested, however, in the V of his crotch, not exactly accessible to her. She heard him begin to hum in time to the music.

Regan thought about Blair and Kat and Sloan. They were bound to be looking for her by now. She didn't know if Sloan would be able to trace the cell phone, or even if he'd gotten the call. She just hoped to God that by now Blair had broken her promise and told Kat and Sloan where she'd gone.

Suddenly, the man hit the brakes, sending her forward with such a jolt that the seat belt locked, cutting painfully into her shoulder.

"Turn off that crap," he yelled. Regan sat frozen, unable to do anything other than stare at him in shock and terror.

Bulgy-eyes was back. "I said, turn off that music. I can't stand that shit."

Regan reached to press the eject button, her stomach queasy all over again. She removed the CD, and the radio came on with a hiss and scratch that hurt her ears. She turned it off.

"Who told you to do that?" the man screamed at her, his face contorted with rage. He picked up the gun and aimed it at her face. "You think you can control me, bitch? You think you can make me do whatever you and your slimy friends want? Well, no more. I'm through with you. From now on, you'll do as I say. You'll dance to my tunes, and," he laughed gutturally "you'll dance till you die."

Regan swallowed. *Dance Till You Die.* Those words had been on the lurid, grisly Internet cartoon. Now she knew who'd sent it. Sloan had remarked that the killer must be a computer genius, smart enough to evade detection even by the sophisticated FBI Carnivore system.

Computer genius.

Kevin Carrington.

Aka Adrian Pierce, et. al.

She had never been around an insane person before, certainly not a wild-eyed crazy killer. He was talking to her as if he knew her, even though he did not. Who, in his crazy, mixed-up mind, did he think she was?

She recalled something Sloan had told her, his theory that the serial killer was murdering women who reminded him of someone he hated and wanted to kill. Someone who'd likely abused him in childhood. Someone he wanted to kill, but for some reason, couldn't. She thought of the image of Liliane LaRue, Kevin's mother, the woman whom she herself strongly resembled.

If this was Kevin Carrington, was he in his insanity trying to kill his mother?

In his sick mind, was she now his mother? She quelled a shudder. She had to do something to calm him down.

"I never meant to control you, Kevin," she said, in a conciliatory tone.

He snorted. "Kevin? I keep telling you, I'm not Kevin. And you're not a very smart bitch, are you?"

Regan bit her lip. Should she say anything else or just keep quiet?

"Answer me, bitch!" he shrieked, waving the gun. "Tell me how really stupid you are."

Sweat prickled her brow and ran down her spine. "I'm really stupid," she murmured. If she agreed, maybe he wouldn't pull the trigger.

They were stopped in the middle of the road, and a car approached from the rear, honking its horn. The-man-who-wasn't-Kevin whipped his head around in fury at the oncoming vehicle. He swung the gun out the window and pulled off a shot that shattered the car's windshield. "Arrogant bastard," the man muttered, stepping on the accelerator and sending Regan back against the seat with the same force she'd been thrown against the seat belt when they stopped.

They drove in silence, the driver taking the dangerous, winding coastal road at breakneck speed. Regan grasped the armrests so tightly that her fingers soon ached. They passed Cambria, and she saw a road sign that read: Carmel, 95 Miles.

The driver smiled when he too saw the road sign. He laid the gun in his lap again and reached for a cell phone she hadn't noticed tucked into a holder above the rearview mirror. He paid no attention to her as he dialed, punching in the numbers as calmly as if he were about to make dinner reservations. He held the phone to his ear, kept the other hand on the wheel, and slowed to a safer speed.

"Dad, hi," he said, and cleared his throat. "This is Kevin."

94

Peter Smith had never been so terrified in his life, nor so unsure of his decisions. But then, he hadn't known the depth of Adrian's hatred, the lethal intensity of his rage. Adrian had eased past him, little by little, and had fooled him into complacency. Peter had had no idea when Adrian had come and gone, or what he did while he was away. Adrian always managed to show up when Peter went looking for him, always had a story that covered his real activities.

But Peter knew now what Adrian had become. He knew that it was Adrian who'd killed those women in San Francisco. And he knew that unless he did something, Adrian would murder Regan.

That's why he'd let Adrian take control for now. Or at least, Adrian thought he was in control. But it was Peter who'd set it all up. Adrian was only the instrument, the means by which Peter could at last end the nightmare. He regretted that Regan had to be involved, but he needed her. She was pivotal to the success of his plan.

He hoped she loved him enough to do what he was about to ask.

When Peter had discovered that Adrian had chosen murder as his revenge, he knew the time had come when they all must face their demons. The horror and the hiding had gone on long enough. Regardless of what Kevin wanted, they must end it, and to end it, they must face the beginning of it. And no matter what happened in the next few hours, Peter swore to protect Regan. He would not let her become yet another victim of the obscenity that had started it all.

Peter kept a close eye on Adrian as he traveled. He'd managed to extract a promise from the rage-bearer that he wouldn't hurt Regan, although he didn't trust Adrian to keep that promise. His rage had spun out of control. Peter lurked just beneath the surface, crouching, watching, keeping vigil on the frightened woman locked in her seat belt next to the man who would destroy them all.

95

Sloan and Kelly charged through the streets of San Francisco, racing against time and the whims of a madman. A helicopter awaited them, along with a team of sharpshooters, at the Ferry Building heliport. They were to be airlifted to a destination south of Carmel, a remote, exclusive community, reportedly the home of Michael Carrington.

Shortly after Blair had unmasked Kevin Carrington, and they'd recognized him as Peter Smith, Sloan's phone had rung again. It was Ron Perkins in Santa Barbara.

"Johnson's awake," he'd told Sloan. "He said he was shot by Kevin Carrington. He gave us a description of the car he's probably driving, a black Lincoln Navigator, company vehicle, by the way, not registered to any of those names you gave me. But we've got the tag number now, and it's out statewide."

"Where's he taking her?" Sloan wanted to know. But Johnson had apparently drawn a blank on that one.

"Could be headed back to San Francisco or Palo Alto. Could be going to Mexico." Perkins also gave Sloan a brief rundown on what had been discovered at the Carrington mansion.

But Sloan's mind wasn't on evidence, no matter how intriguing. His only priority was to find Regan. As he hung up, he mentally went over all that he knew about the killer,

reviewing the data he'd collected in his profile. The pieces
suddenly began to fall into place, the haze that had surrounded the case lifted, and Sloan understood clearly where
Kevin Carrington was headed.

On the Internet, Sloan had read about the tragic death of
Kevin's brother, and that a year later, on the same day, April
4, his mother had committed suicide. Then Blair had told
him that Regan had learned Kevin was estranged from his
father. In his gut, Sloan knew there was more to what had
happened in Kevin's young life than met the eye. Something,
he was certain, to do with Michael Carrington. He was also
certain that it was no coincidence that Carrington had made
his move today. It was April 4.

The photo of Liliane LaRue looked so much like Regan,
it didn't take a rocket scientist to deduct that the mother was
the true target of the killer's rage. But Liliane was dead.
Kevin couldn't kill her again. So he'd killed the others instead. Now, he'd taken Regan. And for some reason known
only to the psychopath, Kevin Carrington had let Regan live,
at least for now. He needed her for something, and that
something, Sloan was certain, had to do with his father.
Kevin was taking Regan home to daddy.

But where was daddy?

It had taken far too long, considering the resources available to him, but Sloan had at last discovered the whereabouts
of the aging movie star who'd fathered a child who'd become a serial killer. He'd been unable to find Carrington's
phone number, however, and there was no time to waste.
His people would keep trying to contact Michael to warn
him of what was about to happen. In the meantime, praying
that the gods were on his side, Sloan raced to get there in
time to save Regan's life.

96

Regan's muscles ached from tension and travel when the driver at last turned off the main highway and made his way up a steep, winding road into the mountains. She'd guessed from his syrupy, apologetic conversation with someone he called Dad, a dialogue that had taken place in an altogether different voice than she'd heard so far from the man, that she must be headed toward Michael Carrington's secret retreat. The speaker, Kevin or whoever-it-was, had been conciliatory and had specifically asked if "Aunt Briana" was there, as he wanted to apologize to her as well for staying gone so long.

The Prodigal Son was returning home.

Regan inhaled a deep, silent breath, bracing for the terror she was certain awaited at the end of this road. Michael Carrington had no idea what was headed his way. He expected a happy reunion with his son. Instead, he was going to be visited by a crazed killer.

The gates to the property swung open as if by magic when they approached, and Regan spotted a security camera mounted on a post nearby. She wondered what Michael Carrington was thinking right now. What was he feeling? And who was Aunt Briana?

They drove a long way into the desolate wilderness, it seemed, observed only by the scrubby vegetation that was native to the mountains. The road was unpaved, and they kicked up a wake of white gravel dust behind the vehicle. At last they turned a bend in the road, and in spite of her terror, Regan drew in a stunned breath at the sight that met her eyes.

The house glimmered white and pristine in the afternoon sun and looked for all the world like some exotic Eastern temple. She'd never seen the Taj Mahal, but those words came to her mind as a fit description of this place. Huge and imposing, the mansion covered most of the open hillside, with turrets and towers topped with tiles of deep blue. Beyond and far below, the Pacific stretched into infinity.

The driver slowed, then came to a halt and surveyed the place, a slight frown creasing his forehead. Had he been here before, Regan wondered, or was this the first time he'd seen his father's palace? Was he as awestruck as she?

Regan saw him grip the gun, then he stepped on the accelerator again. He pulled the Navigator into the circular drive that led to what she guessed was the front of the house, although with this structure, it was hard to tell. This could be the servants' entrance, for all she knew.

She saw the door open, and an unimposing figure dressed in khaki-colored slacks and a polo-style shirt came out of the house. He wasn't particularly handsome, although his features were pleasing enough. His thinning hair was tousled by the wind as he waited at the top of the steps.

This was Michael Carrington, the famous movie star?

"Get out," the man said gruffly and waved the gun at her.

Regan couldn't wait to get out. She opened the door and hopped to terra firma, hoping that somehow this place would offer safety and rescue.

Michael Carrington gave her a curious look, and then he broke into a smile. She knew what he must be thinking, that his son had at long last met a woman and was romantically involved with her. That Kevin had brought his bride-to-be, or maybe his bride, to meet the family. That she was the reason for this unexpected reunion.

She saw his smile fade, however, as he looked past her to the man who approached, aiming a gun at him.

"Hello, Daddy," the man said with an ugly sneer. "What's

the matter? Aren't you going to invite us in?"

Michael Carrington's face turned three shades of pale, and he started to back into the house, but Kevin pulled the trigger, sending a bullet into the white stucco walls. He hadn't aimed at his father, but if he had, he could easily have killed him.

"Kevin. I . . . I don't understand. What're you doing?"

"My name's not Kevin, asshole. You destroyed Kevin a long time ago. He died, the same as Darrin."

"What . . . are you talking about?"

Regan saw the fear in Michael Carrington's eyes, fear not only for his own life, but fear of Kevin's madness.

"Oh, come on, Father dear, let's go inside, and I'll explain it all." The speaker's tone was sarcastic, patronizing. He put the barrel of the gun to the back of Regan's head. "Inside."

Michael, apparently frozen with fear, took halting steps backward into the house, followed by Regan and Kevin. They entered a grand foyer that soared three stories into the air. Brilliant California sunlight poured in through high windows, washing the elegant structure and rendering it with a kind of celestial purity.

Regan wondered with a shudder how much blood that light would soon illuminate on the pristine white walls. She darted her gaze around, looking for a telephone or some other means she might use to contact the outside world. Were there other people here? Should she shout out a warning? She saw no one except Michael Carrington.

The foyer opened onto a long, tiled hallway, a loggia of sorts, that looked out over the sea on the left. On the right, she saw arched doorways and assumed they must lead to rooms along the way. There was no phone anywhere in sight, not that she'd have a chance to use it if there were. The metal of the gun was warming against the skin of her scalp.

If she'd taken a course in self-defense instead of that damned ballroom dancing, she thought cynically, she might have had the ability to disarm him, but she didn't dare try anything. At least not at the moment.

"Where's Briana?" the man asked brusquely.

"She . . . she's on her way. She doesn't live here, you know."

Her captor snorted. "I don't know why not. You've been screwing her for years. Even . . ." He hesitated, then said with deliberate malice, "when Mother was alive."

"Kevin," Michael protested, but the man turned the gun on him, and he shut up.

"I told you, I'm not Kevin."

Regan saw the beads of perspiration on Michael's forehead and noticed the pulse beating heavily in a vein in his neck.

"So . . . who are you, then?" Michael asked.

"I'm Adrian. Adrian Pierce. Don't you have a more comfortable place where we can wait for Briana?"

The little party of terror moved down the hall and into a gracious living area, furnished with an Oriental flair.

"Nice digs, Pop," Adrian said, looking around. "Too bad you never invited Kevin here."

"You . . . I mean Kevin . . . wouldn't have come," Michael replied heavily. Regan saw him glance toward the door and guessed he would try to warn the woman named Briana away if he could. If he did, however, Regan believed Kevin/Adrian would murder him on the spot.

"No, I suppose he wouldn't," Adrian agreed amiably. "Something about being around you makes him nervous. Scared, actually, the silly twit. He's a coward, if you ask me. If he'd let me, I'd have killed you—and the bitch—a long time ago."

"Son, you're not making any sense," Michael protested. "You're Kevin, not someone named Adrian. I've known you all your life."

"You haven't known dick," the man spat out. Regan saw his face begin to mottle with red splotches, and his eyes bulged with rage. "You were never home, Daddykins. You were never around to know what happened to Kevin and Darrin. She killed Darrin, you know. Beat the living shit out of him with his baseball bat when he was trying to protect Kevin from her faggot boyfriend. They used to fuck Darrin and Kevin, did you know that, Daddy?"

Michael Carrington dropped into a chair, his mouth open, gaping at the speaker. Regan took in a sharp breath and held it. She covered her mouth with the back of her hand. This madman . . . Kevin, Adrian . . . was accusing someone of unspeakable horrors. Had he made this up, or was he telling the truth?

With his gun trained steadily on them, Adrian moved away from Regan and went to stand in the doorway. He too was watching for Briana. "That's right, Mr. Carrington," he went on when Michael didn't speak. "While you were off seeing the world and being Mr. Movie Star, Briana and the fags she hung with used your sons like little cunts. Used to make them dance to their obscene music, then poked them and sucked them until Darrin finally had enough. When he stood up to them, they killed him. And you know what else, Mr. Movie Star? They laughed when they did it. Strung out on drugs, bellies full of booze, they just laughed and laughed, and then they took him out and fed him to the fish."

"No," Michael managed at last. "No. You're lying. I don't know why you're making this up, Kevin, but Briana would never do such a thing. She loved you boys. That's why I took her up on her offer to take care of you after Liliane died."

"Liliane." The killer's eyes suddenly misted. "Mother. She never knew what a monster her sister was. Mother would never have left us at all, if *you,* you sorry bastard, hadn't made her go away." The hand that held the gun was shaking violently, and fury underlined every word.

Regan stared at the man and saw a tear slip from his eye and run down his cheek. Her mind was reeling. Briana was Liliane's sister? Michael's lover? Darrin's murderer? Kevin's molester? Surely the madman was making up tales.

Just then she heard the door burst open, and a husky female voice echoed in the hall.

"Kevin! My darling Kevin, you've come for a visit at last!"

Kevin, or Adrian, slowly turned to face her, and her enthusiasm vanished at the sight of the gun. She stopped in mid-stride.

"Kevin?"

97

Kevin Carrington stared at the woman who entered the house calling out his name as if she were his long-lost mother. This couldn't be Briana. This woman was old and dumpy, with faded hair and a puffy, wrinkled face.

"Briana?"

"What's . . . going on here, Kevin?" she asked cautiously.

Kevin wasn't sure what was going on. He didn't exactly know where he was or how he got here. He became aware that there was a gun in his hand, and he nearly dropped it. He looked into the living room and saw his father, or an old man who resembled his father, and a strange woman who looked eerily like his mother.

Kevin returned his gaze to Briana, and a wave of fear swept over him.

"Don't hurt me," he pleaded. In his mind, he was a small child again, a boy with his back to the wall, helpless, defenseless against the attack he knew was to come.

"Hurt you?" Briana said, her expression turning dark. "I would never hurt you, Kevin. Why would you say such a thing?"

But Kevin was gone. Another boy was there to endure the pain and humiliation.

"You can't hurt Kevin," he said. "Kevin isn't here."

He saw a look of confusion on her face. "Who . . . what . . . ?"

The boy laughed. He wasn't afraid of the old witch, because he couldn't feel pain. She couldn't hurt him if she wanted to. And this time, if she tried anything, he had a gun.

"My name's Bobby. You don't know it, but it was me you hurt, not Kevin. It was me you and your buggery boyfriends played with all those nights. But don't worry. I didn't feel a thing." The boy felt a sob welling up inside and wondered who was crying.

"You killed Darrin," a voice said, and rage boiled once again in Adrian's breast as he took over. "You killed Kevin's brother the night I was born."

"You're insane," Briana uttered and took a step back.

Adrian raised the gun and pulled the trigger. "And you're a whore," he replied as she screamed and crumpled to the floor. He lowered the gun and let it drop from his hand. It hit the clay tiles with a loud clatter. But he was unaware of anything but the music that thrummed in his ears.

Hard. Hot. Heavy music, with a cruel, unrelenting rhythm.

Ka-thud. Ka-thud. Ka-thud.

He strode to where Briana had fallen and saw her staring up at him, eyes wide with terror.

Good. She wasn't dead. Yet.

"May I have this dance?" he said.

98

Regan watched the tableau in shock and disbelief. The man picked Briana's substantial body up from the floor as if she weighed nothing. He took her by the shoulders and began to dance with her to the beat of some music only he could hear. Regan knew that dance. She'd seen it before. She'd danced it. And she knew where it would end.

She eyed the gun, then looked at Michael Carrington. The man appeared frozen in a state of dazed shock and seemed unable to move. Adrenaline poured through her veins, and her ears began to ring. What should she do? She wasn't strong enough to fight the man physically. The gun was her only chance.

Could she do it? Could she shoot Kevin Carrington?

Quaking, she edged toward the gun. She had no choice. She had to disable him, or he would kill Briana, and then likely, her as well. Maybe his father. Maybe himself.

He was paying no attention to her as she moved stealthily toward the gun. It was cold and heavy in her hand when she picked it up. She blinked away tears of fear and swallowed the rock that seemed lodged in her throat. She raised the gun and pointed it at Kevin.

Then suddenly, he turned to face her, placing the woman's body in the line of fire. She released the pressure on the trigger but didn't lower the gun. "Let her go," Regan said in a raspy voice. "She can't hurt you anymore."

"She killed him," the man said. "She killed Darrin."

Regan thought he would complete the dance macabre by strangling the nearly limp woman he held at arm's length, but instead, he released her, and she fell again to the floor. He turned and faced Regan.

"End it," he said, and with a chill, she recognized his voice. His face softened, his demeanor changed before her eyes, and he was Peter. "End it," he begged. "Please, for God's sake and mine, pull the trigger."

"Peter?"

"I'm Peter, and I'm Kevin, and Adrian and Bobby and a host of others. Remember those kids I told you about?" He smiled sadly. "I don't expect you to understand, Regan. But I beg you, help me end the nightmare."

Regan stared at Peter, her heart in shreds. "Oh, dear God," she murmured. She wanted to go to him, to draw him into her arms and hold him and rock him and tell him everything was going to be okay. But he wasn't just Peter. He was Adrian, as well. A vicious, insane killer who'd taken many lives, and who would take more given the chance.

"Let me call somebody," she said. "We'll get you help, Peter."

But it was Adrian who now faced her. "Cunt!" he shouted and lunged toward her.

Reflexively, Regan McKinney pulled the trigger, and the bullet slammed into the man's chest, freezing him in mid-stride, like a video that's been put on pause. He gave her a strange, unbelieving look, then fell to his knees. His gaze met hers, and in it, she saw both love and gratitude.

"Peter!" she screamed and ran to him. He collapsed into her arms.

"Regan," he said, barely above a whisper. "I'm sorry."

His body went limp and heavy against hers. "Peter, no. Don't die. I'm sorry . . . I didn't mean to . . ."

But Peter was unconscious. Regan began to shake with tremors of emotion—a release of terror, a renewed horror, a feverish heat, an icy chill—all danced through her body. She didn't understand what had happened. How it could have happened. All she knew was that Peter was dying. She looked down at him, held him closer, and cried while his life faded into a pool of blood on her jeans.

99

Sloan peered out of the bubble of the helicopter at what looked like a fortress perched on the cliff above which the craft hovered. He bit his lip when he saw the black Lincoln Navigator parked in the drive. Was he too late?

"Want me to set it down, sir?" asked the pilot.

Sloan nodded. "Take it as close to the back of the house as you can." The Carrington castle, as he would refer to it ever after, was sited on a large clearing, making it easy for a helicopter to land. He guessed the wealthy recluse probably used helicopters from time to time to get in and out of this remote wilderness. But the openness also made them an easy target if Kevin Carrington had heard their approach.

A parade of police and emergency vehicles from surrounding counties and municipalities were poised at the entrance gate, which had been disarmed and forced open. Sloan radioed the team leader to proceed with caution. He didn't know what they would find in this elegant fortress, or what kind of battle would ensue. He prayed for Regan's safety, but held out little hope.

The chopper landed on the gravel, the blades stirring a cloud of white dust around them. The SWAT team disbursed to the vantage points they'd sighted from the air, weapons ready. Sloan took his gun from his holster, jumped off the aircraft, then signaled for the pilot to take off again. His orders were to hover nearby, out of gunshot range, and wait for the signal to return when the firefight was over.

The police cars and two ambulances raced up to the house and formed a tight arc around the front door. The back of the house overlooked a cliff that dropped several hundred feet to the highway below, and then plummeted on down to the sea. Anyone attempting to escape that way would die trying. Sloan's pulse was pounding heavily as he gave the order for the police to use their bullhorn.

"This is the police," the tinny voice crackled into the late afternoon air. "You are surrounded. Come out with your hands up. I repeat, this is the police. You are surrounded. Come out with your hands up."

From where he crouched at the side of the house, Sloan could see the front door. For a long moment, nothing happened. It was suddenly preternaturally quiet on the hillside. Even the wind had gone still.

And then, the door opened, ever so slowly, and a man raised his hands and stepped out. Kevin Carrington?

This was entirely too easy, Sloan thought, gripping his gun even tighter. Then he realized this man was old enough to be the father, Michael Carrington.

"Don't shoot," the man said, then lowered his hands and covered his face. He fell to his knees, sobbing.

Cautiously, Sloan eased around the corner and ran up the steps, pressing his body against the side of the house.

"Where's Kevin?" he demanded.

The older Carrington shook his head in grief. "He's inside. It's okay. He can't hurt anyone anymore. He's dead."

Sloan wanted to believe Michael Carrington, but he'd been a cop for too many years to trust appearances. He kicked the door open and spun inside, gun extended. He saw three figures on the floor, and his heart contracted with pain. He *was* too late.

But Regan raised her head. "Sloan?"

He ran to her, kneeling beside her. "Are you hurt?"

Her face was white and ravaged by tears. "Only in my heart," she whispered.

He looked at the man slumped in her arms. "Peter Smith?"

She nodded. "And Kevin Carrington. And a bunch of others. Oh, Sam, it's horrible."

It was the first time she'd called him Sam, and her grief went right to his heart. He put his arm around her shoulder, knowing it was little comfort for all she'd endured. Sloan didn't know what she meant by Kevin being more than one person, but he didn't have time to find out at the moment. He turned to the other inert figure. "Who's that?"

"The woman he was trying to kill all along. His aunt, Briana. Is she dead?"

Sloan checked and found a pulse, then glanced in all directions. "Anyone else in the house?"

"I don't think so."

"Stay right there. I'll get the medics."

100

The helicopter raised another swirl of dust as it took off from the scene of the horror, and Regan huddled against Sam Sloan, not caring that she didn't know him very well. She was desperate for human comfort, in whatever form it came. Her body still quaked with uncontrollable spasms, and her head ached with the pressure of her tear-swollen sinuses. She shut her eyes, but all she could see was the tortured face of the man she'd known, and loved, as Peter Smith. The man who'd treated her with kindness and respect, made her feel worthwhile. Who'd made love to her with a magical passion.

The man who was also a killer.

Kat and Blair were waiting for her when the helicopter landed in San Francisco, and Regan ran into their open arms. She allowed herself to be engulfed in their tearful embraces, and her own tears rose again, as if they could wash away the horror of all that had happened. At last, she broke away. She looked gratefully at Kat, brushed a strand of hair behind Blair's ear, and said, "Let's go home."

IOI

Sam Sloan sat in a darkened conference room in the Hall of Justice, his eyes riveted on the large screen on the wall in front of him. Next to him were Regan McKinney, Kat Bowen, Brad Kelly, and numerous other FBI agents and law enforcement officers. Michael Carrington had declined to come. He'd been examined and released at the hospital, but he'd remained with the woman named Briana Jones, who was in critical condition, but who was expected to live.

Also viewing the tape were two psychiatrists, one in private practice who treated patients who suffered from DID, or disassociative identity disorder, also known as multiple personality disorder. The other was a professor at UC Berkeley who was engaged in research of the controversial phenomenon.

If anyone had any doubts about the existence of this particular kind of mental illness, they'd change their mind when they saw this video, Sloan thought.

Either that, or Kevin Carrington was a far more talented actor than his father.

Sloan had seen the video the day before, and he was still stunned and amazed by its content. The Santa Barbara police had discovered it in the Carrington mansion, where Kevin Carrington apparently had been going for some time to record the sad and bizarre tale of his life, a tale that validated the story Regan had heard from the madman's own lips.

There was no question in Sloan's mind that if Regan hadn't been with him the day he drove to his father's house, Kevin would have murdered both Michael Carrington and Briana Jones, his aunt, then taken his own life.

And if what Kevin had told Regan, and what he'd recorded on the tape was true, he wouldn't have blamed him.

An image suddenly filled the screen, preceded by no introduction or soundtrack. This was your basic home movie. Kevin Carrington, dressed in a plaid shirt and baseball cap, looked solemnly into the camera.

"My name is Kevin Carrington," he said, "and I believe I'm losing my mind. There's something inside of me, something dark and frightful I can't seem to control, and I'm afraid I'm going to hurt someone. There are large chunks of time missing from my memory, I hear voices in my head, I see visions, and from time to time, I find evidence that somebody has been in my house. I know this is impossible, for I live a highly protected life. Yet, there's the ice cream, the baseball bats, clothes that aren't mine. The music, that horrible music, I don't know where that's coming from. Sometimes it's inside my head, but then I'll find a CD in the player and don't know how it got there."

This was when the video started to get interesting. Sloan glanced at Regan, whose expression was impassive. His heart went out to her. This was the man she'd thought she'd loved, and under the same circumstances, he thought it would be almost impossible for him to cope with the enormity of what she'd been through. What she was about to see and learn about Peter Smith taxed even the most open of minds.

Kevin Carrington suddenly stood up and threw off the baseball cap. His face turned beet-red, and his eyes bulged, bullfroglike. "I put it there, candyass," the speaker said, and his voice held no resemblance to that of Kevin Carrington. "I put it there to remind me, you, us, of what happened. You don't remember what happened, do you, Kevin? Well, I remember. So do Peter and Bobby and the rest. But you're too chicken to face it. Well, I'm not. Not only am I going to face it, I'm going to kill that bitch who did this to us. So you just cower down there, Kevin old boy, and let good old Adrian handle it." He sneered into the camera.

"I'm the one who's always handled things because the wimp couldn't bear it. I didn't plan on making this little tape, but since I'm here, let me just say that I'm making her pay for what she did. I'll play with her and scare her shitless, like she did Kevin and Darrin. I'll torment her and laugh in her face, and then, I'll kill her and feed her to the fish."

He reached for a button, and the scene faded to black. A low murmur rippled through the room, but the viewers grew quiet again as the second scene began. It was Kevin again, this time sitting with one leg draped over the arm of the chair, swinging rapidly. He didn't have the ball cap on this time, and he was wearing a T-shirt rather than the plaid flannel. He was eating a huge bowl of ice cream. "I'm Bobby. Kevin knows about me, but he doesn't ever talk to me. He buys me ice cream and pretty much lets me do what I want, so I hang around. He thinks he's going crazy, but he's not. He's a normal kind of guy, 'cause he's got all of us going for him. Except he doesn't know about all of us, 'cause we're quite a big family now. There's Erin B., and Johnnyboy, and Skunk and Marcella." He leaned his head back and closed his eyes. "There's Moe, but we don't see her very much, and Markie, he's just a baby." He looked back into the camera, and his expression darkened. "And there's Adrian. I'm afraid of him. So are a lot of the others. I go to Peter whenever Adrian's around. Peter loves me. He takes care of me, of us all. I hope Peter never goes away."

He grew quiet and just sat there, swinging his leg and eating his ice cream. "Fast-forward," Sloan told the technician who was running the video. "He does this for about half an hour."

He turned to Regan. "Are you all right?"

She chewed on her lower lip and shook her head. "No, can't say as I am," she replied.

"Do you want to watch the rest, or is this too difficult for you?"

She inhaled and let her breath out slowly. She reached for her sister's hand. She batted her eyelids as if to clear away tears. "I want to see it all. This was Peter, no matter who or what else he was. I loved Peter, and I believed in him. I . . . it's just so hard to believe this."

"It gets graphic in a little while," he warned her.

But then, she'd already heard that part two days ago, from the mouth of the killer, who revealed that he'd once been the victim.

102

Regan held on to Kat's hand for dear life as the video progressed and she saw Peter "take the stand," so to speak. This was all too overwhelming for her to grasp, and yet she'd witnessed the unholy transformations in the man for herself. How could one physical body hold so many personas? And how on earth did the same body take on such different aspects and forms? It was as if Kevin Carrington were a Claymation figure that was molded by whatever personality was in charge at the time. On camera, Kevin looked and acted like the geeky genius he was. He generally wore the ball cap and plaid shirt. He also wore glasses. But when another personality surfaced and took off the cap, removed the glasses, or wore different clothing, she didn't recognize him as Kevin.

Peter appeared in a blue oxford-cloth button-down shirt, chinos, and brown loafers. Emotion tightened her throat as Regan watched him begin to speak.

"I'm Peter," he said simply, "and it's my job to manage our little family. I was born when Kevin was small, after Darrin died. There was no one Kevin could turn to. His father was gone all the time, and Kevin was left in the care of his mother's sister, Briana Jones. But Briana wasn't the loving auntie Michael Carrington trusted to care for his son. Or did he trust her? Sometimes I wonder if he knew all along what was going on, but didn't step in to stop it." He paused and gave a self-deprecating laugh. "I'm not a psychologist, but I often wonder why Michael didn't listen to Kevin. I know Kevin tried to tell his father, but Michael didn't believe him. Nobody would listen to him. Nobody, it seemed, cared. That's why I'm here. I was born to care."

103

Regan went limp from physical and emotional exhaustion when the tape reached its conclusion. Apparently, Kevin wasn't quite finished with his story when he'd asked Ed Johnson to bring her to Santa Barbara, which triggered the tragic ending to an even more tragic tale.

Had it been Kevin who'd requested she come, she wondered, or had it been Peter? Had he called her in desperation, seeking her help in ending his torment?

End it . . . Please, for God's sake and mine, pull the trigger.

She looked at Kat when the lights came on. Her sister's face was pale, and she'd been crying. "Oh, dear God, those poor, poor boys," she said, wiping her eyes with a tissue. "Could this be true, Sam, or is it just the work of a demented mind?"

Regan had been wondering the same thing. Had Peter been mad all along?

"Let's hear what the experts have to say." Those in the room were grouped around a conference table. "Dr. Amundson," he said, speaking to the private physician. "Could you please give us your opinion of what you just saw?"

The psychiatrist was small of stature, thin and bald and sad-looking, as if his profession had worn him down over the years.

"This man is the son of an actor," he began, "and it's possible this was all staged to prepare his defense should he be caught and charged with the murders." He toyed with the edge of his mustache. "We'll never know for sure, now that he's gone. But if this wasn't a staged production, and I feel strongly that it was not, then you have here a classic example of a severely dissociated personality."

"Could you explain?" Sloan asked.

Regan saw that this was clearly difficult for the doctor.

"In my experience," he said slowly, "patients who suffer from DID have experienced prolonged and severe sexual abuse from an early age. It's the one thing they seem to have in common. Children are sexually undeveloped human beings, and when the sexuality of young children is violated, they lose their feeling of self-efficacy. They no longer believe they have control over their lives. They become anxious, compulsive, and in some cases, they dissociate completely in order to cope.

"When a woman is raped," he continued, "it's a tragedy, and it often takes years for her to overcome the trauma. But when a child is raped, that trauma goes even deeper. Sometimes the child copes by dissociating from the events and people surrounding the abuse. They create 'alters,' separate personalities who take the abuse so they don't have to."

"Do you believe that's what could have happened here?"

Dr. Amundson drummed his fingers on the table. "It sounds to me like 'Bobby' was created to take it when Kevin could no longer handle the horror. And if Kevin endured not only extended sexual abuse as a young boy, but also witnessed the brutal beating death of his brother, I think it's entirely possible that he created other alters, maybe a lot of them. We've met Bobby and Peter and Adrian, but Bobby claims there were even more."

The room grew silent, then Amundson added, "The psyche at whatever age can only endure so much before it breaks."

The second psychiatrist, Dr. Michael Wilson, joined in at this point. "In my research, I've found that people who suffer this dissociative syndrome create their alters according to certain archetypes," he said. "There is usually a child, maybe more than one, who, like Dr. Amundson said, sometimes steps in to take the abuse in place of the victim. I agree with Dr. Amundson. I think this role is clearly Bobby's, the boy who can feel no pain. Then there's the Protector. Peter. The one who sort of runs the show for them all. The Protector generally knows about the other alters, but the others, including the core personality, don't always know about him. The multiples are his 'children,' his wards. He, or she, is charged with the physical safety of the core personality, which protects the safety of the rest, and with making sure the core personality functions as normally as possible in the outside world."

Regan listened, stunned and spellbound. This man had just described what Peter had tried to tell her. He was responsible for the children . . .

"If Peter's job was to protect the physical safety of the core personality," an older FBI agent asked, "it doesn't make sense that he would draw fire on himself, as we've been told by Ms. McKinney he did. Wouldn't he do everything in his power to protect them all from destruction?"

The two doctors exchanged glances. "It's hard to say," Amundson replied. "If Peter knew that one of the alters was a murderer, he might have been honorable enough to choose to let all the personalities, including Kevin, die in order to stop the murders. Especially if he thought that Adrian would kill someone Kevin cared about."

He hadn't chosen to die to protect someone Kevin cared about, Regan thought. He'd chosen to die to protect her. In the end, Peter knew Adrian had been killing women who looked like her, not because she looked like the mother, Liliane, but because she resembled the abusive aunt, Briana. Peter knew that if Adrian did not die, other women would, including Regan. She could never explain to the psychiatrists or cops what she knew in her heart. Peter had begged her to pull the trigger, but when she couldn't, he'd let Adrian surface, knowing she'd have to protect herself or be killed.

104

Regan answered the door to find Sam Sloan standing on the porch.

"I came to say goodbye," he told her, and she was surprised at the dismay she felt. She'd come to depend on him to see them all through the nightmare. He was the rock against which they'd leaned, even though she'd disobeyed his orders and landed in the middle of the horrific affair.

"Come in," she said. He took off his hat and entered Kat's house.

"I was wondering if you'd let me take you to lunch," he asked, and he seemed a little awkward, boyish. "I thought we'd go down to Fisherman's Wharf or somewhere and have some seafood. I haven't had much chance to try the food in San Francisco."

Blair descended the stairs and eyed Sloan quizzically. "Do you believe he was all those people?" she asked.

"I don't know what to believe, Blair, but it seems the most likely explanation."

Kat came from the direction of the kitchen. "Hi, Sam. What's up? Want to stay for lunch?"

He shook his head. "Thanks, Kat, but I've come to see if I can convince your sister to have a bite with me before I catch my flight back to D.C."

"You're leaving?" Blair exclaimed. "So . . . soon?"

"Case is over. DNA still has to prove it, but Kevin Carrington was our man. I've done my job, and it's time for me to go."

Regan too didn't want him to go. "I'll get my purse," she said.

They ate lunch at Fisherman's Grotto 9, a famous wharf restaurant, then strolled along Fisherman's Wharf, watching the boats, tourists, beggars, vendors, and fishermen mingling in a thin springtime sun. Things were back to normal. San Francisco was safe again.

Except that Regan didn't know if she'd ever feel safe again. Or if she'd ever trust her judgment when it came to men. First Adam. Then Peter. From now on, she'd go it alone.

But she knew that wasn't the answer, because with Peter, she'd learned the magical side of love. She would always love Peter, she supposed. Her throat constricted.

"What are you going to do next?" she asked Sam Sloan.

He gave her a wry grin. "Buy some popcorn to feed the seagulls."

She managed a small laugh. "I mean, when you go back to D.C."

He purchased the popcorn before answering. He offered the container to her, and she grasped a handful. "I'm thinking about quitting."

She jerked her head toward him. "What? Quitting what?"

"This job," he replied heavily. "The FBI. I think I've been at it too long. Each case seems to get to me a little more, and I'm losing my edge. I should never have let you keep that cell phone—"

He broke off, and Regan reached out and lightly touched his forearm. She'd seen the sadness in his eyes from time to time when he'd talked to her about his work, but she hadn't considered the emotional toll such a job must take on a man's soul. "I wouldn't have given it over unless you threw me in jail," she told him. "It's not your fault."

He looked into her eyes. "It was. You could have been killed, and if you had, I couldn't have lived with myself knowing it was my fault."

"Sam, you can't save the world. People make their own decisions, stupid or otherwise. I'm the one who made the mistake."

He gave a short laugh and tossed some popcorn out over the bay. Greedy gulls attacked it with noisy cries. "I think I'll quit while I'm ahead. Next time, I might not be so lucky."

Silence fell between them. In the distance, sea lions barked.

Regan had never before been exposed to the hideous kind of crimes that were apparently a way of life for Sam. She couldn't imagine waking up every day to death and horror and grief, blood and gore. She didn't blame him for wanting out.

"What's wrong with our world, Sam, that there's so much crime? How can people like Briana Jones get away with the horrors she perpetrated on those boys?"

It appeared that no charges would be pressed, for there was no one to testify against her. Only a dead man speaking in an insane manner on a videotape.

"It won't stop, unless we start listening to the children," Sam said, popping a kernel into his mouth, then throwing some to the birds. "The Peter alter claimed that Kevin tried to tell his father what was happening, but that either he didn't listen, didn't believe him, or didn't want to hear it. I've been talking to some experts on child abuse, and they tell me that often a parent looks the other way while a child is abused."

"That's horrible."

"Yes, it is. Sometimes the other parent is afraid of the abuser, sometimes in denial. But the child suffers all the same."

Regan grew silent, thinking. "Sam, what can I do to help kids like that?"

"Like you just told me, you can't save everyone. But you could tell their story. Jeff Roundtree seemed to think you're a pretty good writer." He laughed quietly and ran a hand through his hair. "You got one hell of a story about Kevin Carrington, I have to say."

It wasn't funny. But Sloan was putting an idea into Regan's head. "Tell their story? How?"

"You told me you came out here looking for a new life, a career. Why not study to become a journalist? An investigative reporter? Seems to me you're a natural."

Regan slipped on the idea, and it felt good. It also felt good to hear such affirming words from Sam Sloan. She was going to miss him.

"I'll think about it, Sam. And you think about that new life you want, too." She inhaled deeply of the crisp, salty San Francisco air. "The West Coast seems to be where everything's happening these days . . ."

AUTHOR'S NOTE

The diagnosis of dissociative identity disorder, formerly called multiple personality disorder, remains controversial among mental health professionals. Some doubt the existence of the phenomenon, giving patients who evidence different personality traits and the accompanying symptoms—blackouts, headaches, the inability to deal with time—diagnoses other than DID.

However, as more and more psychiatrists and psychologists begin to accept the disorder as valid, they are finding that many patients suffer this psychosis to one degree or another. Few experience the severe dissociation described in this book, although there are documented cases of such on record. One mental health professional I interviewed believes that as many as ten percent of prisoners in the U.S. suffer from this disorder. I do not know of any case, however, in which the dissociated person has committed serial murder. This is, after all, fiction.

The one common denominator among all DID patients is severe and prolonged sexual abuse starting in early childhood. The dissociation, or the creation of "alters," is their means of coping with the atrocities committed upon them. It is difficult and often impossible for those outside the situation to discover the abuse and take action to rescue the child. Incredibly, families often look the other way, not wanting to admit what is happening, or in fear of the perpetrator. The child is also often afraid or ashamed to tell anyone what is happening, if indeed he/she even understands it.

After researching DID for this book, I am convinced it is very real, that many suffer from it to one degree or another, and until we start listening more closely to the children and accepting that something terrible could be happening to them, this travesty of humanity is likely to continue.

For readers wanting to learn more about DID, I recommend the classic, *Sybil*, by Flora Rheta Schreiber, but even more so *When Rabbit Howls*, by Truddi Chase, which is written not only by the core personality, but also by the alters. There is also much available on private Internet sites.